# JUST AFTER SUNSET

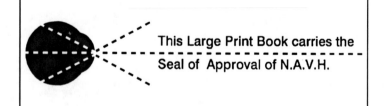

This Large Print Book carries the
Seal of Approval of N.A.V.H.

# JUST AFTER SUNSET

## STEPHEN KING

**LARGE PRINT PRESS**
*A part of Gale, Cengage Learning*

GALE
CENGAGE Learning™

Detroit • New York • San Francisco • New Haven, Conn • Waterville, Maine • London

**GALE**
CENGAGE Learning

Large Print Press, a part of Gale, Cengage Learning.

**LIBRARY OF CONGRESS CATALOGING-IN-PUBLICATION DATA**

King, Stephen, 1947–
    Just after sunset / by Stephen King.
      p. cm. — (Thorndike Press large print basic)
     ISBN-13: 978-1-4104-1060-3 (hardcover : alk. paper)
     ISBN-10: 1-4104-1060-9 (hardcover : alk. paper)
     1. Large type books. I. Title.
    PS3561.I483J87 2008b
    813'.54—dc22                       2008038780

ISBN 13: 978-1-59413-350-3 (pbk. : alk. paper)
ISBN 10: 1-59413-350-6 (pbk. : alk. paper)

Published in 2009 by arrangement with Scribner, an imprint of Simon & Schuster, Inc.

Printed in the United States of America
2 3 4 5 6    13 12 11 10 09
ED321

For Heidi Pitlor

"I can fancy what you saw. Yes; it is horrible enough; but after all, it is an old story, an old mystery played. . . . Such forces cannot be named, cannot be spoken, cannot be imagined except under a veil and a symbol, a symbol to the most of us appearing a quaint, poetic fancy, to some a foolish tale. But you and I, at all events, have known something of the terror that may dwell in the secret place of life, manifested under human flesh; that which is without form taking to itself a form. Oh, Austin, how can it be? How is it that the very sunlight does not turn to blackness before this thing, the hard earth melt and boil beneath such a burden?"

Arthur Machen
*The Great God Pan*

# CONTENTS

# INTRODUCTION

One day in 1972, I came home from work and found my wife sitting at the kitchen table with a pair of gardening shears in front of her. She was smiling, which suggested I wasn't in *too* much trouble; on the other hand, she said she wanted my wallet. That didn't sound good.

Nevertheless, I handed it over. She rummaged out my Texaco gasoline credit card — such things were routinely sent to young marrieds then — and proceeded to cut it into three large pieces. When I protested that the card had been very handy, and we always made at least the minimum payment at the end of the month (sometimes more), she only shook her head and told me that the interest charges were more than our fragile household economy could bear.

"Better to remove the temptation," she said. "I already cut up mine."

And that was that. Neither of us carried a credit card for the next two years.

She was right to do it, *smart* to do it, because at the time we were in our early twenties and had two kids to take care of; financially, we were just keeping our heads above water. I was teaching high school English and working at an industrial laundry during the summer, washing motel sheets and occasionally driving a delivery truck around to those same motels. Tabby was taking care of the kids during her days, writing poems when they took their naps, and working a full shift at Dunkin' Donuts after I came home from school. Our combined income was enough to pay the rent, buy groceries, and keep diapers on our infant son, but not enough to manage a phone; we let that go the way of the Texaco card. Too much temptation to call someone long distance. There was enough left over to occasionally buy books — neither of us could live without those — and to pay for my bad habits (beer and cigarettes), but very little beyond that. Certainly there wasn't money to pay finance charges for the privilege of carrying that convenient but ultimately dangerous rectangle of plastic.

What left-over income we did have usually went for things like car repairs, doctor bills, or what Tabby and I called "kidshit": toys, a second-hand playpen, a few of those maddening Richard Scarry books. And that little bit of extra often came from the short stories

I was able to sell to men's magazines like *Cavalier, Dude,* and *Adam.* In those days it was never about writing literature, and any discussion of my fiction's "lasting value" would have been as much a luxury as that Texaco card. The stories, when they sold (they didn't always), were simply a welcome bit of found money. I viewed them as a series of *piñatas* I banged on, not with a stick but my imagination. Sometimes they broke and showered down a few hundred bucks. Other times, they didn't.

Luckily for me — and believe me when I say that I have led an extremely lucky life, in more ways than this one — my work was also my joy. I was knocking myself out with most of those stories, having a blast. They came one after another, like the hits from the AM rock radio station that was always playing in the combination study-and-laundry-room where I wrote them.

I wrote them fast and hard, rarely looking back after the second rewrite, and it never crossed my mind to wonder where they were coming from, or how the structure of a good short story differed from the structure of a novel, or how one manages issues of character development, backstory, and time-frame. I was flying entirely by the seat of my pants, running on nothing but intuition and a kid's self-confidence. All I cared about was that they were coming. That was all I had to care about. Certainly it never occurred to me that writing short stories is a fragile craft, one that can be forgotten if it isn't used almost constantly. It didn't feel fragile to me then. Most of those stories felt like bulldozers.

Many bestselling novelists in America don't write short stories. I doubt if it's a money issue; financially successful writers don't need to think about that part of it. It might be that when the world of the full-time novelist shrinks to below, say, seventy thousand words, a kind of creative claustrophobia sets in. Or maybe it's just that the knack of miniaturization gets lost along the way. There are lots of things in life that are like riding a bike, but writing short stories isn't one of them. You *can* forget how.

During the late eighties and nineties, I wrote fewer and fewer stories, and the ones I did write were longer and longer (and there are a couple of the longer ones in this book). That was okay. But there were also short stories I wasn't writing because I had some novel or other to finish, and that wasn't so okay — I could feel those ideas in the back of my head crying to be written. Some eventually were; others, I'm sad to say, died and blew away like dust.

Worst of all, there were stories I no longer knew how to write, and that was dismaying. I knew I could have written them in that laundry room, on Tabby's little Olivetti portable, but as a much older man, even with my craft more honed and my tools — this Macintosh I'm writing on tonight, for instance — much more pricey, those stories were eluding me. I remember messing one up and thinking of an aging sword-maker, looking helplessly at a fine Toledo blade and musing, *I used to know how to make this stuff.*

Then one day three or four years ago, I got a letter from Katrina Kenison, who edited the annual *Best American Short Stories* series (she has since been succeeded by Heidi Pitlor, to whom the book you are holding is dedicated). Ms. Kenison asked if I'd be interested in editing the 2006 volume. I didn't need to sleep on it, or even think it over on an afternoon walk. I said yes immediately. For all sorts of reasons, some even altruistic, but I would be a black liar indeed if I didn't admit self-interest played a part. I thought if I read enough short fiction, immersed myself in the best the American literary magazines had to offer, I might be able to recapture some of the effortlessness that had been slipping away. Not because I needed those checks — small but very welcome when you're just starting out — to buy a new muffler for a used car or a birthday present for my wife, but because I didn't see losing my ability to write short stories as a fair exchange for a walletload of credit cards.

I read hundreds of stories during my year

as guest editor, but I won't go into that here; if you're interested, buy the book and read the introduction (you'll also be treating yourself to twenty swell short stories, which is no poke in the eye with a sharp stick). The important thing as it affects the stories that follow is that I got excited all over again, and I started writing stories again in the old way. I had hoped for that, but had hardly dared believe it would happen. The first of those "new" stories was "Willa," which is also the first story in this book.

Are these stories any good? I hope so. Will they help you pass a dull airplane flight (if you're reading) or a long car trip (if you're listening on CD)? I *really* hope so, because when that happens, it's a kind of magic spell.

I loved writing these, I know that. And I hope you like reading them, I know that, too. I hope they take you away. And as long as I remember how to do it, I'll keep at it.

Oh, and one more thing. I know some readers like to hear something about how or why certain stories came to be written. If you are one of those people, you'll find my "liner notes" at the back. But if you go there before you read the stories themselves, shame on you.

And now, let me get out of your way. But before I go, I want to thank you for coming. Would I still do what I do if you didn't? Yes, indeed I would. Because it makes me happy when the words fall together and the picture comes and the make-believe people do things that delight me. But it's better with you, Constant Reader.

Always better with you.

Sarasota, Florida<br>February 25, 2008

# WILLA

You don't see what's right in front of your eyes, she'd said, but sometimes he did. He supposed he wasn't entirely undeserving of her scorn, but he wasn't entirely blind, either. And as the dregs of sunset faded to bitter orange over the Wind River Range, David looked around the station and saw that Willa was gone. He told himself he wasn't sure, but that was only his head — his sinking stomach was sure enough.

He went to find Lander, who liked her a bit. Who called her spunky when Willa said Amtrak was full of shit for leaving them stranded like this. A lot of them didn't care for her at all, stranded by Amtrak or not.

"It smells like wet crackers in here!" Helen Palmer shouted at him as David walked past. She had found her way to the bench in the corner, as she always did, eventually. The Rhinehart woman was minding her for the time being, giving the husband a little break, and she gave David a smile.

"Have you seen Willa?" David asked.

The Rhinehart woman shook her head, still smiling.

"We got fish for supper!" Mrs. Palmer burst out furiously. A knuckle of blue veins beat in the hollow of her temple. A few people looked around. "First one t'ing an' den anudder!"

"Hush, Helen," the Rhinehart woman said. Maybe her first name was Sally, but David thought he would have remembered a name like that; there were so few Sallys these days. Now the world belonged to the Ambers, Ashleys, and Tiffanys. Willa was another endangered species, and just thinking that made his stomach sink down again.

"Like crackers!" Helen spat. "Them dirty old crackers up to camp!"

Henry Lander was sitting on a bench under the clock. He had his arm around his wife. He glanced up and shook his head before David could ask. "She's not here. Sorry. Gone into town if you're lucky. Bugged out for good if you're not." And he made a hitchhiking gesture.

David didn't believe his fiancée would hitchhike west on her own — the idea was crazy — but he believed she wasn't here. Had known even before counting heads, actually, and a snatch of some old book or poem about winter occurred to him: A cry of absence, absence in the heart.

The station was a narrow wooden throat.

Down its length, people either strolled aimlessly or simply sat on benches under the fluorescent lights. The shoulders of the ones who sat had that special slump you saw only in places like this, where people waited for whatever had gone wrong to be made right so the broken journey could be mended. Few people came to places like Crowheart Springs, Wyoming on purpose.

"Don't you go haring after her, David," Ruth Lander said. "It's getting dark, and there's plenty of critters out there. Not just coyotes, either. That book salesman with the limp says he saw a couple of wolves on the other side of the tracks, where the freight depot is."

"Biggers," Henry said. "That's his name."

"I don't care if his name is Jack D. Ripper," Ruth said. "The point is, you're not in Kansas anymore, David."

"But if she went —"

"She went while it was still daylight," Henry Lander said, as if daylight would stop a wolf (or a bear) from attacking a woman on her own. For all David knew, it might. He was an investment banker, not a wildlife expert. A young investment banker, at that.

"If the pick-up train comes and she's gone, she'll miss it." He couldn't seem to get this simple fact into their heads. It wasn't getting traction, in the current lingo of his office back in Chicago.

Henry raised his eyebrows. "Are you telling me that both of you missing it will improve things somehow?"

If they both missed it, they'd either catch a bus or wait for the next train together. Surely Henry and Ruth Lander saw that. Or maybe not. What David mostly saw when he looked at them — what was right in front of his eyes — was that special weariness reserved for people temporarily stuck in West Overalls. And who else cared for Willa? If she dropped out of sight in the High Plains, who besides David Sanderson would spare a thought? There was even some active dislike for her. That bitch Ursula Davis had told him once that if Willa's mother had left the *a* off the end of her name, "it would have been just about perfect."

"I'm going to town and look for her," he said.

Henry sighed. "Son, that's very foolish."

"We can't be married in San Francisco if she gets left behind in Crowheart Springs," he said, trying to make a joke of it.

Dudley was walking by. David didn't know if Dudley was the man's first or last name, only that he was an executive with Staples office supply and had been on his way to Missoula for some sort of regional meeting. He was ordinarily very quiet, so the donkey hee-haw of laughter he expelled into the growing shadows was beyond surprising; it was shocking. "If the train comes and you miss it," he said, "you can hunt up a justice of the peace and get married right here. When you get back east, tell all your friends you had a real Western shotgun wedding. Yeehaw, partner."

"Don't do this," Henry said. "We won't be here much longer."

"So I should leave her? That's nuts."

He walked on before Lander or his wife could reply. Georgia Andreeson was sitting on a nearby bench and watching her daughter caper up and down the dirty tile floor in her red traveling dress. Pammy Andreeson never seemed to get tired. David tried to remember if he had seen her asleep since the train derailed at the Wind River junction point and they had wound up here like someone's forgotten package in the dead letter office. Once, maybe, with her head in her mother's lap. But that might be a false memory, created out of his belief that five-year-olds were supposed to sleep a lot.

Pammy hopped from tile to tile, a prank in motion, seeming to use the squares as a giant hopscotch board. Her red dress jumped around her plump knees. "I knew a man, his name was Danny," she chanted in a monotonous one-note holler. It made David's fillings ache. "He tripped and fell, on his fanny. I knew a man, his name was David. He tripped and fell, on his bavid." She giggled and pointed at David.

"Pammy, stop," Georgia Andreeson said. She smiled at David and brushed her hair from the side of her face. He thought the gesture unutterably weary, and thought she had a long road ahead with the high-spirited Pammy, especially with no Mr. Andreeson in evidence.

"Did you see Willa?" he asked.

"Gone," she said, and pointed to the door with the sign over it reading TO SHUTTLE, TO TAXIS, CALL AHEAD FROM COURTESY PHONE FOR HOTEL VACANCIES.

Here was Biggers, limping toward him. "I'd avoid the great outdoors, unless armed with a high-powered rifle. There are wolves. I've seen them."

"I knew a girl, her name was Willa," Pammy chanted. "She had a headache, and took a pilla." She collapsed to the floor, shouting with laughter.

Biggers, the salesman, hadn't waited for a reply. He was limping back down the length of the station. His shadow grew long, shortened in the glow of the hanging fluorescents, then grew long again.

Phil Palmer was leaning in the doorway beneath the sign about the shuttle and the taxis. He was a retired insurance man. He and his wife were on their way to Portland. The plan was to stay with their oldest son and his wife for a while, but Palmer had confided to David and Willa that Helen would probably never be coming back east. She had cancer as well as Alzheimer's. Willa called it a twofer. When David told her that was a little cruel, Willa had looked at him, started to say something, and then had only shaken her head.

Now Palmer asked, as he always did: "Hey, mutt — got a butt?"

To which David answered, as he always did: "I don't smoke, Mr. Palmer."

And Palmer finished: "Just testing you, kiddo."

As David stepped out onto the concrete platform where detraining passengers waited for the shuttle to Crowheart Springs, Palmer frowned. "Not a good idea, my young friend."

Something — it might have been a large dog but probably wasn't — lifted a howl from the other side of the railway station, where the sage and broom grew almost up to the tracks. A second voice joined it, creating harmony. They trailed off together.

"See what I mean, jellybean?" And Palmer smiled as if he'd conjured those howls just to prove his point.

David turned, his light jacket rippling around him in the keen breeze, and started down the steps. He went fast, before he could change his mind, and only the first step was really hard. After that he just thought about Willa.

"David," Palmer said, not joshing now, not

joking around. "Don't."

"Why not? She did. Besides, the wolves are over there." He jerked a thumb back over his shoulder. "If that's what they are."

"Course that's what they are. And no, they probably won't come at you — I doubt if they're specially hungry this time of year. But there's no need for both of you to spend another God-knows-how-long in the middle of nowhere just because she got to missing the bright lights."

"You don't seem to understand — she's my girl."

"I'm going to tell you a hard truth, my friend: If she really considered herself your girl, she wouldn't have done what she did. You think?"

At first David said nothing, because he wasn't sure what he thought. Possibly because he often didn't see what was right in front of his eyes. Willa had said so. Finally he turned back to look at Phil Palmer leaning in the doorway above him. "I think you don't leave your fiancée stranded in the middle of nowhere. That's what I think."

Palmer sighed. "I almost hope one of those trash-pine lobos does decide to put the bite on your city ass. It might smarten you up. Little Willa Stuart cares for nobody but herself, and everyone sees it but you."

"If I pass a Nite Owl store or a 7-Eleven,

26

you want me to pick you up a pack of cigarettes?"

"Why the fuck not?" Palmer said. Then, just as David was walking across NO PARKING TAXI ZONE painted on the empty curbless street: "David!"

David turned back.

"The shuttle won't be back until tomorrow, and it's three miles to town. Says so, right on the back wall of the information booth. That's six miles, round-trip. On foot. Take you two hours, and that's not counting the time it might take you to track her down."

David raised his hand to indicate he heard, but kept going. The wind was off the mountains, and cold, but he liked the way it rippled his clothes and combed back his hair. At first he watched for wolves, scanning one side of the road and then the other, but when he saw none, his thoughts returned to Willa. And really, his mind had been fixed on little else since the second or third time he had been with her.

She'd gotten to missing the bright lights; Palmer was almost certainly right about that much, but David didn't believe she cared for nobody but herself. The truth was she'd just gotten tired of waiting around with a bunch of sad old sacks moaning about how they were going to be late for this, that, and the other. The town over yonder probably didn't amount to much, but in her mind it must

27

have held some possibility for fun, and that had outweighed the possibility of Amtrak sending a special to pick them up while she was gone.

And where, exactly, would she have gone looking for fun?

He was sure there were no what you'd call nightclubs in Crowheart Springs, where the passenger station was just a long green shed with WYOMING and "THE EQUALITY STATE" painted on the side in red, white, and blue. No nightclubs, no discos, but there were undoubtedly bars, and he thought she'd settle for one of those. If she couldn't go clubbin', she'd go jukin'.

Night came on and the stars unrolled across the sky from east to west like a rug with spangles in it. A half-moon rose between two peaks and sat there, casting a sickroom glow over this stretch of the highway and the open land on both sides of it. The wind whistled beneath the eaves of the station, but out here it made a strange open humming that was not quite a vibration. It made him think of Pammy Andreeson's hopscotch chant.

He walked listening for the sound of an oncoming train behind him. He didn't hear that; what he heard when the wind dropped was a minute but perfectly audible click-click-click. He turned and saw a wolf standing about twenty paces behind him on the broken passing line of Route 26. It was almost as big as a calf, its coat as shaggy as a Russian hat. In the starshine its fur looked black, its eyes a dark urine yellow. It saw David looking and stopped. Its mouth dropped open in a grin, and it began to pant, the sound of a small engine.

There was no time to be afraid. He took a step toward it, clapped his hands, and shouted, "Get out of here! Go on, now!"

The wolf turned tail and fled, leaving a pile of steaming droppings behind on Route 26. David grinned but managed to keep from laughing out loud; he thought that would be tempting the gods. He felt both scared and absurdly, totally cool. He thought of changing his name from David Sanderson to Wolf Frightener. That would be quite the name for an investment banker.

Then he did laugh a little — he couldn't help it — and turned toward Crowheart Springs again. This time he walked looking over his shoulder as well as from side to side, but the wolf didn't come back. What came was a certainty that he would hear the shriek of the special coming to pick up the others; the part of their train that was still on the tracks would have been cleared away from the junction, and soon the people waiting in the station back there would be on their way again — the Palmers, the Landers, the limping Biggers, the dancing Pammy, and all the rest.

Well, so what? Amtrak would hold their luggage in San Francisco; surely they could be trusted to get that much right. He and Willa could find the local bus station. Greyhound must have discovered Wyoming.

He came upon a Budweiser can and kicked it awhile. Then he kicked it crooked, off into the scrub, and as he was debating whether or not to go after it, he heard faint music: a bass line and the cry of a pedal steel guitar, which always sounded to him like chrome teardrops. Even in happy songs.

She was there, listening to that music. Not because it was the closest place with music, but because it was the right place. He knew it. So he left the beer can and walked on toward the pedal steel, his sneakers scuffing up dust that the wind whipped away. The sound of the drum kit came next, then a red neon arrow below a sign that just read 26. Well, why not? This was Route 26, after all. It was a perfectly logical name for a honky-tonk.

It had two parking lots, the one in front paved and packed with pickup trucks and cars, most American and most at least five years old. The lot on the left was gravel. In that one, ranks of long-haul semis stood under brilliant blue-white arc sodiums. By now David could also hear the rhythm and lead guitars, and read the marquee over the door: ONE NIGHT ONLY THE DERAILERS $5 COVER SORRY.

The Derailers, he thought. Well, she certainly found the right group.

David had a five in his wallet, but the foyer of 26 was empty. Beyond it, a big hardwood dance floor was crammed with slow-dancing couples, most wearing jeans and cowboy boots and clutching each other's butts as the band worked its way deeper into "Wasted Days and Wasted Nights." It was loud, lachrymose, and — as far as David Sanderson could tell — note perfect. The smells of beer, sweat, Brut, and Wal-Mart perfume hit him like a punch in the nose. The laughter and conversation — even a footloose yeehaw cry from the far side of the dance floor — were like sounds heard in a dream you have again and again at certain critical turns of life: the dream of being unprepared for a big exam, the dream of being naked in public, the dream of falling, the dream in which you hurry toward a corner in some strange city, sure your fate lies on the far side.

David considered putting his five back in his wallet, then leaned into the ticket booth and dropped it on the desk in there, which was bare except for a pack of Lucky Strikes sitting on a Danielle Steel paperback. Then he went into the crowded main room.

The Derailers swung their way into something upbeat and the younger dancers began to pogo like kids at a punk show. To David's left, two dozen or so older couples began a

31

pair of line dances. He looked again and realized there was only one line-dancing group, after all. The far wall was a mirror, making the dance floor look twice as big as it really was.

A glass shattered. "You pay, partner!" the lead singer called as The Derailers hit the instrumental break, and the dancers applauded his wit, which probably seemed fairly sparkling, David thought, if you were running hot on the tequila highway.

The bar was a horseshoe with a neon replica of the Wind River Range floating overhead. It was red, white, and blue; in Wyoming, they did seem to love their red, white, and blue. A neon sign in similar colors proclaimed YOU ARE IN GOD'S COUNTRY PARTNER. It was flanked by the Budweiser logo on the left and the Coors logo on the right. The crowd waiting to be served was four-deep. A trio of bartenders in white shirts and red vests flashed cocktail shakers like six-guns.

It was a barn of a place — there had to be five hundred people whooping it up — but he had no concerns about finding Willa. My mojo's working, he thought as he cut a corner of the dance floor, almost dancing himself as he avoided various gyrating cowboys and cowgirls.

Beyond the bar and the dance floor was a dark little lounge with high-backed booths.

Quartets were crammed into most of these, usually with a pitcher or two for sustenance, their reflections in the mirrored wall turning each party of four into eight. Only one of the booths wasn't full up. Willa sat by herself, her high-necked flower-print dress looking out of place among the Levi's, denim skirts, and pearl-button shirts. Nor had she bought herself a drink or anything to eat — the table was bare.

She didn't see him at first. She was watching the dancers. Her color was high, and there were deep dimples at the corners of her mouth. She looked nine miles out of place, but he had never loved her more. This was Willa on the edge of a smile.

"Hi, David," she said as he slid in beside her. "I was hoping you'd come. I thought you would. Isn't the band great? They're so loud!" She almost had to yell to be heard, but he could see she liked that, too. And after her initial glance at him, she went back to looking at the dancers.

"They're good, all right," he said. They were, too. He could feel himself responding in spite of his anxiety, which had returned. Now that he'd actually found her, he was worried all over again about missing that damned pick-up train. "The lead singer sounds like Buck Owens."

"Does he?" She looked at him, smiling. "Who's Buck Owens?"

"It doesn't matter. We ought to go back to the station. Unless you want to be stranded here another day, that is."

"That might not be so bad. I kind of like this pla— whoa, look out!"

A glass arched across the dance floor, sparkling briefly green and gold in the stage gels, and shattered somewhere out of sight. There were cheers and some applause — Willa was also applauding — but David saw a couple of beefcakes with the words SECURITY and SERENITY printed on their T-shirts moving in on the approximate site of the missile launch.

"This is the kind of place where you can count on four fistfights in the parking lot before eleven," David said, "and often one free-for-all inside just before last call."

She laughed, pointed her forefingers at him like guns. "Good! I want to see!"

"And I want us to go back," he said. "If you want to go honky-tonking in San Francisco, I'll take you. It's a promise."

She stuck out her lower lip and shook back her sandy-blond hair. "It wouldn't be the same. It wouldn't, and you know it. In San Francisco they probably drink . . . I don't know . . . macrobiotic beer."

That made him laugh. As with the idea of an investment banker named Wolf Frightener, the idea of macrobiotic beer was just too rich. But the anxiety was there, under the laughter;

in fact, wasn't it fueling the laughter?

"We're gonna take a short break and be right back," the lead singer said, wiping his brow. "Y'all drink up, now, and remember — I'm Tony Villanueva, and we are The Derailers."

"That's our cue to put on our diamond shoes and depart," David said, and took her hand. He slid out of the booth, but she didn't come. She didn't let go of his hand, either, though, and he sat down again feeling a touch of panic. Thinking he now knew how a fish felt when it realized it couldn't throw the hook, that old hook was in good and tight and Mr. Trout was bound for the bank, where he would flop his final flop. She was looking at him with those same killer blue eyes and deep dimples: Willa on the edge of a smile, his wife-to-be, who read novels in the morning and poetry at night and thought the TV news was . . . what did she call it? Ephemera.

"Look at us," she said, and turned her head away from him.

He looked at the mirrored wall on their left. There he saw a nice young couple from the East Coast, stranded in Wyoming. In her print dress she looked better than he did, but he guessed that was always going to be the case. He looked from the mirror-Willa to the real thing with his eyebrows raised.

"No, look again," she said. The dimples were still there, but she was serious now —

35

as serious as she could be in this party atmosphere, anyway. "And think about what I told you."

It was on his lips to say, You've told me many things, and I think about all of them, but that was a lover's reply, pretty and essentially meaningless. And because he knew what thing she meant, he looked again without saying anything. This time he really looked, and there was no one in the mirror. He was looking at the only empty booth in 26. He turned to Willa, flabbergasted . . . yet somehow not surprised.

"Didn't you even wonder how a presentable female could be sitting here all by herself when the place is juiced and jumping?" she asked.

He shook his head. He hadn't. There were quite a few things he hadn't wondered, at least until now. When he'd last had something to eat or drink, for instance. Or what time it was, or when it had last been daylight. He didn't even know exactly what had happened to them. Only that the Northern Flyer had left the tracks and now they were by some coincidence here listening to a country-western group called —

"I kicked a can," he said. "Coming here I kicked a can."

"Yes," she said, "and you saw us in the mirror the first time you looked, didn't you? Perception isn't everything, but perception and expectation together?" She winked, then leaned toward him. Her breast pressed against his upper arm as she kissed his cheek, and the sensation was lovely — surely the feel of living flesh. "Poor David. I'm sorry. But you were brave to come. I really didn't think you would, that's the truth."

"We need to go back and tell the others."

Her lips pressed together. "Why?"

"Because —"

Two men in cowboy hats led two laughing women in jeans, Western shirts, and ponytails toward their booth. As they neared it, an identical expression of puzzlement — not quite fear — touched their faces, and they headed back toward the bar instead. They feel us, David thought. Like cold air pushing them away — that's what we are now.

"Because it's the right thing to do."

Willa laughed. It was a weary sound. "You remind me of the old guy who used to sell the oatmeal on TV."

"Hon, they think they're waiting for a train to come and pick them up!"

"Well, maybe there is!" He was almost frightened by her sudden ferocity. "Maybe the one they're always singing about, the gospel train, the train to glory, the one that don't carry no gamblers or midnight ramblers. . . ."

"I don't think Amtrak runs to heaven," David said. He was hoping to make her laugh, but she looked down at her hands almost sullenly, and he had a sudden intuition. "Is there something else you know? Something we should tell them? There is, isn't there?"

"I don't know why we should bother when we can just stay here," she said, and was that petulance in her voice? He thought it was. This was a Willa he had never even suspected. "You may be a little nearsighted, David, but at least you came. I love you for that." And she kissed him again.

"There was a wolf, too," he said. "I clapped my hands and scared it off. I'm thinking of changing my name to Wolf Frightener."

She stared at him for a moment with her mouth open, and David had time to think: I had to wait until we were dead to really surprise the woman I love. Then she dropped against the padded back of the booth, roaring with laughter. A waitress who happened to be passing dropped a full tray of beers with a crash and swore colorfully.

"Wolf Frightener!" Willa cried. "I want to call you that in bed! 'Oh, oh, Wolf Frightener, you so big! You so hairy!' "

The waitress was staring down at the foaming mess, still cursing like a sailor on shore leave. All the while keeping well away from that one empty booth.

David said, "Do you think we still can? Make love, I mean?"

Willa wiped at her streaming eyes and said,

"Perception and expectation, remember? Together they can move mountains." She took his hand again. "I still love you, and you still love me. Don't you?"

"Am I not Wolf Frightener?" he asked. He could joke, because his nerves didn't believe he was dead. He looked past her, into the mirror, and saw them. Then just himself, his hand holding nothing. Then they were both gone. And still . . . he breathed, he smelled beer and whiskey and perfume.

A busboy had come from somewhere and was helping the waitress mop up the mess. "Felt like I stepped down," David heard her saying. Was that the kind of thing you heard in the afterlife?

"I guess I'll go back with you," she said, "but I'm not staying in that boring station with those boring people when this place is around."

"Okay," he said.

"Who's Buck Owens?"

"I'll tell you all about him," David said. "Roy Clark, too. But first tell me what else you know."

"Most of them I don't even care about," she said, "but Henry Lander's nice. So's his wife."

"Phil Palmer's not bad, either."

She wrinkled her nose. "Phil the Pill."

"What do you know, Willa?"

"You'll see for yourself, if you really look."

"Wouldn't it be simpler if you just —"

Apparently not. She rose until her thighs pressed against the edge of the table, and pointed. "Look! The band is coming back!"

The moon was high when he and Willa walked back to the road, holding hands. David didn't see how that could be — they had stayed for only the first two songs of the next set — but there it was, floating all the way up there in the spangled black. That was troubling, but something else troubled him even more.

"Willa," he said, "what year is it?"

She thought it over. The wind rippled her dress as it would the dress of any live woman. "I don't exactly remember," she said at last. "Isn't that odd?"

"Considering I can't remember the last time I ate a meal or drank a glass of water? Not too odd. If you had to guess, what would you say? Quick, without thinking."

"Nineteen . . . eighty-eight?"

He nodded. He would have said 1987 himself. "There was a girl in there wearing a T-shirt that said CROWHEART SPRINGS HIGH SCHOOL, CLASS OF '03. And if she was old enough to be in a roadhouse —"

"Then '03 must have been at least three years ago."

"That's what I was thinking." He stopped. "It can't be 2006, Willa, can it? I mean, the twenty-first century?"

Before she could reply, they heard the click-click-click of toenails on asphalt. This time more than just one set; this time there were four wolves behind them on the highway. The biggest, standing in front of the others, was the one that had come up behind David on his walk toward Crowheart Springs. He would have known that shaggy black pelt anywhere. Its eyes were brighter now. A half-moon floated in each like a drowned lamp.

"They see us!" Willa cried in a kind of ecstasy. "David, they see us!" She dropped to one knee on a white dash of the broken passing line and held out her right hand. She made a clucking noise and said, "Here, boy! Come on!"

"Willa, I don't think that's such a good idea."

She paid no attention, a very Willa thing to do. Willa had her own ideas about things. It was she who had wanted to go from Chicago to San Francisco by rail — because, she said, she wanted to know what it felt like to fuck on a train. Especially one that was going fast and rocking a little.

"Come on, big boy, come to your mama!"

The big lobo came, trailed by its mate and their two . . . did you call them yearlings? As it stretched its muzzle (and all those shining teeth) toward the slim outstretched hand, the moon filled its eyes perfectly for a moment, turning them silver. Then, just before its long snout could touch her skin, the wolf uttered a series of piercing yips and flung itself backward so sharply that for a moment it rose on its rear legs, front paws boxing the air and the white plush on its belly exposed. The others scattered. The big lobo executed a midair twist and ran into the scrubland to the right of the road, still yipping, with his tail tucked. The rest followed.

Willa rose and looked at David with an expression of hard grief that was too much to bear. He dropped his eyes to his feet instead. "Is this why you brought me out into the dark when I was listening to music?" she asked. "To show me what I am now? As if I didn't know!"

"Willa, I'm sorry."

"Not yet, but you will be." She took his hand again. "Come on, David."

Now he risked a glance. "You're not mad at me?"

"Oh, a little — but you're all I've got now, and I'm not letting you go."

Shortly after seeing the wolves, David spied a Budweiser can lying on the shoulder of the road. He was almost positive it was the one he had kicked along ahead of him until he'd kicked it crooked, out into the sage. Here it was again, in its original position . . . because he had never kicked it at all, of course. Perception isn't everything, Willa had said, but perception and expectation together? Put them together and you had a Reese's peanut butter cup of the mind.

He kicked the can out into the scrubland, and when they were past that spot, he looked back and there it lay, right where it had been since some cowboy — maybe on his way to 26 — had chucked it from the window of his pickup truck. He remembered that on *Hee Haw* — that old show starring Buck Owens and Roy Clark — they used to call pickup trucks cowboy Cadillacs.

"What are you smiling about?" Willa asked him.

"Tell you later. Looks like we're going to have plenty of time."

They stood outside the Crowheart Springs railway station, holding hands in the moonlight like Hansel and Gretel outside the candy house. To David the long building's green paint looked ashy gray in the moonlight, and although he knew WYOMING and "THE EQUALITY STATE" were printed in red, white, and blue, they could have been any colors at all. He noticed a sheet of paper, protected from the elements by plastic, stapled to one of the posts flanking the wide steps leading up to the double doors. Phil Palmer still leaned there.

"Hey, mutt!" Palmer called down. "Got a butt?"

"Sorry, Mr. Palmer," David said.

"Thought you were going to bring me back a pack."

"I didn't pass a store," David said.

"They didn't sell cigarettes where you were, doll?" Palmer asked. He was the kind of man who called all women of a certain age doll; you knew that just looking at him, as you knew that if you happened to pass the time of day with him on a steamy August afternoon, he'd tip his hat back on his head to wipe his brow and tell you it wasn't the heat, it was the humidity.

"I'm sure they did," Willa said, "but I would have had trouble buying them."

"Want to tell me why, sugarpie?"

"Why do you think?"

But Palmer crossed his arms over his narrow chest and said nothing. From somewhere inside, his wife cried, "We got fish for supper! First one t'ing an' den anudder! I hate the smell of this place! Crackers!"

"We're dead, Phil," David said. "That's why. Ghosts can't buy cigarettes."

Palmer looked at him for several seconds, and before he laughed, David saw that Palmer more than believed him: Palmer had known all along. "I've heard plenty of reasons for not bringing someone what he asked for," he said, "but I have to think that takes the prize."

"Phil —"

From inside: "Fish for supper! Oh, gah-

44

dammit!"

"Excuse me, kiddies," Palmer said. "Duty calls." And he was gone. David turned to Willa, thinking she'd ask him what else he had expected, but Willa was looking at the notice posted beside the stairs.

"Look at that," she said. "Tell me what you see."

At first he saw nothing, because the moon was shining on the protective plastic. He took a step closer, then one to the left, moving Willa aside to do it.

"At the top it says NO SOLICITING BY ORDER OF SUBLETTE COUNTY SHERIFF, then some fine print — blah-blah-blah — and at the bottom —"

She gave him an elbow. Not gently, either. "Stop shitting around and look at it, David. I don't want to be here all night."

*You don't see what's right in front of your eyes.*

He turned away from the station and stared at the railroad tracks shining in the moonlight. Beyond them was a thick white neck of stone with a flat top — that thar's a mesa, pardner, jest like in them old John Ford movies.

He looked back at the posted notice, and wondered how he ever could have mistaken TRESPASSING for SOLICITING, a big bad investment banker like Wolf Frightener Sanderson.

"It says NO TRESPASSING BY ORDER OF SUBLETTE COUNTY SHERIFF," he said.

"Very good. And under the blah-blah-blah, what about there?"

At first he couldn't read the two lines at the bottom at all; at first those two lines were just incomprehensible symbols, possibly because his mind, which wanted to believe none of this, could find no innocuous translation. So he looked away to the railroad tracks once more and wasn't exactly surprised to see that they no longer gleamed in the moonlight; now the steel was rusty, and weeds were growing between the ties. When he looked back again, the railway station was a slumped derelict with its windows boarded up and most of the shingles on its roof gone. NO PARKING TAXI ZONE had disappeared from the asphalt, which was crumbling and full of potholes. He could still read WYOMING and "THE EQUALITY STATE" on the side of the building, but now the words were ghosts. Like us, he thought.

"Go on," Willa said — Willa, who had her own ideas about things, Willa who saw what was in front of her eyes and wanted you to see too, even when seeing was cruel. "That's your final exam. Read those two lines at the bottom and then we can get this show on the road."

He sighed. "It says THIS PROPERTY IS CONDEMNED. And then DEMOLITION

46

SCHEDULED IN JUNE 2007."

"You get an A. Now let's go see if anyone else wants to go to town and hear The Derailers. I'll tell Palmer to look on the bright side — we can't buy cigarettes, but for people like us there's never a cover charge."

Only nobody wanted to go to town.

"What does she mean, we're dead? Why does she want to say an awful thing like that?" Ruth Lander asked David, and what killed him (so to speak) wasn't the reproach in her voice but the look in her eyes before she pressed her face against the shoulder of Henry's corduroy jacket. Because she knew too.

"Ruth," he said, "I'm not telling you this to upset you —"

"Then stop!" she cried, her voice muffled.

David saw that all of them but Helen Palmer were looking at him with anger and hostility. Helen was nodding and muttering between her husband and the Rhinehart woman, whose first name was probably Sally. They were standing under the fluorescents in little groups . . . only when he blinked, the fluorescents were gone. Then the stranded passengers were just dim figures standing in the shattered moonlight that managed to find its way in through the boarded-up windows. The Landers weren't sitting on a bench; they were sitting on a dusty floor near a little cluster of empty crack vials — yes, it seemed that crack had managed to find its way even out here to John Ford country — and there was a faded circle on one wall not far from the corner where Helen Palmer squatted and muttered. Then David blinked again and the fluorescents were back. So was the big clock, hiding that faded circle.

Henry Lander said, "Think you better go along now, David."

"Listen a minute, Henry," Willa said.

Henry switched his gaze to her, and David had no trouble reading the distaste that was there. Any liking Henry might once have had for Willa Stuart was gone now.

"I don't want to listen," Henry said. "You're upsetting my wife."

"Yeah," a fat young man in a Seattle Mariners cap said. David thought his name was O'Casey. Something Irish with an apostrophe in it, anyway. "Zip it, baby girl!"

Willa bent toward Henry, and Henry recoiled from her slightly, as if her breath were bad. "The only reason I let David drag me back here is because they are going to demolish this place! Can you say wrecking ball, Henry? Surely you're bright enough to get your head around that concept."

"Make her stop!" Ruth cried, her voice muffled.

Willa leaned even closer, eyes bright in her narrow, pretty face. "And when the wrecking

48

ball leaves and the dump trucks haul away the crap that used to be this railway station — this old railway station — where will you be?"

"Leave us alone, please," Henry said.

"Henry — as the chorus girl said to the archbishop, denial is not a river in Egypt."

Ursula Davis, who had disliked Willa from the first, stepped forward, leading with her chin. "Fuck off, you troublesome bitch."

Willa swung around. "Don't any of you get it? You're dead, we're all dead, and the longer you stay in one place, the harder it's going to be to ever go anywhere else!"

"She's right," David said.

"Yeah, and if she said the moon was cheese, you'd say provolone," Ursula said. She was a tall, forbiddingly handsome woman of about forty. "Pardon my French, but she's got you so pussy-whipped it isn't funny."

Dudley let out that startling donkey bray again, and the Rhinehart woman began to sniffle.

"You're upsetting the passengers, you two." This was Rattner, the little conductor with the apologetic face. He hardly ever spoke. David blinked, the station lensed dark and moonlit again for another moment, and he saw that half of Rattner's head was gone. The rest of his face had been burned black.

"They're going to demolish this place and you'll have nowhere to go!" Willa cried.

49

"Fucking . . . nowhere!" She dashed angry tears from her cheeks with both fists. "Why don't you come to town with us? We'll show you the way. At least there are people . . . and lights . . . and music."

"Mumma, I want to hear some music," Pammy Andreeson said.

"Hush," her mother said.

"If we were dead, we'd know it," Biggers said.

"He's got you there, son," Dudley said, and dropped David a wink. "What happened to us? How did we get dead?"

"I . . . don't know," David said. He looked at Willa. Willa shrugged her shoulders and shook her head.

"You see?" Rattner said. "It was a derailment. Happens . . . well, I was going to say all the time, but that's not true, even out here where the rail system needs a fair amount of work, but every now and then, at one of the junction points —"

"We faw down," Pammy Andreeson said. David looked at her, really looked, and for a moment saw a corpse, burned bald, in a rotting rag of a dress. "Down and down and down. Then —" She made a growling, rattling sound in her throat, put her small, grimy hands together, and tossed them apart: every child's sign language for explosion.

She seemed about to say something more, but before she could, her mother suddenly slapped her across the face hard enough to expose her teeth in a momentary sneer and drive spit from the corner of her mouth. Pammy stared up for a moment in shocked disbelief, then broke into a strident, one-note wail even more painful than her hopscotch chant.

"What do we know about lying, Pamela?" Georgia Andreeson yelled, grabbing the child by her upper arm. Her fingers sank in almost out of sight.

"She's not lying!" Willa said. "We went off the tracks and into the gorge! Now I remember, and you do too! Don't you? Don't you? It's on your face! It's on your fucking face!"

Without looking in her direction, Georgia Andreeson flipped Willa the bird. Her other hand shook Pammy back and forth. David saw a child flop in one direction, a charred corpse in the other. What had caught fire? Now he remembered the drop, but what had caught fire? He didn't remember, perhaps because he didn't want to remember.

"What do we know about lying?" Georgia Andreeson shouted.

"It's wrong, Mama!" the child blubbered.

The woman dragged her off into the darkness, the child still screaming that one monotonous note.

There was a moment of silence in their wake — all of them listening to Pammy being dragged into exile — and then Willa turned to David. "Had enough?"

"Yes," he said. "Let's go."

"Don't let the doorknob hitcha where the good Lord splitcha!" Biggers advised, madly exuberant, and Dudley yodeled laughter.

David let Willa lead him toward the double doors, where Phil was leaning just inside, his arms still crossed on his chest. Then David pulled free of Willa's hand and went to Helen Palmer sitting in the corner, rocking back and forth. She looked up at him with dark, bewildered eyes. "We got fish for supper," she said in what was little more than a whisper.

"I don't know about that," he said, "but you were right about the smell of the place. Old dirty crackers." He looked back and saw the rest of them staring at him and Willa in the moonlit dimness that could be fluorescent light if you wanted it to be badly enough. "It's the smell places get when they've been closed up a long time, I guess," he said.

"Better buzz, cuz," Phil Palmer said. "No one wants to buy what you're selling."

"Don't I know it," David said, and followed Willa into the moonlit dark. Behind him, like a rueful whisper of wind, he heard Helen Palmer say, "First one t'ing an' den anudder."

The miles back to 26 made their score nine for the night, but David wasn't a bit tired. He supposed ghosts didn't get tired, just as they didn't get hungry or thirsty. Besides, it was a different night. The moon was full now, shining like a silver dollar high in the sky, and 26's front parking lot was empty. In the gravel lot around to the side, a few semis stood silent, and one rumbled sleepily with its running lights glowing. The marquee sign now read: COMING THIS WEEKEND THE NIGHTHAWKS BRING YOUR HONEY SPEND YOUR MONEY.

"That's cute," Willa said. "Will you bring me, Wolf Frightener? Am I not your honey?"

"You are and I will," David said. "The question is what do we do now? Because the honky-tonk is closed."

"We go in anyway, of course," she said.

"It'll be locked up."

"Not if we don't want it to be. Perception, remember? Perception and expectation."

He remembered, and when he tried the door, it opened. The barroom smells were still there, now mixed with the pleasant odor of some pine-scented cleaner. The stage was empty and the stools were on the bar with their legs sticking up, but the neon replica of the Wind River Range was still on, either because the management left it that way after closing or because that was the way he and Willa wanted it. That seemed more likely. The dance floor seemed very big now that it was empty, especially with the mirror wall to double it. The neon mountains shimmered upside down in its polished depths.

Willa breathed deep. "I smell beer and perfume," she said. "A hot rod smell. It's lovely."

"You're lovely," he said.

She turned to him. "Then kiss me, cowboy."

He kissed her there on the edge of the dance floor, and judging by what he was feeling, lovemaking wasn't out of the question. Not at all.

She kissed both corners of his mouth, then stepped back. "Put a quarter in the jukebox, would you? I want to dance."

David went over to the juke at the end of the bar, dropped a quarter, and played D19 — "Wasted Days and Wasted Nights," the Freddy Fender version. Out in the parking lot, Chester Dawson, who had decided to lay over here a few hours before resuming his journey to Seattle with a load of electronics, raised his head, thinking he heard music, decided it was part of a dream he'd been having, and went back to sleep.

David and Willa moved slowly around the empty floor, sometimes reflected in the mirror wall and sometimes not.

"Willa —"

"Hush a little, David. Baby wants to dance."

David hushed. He put his face in her hair and let the music take him. He thought they would stay here now, and that from time to time people would see them. 26 might even get a reputation for being haunted, but probably not; people didn't think of ghosts much while they were drinking, unless they were drinking alone. Sometimes when they were closing up, the bartender and the last waitress (the one with the most seniority, the one responsible for splitting the tips) might have an uneasy sense of being watched. Sometimes they'd hear music even after the music had stopped, or catch movement in the mirror next to the dance floor or the one in the lounge. Usually just from the tail of the eye. David thought they could have finished up in better places, but on the whole, 26 wasn't bad. Until closing there were people. And there would always be music.

He did wonder what would become of the others when the wrecking ball tore apart their illusion — and it would. Soon. He thought of Phil Palmer trying to shield his terrified, howling wife from falling debris that couldn't hurt her because she was not, properly speaking, even there. He thought of Pammy Andreeson cowering in her shrieking mother's arms. Rattner, the soft-spoken conductor, saying, Just be calm, folks, in a voice that couldn't be heard over the roar of the big yellow machines. He thought of the book salesman, Biggers, trying to run away on his bad leg, lurching and finally falling while the wrecking ball swung and the dozers snarled and bit and the world came down.

He liked to think their train would come before then — that their combined expectation would make it come — but he didn't really believe it. He even considered the idea that the shock might extinguish them and they'd simply whiff out like candle flames in a strong gust of wind, but he didn't believe that, either. He could see them too clearly after the bulldozers and dump trucks and back-end loaders were gone, standing by the rusty disused railway tracks in the moonlight while a wind blew down from the foothills, whining around the mesa and beating at the broomgrass. He could see them huddled together under a billion High Country stars, still waiting for their train.

"Are you cold?" Willa asked him.

"No — why?"

"You shivered."

"Maybe a goose walked over my grave," he said. He closed his eyes, and they danced together on the empty floor. Sometimes they were in the mirror, and when they slipped from view there was only a country song playing in an empty room lit by a neon mountain range.

# THE
# GINGERBREAD GIRL

## -1-

**Only fast running would do.**

After the baby died, Emily took up running. At first it was just down to the end of the driveway, where she would stand bent over with her hands clutching her legs just above the knees, then to the end of the block, then all the way to Kozy's Qwik-Pik at the bottom of the hill. There she would pick up bread or margarine, maybe a Ho Ho or a Ring Ding if she could think of nothing else. At first she only walked back, but later she ran that way, too. Eventually she gave up the snack foods. It was surprisingly hard to do. She hadn't realized that sugar eased grief. Or maybe the snacks had become a fetish. Either way, in the end the Ho Hos had to go go. And did. Running was enough. Henry called the *running* a fetish, and she supposed he was right.

"What does Dr. Steiner say about it?" he asked.

"Dr. Steiner says run your ass off, get those endorphins going." She hadn't mentioned the running to Susan Steiner, hadn't even seen her since Amy's funeral. "She says she'll put it on a prescription pad, if you want."

Emily had always been able to bluff Henry. Even after Amy died. *We can have another one,* she had said, sitting beside him on the bed as he lay there with his ankles crossed and tears streaming down the sides of his face.

It eased him and that was good, but there was never going to be another baby, with the attendant risk of finding said infant gray and still in its crib. Never again the fruitless CPR, or the screaming 911 call with the operator saying *Lower your voice, ma'am, I can't understand you.* But Henry didn't need to know that, and she was willing to comfort him, at least at the start. She believed that comfort, not bread, was the staff of life. Maybe eventually she would be able to find some for herself. In the meantime, she had produced a defective baby. That was the point. She would not risk another.

Then she started getting headaches. Real blinders. So she *did* go to a doctor, but it was Dr. Mendez, their general practitioner, not Susan Steiner. Mendez gave her a prescription for some stuff called Zomig. She took the bus to the family practice where Mendez hung out, then ran to the drugstore to get the scrip filled. After that she jogged home — it was two miles — and by the time she got there, she had what felt like a steel fork planted high up in her side, between the top of her ribs and her armpit. She didn't let it concern her. That was pain that would go away. Besides, she was exhausted and felt as if she could sleep for a while.

She did — all afternoon. On the same bed where Amy had been made and Henry had cried. When she woke up, she could see ghostly circles floating in the air, a sure sign that she was getting one of what she liked to call Em's Famous Headaches. She took one of her new pills, and to her surprise — almost shock — the headache turned tail and slunk away. First to the back of her head, then gone. She thought there ought to be a pill like that for the death of a child.

She thought she needed to explore the limits of her endurance, and she suspected the exploration would be a long one. There was a JuCo with a cinder track not too far from the house. She began to drive over there in the early mornings just after Henry left for work. Henry didn't understand the running. Jogging, sure — lots of women jogged. Keep those extra four pounds off the old fanny, keep those extra two inches off the old waistline. But Em didn't have an extra four pounds on her backside, and besides, jogging was no longer enough. She had to run, and fast. Only fast running would do.

She parked at the track and ran until she could run no more, until her sleeveless FSU sweatshirt was dark with sweat down the front and back and she was shambling and sometimes puking with exhaustion.

Henry found out. Someone saw her there, running all by herself at eight in the morning, and told him. They had a discussion about it. The discussion escalated into a marriage-ending argument.

"It's a hobby," she said.

"Jodi Anderson said you ran until you fell down. She was afraid you'd had a heart attack. That's not a hobby, Em. Not even a fetish. It's an obsession."

And he looked at her reproachfully. It would be a little while yet before she picked up the book and threw it at him, but that was what really tore it. That reproachful look. She could no longer stand it. Given his rather long face, it was like having a sheep in the house. *I married a Dorset gray,* she thought, *and now it's just baa-baa-baa, all day long.*

But she tried one more time to be reasonable about something she knew in her heart had no reasonable core. There was magical thinking; there was also magical doing. Running, for instance.

"Marathoners run until they fall down," she said.

"Are you planning to run in a marathon?"

"Maybe." But she looked away. Out the window, at the driveway. The driveway called her. The driveway led to the sidewalk, and the sidewalk led to the world.

"No," he said. "You're not going to run in a marathon. You have no plans to run in a marathon."

It occurred to her — with that sense of brilliant revelation the obvious can bring — that this was the essence of Henry, the fucking *apotheosis* of Henry. During the six years of their marriage he had always been perfectly aware of what she was thinking, feeling, planning.

*I comforted you,* she thought — not furious yet but beginning to be furious. *You lay there on the bed,* leaking, *and I comforted you.*

"The running is a classic psychological response to the pain you feel," he was saying in that same earnest way. "It's called avoidance. But, honey, if you don't feel your pain, you'll never be able to —"

That's when she grabbed the object nearest at hand, which happened to be a paperback copy of The Memory Keeper's Daughter. This was a book she had tried and rejected, but Henry had picked it up and was now about three quarters of the way through, judging from the bookmark. *He even has the reading tastes of a Dorset gray,* she thought, and hucked it at him. It struck him on the shoulder. He stared at her with wide, shocked eyes, then grabbed at her. Probably just to hug her, but who knew? Who really knew anything?

If he had grabbed a moment earlier, he might have caught her by the arm or the wrist or maybe just the back of her T-shirt. But that moment of shock undid him. He missed, and she was running, slowing only to snatch her fanny pack off the table by the front door. Down the driveway, to the sidewalk. Then down the hill, where she had briefly pushed a pram with other mothers who now shunned her. This time she had no intention of stopping or even slowing. Dressed only in shorts, sneakers, and a T-shirt reading SAVE THE CHEERLEADER, Emily ran out into the world. She put her fanny pack around her waist and snapped the catch as she pelted down the hill. And the feeling?

Exhilaration. Pure pow.

She ran downtown (two miles, twenty-two minutes), not even stopping when the light was against her; when that happened, she jogged in place. A couple of boys in a top-down Mustang — it was just getting to be top-down weather — passed her at the corner of Main and Eastern. One whistled. Em gave him the finger. He laughed and applauded as the Mustang accelerated down Main.

She didn't have much cash, but she had a pair of credit cards. The American Express was the prize, because with it she could get traveler's checks.

She realized she wasn't going home, not for a while. And when the realization caused a feeling of relief — maybe even fugitive excitement — instead of sorrow, she suspected this was not a temporary thing.

She went into the Morris Hotel to use the phone, then decided on the spur of the moment to take a room. Did they have anything for just the one night? They did. She gave the desk clerk her AmEx card.

"It doesn't look like you'll need a bellman," the clerk said, taking in her shorts and T-shirt.

"I left in a hurry."

"I see." Spoken in the tone of voice that said he didn't see at all. She took the key he slid to her and hurried across the wide lobby to the elevators, restraining the urge to run.

-2-

**You sound like you might be crying.**
She wanted to buy some clothes — a couple of skirts, a couple of shirts, two pairs of jeans, another pair of shorts — but before shopping she had calls to make: one to Henry and one to her father. Her father was in Tallahassee. She decided she had better call him first. She couldn't recall the number of his office phone in the motor pool but had his cell-phone

number memorized. He answered on the first ring. She could hear engines revving in the background.

"Em! How are you?"

That should have been a complex question, but wasn't. "I'm fine, Dad. But I'm in the Morris Hotel. I guess I've left Henry."

"Permanently or just a kind of trial balloon?" He didn't sound surprised — he took things in stride; she loved that about him — but the sound of the revving motors first faded, then disappeared. She imagined him going into his office, closing the door, perhaps picking up the picture of her that stood on his cluttered desk.

"Can't say yet. Right now it doesn't look too good."

"What was it about?"

"Running."

*"Running?"*

She sighed. "Not really. You know how sometimes a thing is about something else? Or a whole bunch of something elses?"

"The baby." Her father had not called her Amy since the crib death. Now it was always just *the baby.*

"And the way I'm handling it. Which is not the way Henry wants me to. It occurred to me that I'd like to handle things in my own way."

"Henry's a good man," her father said, "but he has a way of seeing things. No doubt."

She waited.

"What can I do?"

She told him. He agreed. She knew he would, but not until he heard her all the way out. The hearing out was the most important part, and Rusty Jackson was good at it. He hadn't risen from one of three mechanics in the motor pool to maybe one of the four most important people at the Tallahassee campus (and she hadn't heard that from him; he'd never say something like that to her or anyone else) by not listening.

"I'll send Mariette in to clean the house," he said.

"Dad, you don't need to do that. I can clean."

"I want to," he said. "A total top-to-bottom is overdue. Damn place has been closed up for almost a year. I don't get down to Vermillion much since your mother died. Seems like I can always find some more to do up here."

Em's mother was no longer Debra to him, either. Since the funeral (ovarian cancer), she was just *your mother.*

Em almost said, *Are you sure you don't mind this?* but that was the kind of thing you said when a stranger offered to do you a favor. Or a different kind of father.

"You going there to run?" he asked. She could hear a smile in his voice. "There's plenty of beach to run on, and a good long stretch of road, too. As you well know. And you won't have to elbow people out of your way. Between now and October, Vermillion is as quiet as it ever gets."

"I'm going there to think. And — I guess — to finish mourning."

"That's all right, then," he said. "Want me to book your flight?"

"I can do that."

"Sure you can. Emmy, are you okay?"

"Yes," she said.

"You sound like you might be crying."

"A little bit," she said, and wiped her face. "It all happened very fast." *Like Amy's death,* she could have added. She had done it like a little lady; never a peep from the baby monitor. *Leave quietly, don't slam the door,* Em's own mother often said when Em was a teenager.

"Henry won't come there to the hotel and bother you, will he?"

She heard a faint, delicate hesitation before he chose *bother,* and smiled in spite of her tears, which had pretty well run their course, anyway. "If you're asking if he's going to come and beat me up . . . that's not his style."

"A man sometimes finds a different style when his wife up and leaves him — just takes off running."

"Not Henry," she said. "He's not a man to cause trouble."

"You sure you don't want to come to Tallahassee first?"

She hesitated. Part of her did, but —

"I need a little time on my own. Before anything else." And she repeated, "All this happened very fast." Although she suspected it had been building for quite some time. It might even have been in the DNA of the marriage.

"All right. Love you, Emmy."

"Love you, too, Dad. Thank you." She swallowed. "So much."

Henry didn't cause trouble. Henry didn't even ask where she was calling from. Henry said, "Maybe you're not the only one who needs a little time apart. Maybe this is for the best."

She resisted an urge — it struck her as both normal and absurd — to thank him. Silence seemed like the best option. What he said next made her glad she'd chosen it.

"Who'd you call for help? The Motor-Pool King?"

This time the urge she resisted was to ask if he'd called his mother yet. Tit for tat never solved anything.

She said — evenly, she hoped: "I'm going to Vermillion Key. My dad's place there."

"The conch shack." She could almost hear him sniff. Like Ho Hos and Twinkies, houses with only three rooms and no garage were not a part of Henry's belief system.

Em said, "I'll call you when I get there."

A long silence. She imagined him in the kitchen, head leaning against the wall, hand gripping the handset of the phone tight enough to turn his knuckles white, fighting to reject anger. Because of the six mostly good years they'd had together. She hoped he would make it. If that was indeed what was going on.

When he spoke next, he sounded calm but tired out. "Got your credit cards?"

"Yes. And I won't overuse them. But I want my half of —" She broke off, biting her lip. She had almost called their dead child *the baby,* and that wasn't right. Maybe it was for her father, but not for her. She started again.

"My half of Amy's college money," she said. "I don't suppose there's much, but —"

"There's more than you think," he said. He was starting to sound upset again. They had begun the fund not when Amy was born, or even when Em got pregnant, but when they first started trying. Trying had been a four-year process, and by the time Emily finally kindled, they were talking about fertility treatments. Or adoption. "Those investments weren't just good, they were blessed by heaven — especially the software stocks. Mort got us in at the right time and out at the absolute golden moment. Emmy, you don't want to take the eggs out of that nest."

There he was again, telling her what she wanted to do.

"I'll give you an address as soon as I have one," she said. "Do whatever you want with your half, but make mine a cashier's check."

"Still running," he said, and although that professorial, observational tone made her wish he was here so she could throw another book at him — a hardcover this time — she held her silence.

At last he sighed. "Listen, Em, I'm going to clear out of here for a few hours. Come on in and get your clothes or your whatever. And I'll leave some cash for you on the dresser."

For a moment she was tempted; then it occurred to her that leaving money on the dresser was what men did when they went to whores.

"No," she said. "I want to start fresh."

"Em." There was a long pause. She guessed he was struggling with his emotions, and the thought of it caused her own eyes to blur over again. "Is this the end of us, kiddo?"

"I don't know," she said, working to keep her own voice straight. "Too soon to tell."

"If I had to guess," he said, "I'd guess yes. Today proves two things. One is that a healthy woman can run a long way."

"I'll call you," she said.

"The other is that living babies are glue when it comes to marriage. Dead ones are acid."

That hurt more than anything else he might have said, because it reduced Amy to an ugly metaphor. Em couldn't do that. She didn't think she'd ever be able to do that. "I'll call you," she said, and hung up.

## -3-

**Vermillion Key lay dazed and all but deserted.**

So Emily Owensby ran down to the end of the driveway, then down the hill to Kozy's Qwik-Pik, and then at the Cleveland South Junior College track. She ran to the Morris Hotel. She ran out of her marriage the way a woman can run out of a pair of sandals when she decides to let go and really dash. Then she ran (with the help of Southwest Airlines) to Fort Myers, Florida, where she rented a car and drove south toward Naples. Vermillion Key lay dazed and all but deserted under the baking June light. Two miles of road ran along Vermillion Beach from the drawbridge to the stub of her father's driveway. At the end of the driveway stood the unpainted conch shack, a slummy-looking thing with a blue roof and peeling blue shutters on the outside, air-conditioned and comfy on the inside.

When she turned off the engine of her Avis Nissan, the only sounds were waves crashing on the empty beach, and, somewhere nearby, an alarmed bird shouting *Uh-oh! Uh-oh!* over and over.

Em lowered her head against the steering wheel and cried for five minutes, letting out all the strain and horror of the last half year. Trying to, anyway. There was no one in earshot except for the uh-oh bird. When she was finally done, she took off her T-shirt and wiped everything away: the snot, the sweat, the tears. She wiped herself clean all the way down to the top of her plain gray sports bra. Then she walked to the house, shells and bits of coral crunching under her sneakers. As she bent to get the key from the Sucrets box hidden beneath the charming-in-spite-of-itself lawn gnome with its faded red hat, it occurred to her that she hadn't had one of her headaches in over a week. Which was a good thing, since her Zomig was more than a thousand miles away.

Fifteen minutes later, dressed in shorts and one of her father's old shirts, she was running on the beach.

For the next three weeks, her life became one of stark simplicity. She drank coffee and orange juice for breakfast, ate huge green salads for lunch, and devoured Stouffer's cuisine for dinner, usually macaroni and cheese or boil-in-the-bag chipped beef on toast — what her dad called shit on a shingle. The carbs came in handy. In the morning, when it was cool, she ran barefoot on the beach, down close to the water where the sand was firm and wet and mostly free of shells. In the afternoon, when it was hot (and frequently showery), she ran on the road, which was shady for most of its length. Sometimes she got soaked. On these occasions she ran on through the rain, often smiling, sometimes even laughing, and when she got back, she stripped in the foyer and dumped her soaking clothes in the washer, which was — conveniently — only three steps from the shower.

At first she ran two miles on the beach and a mile on the road. After three weeks, she was doing three miles on the beach and two on the road. Rusty Jackson was pleased to call his getaway place the Little Grass Shack, after some old song or other. It was at the extreme north end, and there was nothing like it on Vermillion; everything else had been taken over by the rich, the superrich, and, at the extreme south end, where there were three McMansions, the absurdly rich. Trucks filled with groundskeeping gear sometimes passed Em on her road runs, but rarely a car. The houses she passed were all closed up, their driveways chained, and they would stay that way until at least October, when the owners started to trickle back. She began to make up names for them in her head: the one with the columns was Tara, the one behind the high, barred iron fence was Club Fed, the big one hiding behind an ugly gray concrete wall was the Pillbox. The only other small one, mostly screened by palmettos and traveler palms, was the Troll House — where, she imagined, the in-season inhabitants subsisted on Troll House cookies.

On the beach, she sometimes saw volunteers from Turtle Watch, and soon came to hail them by name. They would give her a "Yo, Em!" in return as she ran past. There was rarely anyone else, although once a helicopter buzzed her. The passenger — a young man — leaned out and waved. Em waved back, her face safely masked by the shadow of her FSU 'Noles cap.

She shopped at the Publix five miles north on U.S. 41. Often on her ride home, she would stop at Bobby Trickett's Used Books, which was far bigger than her dad's little retreat but still your basic conch shack. There she bought old paperback mysteries by Raymond Chandler and Ed McBain, their pages dark brown at the edges and yellow inside, their smell sweet and as nostalgic as the old Ford woody station wagon she sighted one day tooling down 41 with two lawn chairs strapped to the roof and a beat-to-shit surfboard sticking out the back. There was no need to buy any John D. MacDonalds; her father had the whole set packed into his orange-crate bookcases.

By the end of July she was running six and

sometimes seven miles a day, her boobs no more than nubs, her butt mostly nonexistent, and she had lined two of her dad's empty shelves with books that had titles like *Dead City* and *Six Bad Things.* The TV never went on at night, not even for the weather. Her father's old PC stayed dark. She never bought a newspaper.

Her father called her every second day, but stopped asking if she wanted him to "yank free" and come on down after she told him that when she was ready to see him, she'd tell him so. In the meantime, she said, she wasn't suicidal (true), not even depressed (not true), and she was eating. That was good enough for Rusty. They had always been straight up with each other. She also knew that summer was a busy time for him — everything that couldn't be done when kids were crawling all over the campus (which he always called *the plant*) had to be done between June 15 and September 15, when there was nobody around but summer students and whatever academic conferences the administration could pull in.

Also, he had a lady friend. Melody, her name was. Em didn't like to go there — it made her feel funny — but she knew Melody made her dad happy, so she always asked after her. *Fine,* her dad invariably replied. *Mel's as dandy as a peach.*

Once she called Henry, and once Henry

called her. The night he called her, Em was pretty sure he was drunk. He asked her again if they were over, and she told him again that she didn't know, but that was a lie. *Probably* a lie.

Nights, she slept like a woman in a coma. At first she had bad dreams — reliving the morning they had found Amy dead over and over again. In some of the dreams, her baby had turned as black as a rotten strawberry. In others — these were worse — she found Amy struggling for breath and saved her by administering mouth-to-mouth. They were worse because she woke to the realization that Amy was actually the same old dead. She came from one of these latter dreams during a thunderstorm and slid naked from the bed to the floor, crying with her elbows propped on her knees and her palms pushing her cheeks up in a smile while lightning flashed over the Gulf and made momentary blue patterns on the wall.

As she extended herself — exploring those fabled limits of endurance — the dreams either ceased or played themselves out far below the eye of her memory. She began to awaken feeling not so much refreshed as unwound all the way to the core of herself. And although each day was essentially the same as the day before, each began to seem like a new thing — its own thing — instead of an extension of the old thing. One day she woke realizing that Amy's death had begun to be something that *had* happened instead of something that *was* happening.

She decided she would ask her father to come down — and bring Melody if he wanted to. She would give them a nice dinner. They could stay over (what the hell, it *was* his house). And then she'd start thinking about what she wanted to do with her real life, the one she would soon resume on the other side of the drawbridge: what she wanted to keep and what she wanted to cast away.

She would make that call soon, she thought. In a week. Two, at the most. It wasn't quite time yet, but almost. Almost.

## -4-

**Not a very nice man.**

One afternoon not long after July became August, Deke Hollis told her she had company on the island. He called it *the island,* never the key.

Deke was a weathered fifty, or maybe seventy. He was tall and rangy and wore a battered old straw hat that looked like an inverted soup bowl. From seven in the morning until seven at night, he ran the drawbridge between Vermillion and the mainland. This was Monday to Friday. On weekends, "the kid" took over (said kid being about thirty).

76

Some days when Em ran up to the draw-bridge and saw the kid instead of Deke in the old cane chair outside the gatehouse, reading *Maxim* or *Popular Mechanics* rather than *The New York Times,* she was startled to realize that Saturday had come around again.

This afternoon, though, it was Deke. The channel between Vermillion and the mainland — which Deke called *the thrut* (throat, she assumed) — was deserted and dark under a dark sky. A heron stood on the drawbridge's Gulf-side rail, either meditating or looking for fish.

"Company?" Em said. "I don't have any company."

"I didn't mean it that way. Pickering's back. At 366? Brought one of his 'nieces.' " The punctuation for *nieces* was provided by a roll of Deke's eyes, of a blue so faded they were nearly colorless.

"I didn't see anyone," Em said.

"No," he agreed. "Crossed over in that big red M'cedes of his about an hour ago, while you were probably still lacin' up your ten-nies." He leaned forward over his newspaper; it crackled against his flat belly. She saw he had the crossword about half completed. "Different niece every summer. Always young." He paused. "Sometimes *two* nieces, one in August and one in September."

"I don't know him," Em said. "And I didn't see any red Mercedes." Nor did she know

77

which house belonged to 366. She noticed the houses themselves, but rarely paid attention to the mailboxes. Except, of course, for 219. That was the one with the little line of carved birds on top of it. (The house behind it was, of course, Birdland.)

"Just as well," Deke said. This time instead of rolling his eyes, he twitched down the corners of his mouth, as if he had something bad tasting in there. "He brings 'em down in the M'cedes, then takes 'em back to St. Petersburg in his boat. Big white yacht. The *Playpen.* Went through this morning." The corners of his mouth did that thing again. In the far distance, thunder mumbled. "So the nieces get a tour of the house, then a nice little cruise up the coast, and we don't see Pickering again until January, when it gets cold up in Chicagoland."

Em thought she might have seen a moored white pleasure craft on her morning beach run but wasn't sure.

"Day or two from now — maybe a week — he'll send out a couple of fellas, and one will drive the M'cedes back to wherever he keeps it stored away. Near the private airport in Naples, I imagine."

"He must be very rich," Em said. This was the longest conversation she'd ever had with Deke, and it was interesting, but she started jogging in place just the same. Partly because she didn't want to stiffen up, mostly because her body was calling on her to run.

"Rich as Scrooge McDuck, but I got an idea Pickering actually *spends* his. Probably in ways Uncle Scrooge never imagined. Made it off some kind of computer thing, I heard." The eye roll. "Don't they all?"

"I guess," she said, still jogging in place. The thunder cleared its throat with a little more authority this time.

"I know you're anxious to be off, but I'm talking to you for a reason," Deke said. He folded up his newspaper, put it beside the old cane chair, and stuck his coffee cup on top of it as a paperweight. "I don't ordinarily talk out of school about folks on the island — a lot of 'em's rich and I wouldn't last long if I did — but I like you, Emmy. You keep yourself to yourself, but you ain't a bit snooty. Also, I like your father. Him and me's lifted a beer, time to time."

"Thanks," she said. She was touched. And as a thought occurred to her, she smiled. "Did my dad ask you to keep an eye on me?"

Deke shook his head. "Never did. Never would. Not R. J.'s style. He'd tell you the same as I am, though — Jim Pickering's not a very nice man. I'd steer clear of him. If he invites you in for a drink or even just a cup of coffee with him and his new 'niece,' I'd say no. And if he were to ask you to go cruising with him, I would *definitely* say no."

"I have no interest in cruising anywhere,"

she said. What she was interested in was finishing her work on Vermillion Key. She felt it was almost done. "And I better get back before the rain starts."

"Don't think it's coming until five, at least," Deke said. "Although if I'm wrong, I think you'll still be okay."

She smiled again. "Me too. Contrary to popular opinion, women don't melt in the rain. I'll tell my dad you said hello."

"You do that." He bent down to get his paper, then paused, looking at her from beneath that ridiculous hat. "How're you doing, anyway?"

"Better," she said. "Better every day." She turned and began her road run back to the Little Grass Shack. She raised her hand as she went, and as she did, the heron that had been perched on the drawbridge rail flapped past her with a fish in its long bill.

Three sixty-six turned out to be the Pillbox, and for the first time since she'd come to Vermillion, the gate was standing ajar. Or had it been ajar when she ran past it toward the bridge? She couldn't remember — but of course she had taken up wearing a watch, a clunky thing with a big digital readout, so she could time herself. She had probably been looking at that when she went by.

She almost passed without slowing — the thunder was closer now — but she wasn't exactly wearing a thousand-dollar suede skirt from Jill Anderson, only an ensemble from the Athletic Attic: shorts and a T-shirt with the Nike swoosh on it. Besides, what had she said to Deke? *Women don't melt in the rain.* So she slowed, swerved, and had a peek. It was simple curiosity.

She thought the Mercedes parked in the courtyard was a 450 SL, because her father had one like it, although his was pretty old now and this one looked brand-new. It was candy-apple red, its body brilliant even under the darkening sky. The trunk was open. A sheaf of long blond hair hung from it. There was blood in the hair.

Had Deke said the girl with Pickering was a blond? That was her first question, and she was so shocked, so fucking *amazed,* that there was no surprise in it. It seemed like a perfectly reasonable question, and the answer was Deke hadn't said. Only that she was young. And a niece. With the eye roll.

Thunder rumbled. Almost directly overhead now. The courtyard was empty except for the car (and the blond in the trunk, there was her). The house looked deserted, too: buttoned up and more like a pillbox than ever. Even the palms swaying around it couldn't soften it. It was too big, too stark, too gray. It was an ugly house.

Em thought she heard a moan. She ran through the gate and across the yard to the open trunk without even thinking about it. She looked in. The girl in the trunk hadn't moaned. Her eyes were open, but she had been stabbed in what looked like dozens of places, and her throat was cut ear to ear.

Em stood looking in, too shocked to move, too shocked to even breathe. Then it occurred to her that this was a *fake* dead girl, a movie prop. Even as her rational mind was telling her that was bullshit, the part of her that specialized in rationalization was nodding frantically. Even making up a story to back-stop the idea. Deke didn't like Pickering, and Pickering's choice of female companionship? Well guess what, Pickering didn't like Deke, either! This was nothing but an elaborate practical joke. Pickering would go back across the bridge with the trunk deliberately ajar, that fake blond hair fluttering, and —

But there were smells rising out of the trunk now. They were the smells of shit and blood. Em reached forward and touched the cheek below one of those staring eyes. It was cold, but it was skin. Oh God, it was human skin.

There was a sound behind her. A footstep. She started to turn, and something came down on her head. There was no pain, but brilliant white seemed to leap across the world. Then the world went dark.

**He looked like he was trying to play creep-mouse with her.**

When she woke up, she was duct-taped to a chair in a big kitchen filled with terrible steel objects: sink, fridge, dishwasher, a stove that looked like it belonged in the kitchen of a restaurant. The back of her head was sending long, slow waves of pain toward the front of her head, each one seeming to say *Fix this! Fix this!*

Standing at the sink was a tall, slender man in khaki shorts and an old Izod golf shirt. The kitchen's fluorescent fixtures sent down a merciless light, and Em could see the deepening crow's-foot at the corner of his eye, the smattering of gray along the side of his short power haircut. She put him at about fifty. He was washing his arm in the sink. There appeared to be a puncture wound in it, just below the elbow.

He snapped his head around. There was an animal quickness to him that made her stomach sink. His eyes were of a blue much more vivid than Deke Hollis's. She saw nothing in them she recognized as sanity, and her heart sank further. On the floor — the same ugly gray as the outside of the house, only tile instead of cement — there was a dark, filmy track about nine inches wide. Em thought it was probably blood. It was very easy to imagine the blond girl's hair making it as Pickering dragged her through the room by her feet, to some unknown destination.

"You're awake," he said. "Good deal. *Awesome.* Think I wanted to kill her? I didn't want to kill her. She had a knife in her goshdamn *sock!* I pinched her on the arm, that's all." He seemed to consider this, and while he did, he blotted the dark, blood-filled gash below his elbow with a wad of paper towels. "Well, also on the tit. But all girls expect that. Or should. It's called *FORE-play.* Or in this case, *WHORE-play.*"

He made quotation marks with the first and second fingers of his hands each time. To Em, he looked like he was trying to play creepmouse with her. He also looked crazy. In fact, there was no doubt about his state of mind. Thunder crashed overhead, loud as a load of dropped furniture. Em jumped — as well as she could, bound to a kitchen chair — but the man standing by the stainless-steel double-basin sink didn't glance up at the sound. It was as though he hadn't heard. His lower lip was thrust out.

"So I took it away from her. And then I lost my head. I admit it. People think I'm Mr. Cool, and I try to live up to that. I do. I try to live up to that. But any man can lose his head. That's what they don't realize. Any man. Under the right set of circumstances."

Rain poured down as if God had pulled the chain up there in His own personal WC.

"Who could reasonably assume you're here?"

"Lots of people." This answer came without hesitation.

He was across the room in a flash. *Flash* was the word. At one moment he was by the sink, at the next beside her and whacking her face hard enough to make white spots explode in front of her eyes. These shot around the room, drawing bright cometary tails after them. Her head snapped to the side. Her hair flew against her cheek, and she felt blood begin to flow into her mouth as her lower lip burst. The inner lining had been cut by her teeth, and deep. Almost all the way through, it felt like. Outside, the rain rushed down. *I'm going to die while it's raining,* Em thought. But she didn't believe it. Maybe no one did, when the deal actually came down.

*"Who knows?"* He was leaning over, bellowing into her face.

"*Lots* of people," she reiterated, and the words came out *losh of people* because her lower lip was swelling. And she felt blood spilling down her chin in a small stream. Still, her *mind* wasn't swelling, in spite of the pain and fear. It knew her one chance at life was making this man believe he'd be caught if he killed her. Of course he would also be caught if he let her go, but she would deal with that later. One nightmare at a time.

"*Losh* of people!" she said again, defiantly.

He flashed back to the sink and when he returned, he had a knife in his hand. A little one. Very likely the one the dead girl had taken from her sock. He put the tip on Em's lower eyelid and pulled it down. That was when her bladder let go, all at once, in a rush.

An expression of somehow prissy disgust momentarily tightened Pickering's face, yet he also seemed delighted. Some part of Em's mind wondered how any person could hold two such conflicting emotions in his mind at the same time. He took a half step back, but the point of the knife didn't waver. It still dimpled into her skin, simultaneously pulling down her lower eyelid and pushing her eyeball up gently in its socket.

"Nice," he said. "Another mess to clean up. Not unexpected, though. No. And like the man said, there's more room out than there is in. That's what the man said." He actually laughed, one quick yip, and then he leaned forward, his vivid blue eyes staring into her hazel ones. "Tell me one person who knows you're here. Don't hesitate. Do *not* hesitate. If you hesitate I'll know you're making something up and I'll lift your eye right out of its socket and flip it into the sink. I can do it. So tell me. *Now.*"

"Deke Hollis," she said. It was tattling, *bad* tattling, but it was also nothing but reflex.

She didn't want to lose her eye.

"Who else?"

No name occurred to her — her mind was a roaring blank — and she believed him when he said hesitating would cost her her left eye. *"No one, okay?"* she cried. And surely Deke would be enough. Surely one person would be enough, unless he was so crazy that —

He drew the knife away, and although her peripheral vision couldn't quite pick it up, she felt a tiny seed pearl of blood blooming there. She didn't care. She was just glad to still *have* peripheral vision.

"Okay," Pickering said. "Okay, okay, good, okay." He walked back to the sink and tossed the little knife into it. She started to be relieved. Then he opened one of the drawers beside the sink and brought out a bigger one: a long, pointed butcher knife.

"Okay." He came back to her. There was no blood on him that she could see, not even a spot. How was that possible? How long had she been out?

"Okay, okay." He ran the hand not holding the knife through the short, stupidly expensive tailoring of his hair. It sprang right back into place. "Who's Deke Hollis?"

"The drawbridge keeper," she said. Her voice was unsteady, wavering. "We *talked* about you. That's why I stopped to look in." She had a burst of inspiration. "He saw the girl! Your niece, he called her!"

"Yeah, yeah, the girls always go back by boat, that's all he knows. That's all he knows in the world. Are people ever nosy! Where's your car? Answer me *now* or you get the new special, a breast amputation. Quick but *not* painless."

"The Grass Shack!" It was all she could think of to say.

"What's that?"

"The little conch house at the end of the key. It's my dad's." She had another burst of inspiration. "*He* knows I'm here!"

"Yeah, yeah." This didn't seem to interest Pickering. "Yeah, okay. Right, big-time. Are you saying you *live* here?"

"Yes . . ."

He looked down at her shorts, now a darker blue. "Runner, are you?" She didn't answer this, but Pickering didn't seem to care. "Yeah, you're a runner, damn right you are. Look at those legs." Incredibly, he bowed at the waist — as if meeting royalty — and with a loud smack kissed her left thigh just below the hem of her shorts. When he straightened up, she observed with a sinking heart that the front of his pants were sticking out. Not good.

"You run up, you run back." He flicked the blade of the butcher knife in an arc, like a conductor with a baton. It was hypnotic. Outside, the rain continued to pour down. It would go on that way for forty minutes, maybe an hour, and then the sun would come back out. Em wondered if she would be alive to see it. She didn't think so. Yet this was still hard to believe. Impossible, really.

"You run up, you run back. Up and back. Sometimes you pass the time of day with that old man in the straw hat, but you don't pass it with anyone else." She was scared, but not too scared to realize he wasn't talking to her. "Right. Not with anyone else. Because there's nobody else here. If any of the tree-planting, grass-cutting beaners who work down here saw you on your afternoon run, will they remember? Will they?"

The knife blade ticked back and forth. He eyed the tip, seeming to depend on this for an answer.

"No," he said. "No, and I'll tell you why. Because you're just another rich gringa running her buns off. They're everywhere. See 'em every day. Health nuts. Have to kick 'em out of your way. If not running, on bikes. Wearing those dumb little potty helmets. Okay? Okay. Say your prayers, Lady Jane, but make it quick. I'm in a hurry. Big, big hurry."

He raised the knife to his shoulder. She saw his lips tighten down in anticipation of the killing stroke. For Em, the whole world suddenly came clear; everything stood out with exclamatory brilliance. She thought: *I'm coming, Amy.* And then, absurdly, something she might have heard on ESPN: *Be there, baby.*

But then he paused. He looked around,

89

exactly as if someone had spoken. "Yeah," he said. Then: "Yeah?" And then: "Yeah." There was a Formica-topped island in the middle of the room, for food preparation. He dropped the knife on it with a clatter instead of sticking it into Emily.

He said, "Sit there. I'm not going to kill you. I changed my mind. Man can change his mind. I got nothing from Nicole but a poke in the arm."

There was a depleted roll of duct tape on the island. He picked it up. A moment later he was kneeling in front of her, the back of his head and the naked nape of his neck exposed and vulnerable. In a better world — a fairer world — she could have laced her hands together and brought them down on that exposed nape, but her hands were bound at the wrists to the chair's heavy maple arms. Her torso was bound to the back by more duct tape, thick corsets of the stuff at the waist and just below her breasts. Her legs were bound to the chair's legs at the knees, the upper calves, the lower calves, and the ankles. He had been very thorough.

The legs of the chair were taped to the floor, and now he put on fresh layers, first in front of her, then behind. When he was finished, all the tape was gone. He stood up and put the empty cardboard core on the Formica island. "There," he said. "Not bad. Okay. All set. You wait here." He must have found something funny in this, because he cocked his head upward and loosed another of those brief, yapping laughs. "Don't get bored and run off, okay? I need to go take care of your nosy old friend, and I want to do it while it's still raining."

This time he flashed to a door that proved to be a closet. He yanked out a yellow slicker. "Knew this was in here somewhere. Everybody trusts a guy in a raincoat. I don't know why. It's just one of those mystery facts. Okay, girlfriend, sit tight." He uttered another of those laughs that sounded like the bark of an angry poodle, and then he was gone.

## -6-

**Still 9:15.**
When the front door slammed and Em knew he had really left, that abnormal brightness in the world started to turn gray, and she realized she was on the verge of fainting. She could not afford to faint. If there was an afterlife and she eventually saw her father there, how could she explain to Rusty Jackson that she had wasted her last minutes on earth in unconsciousness? He would be disappointed in her. Even if they met in heaven, standing ankle-deep in clouds while angels all around them played the music of the spheres (arranged for harp), he would be

disappointed in her for wasting her only chance in a Victorian swoon.

Em deliberately ground the lacerated lining of her lower lip against her teeth . . . then bit down, bringing fresh blood. The world jumped back to brightness. The sound of the wind and down-rushing rain swelled like strange music.

How long did she have? It was a quarter of a mile from the Pillbox to the drawbridge. Because of the slicker, and because she hadn't heard the Mercedes start up, she had to think he was running. She knew she might not have heard the engine over the rain and thunder, but she just didn't believe he would take his car. Deke Hollis knew the red Mercedes and didn't like the man who drove it. The red Mercedes might put Deke on his guard. Emily believed Pickering would know that. Pickering was crazy — part of the time he'd been talking to himself, but at least some of the time he'd been talking to someone he could see but she couldn't, an invisible partner in crime — but he wasn't stupid. Neither was Deke, of course, but he would be alone in his little gatehouse. No cars passing, no boats waiting to go through, either. Not in this downpour.

Plus, he was old.

"I have maybe fifteen minutes," she said to the empty room — or perhaps it was the bloodstain on the floor she was talking to. He hadn't gagged her, at least; why bother? There would be no one to hear her scream, not in this ugly, boxy, concrete fortress. She thought she could have stood in the middle of the road, screaming at the top of her lungs, and *still* no one would have heard her. Right now even the Mexican groundskeepers would be under cover, sitting in the cabs of their trucks drinking coffee and smoking cigarettes.

"Fifteen minutes at most."

Yes. Probably. Then Pickering would come back and rape her, as he had been planning to rape Nicole. After that he would kill her, as he had already killed Nicole. Her and how many other "nieces"? Em didn't know, but she felt certain this was not — as Rusty Jackson might have said — his first rodeo.

Fifteen minutes. Maybe just ten.

She looked down at her feet. They weren't duct-taped to the floor, but the feet of the chair were. Still . . .

You're a runner; damn right you are. Look at those legs.

They were good legs, all right, and she didn't need anyone to kiss them to make her aware of it. Especially not a lunatic like Pickering. She didn't know if they were good in the sense of being beautiful, or sexy, but in utilitarian terms, they were very good. They had carried her a long way since the morning she and Henry had found Amy dead in her crib. Pickering clearly had great faith in the powers of duct tape, had probably seen it employed by dozens of psycho killers in dozens of movies, and none of his "nieces" had given him any cause to doubt its efficacy. Maybe because he hadn't given them a chance, maybe because they were too frightened. But maybe . . . especially on a wet day, in an unaired house so damp she could smell the mildew . . .

Em leaned forward as far as the corsets binding her would allow and gradually began to flex the muscles of her thighs and calves: those new runner's muscles the lunatic had so admired. First just a little flex, then up to half. She was approaching full flex, and starting to lose hope, when she heard a sucking sound. It was low at first, barely more than a wish, but it got louder. The tape had been wrapped and then rewrapped in crisscrossing layers, it was hellishly strong, but it was pulling free of the floor just the same. But slowly. Dear God, so slowly.

She relaxed, breathing hard, sweat now breaking on her forehead, under her arms, between her breasts. She wanted to go again at once, but her experience running the Cleveland South track told her she must wait and let her rapidly pumping heart flush the lactic acid from her muscles. Her next effort would generate less force and be less successful if she didn't. But it was hard. Waiting was hard. She had no idea how long he had been gone. There was a clock on the wall — a sunburst executed in stainless steel (like seemingly everything else in this horrible, heartless room, except the red maple chair she was bound to) — but it had stopped at 9:15. Probably it was a battery job and its battery had died.

She tried to remain still until she had counted to thirty (with a *delightful Maisie* after each number), and could only hold out to seventeen. Then she flexed again, pushing down with all her might. This time the sucking sound was immediate and louder. She felt the chair begin to *lift.* Just a little, but it was definitely rising.

Em strained, her head thrown back, her teeth bared, fresh blood running down her chin from her swollen lip. The cords on her neck stood out. The sucking sound became louder still, and now she also heard a low ripping sound.

Hot pain bloomed suddenly in her right calf, tightening it. For a moment Em almost kept on straining — the stakes were high, after all, the stakes were her *life* — but then she relaxed within her bonds again, gasping for air. And counting.

"*One,* delightful Maisie. *Two,* delightful Maisie. *Three . . .*"

Because she could probably pull the chair free of the floor in spite of that warning tightness. She was almost sure she could. But if she did so at the expense of a charley horse in her right calf (she'd had them there before; on a couple of occasions they'd hit so hard the muscle had felt like stone rather than flesh), she would lose more time than she gained. And she'd still be bound to the fucking chair. *Glued* to the fucking chair.

She knew the clock on the wall was dead, but she looked at it anyway. It was a reflex. Still 9:15. Was he at the drawbridge yet? She had a sudden wild hope: Deke would blow the warning horn and scare him off. Could a thing like that happen? She thought it could. She thought Pickering was like a hyena, only dangerous when he was sure he had the upper hand. And, probably like a hyena, wasn't able to imagine not having it.

She listened. She heard thunder, and steadily whooshing rain, but not the blare of the air horn mounted beside the drawbridge keeper's cabin.

She tried pulling the chair off the floor again, and almost went catapulting facefirst into the stove when it came free almost at once. She staggered, tottered, almost fell over, and backed against the Formica-topped service island in the middle of the kitchen to keep from doing so. Her heart was now running so fast, she couldn't detect the individual beats; it seemed to be just a steady hard hum in her chest and high in her neck, below the points of her jaw. If she had fallen over, she would have been like a turtle lying on its back. There wouldn't have been a chance in the world of getting up again.

*I'm all right,* she thought. *It didn't happen.*

No. But she could see herself lying there all the same, and with hellish clarity. Lying there with only the swash of blood made by Nicole's hair for company. Lying there and waiting for Pickering to come back and have his fun with her before ending her life. And he would be back when? In seven minutes? Five? Only three?

She looked at the clock. It was 9:15.

She hunched beside the counter, gasping for breath, a woman who had grown a chair out of her back. There was the butcher knife on the counter, but she couldn't reach it with her hands bound to the chair's arms. Even if she could have grasped it, what then? Just stand there, hunched over, with it in her hand. There was nothing she could reach with it, nothing she could cut with it.

She looked at the stove, and wondered if she could turn on one of the burners. If she could do that, then maybe . . .

Another hellish vision came to her: trying to burn through the tape and having her clothes catch on fire from the gas ring instead. She wouldn't risk it. If someone had offered her pills (or even a bullet in the head) to escape the possibility of rape, torture, and death — likely a slow one, preceded by

97

unspeakable mutilations — she might have overcome the dissenting voice of her father (*"Never give up, Emmy, good things are always just around some corner or other"*) and gone for it. But risking the possibility of third-degree burns all over the upper half of her body? Lying half-baked on the floor, waiting for Pickering to come back, *praying* for him to come back and put her out of her misery?

No. She wouldn't do that. But what did that leave? She could feel time fleeting, fleeting. The clock on the wall still said 9:15, but she thought the beat of the rain had slacked off a bit. The idea filled her with horror. She pushed it back. Panic would get her killed.

The knife was a can't and the stove was a won't. What did that leave?

The answer was obvious. It left the chair. There weren't any others in the kitchen, only three high stools like barstools. She guessed he must have imported this one from a dining room she hoped never to see. Had he bound other women — other "nieces" — to heavy red maple chairs that belonged around a dining-room table? Maybe to this very one? In her heart she was sure he had. And he trusted it even though it was wood instead of metal. What had worked once must work again; she was sure he thought like a hyena in that way, too.

She had to demolish the prison that held her. It was the only way, and she had only minutes to do it.

**It's probably going to hurt.**
She was close to the center island, but the counter stuck out slightly, creating a kind of lip, and she didn't trust it. She didn't want to move — didn't want to risk falling over and becoming a turtle — but she did want a surface wider than that projecting lip to beat against. And so she started toward the refrigerator, which was also stainless steel . . . and big. All the beating surface a girl could want.

She shuffled along with the chair bound to her back and bottom and legs. Her progress was agonizingly slow. It was like trying to walk with a weird, form-fitting coffin strapped to her back. And it *would* be her coffin, if she fell over. Or if she was still whacking it fruitlessly against the front of the KitchenAid when the man of the house returned.

Once she tottered on the edge of falling over — on her face — and managed to keep her balance by what seemed like willpower alone. The pain in her calf came back, once more threatening to become a charley horse and render her right leg useless. She willed that away, too, closing her eyes to do it. Sweat rolled down her face, washing away dried tears she did not remember crying.

How much time was passing? How much? The rain had slackened still more. Soon she would start to hear dripping instead of raining. Maybe Deke was putting up a fight. Maybe he even had a gun in a drawer of his cluttered old desk and had shot Pickering the way you'd shoot a rabid dog. Would she hear a gunshot in here? She didn't think so; the wind was still blowing pretty hard. More likely Pickering — twenty years younger than Deke, and obviously in shape — would take away any weapon Deke might produce and use it on the old man.

She tried to sweep all these thoughts away, but it was hard. It was hard even though they were useless. She shuffled forward with her eyes still closed and her pale face — swollen at the mouth — drawn down in effort. One baby step, two baby steps. *May I take another six baby steps?* Yes, you may. But on the fourth one, her knees — bent almost into a squat — bumped against the front of the refrigerator.

Em opened her eyes, unable to believe she had actually made this arduous safari safely — a distance an unbound person could have covered in three ordinary steps, but a safari for her. A fucking *trek.*

There was no time to waste congratulating herself, and not just because she might hear the Pillbox's front door open anytime. She had other problems. Her muscles were strained and trembling from trying to walk in what was almost a sitting position; she felt like an out-of-condition amateur attempting some outrageous tantra yoga position. If she didn't do this at once, she wouldn't be able to do it at all. And if the chair was as strong as it looked —

But she pushed this thought away.

"It's probably going to hurt," she panted. "You know that, don't you?" She knew, but thought Pickering might have even worse things in mind for her.

"Please," she said, turning sideways to the refrigerator, giving it her profile. If that was praying, she had an idea it was her dead daughter she was praying to. *"Please,"* she said again, and swung her hips sideways, smacking the parasite she was wearing against the front of the fridge.

She wasn't as surprised as when the chair had come free of the floor all at once, almost causing her to flip headfirst onto the stove, but almost. There was a loud cracking sound from the chair back, and the seat slewed sideways on her bottom. Only the legs held firm.

"It's *rotten!*" she cried to the empty kitchen. "The damn thing's *rotten!*" Maybe not actually, but — God bless the Florida climate — it sure wasn't as strong as it looked. Finally, a little stroke of luck . . . and if he came in now, just as she'd had it, Emily thought she would go insane.

How long now? How long had he been gone? She had no idea. She had always had a fairly accurate clock in her head, but now it was as useless as the one on the wall. It was uniquely horrible to have lost track of time so completely. She remembered her big clunky watch and looked down, but the watch was gone. There was just a pale patch where it had been. He must have taken it.

She almost swung sideways into the fridge again, then had a better idea. Her bottom was partly free of the chair seat now, and that gave her extra leverage. She strained with her back as she had strained with her thighs and calves while working to free the chair from the floor, and this time when she felt a warning pain way down low, just above the base of her spine, she didn't relax and wait and recycle. She didn't think she had the luxury of waiting anymore. She could see him coming back, running right down the center of the deserted road, his feet spatting up sprays of water, the yellow slicker flapping. And, in one hand, some sort of a tool. A tire iron, perhaps, that he had snatched from the bloodstained trunk of his Mercedes.

Em strained upward. The pain in the small of her back deepened, took on a glassy intensity. But she could hear that ripping sound again as duct tape let go — not of the chair, but of itself. Of the overlapping layers of itself. Loosening. Loosening wasn't as good as freeing, but it was still good. It gave her more leverage.

She swung her hips against the refrigerator again, letting out a little scream of effort. The shock jarred through her. This time the chair didn't move. The chair clung to her like a limpet. She swung her hips again, harder, screaming louder: tantra yoga meets S&M disco. There was another *crack,* and this time the chair slewed to the right on her back and hips.

She swung again . . . again . . . again, pivoting on her increasingly tired hips and *smashing.* She lost count. She was crying again. She had split her shorts up the back. They had slid down crooked over one hip, and the hip itself was bleeding. She thought she had taken a splinter in it.

She took a deep breath, trying to calm her runaway heart (small chance of that), and whacked herself and her wooden prison into the refrigerator again, as hard as she could. This time she finally struck the lever of the recessed automatic ice dispenser, releasing a jackpot of cubes onto the tiled floor. There was another crack, a sag, and all at once her left arm was free. She looked down at it, stupid-eyed with amazement. The arm of the chair was still bound to her forearm, but now the body of the chair hung askew on that side, held to her by long gray strips of duct tape. It was like being caught in a cobweb. And of course she was; the crazy bastard in the khaki shorts and Izod shirt was the spider. She still wasn't free, but now she could use the knife. All she had to do was shuffle back to the center island and get it.

"Don't step on the cubes," she advised herself in a ragged voice. She sounded — to her own ears, at least — like a manic grad student who had studied herself to the edge of a nervous breakdown. "This would be a very bad time to go skating."

She avoided the ice, but as she bent for the knife, her overstrained back gave a warning creak. The chair, much looser now but still bound to her midsection by those corsets of tape (and at the legs, as well), banged into the side of the island. She paid no attention. She was able to grasp the knife with her newly freed left hand and use it to saw through the tape binding her right arm, sobbing for breath and casting small darting glances at the swing door between the kitchen and whatever lay beyond — the dining room and the front hall, she assumed; it was the way he had gone out, and the way he would probably come back in. When her right hand was free, she tore off the broken chunk of chair still bound to her left arm and tossed it on the center island.

"Stop looking for him," she told herself in the gray, shadowy kitchen. "Just do your work." It was good advice, but hard to follow when you knew your death might come through that door, and soon.

She sawed through the band of tape just below her breasts. This should have been slow, careful work, but she couldn't afford to go slow and nicked herself repeatedly with the tip of the knife. She could feel blood spreading on her skin.

The knife was sharp. The bad news about that were those repeated nicks just below her breastbone. The good news was that the duct tape split away without much argument, layer after layer. Finally it was cut through from top to bottom, and the chair sagged away from her back a little more. She set to work on the wide band of tape around her waist. Now she could bend further, and the work went faster, with less damage to her body. She cut all the way through at last, and the chair fell backward. But its legs were still bound to her legs, and the wooden feet suddenly shifted, digging in low on her calves where the Achilles tendons surfaced like cables just below the skin. The pain was excruciating, and she moaned miserably.

Em reached around and used her left hand to push the chair against her back again, relieving that horrible, digging pressure. It was a filthy angle, all wrong for her arm, but she continued to press the chair to her while she shuffled around so she was once more facing the stove. Then she leaned back, using the center island to relieve the pressure. Gasping for breath, crying again (she wasn't aware of the tears), she leaned forward and began to saw through the tape binding her ankles. Her exertions had loosened these bands and the others binding her lower body to the fucking chair; consequently the work went faster and she cut herself less frequently, although she managed to give herself a fairly good slash on the right calf — as if some mad part of her were trying to punish it for seizing up while she was trying to push the chair free of the floor.

She was working on the tape holding her knees — the last ones left — when she heard the front door open and close. "I'm home, honey!" Pickering called cheerfully. "Miss me?"

Em froze, bent over with her hair hanging in her face, and it took every last scrap of will to get moving again. No time for finesse now; she jammed the blade of the butcher knife under the belt of gray tape binding her right knee, miraculously avoided stabbing the tip into her own kneecap, and hauled upward with all her strength.

In the hall, there was a heavy *cluck* sound, and she knew he had just turned a key in a lock — a big lock, from the sound. Pickering wanted no interruptions, probably thought there had been interruptions enough for one day. He started up the hall. He must have been wearing sneakers (she hadn't noticed before), because she could hear them squelching.

He was whistling "O Susanna."

The tape holding her right knee parted, bottom to top, and the chair fell backward against the counter with a noisy clatter, now bound to her only at the left knee. For a moment the footsteps beyond the swing door — very close, now — stopped, and then they broke into a run. After that it all happened very, very fast.

He hit the door two-handed, and it burst open with a loud thump; those hands were still outstretched as he came racing into the kitchen. They were empty — no sign of the tire iron she had imagined. The sleeves of the yellow slicker were pulled halfway up his arms, and Em had time to think, *That's too small for you, asshole — a wife would tell you, but you don't have a wife, do you?*

The hood of the slicker was pushed back. His power haircut was finally in disarray — *mild* disarray; it was too short for anything else — and rainwater dripped down the sides of his face and into his eyes. He took in the situation at a glance, seemed to understand everything. *"Oh, you annoying bitch!"* he bellowed, and ran around the counter to grab her.

She stabbed out with the butcher knife. The

blade shot between the first and second fingers of his splayed right hand and sawed deep into the flesh at the bottom of the V. Blood poured down. Pickering screamed in pain and surprise — mostly surprise, she thought. Hyenas don't expect their victims to turn on th—

He reached out with his left hand, grabbed her wrist, twisted it. Something creaked. Or maybe snapped. Either way, pain bolted up her arm, as bright as light. She tried to hold on to the knife, but there was no chance. It went flying all the way across the room, and when he let go of her wrist, her right hand flopped, fingers splayed.

He bored in on her and Em pushed him backward, using both hands and ignoring the fresh scream of pain from her strained wrist. It was instinct only. Her rational mind would have told her that a push wasn't going to stop this guy, but her rational mind was now cringing in a corner of her head, able to do nothing but hope for the best.

He outweighed her, but her bottom was pressed against the chipped lip of the center island. He went staggering backward with a look of startlement that would have been comical in other circumstances, and came down on either one ice cube or a bunch of them. For a moment he looked like a cartoon character — Road Runner, perhaps — sprinting in place in an effort to stay on his feet.

Then he stepped on more ice cubes (she saw them go spinning and glinting across the floor), went down hard, and rapped the back of his head against his newly dented refrigerator.

He held up his bleeding hand and looked at it. Then he looked at her. "You *cut* me," he said. "You bitch, you dumb bitch, look at this, you *cut* me. Why did you cut me?"

He tried to scramble to his feet, but more ice cubes went zipping out from beneath him and he thumped down again. He pivoted on one knee, meaning to rise that way, and for a moment his back was to her. Em seized the chair's broken left arm from the center island. Ragged strands of duct tape still dangled from it. Pickering got to his feet and turned toward her. Emily was waiting. She brought the arm down on his forehead using both hands — her right one didn't want to close, but she made it. Some atavistic, survival-oriented part of her even remembered to choke up on the red maple rod, knowing it would maximize the force, and maximum force was good. It was a chair arm, after all, not a baseball bat.

There was a thump. It wasn't as loud as the swing door had been when he hit it coming in, but it still sounded loud enough, perhaps because the rain had slackened even more. For a moment nothing else happened, and then blood began to run out of his power haircut and over his forehead. She stared at him, into his eyes. He stared back with dazed incomprehension.

"Don't," he said feebly, and reached out one hand to take the chair arm from her.

"Yes," she said, and swung again, this time from the side: a slicing two-handed blow, her right hand giving up and letting go at the last moment, her left one holding firm. The end of the arm — ragged where it had broken, splinters sticking out — hammered into Pickering's right temple. This time the blood burst at once as his head snapped to the side, all the way to his left shoulder. Bright drops ran down his cheek and pattered onto the gray tile.

"Stop," he said thickly, pawing at the air with one hand. He looked like a drowning man begging for rescue.

"No," she said, and brought the arm down on his head again.

Pickering screamed and staggered away from her in a head-tucked hunch, trying to put the center island between them. He stepped on more ice cubes and skidded, but this time managed to stay upright. Only by luck, she had to believe, since he had to be all but out on his feet.

For a moment she almost let him go, thinking he would run out through the swing door. It was what she would have done. Then her dad spoke up, very calmly, in her head: *"He's after the knife, sweetie."*

*"No,"* she said, snarling it this time. "No, you *won't.*"

She tried to run around the other side of the island and head him off, but she couldn't run, not while she was dragging the shattered remains of the chair behind her like a ball and fucking chain — it was still duct-taped to her left knee. It banged against the island, slammed her in the butt, tried to get between her legs and trip her. The chair seemed to be on *his* side, and she was glad she had broken it.

Pickering got to the knife — it was lying against the bottom of the swing door — and fell on it like a football tackle covering a loose ball. He was making a guttural wheezing sound deep in his throat. Em reached him just as he started to turn over. She hammered him with the chair arm again and again, shrieking, aware in some part of her mind that it wasn't heavy enough and she wasn't generating anywhere near the amount of force she *wanted* to generate. She could see her right wrist, already puffing up, trying to address the outrage perpetrated on it just as if it expected to survive this day.

Pickering collapsed on the knife and lay still. She backed away a little, gasping for breath, those little white comets once more flying across her field of vision.

Men spoke in her mind. This was not

uncommon with her, and not always unwelcome. Sometimes, but not always.

Henry: *"Get that damned knife and put it right between his shoulder blades."*

Rusty: *"No, honey. Don't go close to him. That's what he expects. He's playing possum."*

Henry: *"Or the back of his neck. That's good, too. His stinking neck."*

Rusty: *"Reaching under him would be like sticking your hand into a hay baler, Emmy. You've got two choices. Beat him to death —"*

Henry, sounding reluctant but convinced: *"— or run."*

Well, maybe. And maybe not.

There was a drawer on this side of the island. She yanked it open, hoping for another knife — for *lots* of them: carving knives, filleting knives, steak knives, serrated bread knives. She would settle for a goddam *butter* knife. What she saw was mostly an array of fancy black plastic cooking tools: a pair of spatulas, a ladle, and one of those big serving spoons full of holes. There was some other bric-a-brac, but the most dangerous-looking thing her eye fell on was a potato peeler.

"Listen to me," she said. Her voice was hoarse, almost guttural. Her throat was dry. "I don't want to kill you, but I will if you make me. I've got a meat fork here. If you try to turn over, I'll stick it in the back of your neck and keep pushing until it comes out the front."

Did he believe her? That was one question. She was sure he'd removed all the knives except for the one underneath him on purpose, but could he be sure he'd gotten all the other sharp objects? Most men had no idea what was in the drawers of their kitchens — she knew this from life with Henry, and before Henry from life with father — but Pickering wasn't most men and this wasn't most kitchens. She had an idea it was more like an operating theater. Still, given how dazed he was (*was* he dazed?), and how he must surely believe that a lapse of memory could get him killed, she thought the bluff might run. Only there was another question: Was he even hearing her? Or understanding her if he did? A bluff couldn't work if the person you were trying to bluff didn't understand the stakes.

But she wasn't going to stand here debating. That would be the worst thing she could do. She bent over, never taking her eyes from Pickering, and hooked her fingers under the last band of tape still binding her to the chair. The fingers of her right hand wanted even less to work now, but she made them. And her sweat-drenched skin helped. She shoved downward, and the tape started coming free with another ill-tempered ripping sound. She supposed it hurt, it left a bright-red band across her kneecap (for some reason the word *Jupiter* floated randomly through her mind), but she was far past feeling such things. It let go all at once and slid down to her ankle, wrinkled and twisted and sticking to itself. She shook it off her foot and sidled backward, free. Her head was pounding, either from exertion or from where he'd hit her while she was looking at the dead girl in the trunk of his Mercedes.

"Nicole," she said. "Her name was Nicole."

Naming the dead girl seemed to bring Em back to herself a little. Now the idea of trying to get the butcher knife out from under him seemed like madness. The part of herself that sometimes talked in her father's voice was right — just staying in the same room with Pickering was pressing her luck. Which left leaving. Only that.

"I'm going now," she said. "Do you hear me?"

He didn't move.

"I've got the meat fork. If you come after me, I'll stab you with it. I'll . . . I'll poke your eyes out. What you want to do is stay right where you are. Have you got that?"

He didn't move.

Emily backed away from him, then turned and left the kitchen by the door on the other side of the room. She was still holding the bloody chair arm.

**There was a photograph on the wall by the bed.**

It was the dining room on the other side. There was a long table with a glass top. Around it were seven red maple chairs. The spot where the eighth belonged was vacant. Of course. As she studied the empty place at the "mother" end of the table, a memory came to her: blood blooming in a tiny seed pearl below her eye as Pickering said, *Okay, good, okay.* He had believed her when she said only Deke could know she might be inside the Pillbox, so he had thrown the little knife — Nicole's little knife, she had thought then — into the sink.

So there had been a knife to threaten him with all along. Still was. In the sink. But she wasn't going back in there now. No way.

She crossed the room and went down a hall with five doors, two on each side and one at the end. The first two doors she passed were open, on her left a bathroom and on her right a laundry room. The washing machine was a top loader, its hatch open. A box of Tide stood on the shelf next to it. A bloodstained shirt was lying halfway in and halfway out of the hatch. Nicole's shirt, Emily was quite sure, although she couldn't be positive. And if it *was* hers, why had Pickering been planning to wash it? Washing wouldn't take out the holes. Emily remembered thinking there had been dozens, although that surely wasn't possible. Was it?

She thought it was, actually: Pickering in a frenzy.

She opened the door beyond the bathroom and saw a guest room. It was nothing but a dark and sterile box starring a king bed so stringently neat, you could no doubt bounce a nickel on the counterpane. And had a maid made up that bed? *Our survey says no,* Em thought. *Our survey says no maid has ever set foot in this house. Only "nieces."*

The door across from the guest room gave way to a study. It was every bit as sterile as the room it faced across the hall. There were two filing cabinets in one corner. There was a big desk with nothing on it but a Dell PC hooded with a transparent plastic dust cover. The floor was plain oak planks. There was no rug. There were no pictures on the wall. The single big window was shuttered, admitting only a few dull spokes of light. Like the guest room, this place looked dim and forgotten.

*He has never worked in here,* she thought, and knew it was true. It was stage dressing. The whole house was, including the room from which she had escaped — the room that looked like a kitchen but was actually an operating theater, complete with easy-clean counters and floors.

The door at the end of the hall was closed, and as she approached it, she knew it would be locked. She would be trapped at the end of this corridor if he entered it from the kitchen/dining-room end. Trapped with nowhere to run, and these days running was the only thing she was good at, the only thing she was good *for.*

She hitched up her shorts — they felt like they were floating on her now, with the back seam split open — and grasped the knob. She was so full of her premonition that for a moment she couldn't believe it when the knob turned in her hand. She pushed the door open and stepped into what had to be Pickering's bedroom. It was almost as sterile as the guest room, but not quite. For one thing, there were two pillows instead of just one, and the counterpane of the bed (which looked like a twin of the guest-room bed) had been turned back in a neat triangle, ready to admit the owner to the comfort of fresh sheets after a hard day's work. And there was a carpet on the floor. Just a cheap nylon-pile thing, but wall-to-wall. Henry no doubt would have called it a Carpet Barn special, but it matched the blue walls and made the room look less skeletal than the others. There was also a small desk — it looked like an old school desk — and a plain wooden chair. And although this was pretty small shakes compared to the study setup, with its big (and unfortunately shuttered) window and expensive computer, she had a feeling this desk had been *used.* That Pickering sat there writing longhand, hunched over like a child in a country schoolroom. Writing what she did not like to think.

The window in here was also big. And unlike the windows in the study and the guest room, it wasn't shuttered. Before Em could look out and see what lay beyond, her attention was drawn to a photograph on the wall by the bed. Not hung and certainly not framed, only tacked there with a pushpin. There were other tiny holes on the wall around it, as if other pictures had been pinned there over the years. This one was a color shot with 4-19-07 printed digitally in the right corner. Taken by an old-fashioned camera rather than a digital one, by the look of the paper, and not by anyone with much flair for photography. On the other hand, perhaps the photographer had been excited. The way hyenas might get excited, she supposed, when sundown comes and there's fresh prey in the offing. It was blurry, as if taken with a telephoto lens, and the subject wasn't centered. The subject was a long-legged young woman wearing denim shorts and a cropped top that said BEER O'CLOCK BAR. She had a tray balanced on the fingers of her left hand, like a waitress in a jolly old Norman Rockwell painting. She was laughing. Her hair was blond. Em couldn't be sure it was Nicole, not from this blurred photo and those few shocked instants when she had been looking down at the dead girl in the trunk of the Mercedes . . . but she *was* sure. Her heart was sure.

Rusty: *"It doesn't matter, sweetie. You have to get out of here. You have to get yourself some running room."*

As if to prove it, the door between the kitchen and the dining room banged open — almost hard enough to tear it from the hinges, it sounded like.

*No,* she thought. All the sensation went out of her middle. She didn't think she wet herself again, but wouldn't have been able to tell if she had. *No, it can't be.*

"Want to play rough?" Pickering called. His voice sounded dazed and cheerful. "Okay, I can play rough. Sure. Not a problem. You want it? You bet. Daddy's gonna bring it."

Coming. Crossing the dining room. She heard a thump followed by a rough clatter as he stumbled into one of the other chairs (perhaps the one at the "father" end of the table) and shoved it aside. The world swam away from her, growing gray even though this room was relatively bright now that the storm was unraveling.

She bit down on her split lip. This sent a fresh stream of blood down her chin, but it also brought color and reality back into the world. She slammed the door and grabbed for the lock. There *was* no lock. She looked around and spied the humble wooden chair sitting before the humble wooden desk. As Pickering broke into a shambling run past his laundry room and study — and did he have the butcher knife clutched in one hand? Of course he did — she snatched the chair, placed it under the knob, and tilted it. Only an instant later, he hit the door with both hands.

She thought that if this floor had also been oak planking, the chair would have skidded away like a shuffleboard weight. Perhaps she would have grabbed it and stood him off with it: Em the Fearless Lion Tamer. She didn't think so. In any case, there was that carpet. Cheap nylon pile, but deep — it had that going for it, at least. The tilted legs of the chair dug in and held, although she saw a ripple go through the carpet.

Pickering roared and began to beat on the door with his fists. She hoped he was still holding on to the knife as he did it; maybe he would inadvertently cut his own throat.

"Open this door!" he shouted. "Open it! You're only making it worse for yourself!"

*Like I could,* Emily thought, backing away. And looking around. What now? The window? What else? There was only the one door, so it had to be the window.

"You're making me mad, Lady Jane!"

*No, you were already mad. As in hatter.*

She could see the window was a Florida special, the kind made only for looking out of, not for opening. Because of the air-conditioning. So what was next? Hurtle through it like Clint Eastwood in one of those old spaghetti westerns? Sounded possible; it was certainly the kind of thing that had appealed to her as a kid, but she had an idea she'd cut herself to ribbons if she actually tried it. Clint Eastwood and The Rock and Steven Seagal had stuntmen going for them when it came to things like the old through-the-saloon-window sequences. And the stuntmen had special glass going for *them.*

She heard the rapid thump of footfalls beyond the door as he first backed up and then ran at it again. It was a heavy door, but Pickering wasn't kidding, and it shuddered in its frame. This time the chair jerked backward an inch or two before holding. Worse, that ripple went through the rug again and she heard a tearing sound that was not unlike the sound of duct tape letting go. He was remarkably lively for someone who had been beaten about the head and shoulders with a stout piece of red maple, but of course he was both crazy and just sane enough to know that if she got away, he wouldn't. She supposed that was a strong motivator.

*I should have used the whole fucking chair on him,* she thought.

"Want to play?" he panted. "*I'll* play. Sure. Bet your butt. But you're on *my* playground, okay? And here . . . I . . . *come!*" He hit the door again. It bucked in its frame, loose on its hinges now, and the chair jumped back another two or three inches. Em could see dark teardrop shapes between the tilted legs and the door: rips in the cheap carpet.

Out the window then. If she was going to die bleeding from Christ alone knew how many wounds, she would rather inflict them herself. Maybe . . . if she wrapped herself in the coverlet . . .

Then her eye fell on the desk.

"Mr. Pickering!" she called, grasping the desk by the sides. "Wait! I want to make a deal with you!"

"No deals with bitches, okay?" he said petulantly, but he had stopped for a moment — perhaps to get his breath back — and it gave her time. Time was all she wanted. Time was all she could possibly get from him; she didn't really need him to tell her he wasn't the sort of man who made deals with bitches. "What's your big plan? Tell Daddy Jim."

Currently the desk was her plan. She picked it up, half certain her strained lower back would just pop like a balloon. But the desk was light, and lighter still when several rubber-banded stacks of what looked like university blue books came tumbling out.

"What are you doing?" he asked sharply,

and then: "Don't do that!"

She ran at the window, then stopped short and threw the desk. The sound of the breaking glass was enormous. Without pausing to think or look — thinking would do her no good at this point, and looking would only scare her if the drop was far — she yanked the coverlet from the bed.

Pickering hit the door again, and although the chair held again (she knew this; if it let go he would have been running across the room and grabbing for her), something gave a loud wooden crack.

Em wrapped the coverlet around her from chin to feet, for a moment looking like an N.C. Wyeth Indian woman about to set off into a snowstorm. Then she leaped through the jagged hole in the window just as the door crashed open behind her. Several arrows of glass sticking out of the frame wounded the coverlet, but not a single one touched Em.

*"Oh, you fucking annoying bitch!"* Pickering screamed behind her — *close* behind her — and then she was sailing.

### -9-

**Gravity is everyone's mother.**
She had been a tomboy as a kid, preferring boy's games (the best one was simply called Guns) in the woods behind their house in

suburban Chicago to goofing around with Barbie and Ken on the front porch. She lived in her Toughskins and shell tops, hair scrooped back behind her head in a ponytail. She and her bestfriend Becka watched old Eastwood and Schwarzenegger movies on TV instead of the Olsen twins, and when they watched *Scooby-Doo,* they identified with the dog rather than Velma or Daphne. For two years in grammar school, their lunches were Scooby Snacks.

And they climbed trees, of course. Emily seemed to remember her and Becka hanging out in the trees in their respective backyards for one whole summer. They might have been nine that year. Other than her father's lesson on how to fall, the only thing Em remembered clearly about the tree-climbing summer was her mother putting some kind of white cream on her nose every morning and telling her, *"Don't wipe that off, Emmy!"* in her obey-me-or-die voice.

One day, Becka lost her balance and came very close to falling fifteen feet to the Jackson lawn (maybe only ten, but at the time it had looked to the girls like twenty-five . . . even fifty). She saved herself by grabbing a branch, but then hung there, wailing for help.

Rusty had been mowing the lawn. He strolled over — yes, strolled; he even took time to kill the Briggs & Stratton — and held out his arms. "Drop," he said, and Becka, only two years past her belief in Santa and still sublimely trusting, dropped. Rusty caught her easily, then called Em down from the tree. He made both girls sit at the base. Becka was crying a little, and Em was scared — mostly that tree climbing would now become an act that was *forbidden,* like walking down to the corner store alone after seven p.m.

Rusty did not forbid them (although Emily's mother might have, if she had been looking out the kitchen window). What he did was teach them how to fall. And then they practiced for almost an hour.

What a cool day that had been.

As she went out through the window, Emily saw it was a damned good distance to the flagged patio below. Maybe only ten feet, but it looked like twenty-five as she dropped with the shredded coverlet fluttering around her. Or fifty.

*Let your knees give way,* Rusty had told them sixteen or seventeen years before, during Tree-Climbing Summer, also known as the Summer of the White Nose. *Don't ask them to take the shock. They will — in nine cases out of ten, if the drop isn't too far, they will — but you could end up with a broken bone. Hip, leg, or ankle. Ankle, most likely. Remember that gravity is everyone's mother. Give in to her. Let her hug you. Let your knees give way, then tuck and roll.*

Em hit the red Spanish-style flagstones and let her knees give way. At the same time she shoulder-checked the air, throwing her weight to the left. She tucked her head and rolled. There was no pain — no *immediate* pain — but a vast jarring went through her, as if her body had become an empty shaft and someone had dropped some large piece of furniture right down the center. But she kept her head from rapping the flagstones. And she didn't think she had broken either leg, although only standing would prove her right.

She struck a metal patio table hard enough to knock it over. Then she got to her feet, still not entirely sure her body was intact enough to do this until it actually did. She looked up and saw Pickering peering out the broken window. His face was cramped into a grimace, and he was brandishing the knife.

*"Stop it!"* he shouted. "Stop running away and *hold still!"*

*As if,* Em thought. The last of that afternoon's rain had turned to fog, dotting her upturned face with dew. It felt heavenly. She gave him the finger, then shook it for emphasis.

Pickering roared, *"Don't you flip me the bird, you cunt!"* and threw the knife at her. It didn't even come close. It struck the flagstones with a clang and skittered away beneath his gas grill in two pieces, blade and handle. When

126

she looked up again, the shattered window was vacant.

Her dad's voice told her Pickering was coming, but Em hardly needed that update. She went to the edge of the patio — walking easily, not limping, although she supposed she might owe that to the adrenaline surge — and looked down. Three measly feet to the sand and sea oats. A bunny compared to the drop she had just survived. Beyond the patio was the beach, where she had done so many morning runs.

She looked the other way, toward the road, but that was no good. The ugly concrete wall was too high. And Pickering was coming. Of course he was.

She braced one hand on the ornamental brickwork, then dropped to the sand. Sea oats tickled her thighs. She hurried up the dune between the Pillbox and the beach, hitching at her ruined shorts and looking repeatedly back over her shoulder. Nothing . . . still nothing . . . and then Pickering burst out through the back door, yelling at her to stop right where she was. He had ditched the yellow slicker and had grabbed some other sharp object. He was waving it in his left hand as he ran down the walk to the patio. She couldn't see what it was, and didn't want to. She didn't want him that close.

She could outrun him. Something in his gait said he would be fast for a little while and then flag, no matter how strongly his insanity and his fear of exposure pricked him on.

She thought: *It's as if I was in training for this all along.*

Yet she almost made a crucial mistake when she got to the beach, almost turned south. That would have taken her to the end of Vermillion Key in less than a quarter of a mile. Of course she could hail the drawbridge gatehouse when she got there (scream her lungs out for help, actually), but if Pickering had done something to Deke Hollis — and she was afraid that was the case — she would then be toast. There might be a passing boat she could scream to, but she had an idea Pickering was far past any restraint; at this point he would probably be willing to stab her to death on the stage of Radio City Music Hall as the Rockettes looked on.

So she turned north instead, where almost two miles of empty beach lay between her and the Grass Shack. She stripped off her sneakers and began to run.

## -10-

**What she had not expected was the beauty.** This wasn't the first time she had run on the beach after one of these brief but powerful afternoon storms, and the feeling of wetness accumulating on her face and arms was familiar. So was the heightened sound of the surf (the tide was on the come now, the beach narrowing to a stripe) and the heightened aromas: salt, seaweed, flowers, even wet wood. She had expected to be frightened — the way she supposed people in combat were frightened while doing dangerous jobs that usually (but not always) came out all right. What she had not expected was the beauty.

The fog had come in from the Gulf. The water was a dull green phantom, heaving shoreward through the white. The fish must have been running, because it was a pelican all-you-can-eat buffet out there. She saw most as projected shadows, folding their wings and plummeting at the water. A few others bobbed up and down on the waves closer in, seemingly as dead as decoys, but watching her. Out there to her left, the sun was a small orange-yellow coin peering dully.

She was afraid her calf would cramp up again — if that happened, she was done, finished. But this was work it had become used to, and it felt loose enough, if a little too warm. Her lower back was more worrisome, broadcasting a twinge with every third or fourth stride and sending out a heavier flash of pain every two dozen or so. But she talked to it inside her head, babied it, promised it hot baths and shiatsu massages when this was over and the feral creature behind her was safely incarcerated in the Collier County jail. It seemed to work. Either that or running was itself a kind of massage. She had reasons to think this was so.

Pickering bellowed twice more for her to stop, then fell silent, saving his breath for the chase. She looked back once and thought he was perhaps seventy yards behind, the only thing about him standing out in the misty late afternoon his red Izod shirt. She looked again and he was clearer; she could see his blood-splattered khaki shorts. Fifty yards behind. But panting. Good. Panting was good.

Emily leaped over a tangle of driftwood and her shorts slid down, threatening to hobble or even trip her up. She didn't have time to stop and take them off so she yanked them up savagely, wishing there was a drawstring she could pull, maybe even clutch in her teeth.

There was a yell from behind her and she thought there was fear as well as fury in it. It sounded as though Pickering was finally realizing this might not go his way. She risked another look back, hoping, and her hope was not in vain. He had tripped over the driftwood she had skipped over and gone to his knees. His new weapon lay before him, making an X in the sand. Scissors, then. Kitchen scissors. The big kind cooks used to snip gristle and bone. He snatched them up and scrambled to his feet.

Emily ran on, increasing her speed a little bit at a time. She didn't plan on doing this, but she didn't think it was her body taking over, either. There was something between body and mind, some interface. That was the part of her that wanted to be in charge now, and Em let it take over. That part wanted her to turn it on just bit by bit, almost gently, so that the animal behind her wouldn't realize what she was doing. That part wanted to tease Pickering into increasing his own speed to keep up with her, maybe even close the gap a little. That part wanted to use him up and blow him out. That part wanted to hear him gasping and wheezing. Maybe even coughing, if he was a smoker (although that seemed too much to hope for). Then she would put herself into the overdrive gear she now had but rarely used; that gear always seemed like tempting fate, somehow — like donning wax wings on a sunny day. But now she had no choice. And if she had tempted fate, it had been when she'd swerved to look into the Pillbox's flagged courtyard in the first place.

*And what choice did I have, once I saw her hair? Maybe it was fate that tempted me.*

She ran on, her feet printing the sand with her passing. She looked back again and saw Pickering only forty yards behind, but forty yards was okay. Given how red and strained his face was, forty was very okay.

To the west and directly overhead, the clouds tore open with tropical suddenness, instantly brightening the fog from dreary gray to dazzling white. Patches of sun dotted the beach with spotlights; Em ran into one and then out in a single stride, feeling the temperature spike with returning humidity and then drop again as the fog once more took her in. It was like running past an open Laundromat door on a cold day. Ahead of her, hazy blue opened in a long cat's eye. A double rainbow leaped out above it, each color blazing and distinct. The westward legs plunged into the unraveling fog and doused themselves in the water; those curving down toward the mainland disappeared into the palms and waxy fiddlewoods.

Her right foot clipped her left ankle and she stumbled. For a moment she was on the verge of falling, and then she regained her balance. But now he was just thirty yards behind, and thirty was too close. No more looking at rainbows. If she didn't take care of business, the ones up ahead would be her last.

She faced forward again and there was a man there, standing ankle-deep in the surf and staring at them. He was wearing nothing but a pair of cutoff denim shorts and a sopping red neckerchief. His skin was brown; his hair and eyes were dark. He was short, but his body was as trim as a glove. He walked out of the water, and she could see the concern on his face. Oh, thank God, she could see the concern.

"Help!" she screamed. *"Help me!"*

The look of concern deepened. *"Señora? Qué ha pasado? Qué es lo que va mal?"*

She knew some Spanish — driblets and drablets — but at the sound of his, all of hers went out of her mind. It didn't matter. This was almost certainly one of the groundskeepers from one of the big houses. He had taken advantage of the rain to cool off in the Gulf. He might not have a green card, but he didn't need one to save her life. He was a man, he was clearly strong, and he was concerned. She threw herself into his arms and felt the water on him soak onto her skin and shirt.

"He's crazy!" she shouted into his face. She could do this because they were almost exactly the same height. And at least one Spanish word came back to her. A valuable one, she thought, in this situation. *"Loco! Loco, loco!"*

The guy turned, one arm firmly around her. Emily looked where he was looking and saw Pickering. Pickering was grinning. It was an easy grin, rather apologetic. Even the blood spattered on his shorts and swelling face didn't render the grin entirely unconvincing. And there was no sign of the scissors, that was the worst. His hands — the right one slashed and now clotting between the first two fingers — were empty.

"*Es mi esposa,*" he said. His tone was as apologetic — and as convincing — as his grin. Even the fact that he was panting seemed all right. "*No te preocupes. Ella tiene . . .*" His Spanish either failed him or seemed to fail him. He spread his hands, still grinning. "Problems? She has problems?"

The Latino's eyes lit with comprehension and relief. "*Problemas?*"

"*Sí,*" Pickering agreed. Then one of his spread hands went to his mouth and made a bottle-tipping gesture.

"Ah!" the Latino said, nodding. "*Dreenk!*"

"No!" Em cried, sensing the guy was about to actually push her into Pickering's arms, wanting to be free of this unexpected *problema,* this unexpected *señora.* She blew breath into the man's face to show there was no liquor on it. Then inspiration struck and she tapped her swollen mouth. "*Loco!* He did this!"

"Nah, she did it to herself, mate," Pickering said. "Okay?"

"Okay," the Latino said, and nodded, but he didn't push Emily toward Pickering after all. Now he seemed undecided. And another word came to Emily, something dredged up from some educational children's show she had watched — probably with the faithful Becka — when she wasn't watching *Scooby-Doo.*

"*Peligro,*" she said, forcing herself not to shout. Shouting was what crazy *esposas* did. She pinned the Latino swimmer's eyes with her own. "*Peligro.* Him! *Señor Peligro!*"

Pickering laughed and reached for her. Panicked at how close he was (it was like having a hay baler suddenly grow hands), she pushed him. He wasn't expecting it, and he was still out of breath. He didn't fall down but did stagger back a step, eyes widening. And the scissors fell out from between the waistband of his shorts and the small of his back, where he had stashed them. For a moment all three of them stared at the metal X on the sand. The waves roared monotonously. Birds cried from inside the unraveling fog.

### -11-

**Then she was up and running again.**

Pickering's easy grin — the one he must have used on so many "nieces" — resurfaced. "I can explain that, but I don't have enough of the lingo. Perfectly good explanation, okay?" He tapped his chest like Tarzan. "*No Señor Loco, no Señor Peligro,* okay?" And it might have flown. But then, still smiling, pointing at Em, he said: "*Ella es bobo perra.*"

135

She had no idea what *bobo perra* was, but she saw the way Pickering's face changed when he said it. Mostly it had to do with his upper lip, which wrinkled and then lifted, as the top half of a dog's snout does when it snarls. The Latino pushed Em a step backward with a sweep of his arm. Not completely behind him, but almost, and the meaning was clear: protection. Then he bent down, reaching for the metal X on the sand.

If he had reached before pushing Em back, things might still have worked out. But Pickering saw things tilting away from him and went for the scissors himself. He got them first, fell on his knees, and stabbed the points through the Latino's sand-caked left foot. The Latino shrieked, his eyes flying wide open.

He reached for Pickering, but Pickering first fell to one side, then got up (*Still so quick,* Em thought) and danced away. Then he moved back in. He curled an arm around the Latino's trim shoulders in a just-pals embrace, and drove the scissors into the Latino's chest. The Latino tried to back away, but Pickering held him fast, stabbing and stabbing. None of the strokes went deep — Pickering was working too fast for that — but blood flowed everywhere.

*"No!"* Emily screamed. *"No, stop it!"*

Pickering turned toward her for just an instant, eyes bright and unspeakable, then stabbed the Latino in the mouth, the scissors going deep enough for the steel finger loops to clash on the man's teeth. "Okay?" he asked. "Okay? That okay? That work for you, you fucking beaner?"

Emily looked around for anything, a single piece of driftwood to strike him with, and there was nothing. When she looked back, the scissors were sticking out of the Latino's eye. He crumpled slowly, almost seeming to bow from the waist, and Pickering bent with him, trying to pull the scissors free.

Em ran at him, screaming. She lowered her shoulder and hit him in the gut, realizing in some distant part of her consciousness that it was a soft gut — a lot of good meals had been stored there.

Pickering went sprawling on his back, panting for breath, glaring at her. When she tried to pull away, he grasped her left leg and dug in with his fingernails. Beside her, the Latino man lay on his side, twitching and covered with blood. The only feature she could still make out on a face that had been handsome thirty seconds before was his nose.

"Come here, Lady Jane," Pickering said, and pulled her toward him. "Let me entertain you, okay? Entertainment okay with you, you useless bitch?" He was strong, and although she clawed at the sand, he was winning. She felt hot breath on the ball of her foot, and then his teeth sank gum-deep into her heel.

There had never been such pain; it made every grain on the beach jump clear in her wide eyes. Em screamed and lashed out with her right foot. Mostly by luck — she was far beyond such things as aim — she struck him, and hard. He howled (a muffled howl), and the needling agony in her left heel stopped as suddenly as it had begun, leaving only a burning hurt. Something had snapped in Pickering's face. She both felt it and heard it. She thought his cheekbone. Maybe his nose.

She rolled to her hands and knees, her swollen wrist bellowing with pain that almost rivaled the pain in her foot. For a moment she looked, even with her torn shorts once more sagging from her hips, like a runner in the blocks, waiting for the gun. Then she was up and running again, only now at a kind of skipping limp. She angled closer to the water. Her head was roaring with incoherencies (that she must look like the limping deputy in some old TV western or other, for instance — the thought just whipping through her head, there and then gone), but the survival-oriented part of her was still lucid enough to want packed sand to run on. She yanked frantically at her shorts, and saw that her hands were covered with sand and blood. With a sob, she wiped first one and then the other against her T-shirt. She threw one glance back over her right shoulder, hoping against hope, but he was coming again.

She tried as hard as she could, *ran* as hard as she could, and the sand — cold and wet where she was running — soothed her fiery heel a little, but she could still get into nothing resembling her old gait. She looked back and saw him gaining, putting everything he had into a final sprint. Ahead of her the rainbows were fading as the day grew relentlessly brighter and hotter.

She tried as hard as she could and knew it wasn't going to be enough. She could outrun an old lady, she could outrun an old man, she could outrun her poor sad husband, but she couldn't outrun the mad bastard behind her. He was going to catch her. She looked for a weapon to hit him with when he did, but there was still nothing. She saw the charred remains of someone's beach-party campfire, but it was too far ahead and too far inland, just below the place where the dunes and sea oats took over from the beach. He would catch her even sooner if she diverted in that direction, where the sand was soft and treacherous. Things were bad enough down here by the water. She could hear him closing in, panting harshly and snorting back blood from his broken nose. She could even hear the rapid whack of his sneakers on the damp sand. She wished so hard for someone else on the beach that for a moment she hallucinated a tall, white-haired guy with a big bent nose and rough dark skin. Then she realized her yearning mind had conjured her own father — a last hope — and the illusion blew away.

He got close enough to reach out for her. His hand batted the back of her shirt, almost caught the fabric, fell away. Next time it wouldn't. She swerved into the water, splashing in first to her ankles, then to her calves. It was the only thing she could think of, the last thing. She had an idea — unformed, inarticulate — of either swimming away from him or at least facing him in the water, where they might be on more even terms; if nothing else, water might slow the strokes of the awful scissors. If she could get deep enough.

Before she could throw herself forward and begin stroking — before she could even get as far in as her thighs — he grabbed her by the neck of her shirt and pulled her backward, dragging her toward the shore again.

Em saw the scissors appear over her left shoulder and grabbed them. She tried to twist, but it was hopeless. Pickering had braced himself in knee-deep water, his legs apart, his feet planted firmly against the sand-sucking rush of the retreating waves. She tripped over one of them and fell against him. They splashed down together.

Pickering's reaction was fast and unmistakable, even in the wet confusion: pushing and bucking and convulsive thrashing. Truth lit up in her head like fireworks on a dark night.

He couldn't swim. Pickering couldn't swim. He had a house by the Gulf of Mexico, but he couldn't swim. And it made perfect sense. His visits to Vermillion Key had been dedicated to indoor sports.

She rolled away from him and he didn't try to grab her. He was sitting chest-deep in the rolling boil of the waves, which were still agitated from the storm, and all his efforts were focused on scrambling up and getting his precious respiration away from a medium it had never learned how to cope with.

Em would have spoken to him if she could have wasted the breath. Would have said, *If I'd known, we could have ended this right away. And that poor man would still be alive.*

Instead, she waded forward, reached out, and grabbed him.

*"No!"* he screamed. He beat at her with both hands. They were empty — he must have lost the scissors when he fell — and he was too scared and disorganized to even make fists. *"No, don't! Let go, you bitch!"*

Em didn't. She dragged him deeper instead. He could have broken her hold, and easily, if he had been able to control his panic, but he couldn't. And she realized it was probably more than the inability to swim; he was having some sort of phobic reaction.

*What kind of a man with a water phobia would own a house on the Gulf? He'd have to be crazy.*

That actually got her laughing, although he was beating on her, his madly waving hands slapping first her right cheek then hard on the left side of her head. A surge of green water slopped into her mouth and she spluttered it back out. She dragged him deeper, saw a big wave coming — smooth and glassy, just a little foam starting to break at the top — and shoved him into it, facefirst. His screams became choked gurgles that disappeared as he went under. He thrust and bucked and twisted in her grip. The big wave washed over her and she held her breath. For a moment they were both under and she could see him, his face contorted into a pale mask of fear and horror that rendered it inhuman, and so turned him into what he really was. A galaxy of grit lazed between them in the green. One small, clueless fish zipped past. Pickering's eyes bulged from their sockets. His power haircut wafted, and this was what she watched. She watched it closely as a silver track of bubbles drifted up from her nose. And when the strands of hair reversed direction, drifting in the direction of Texas rather than that of Florida, she shoved him with all of her might and let him go. Then she planted her feet on the sandy bottom and pistoned upward.

She rose into brilliant air, gasping. She tore breath after breath out of it, then began to walk backward a step at a time. It was hard going, even in close to shore. The retreating wave sucking past her hips and between her legs was almost strong enough to qualify as an undertow. A little farther out, it *would* be. Farther out still it would become a rip, and there even a strong swimmer would have little chance, unless he kept his head and stroked sideways, cutting a long slow angle back to safety.

She floundered, lost her balance, sat down, and another wave drenched her. It felt wonderful. Cold and wonderful. For the first time since Amy's death, she had a moment of feeling good. Better than good, actually; every part of her hurt, and she understood that she was crying again, but she felt divine.

Em struggled to her feet, shirt sopping and stuck to her midriff. She saw some faded blue thing floating away, looked down at herself, looked back, and realized she had lost her shorts.

"That's all right, they were ruined anyway," she said, and began to laugh as she backed toward the beach: now kneedeep, now shindeep, now with only her feet in the boil. She could have stood there for a long time. The cold water almost doused the pain in her burning heel, and she was sure the salt was good for the wound; didn't they say the human mouth was the most germ-laden living thing on earth?

"Yes," she said, still laughing, "but who the

hell is th—"

Then Pickering surfaced, screaming. He was now about twenty-five feet out. He waved wildly with both hands. *"Help me!"* he screamed. *"I can't swim!"*

"I know," Em said. She raised one hand in a bon voyage wave and twiddled the fingers. "And you may even meet a shark. Deke Hollis told me last week they're running."

*"Help —"* A wave buried him. She thought he might not emerge, but he did. He was now thirty feet out. Thirty, at least. *"— me! Please!"*

His vitality was nothing short of amazing, especially since what he was doing — flailing his arms at the water, mostly, as if he thought he could fly away like a seagull — was counterproductive, but he was drifting out farther all the time, and there was no one on the beach to save him.

No one but her.

There was really no way he could get back in, she was sure of it, but she limped her way up to the remains of the beach-party campfire and plucked up the largest of the charred logs, just the same. Then she stood there with her shadow trailing out behind her and just watched.

**I suppose I prefer to think that.**

He lasted a long time. She had no idea exactly how long, because he had taken her watch. After a while he stopped screaming. Then he was just a white circle above the dark red blot of his Izod shirt, and pale arms that were trying to fly. Then all at once he was gone. She thought there might be one more sighting of an arm, surfacing like a periscope and waving around, but there wasn't. He was just gone. *Glub.* She was actually disappointed. Later she would be her real self again — a better self, maybe — but right now she wanted him to keep suffering. She wanted him to die in terror, and not quickly. For Nicole and all the other nieces there might have been before Nicole.

*Am I a niece now?*

She supposed in a way she was. The last niece. The one who had run as fast as she could. The one who had survived. She sat down by the ruins of the campfire and cast the burned butt end of log away. It probably wouldn't have made a very good weapon, anyhow; probably would have shattered like an artist's charcoal stick when she fetched him the first lick. The sun was a deepening orange, kindling the western horizon. Soon the horizon would catch fire.

She thought about Henry. She thought about Amy. There was nothing there, but there had been once — something as beautiful as a double rainbow over the beach — and that was nice to know, nice to remember. She thought of her father. Soon she would get up, and trudge down to the Grass Shack, and call him. But not yet. Not quite yet. For now it was all right to sit with her feet planted in the sand and her aching arms around her drawn-up knees.

The waves came in. There was no sign of her torn blue shorts or Pickering's red golf shirt. The Gulf had taken them both. Had he drowned? She supposed that was the likeliest thing, but the way he had gone down so suddenly, without so much as a final wave . . .

"I think something got him," she said to the deepening air. "I suppose I prefer to think that. God knows why."

*"Because you're human, sweetie,"* her father said. *"Only that."* And she supposed it was that true and that simple.

In a horror movie, Pickering would make one last stand: either come roaring out of the surf or be waiting for her, dripping but still his old lively self, in the bedroom closet when she got back. But this wasn't a horror movie, it was her life. Her own little life. She would live it, starting with the long, limping walk back to where there was a house and a key to fit it hidden in a Sucrets box under the old

146

ugly gnome with the faded red hat. She would use it, and she would use the telephone, too. She would call her father. Then she would call the police. Later, she supposed, she would call Henry. She guessed Henry still had a right to know she was all right, although he would not have it always. Or, she guessed, even want to have it.

On the Gulf, three pelicans swooped low, skimming the water, then rose, looking down. She watched them, holding her breath, as they reached a point of perfect equilibrium in the orange air. Her face — mercifully she didn't know this — was that of the child who might have lived to climb trees.

The three birds folded their wings and dove in formation.

Emily applauded, even though it hurt her swollen right wrist, and cried, *"Yo, pelicans!"*

Then she wiped her arm across her eyes, pushed back her hair, got to her feet, and began to walk home.

# HARVEY'S DREAM

Janet turns from the sink and, boom, all at once her husband of nearly thirty years is sitting at the kitchen table in a white T-shirt and a pair of Big Dog boxers, watching her.

More and more often she has found this weekday commodore of Wall Street in just this place and dressed in just this fashion come Saturday morning: slumped at the shoulder and blank in the eye, a white scruff showing on his cheeks, man-tits sagging out the front of his T, hair standing up in back like Alfalfa of the Little Rascals grown old and stupid. Janet and her friend Hannah have frightened each other lately (like little girls telling ghost stories during a sleepover) by swapping Alzheimer's tales: who can no longer recognize his wife, who can no longer remember the names of her children.

But she doesn't really believe these silent Saturday-morning appearances have anything to do with early-onset Alzheimer's; on any given weekday morning Harvey Stevens is ready and raring to go by six-forty-five, a man of sixty who looks fifty (well, fifty-four) in either of his best suits, and who can still cut a trade, buy on margin, or sell short with the best of them.

No, she thinks, this is merely practicing to be old, and she hates it. She's afraid that when he retires it will be this way every morning, at least until she gives him a glass of orange juice and asks him (with an increasing impatience she won't be able to help) if he wants cereal or just toast. She's afraid she'll turn from whatever she's doing and see him sitting there in a bar of far too brilliant morning sun, Harvey in the morning, Harvey in his T-shirt and his boxer shorts, legs spread apart so she can view the meagre bulge of his basket (should she care to) and see the yellow calluses on his great toes, which always make her think of Wallace Stevens having on about the Emperor of Ice Cream. Sitting there silent and dopily contemplative instead of ready and raring, psyching himself up for the day. God, she hopes she's wrong. It makes life seem so thin, so stupid somehow. She can't help wondering if this is what they fought through for, raised and married off their three girls for, got past his inevitable middle-aged affair for, worked for, and sometimes (let's face it) grabbed for. If this is where you come out of the deep dark woods, Janet thinks, this . . . this parking lot . . . then why does anyone do it?

But the answer is easy. Because you didn't know. You discarded most of the lies along the way but held on to the one that said life *mattered.* You kept a scrapbook devoted to the girls, and in it they were still young and still interesting in their possibilities: Trisha, the eldest, wearing a top hat and waving a tinfoil wand over Tim, the cocker spaniel; Jenna, frozen in mid-jump halfway through the lawn sprinkler, her taste for dope, credit cards, and older men still far over the horizon; Stephanie, the youngest, at the county spelling bee, where *cantaloupe* turned out to be her Waterloo. Somewhere in most of these pictures (usually in the background) were Janet and the man she had married, always smiling, as if it were against the law to do anything else.

Then one day you made the mistake of looking over your shoulder and discovered that the girls were grown and that the man you had struggled to stay married to was sitting with his legs apart, his fish-white legs, staring into a bar of sun, and by God maybe he looked fifty-four in either of his best suits, but sitting there at the kitchen table like that he looked seventy. Hell, seventy-five. He looked like what the goons on *The Sopranos* called a mope.

She turns back to the sink and sneezes delicately, once, twice, a third time.

"How are they this morning?" he asks, meaning her sinuses, meaning her allergies. The answer is not very good, but, like a surprising number of bad things, her summer allergies have their sunny side. She no longer has to sleep with him and fight for her share of the covers in the middle of the night; no longer has to listen to the occasional muffled fart as Harvey soldiers ever deeper into sleep. Most nights during the summer she gets six, even seven hours, and that's more than enough. When fall comes and he moves back in from the guest room, it will drop to four, and much of that will be troubled.

One year, she knows, he won't move back in. And although she doesn't tell him so — it would hurt his feelings, and she still doesn't like to hurt his feelings; this is what now passes for love between them, at least going from her direction to his — she will be glad.

She sighs and reaches into the pot of water in the sink. Gropes around in it. "Not so bad," she says.

And then, just when she is thinking (and not for the first time) about how this life holds no more surprises, no unplumbed marital depths, he says in a strangely casual voice, "It's a good thing you weren't sleeping with me last night, Jax. I had a bad dream. I actually screamed myself awake."

She's startled. How long has it been since he called her Jax instead of Janet or Jan? The

152

last is a nickname she secretly hates. It makes her think of that syrupy-sweet actress on *Lassie* when she was a kid, the little boy (Timmy, his name was Timmy) always fell down a well or got bitten by a snake or trapped under a rock, and what kind of parents put a kid's life in the hands of a fucking collie?

She turns to him again, forgetting the pot with the last egg still in it, the water now long enough off the boil to be lukewarm. He had a bad dream? Harvey? She tries to remember when Harvey has mentioned having had any kind of dream and has no luck. All that comes is a vague memory of their courtship days, Harvey saying something like "I dream of you," she herself young enough to think it sweet instead of lame.

"You what?"

"Screamed myself awake," he says. "Did you not hear me?"

"No." Still looking at him. Wondering if he's kidding her. If it's some kind of bizarre morning joke. But Harvey is not a joking man. His idea of humor is telling anecdotes at dinner about his Army days. She has heard all of them at least a hundred times.

"I was screaming words, but I wasn't really able to say them. It was like . . . I don't know . . . I couldn't close my mouth around them. I sounded like I'd had a stroke. And my voice was lower. Not like my own voice at

153

all." He pauses. "I heard myself, and made myself stop. But I was shaking all over, and I had to turn on the light for a little while. I tried to pee, and I couldn't. These days it seems like I can always pee — a little, anyway — but not this morning at two-forty-seven." He pauses, sitting there in his bar of sun. She can see dust motes dancing in it. They seem to give him a halo.

"What was your dream?" she asks, and here is an odd thing: for the first time in maybe five years, since they stayed up until midnight discussing whether to hold the Motorola stock or sell it (they wound up selling), she's interested in something he has to say.

"I don't know if I want to tell you," he says, sounding uncharacteristically shy. He turns, picks up the pepper mill, and begins to toss it from hand to hand.

"They say if you tell your dreams they won't come true," she says to him, and here is Odd Thing No. 2: all at once Harvey looks there, in a way he hasn't looked to her in years. Even his shadow on the wall above the toaster oven looks somehow more there. She thinks, He looks as though he matters, and why should that be? Why, when I was just thinking that life is thin, should it seem thick? This is a summer morning in late June. We are in Connecticut. When June comes we are always in Connecticut. Soon one of us will get the newspaper, which will be divided into

154

three parts, like Gaul.

"Do they say so?" He considers the idea, eyebrows raised (she needs to pluck them again, they are getting that wild look, and he never knows), tossing the pepper mill from hand to hand. She would like to tell him to stop doing that, it's making her nervous (like the exclamatory blackness of his shadow on the wall, like her very beating heart, which has suddenly begun to accelerate its rhythm for no reason at all), but she doesn't want to distract him from whatever is going on in his Saturday-morning head. And then he puts the pepper mill down anyway, which should be all right but somehow isn't, because it has its own shadow — it runs out long on the table like the shadow of an oversized chess piece, even the toast crumbs lying there have shadows, and she has no idea why that should frighten her but it does. She thinks of the Cheshire Cat telling Alice, "We're all mad here," and suddenly she doesn't want to hear Harvey's stupid dream, the one from which he awakened himself screaming and sounding like a man who has had a stroke. Suddenly she doesn't want life to be anything but thin. Thin is okay, thin is good, just look at the actresses in the movies if you doubt it.

Nothing must announce itself, she thinks feverishly. Yes, feverishly; it's as if she's having a hot flash, although she could have sworn all that nonsense ended two or three years ago. Nothing must announce itself, it's Saturday morning and nothing must announce itself.

She opens her mouth to tell him she got it backward, what they really say is that if you tell your dreams they will come true, but it's too late, he's already talking, and it occurs to her that this is her punishment for dismissing life as thin. Life is actually like a Jethro Tull song, thick as a brick, how could she have ever thought otherwise?

"I dreamed it was morning and I came down to the kitchen," he says. "Saturday morning, just like this, only you weren't up yet."

"I'm always up before you on Saturday morning," she says.

"I know, but this was a dream," he says patiently, and she can see the white hairs on the insides of his thighs, where the muscles are wasted and starved. Once he played tennis, but those days are done. She thinks, with a viciousness that is entirely unlike her, You will have a heart attack, white man, that's what will finish you, and maybe they'll discuss giving you an obit in the *Times,* but if a B-movie actress from the fifties died that day, or a semi-famous ballerina from the forties, you won't even get that.

"But it was like this," he says. "I mean, the sun was shining in." He raises a hand and stirs the dust motes into lively life around his head and she wants to scream at him not to do that.

"I could see my shadow on the floor and it never looked so bright or so thick." He pauses, then smiles, and she sees how cracked his lips are. "*Bright*'s a funny word to use for a shadow, isn't it? *Thick,* too."

"Harvey —"

"I crossed to the window," he says, "and I looked out, and I saw there was a dent in the side of the Friedmans' Volvo, and I knew — somehow — that Frank had been out drinking and that the dent happened coming home."

She suddenly feels that she will faint. She saw the dent in the side of Frank Friedman's Volvo herself, when she went to the door to see if the newspaper had come (it hadn't), and she thought the same thing, that Frank had been out at the Gourd and scraped something in the parking lot. How does the other guy look? had been her exact thought.

The idea that Harvey has also seen this comes to her, that he is goofing with her for some strange reason of his own. Certainly it's possible; the guest room where he sleeps on summer nights has an angle on the street. Only Harvey isn't that sort of man. "Goofing" is not Harvey Stevens's "thing."

There is sweat on her cheeks and brow and neck, she can feel it, and her heart is beating faster than ever. There really is a sense of something looming, and why should this be happening now? Now, when the world is quiet, when prospects are tranquil? If I asked for this, I'm sorry, she thinks . . . or maybe she's actually praying. Take it back, please take it back.

"I went to the refrigerator," Harvey is saying, "and I looked inside, and I saw a plate of devilled eggs with a piece of Saran wrap over them. I was delighted — I wanted lunch at seven in the morning!"

He laughs. Janet — Jax that was — looks down into the pot sitting in the sink. At the one hard-boiled egg left in it. The others have been shelled and neatly sliced in two, the yolks scooped out. They are in a bowl beside the drying rack. Beside the bowl is the jar of mayonnaise. She has been planning to serve the devilled eggs for lunch, along with a green salad.

"I don't want to hear the rest," she says, but in a voice so low she can barely hear it herself. Once she was in the Dramatics Club and now she can't even project across the kitchen. The muscles in her chest feel all loose, the way Harvey's legs would if he tried to play tennis.

"I thought I would have just one," Harvey says, "and then I thought, No, if I do that she'll yell at me. And then the phone rang. I dashed for it because I didn't want it to wake you up, and here comes the scary part. Do you want to hear the scary part?"

No, she thinks from her place by the sink. I don't want to hear the scary part. But at the same time she does want to hear the scary part, everyone wants to hear the scary part, we're all mad here, and her mother really did say that if you told your dreams they wouldn't come true, which meant you were supposed to tell the nightmares and save the good ones for yourself, hide them like a tooth under the pillow. They have three girls. One of them lives just down the road, Jenna the gay divorcée, same name as one of the Bush twins, and doesn't Jenna hate that; these days she insists that people call her Jen. Three girls, which meant a lot of teeth under a lot of pillows, a lot of worries about strangers in cars offering rides and candy, which had meant a lot of precautions, and oh how she hopes her mother was right, that telling a bad dream is like putting a stake in a vampire's heart.

"I picked up the phone," Harvey says, "and it was Trisha." Trisha is their oldest daughter, who idolized Houdini and Blackstone before discovering boys. "She only said one word at first, just 'Dad,' but I knew it was Trisha. You know how you always know?"

Yes. She knows how you always know. How you always know your own, from the very first word, at least until they grow up and become someone else's.

"I said, 'Hi, Trish, why you calling so early,

hon? Your mom's still in the sack.' And at first there was no answer. I thought we'd been cut off, and then I heard these whispering whimpering sounds. Not words but half-words. Like she was trying to talk but hardly anything could come out because she wasn't able to muster any strength or get her breath. And that was when I started being afraid."

Well, then, he's pretty slow, isn't he? Because Janet — who was Jax at Sarah Lawrence, Jax in the Dramatics Club, Jax the truly excellent French-kisser, Jax who smoked Gitanes and affected enjoyment of tequila shooters — Janet has been scared for quite some time now, was scared even before Harvey mentioned the dent in the side of Frank Friedman's Volvo. And thinking of that makes her think of the phone conversation she had with her friend Hannah not even a week ago, the one that eventually progressed to Alzheimer's ghost stories. Hannah in the city, Janet curled up on the window seat in the living room and looking out at their one-acre share of Westport, at all the beautiful growing things that make her sneeze and water at the eyes, and before the conversation turned to Alzheimer's they had discussed first Lucy Friedman and then Frank, and which one of them had said it? Which one of them had said, "If he doesn't do something about his drinking and driving, he's eventually going to kill somebody"?

"And then Trish said what sounded like 'lees' or 'least,' but in the dream I knew she was . . . eliding? . . . is that the word? Eliding the first syllable, and that what she was really saying was 'police.' I asked her what about the police, what was she trying to say about the police, and I sat down. Right there." He points to the chair in what they call the telephone nook. "There was some more silence, then a few more of those half-words, those whispered half-words. She was making me so mad doing that, I thought, Drama queen, same as it ever was, but then she said, 'number,' just as clear as a bell. And I knew — the way I knew she was trying to say 'police' — that she was trying to tell me the police had called her because they didn't have our number."

Janet nods numbly. They decided to unlist their number two years ago because reporters kept calling Harvey about the Enron mess. Usually at dinnertime. Not because he'd had anything to do with Enron per se but because those big energy companies were sort of a specialty of his. He'd even served on a Presidential commission a few years earlier, when Clinton had been the big kahuna and the world had been (in her humble opinion, at least) a slightly better, slightly safer place. And while there were a lot of things about Harvey she no longer liked, one thing she knew perfectly well was that he had more integrity in his little finger than all those Enron sleazebags put together. She might sometimes be bored by integrity, but she knows what it is.

But don't the police have a way of getting unlisted numbers? Well, maybe not if they're in a hurry to find something out or tell somebody something. Plus, dreams don't have to be logical, do they? Dreams are poems from the subconscious.

And now, because she can no longer bear to stand still, she goes to the kitchen door and looks out into the bright June day, looks out at Sewing Lane, which is their little version of what she supposes is the American dream. How quiet this morning lies, with a trillion drops of dew still sparkling on the grass! And still her heart hammers in her chest and the sweat rolls down her face and she wants to tell him he must stop, he must not tell this dream, this terrible dream. She must remind him that Jenna lives right down the road — Jen, that is, Jen who works at the Video Stop in the village and spends all too many weekend nights drinking at the Gourd with the likes of Frank Friedman, who is old enough to be her father. Which is undoubtedly part of the attraction.

"All these whispered little half-words," Harvey is saying, "and she would not speak up. Then I heard 'killed,' and I knew that one of the girls was dead. I just knew it. Not Trisha,

162

because it was Trisha on the phone, but either Jenna or Stephanie. And I was so scared. I actually sat there wondering which one I wanted it to be, like Sophie's fucking Choice. I started to shout at her. 'Tell me which one! Tell me which one! For God's sake, Trish, tell me which one!' Only then the real world started to bleed through . . . always assuming there is such a thing. . . ."

Harvey utters a little laugh, and in the bright morning light Janet sees there is a red stain in the middle of the dent on the side of Frank Friedman's Volvo, and in the middle of the stain is a dark smutch that might be dirt or even hair. She can see Frank pulling up crooked to the curb at two in the morning, too drunk even to try the driveway, let alone the garage — strait is the gate, and all that. She can see him stumbling to the house with his head down, breathing hard through his nose. Viva ze bool.

"By then I knew I was in bed, but I could hear this low voice that didn't sound like mine at all, it sounded like some stranger's voice, and it couldn't put corners on any of the words it was saying. 'Ell-ee itch-un, ell-ee itch-un,' that's what it sounded like. 'Ell-ee itch-un, Ish!' "

Tell me which one. Tell me which one, Trish.

Harvey falls silent, thinking. Considering. The dust motes dance around his face. The

163

sun makes his T-shirt almost too dazzling to look at; it is a T-shirt from a laundry-detergent ad.

"I lay there waiting for you to run in and see what was wrong," he finally says. "I lay there all over goosebumps, and trembling, telling myself it was just a dream, the way you do, of course, but also thinking how real it was. How marvelous, in a horrible way."

He stops again, thinking how to say what comes next, unaware that his wife is no longer listening to him. Jax-that-was is now employing all her mind, all her considerable powers of thought, to make herself believe that what she is seeing is not blood but just the Volvo's undercoating where the paint has been scraped away. *Undercoating* is a word her subconscious has been more than eager to cast up.

"It's amazing, isn't it, how deep imagination goes?" he says finally. "A dream like that is how a poet — one of the really great ones — must see his poem. Every detail so clear and so bright."

He falls silent and the kitchen belongs to the sun and the dancing motes; outside, the world is on hold. Janet looks at the Volvo across the street; it seems to pulse in her eyes, thick as a brick. When the phone rings, she would scream if she could draw breath, cover her ears if she could lift her hands. She hears Harvey get up and cross to the nook as it rings again, and then a third time.

It is a wrong number, she thinks. It has to be, because if you tell your dreams they don't come true.

Harvey says, "Hello?"

# REST STOP

He supposed that at some point between Jacksonville and Sarasota he did a literary version of the old Clark-Kent-in-the-phone-booth routine, but he wasn't sure just where or how. Which suggested it wasn't very dramatic. So did it even matter?

Sometimes he told himself the answer to that was no, the whole Rick Hardin/John Dykstra thing was nothing but an artificial construct, pure press agentry, no different from Archibald Bloggert (or whatever his real name might have been) performing as Cary Grant, or Evan Hunter (whose actual birth name had been Salvatore something-or-other) writing as Ed McBain. And those guys had been his inspiration . . . along with Donald E. Westlake, who wrote hard-boiled "caper" novels as Richard Stark, and K. C. Constantine, who was actually . . . well, no one really knew, did they? As was the case with the mysterious Mr. B. Traven, who had written *Treasure of the Sierra Madre.* No one really knew, and that was a large part of the fun.

Name, name, what's in a name?

Who, for instance, was he on his biweekly ride back to Sarasota? He was Hardin when he left the Pot o' Gold in Jax, for sure, no doubt. And Dykstra when he let himself into his canal-side house on Macintosh Road, certainly. But who was he on Route 75, as he flowed from one town to the other beneath the bright turnpike lights? Hardin? Dykstra? No one at all? Was there maybe a magic moment when the literary werewolf who earned the big bucks turned back into the inoffensive English professor whose specialty was twentieth-century American poets and novelists? And did it matter as long as he was right with God, the IRS, and the occasional football players who took one of his two survey courses?

None of that mattered just south of Ocala. What did was that he had to piss like a racehorse, whoever he was. He'd gone two beers over his usual limit at the Pot o' Gold (maybe three) and had set the Jag's cruise control at sixty-five, not wanting to see any strobing red lights in his rearview mirror tonight. He might have paid for the Jag with books written under the Hardin name, but it was as John Andrew Dykstra that he lived the majority of his life, and that was the name the flashlight would shine on if he was asked for his operator's license. And *Hardin* might have drunk the beers in the Pot o' Gold, but if a Florida state trooper produced the dreaded Breathalyzer kit in its little blue plastic case, it was Dykstra's intoxicated molecules that would wind up inside the gadget's educated guts. And on a Thursday night in June, he would be easy pickings no matter who he was, because all the snowbirds had gone back to Michigan and he had I-75 pretty much to himself.

Yet there was a fundamental problem with beer any undergraduate understood: You couldn't buy it, only rent it. Luckily, there was a rest stop just six or seven miles south of Ocala, and there he would make a little room.

Meanwhile, though, who was he?

Certainly he had come to Sarasota sixteen years before as John Dykstra, and it was under that name that he had taught English at the Sarasota branch of FSU since 1990. Then, in 1994, he'd decided to skip teaching summer classes and have a fling at writing a suspense novel instead. This had not been his idea. He had an agent in New York, not one of the superstuds, but an honest enough guy with a reasonable track record, who had been able to sell four of his new client's short stories (under the Dykstra name) to various literary magazines that paid in the low hundreds. The agent's name was Jack Golden, and while he had nothing but praise for the stories, he dismissed the resulting checks as "grocery money." It had been Jack who'd pointed out that all John Dykstra's published stories had "a high narrative line" (which was agentese for a plot, as far as Johnny could tell) and suggested his new client might be able to make $40,000 or $50,000 a whack writing suspense novels of a hundred thousand words.

"You could do that in a summer if you found a hook to hang your hat on and then stuck to it," he'd told Dykstra in a letter. (They hadn't progressed to using the phone and the fax at that point.) "And it would be twice as much as you'd make teaching classes in the June and August sessions down there at Mangrove U. If you're going to try it, my friend, now is the time — before you find yourself with a wife and two-point-five children."

There had been no potential wife on the horizon (nor was there now), but Dykstra had taken Jack's point; rolling the dice did not get easier as one grew older. And a wife and kids weren't the only responsibilities one took on as time slipped quietly by. There was always the lure of the credit cards, for instance. Credit cards put barnacles on your hull and slowed you down. Credit cards were agents of the norm and worked in favor of the sure thing.

When the summer-teaching contract came in January of '94, he had returned it unsigned to the department head with a brief explanatory note: *I thought this summer I'd try to write a novel instead.*

Eddie Wasserman's reply had been friendly but firm: *That's fine, Johnny, but I can't guarantee the position will be there next summer. The man in the chair always gets right of first refusal.*

Dykstra had considered this, but only briefly; by then he had an idea. Better still, he had a *character:* The Dog, literary father of Jaguars and houses on Macintosh Road, was waiting to be born, and God bless the Dog's homicidal heart.

Ahead of him was the white arrow on the blue sign twinkling in his headlights, and the ramp curving off to the left, and the high-intensity arc-sodium lights illuminating the pavement so brightly that the ramp looked like part of a stage set. He put on his blinker, slowed to forty, and left the interstate.

Halfway up, the ramp branched: trucks and Winnebagos to the right, folks in Jaguars straight ahead. Fifty yards beyond the split was the rest stop, a low building of beige cinder block that also looked like a stage set under the brilliant lights. What would it be in a movie? A missile-command center, maybe? Sure, why not. A missile-command center way out in the boonies, and the guy in charge is suffering from some sort of carefully concealed (but progressive) mental illness. He's seeing Russians everywhere, Russians coming out of the damn woodwork . . . or make it Al Qaeda terrorists, that was probably more au courant. The Russians were sort of out as potential villains these days unless they were pushing dope or teenage hookers. And the villain doesn't matter anyway, it's all a fantasy, but the guy's finger is nevertheless itching to push the red button, and . . .

And he needed to pee, so put the imagination on the back burner for a while, please and thank you. Besides, there was no place for the Dog in a story like that. The Dog was more of an urban warrior, as he'd said at the Pot o' Gold earlier tonight. (Nice phrase, too.) Still, the idea of that crazy missile-silo commander had some power, didn't it? A handsome guy . . . the men love him . . . looks perfectly normal on the outside . . .

There was only one other car in the sprawling parking area at this hour, one of those PT Cruisers that never failed to amuse him — they looked like toy gangster cars out of the 1930s.

He parked four or five slots down from it, turned off the engine, then paused to give the deserted parking lot a quick scan before getting out. This wasn't the first time he'd stopped at this particular rest area on his way back from the Pot, and once he'd been both amused and horrified to see an alligator lumbering across the deserted pavement toward the sugar pines beyond the rest area, looking somehow like an elderly, overweight businessman on his way to a meeting. There was no gator tonight, and he got out, cocking his key-pak over his shoulder and pushing the padlock icon. Tonight there was only him and Mr. PT Cruiser. The Jag gave an obedient twitter, and for a moment he saw his shadow in the brief flash of its headlights . . . only whose shadow was it? Dykstra's or Hardin's?

Johnny Dykstra's, he decided. Hardin was gone now, left behind thirty or forty miles back. But this had been his night to give the brief (and mostly humorous) after-dinner presentation to the rest of the Florida Thieves, and he thought Mr. Hardin had done a fairly good job, ending with a promise to send the Dog after anyone who didn't contribute generously to this year's charity, which happened to be Sunshine Readers, a non-profit that provided audiotape texts and articles for blind scholars.

He walked across the parking lot to the building, the heels of his cowboy boots clocking. John Dykstra never would have worn faded jeans and cowboy boots to a public function, especially one where he was the featured speaker, but Hardin was a different breed of hot rod. Unlike Dykstra (who could be fussy), Hardin didn't care much what people thought of his appearance.

The rest-area building was divided into three parts: the women's room on the left, the men's room on the right, and a big porch-like portico in the middle where you could pick up pamphlets on various central- and south-Florida attractions. There were also snack machines, two soft-drink machines, and a coin-op map dispenser that took a ridiculous number of quarters. Both sides of the short cinder-block entryway were papered with missing-child posters that always gave Dykstra a chill. How many of the kids in the photos, he always wondered, were buried in the damp, sandy soil or feeding the gators in the Glades? How many of them were growing up in the belief that the drifters who had snatched them (and from time to time sexually molested them or rented them out) were their mothers or fathers? Dykstra did not like to look at their open, innocent faces or consider the desperation underlying the absurd reward numbers — $10,000, $20,000, $50,000, in one case $100,000 (that last one for a smiling towheaded girl from Fort Myers who had disappeared in 1980 and would now be a woman in young middle age, if she was still alive at all . . . which she almost certainly was not). There was also a sign informing the public that barrel-picking was prohibited, and another stating that loitering longer than an hour in this rest area was prohibited — PO-LICE TAKE NOTICE.

*Who'd want to loiter here?* Dykstra thought, and listened to the night wind rustle through the palms. A crazy person, that was who. A person to whom a red button would start to look good as the months and years snored past with the sound of sixteen-wheelers in the passing lane at one in the morning.

He turned toward the men's room and then froze in midstep as a woman's voice, slightly distorted by echo but dismayingly close, spoke unexpectedly from behind him.

"No, Lee," she said. "No, honey, don't."

There was a slap, followed by a thump, a muffled meat thump. Dykstra realized he was listening to the unremarkable sounds of abuse. He could actually see the red hand shape on the woman's cheek and her head, only slightly cushioned by her hair (blond? dark?), bouncing off the wall of beige tile. She began to cry. The arc sodiums were bright enough for Dykstra to see that his arms had broken out in gooseflesh. He began to bite his lower lip.

"Fuckin' hoor."

Lee's voice was flat, declamatory. Hard to tell how you could know immediately that he was drunk, because each word was perfectly articulated. But you did know, because you had heard men speak that way before — at ballparks, at carnivals, sometimes through a thin motel-room wall (or drifting down through the ceiling) late at night, after the moon was down and the bars were closed. The female half of the conversation — could you call it a conversation? — might be drunk, too, but mostly she sounded scared.

Dykstra stood there in the little notch of an entryway, facing the men's room, his back turned toward the couple in the women's room. He was in shadow, surrounded on both sides by pictures of missing children that rustled faintly, like the fronds of the palm trees, in the night breeze. He stood there waiting, hoping there would be no more. But of course there was. The words of some country-music singer came to him, nonsensical and portentous: "By the time I found out I was no good, I was too rich to quit."

There was another meaty smack and another cry from the woman. There was a beat of silence, and then the man's voice came again, and you knew he was uneducated as well as drunk; it was the way he said *hoor* when he meant *whore.* You knew all sorts of things about him actually: that he'd sat at the back of the room in his high school English classes, that he drank milk straight out of the carton when he got home from school, that he'd dropped out in his sophomore or junior year, that he did the sort of job for which he needed to wear gloves and carry an X-Acto

176

knife in his back pocket. You weren't supposed to make such generalizations — it was like saying all African-Americans had natural rhythm, that all Italians cried at the opera — but here in the dark at eleven o'clock, surrounded by posters of missing children, for some reason always printed on pink paper, as if that were the color of the missing, you knew it was true.

"Fuckin' little hoor."

*He has freckles,* Dykstra thought. *And he sunburns easily. The sunburn makes him look like he's always mad, and usually he is mad. He drinks Kahlúa when he's in funds, as we say, but mostly he drinks b—*

"Lee, don't," came the voice of the woman. She was crying now, pleading, and Dykstra thought: *Don't do that, lady. Don't you know that only makes it worse? Don't you know he sees that runner of snot hanging out of your nose, and it makes him madder than ever?*

"Don't hit me no more, I'm s—"

*Whap!*

It was followed by another thump and a sharp cry, almost a dog's yelp, of pain. Old Mr. PT Cruiser had once more smoked her hard enough to bounce the back of her head off the tiled bathroom wall, and what was that old joke? Why are there three hundred thousand cases of spousal abuse in America each year? *Because they won't . . . fuckin' . . . listen.*

"Fuckin' hoor." That was Lee's scripture tonight, right out of Second Drunkalonians, and what was scary in that voice — what Dykstra found utterly terrifying — was the lack of emotion. Anger would have been better. Anger would have been safer for the woman. Anger was like a flammable vapor — a spark could ignite it and burn it off in a single quick and gaudy burst — but this guy was just . . . dedicated. He wasn't going to hit her again and then apologize, perhaps starting to cry as he did so. Maybe he had on other nights, but not tonight. Tonight he was going for the long bomb. Hail Mary fulla grace, help me win this stock-car race.

*So what do I do? What's my place in it? Do I have one?*

He certainly wasn't going to go into the men's room and take the long, leisurely piss he had planned and looked forward to; his nuts were drawn up like a couple of hard little stones, and the pressure in his kidneys had spread both up his back and down his legs. His heart was hurrying in his chest, thudding along at a rapid jog-trot that would probably become a sprint at the sound of the next blow. It would be an hour or more before he'd be able to piss again, no matter how badly he had to, and then it would come in a series of unsatisfying little squirts. And God, how he wished that hour had already gone by, that he was sixty or seventy miles down the road from here!

*What do you do if he hits her again?*

Another question occurred: What would he do if the woman took to her heels and Mr. PT Cruiser followed her? There was only one way out of the women's room, and John Dykstra was standing in the middle of it. John Dykstra in the cowboy boots Rick Hardin had worn to Jacksonville, where once every two weeks a group of mystery writers — many of them plump women in pastel pantsuits — met to discuss techniques, agents, and sales, and to gossip about one another.

"Lee-Lee, don't hurt me, okay? Please don't hurt me. Please don't hurt the baby."

Lee-Lee. Jesus wept.

Oh, and another one; score one more. *The baby. Please don't hurt the baby.* Welcome to the fucking Lifetime Channel.

Dykstra's rapidly beating heart seemed to sink an inch in his chest. It felt as if he had been standing here in this little cinder-block notch between the men's room and the women's for at least twenty minutes, but when he looked at his watch, he wasn't surprised to see that not even forty seconds had passed since the first slap. It was the subjective nature of time and the eerie speed of thought when the mind was suddenly put under pressure. He had written about both many times. He supposed most quote-unquote suspense novelists had. It was a goddam staple. The next time it was his turn to address the Florida Thieves, perhaps he would take that as his subject and begin by telling them about this incident. About how he'd had time to think, *Second Drunkalonians.* Although he supposed it might be a little heavy for their biweekly get-togethers, a little —

A perfect flurry of blows interrupted this train of thought. Lee-Lee had snapped. Dykstra listened to the particular sound of these blows with the dismay of a man who understands he's hearing sounds he will never forget, not movie-soundtrack Foleys but a fists-hitting-a-feather-pillow sound, surprisingly light, actually almost delicate. The woman screamed once in surprise and once in pain. After that she was reduced to puffing little cries of pain and fear. Outside in the dark, Dykstra thought of all the public-service spots he'd seen about preventing domestic violence. They did not hint at this, how you could hear the wind in the palm trees in one ear (and the rustle of the missing-child posters, don't forget that) and those little groaning sounds of pain and fear in the other.

He heard shuffling feet on the tiles and knew Lee (Lee-Lee, the woman had called him, as if a pet name might defuse his rage) was closing in. Like Rick Hardin, Lee was boots. The Lee-Lees of the world tended to be Georgia Giant guys. They were Dingo men. The woman was in sneakers, white low-tops. He knew it.

"Bitch, you fuckin' bitch, I seen you talkin' to him, tossin' your tits at him, you fuckin' hoor —"

"No, Lee-Lee, I never —"

The sound of another blow, and then a hoarse expectoration that was neither male nor female. Retching. Tomorrow, whoever cleaned these restrooms would find vomit drying on the floor and one of the tiled walls in the women's, but Lee and his wife or girlfriend would be long departed, and to the cleaner it would be just another mess to clean up, the story of the puke both unclear and uninteresting, and what was Dykstra supposed to do? Jesus, did he have the sack to go in there? If he didn't, Lee might finish beating her up and call it good, but if a stranger interfered —

*He could kill both of us.*

But . . .

*The baby. Please don't hurt the baby.*

Dykstra clenched his fists and thought, *Fucking Lifetime Channel!*

The woman was still retching.

"Stop that, Ellen."

*"I can't!"*

"No? Okay, good. I'll stop it for you. Fuckin' . . . *hoor*."

Another *whap!* punctuated *hoor*. Dykstra's

181

heart sank even lower. He would not have thought it possible. Soon it would be beating in his belly. If only he could channel the Dog! In a story it would work — he'd even been thinking about identity before making the evening's great mistake of turning into this rest area, and if that wasn't what the writing manuals called foreshadowing, then what was?

Yes, he would turn into his hit man, stride into the women's room, beat the living shit out of Lee, then go on his way. Like Shane in that old movie with Alan Ladd.

The woman retched again, the sound of a machine turning stones into gravel, and Dykstra knew he wasn't going to channel the Dog. The Dog was make-believe. This was reality, rolling out right here in front of him like a drunk's tongue.

"Do it again and see what it gets you," Lee invited, and now there was something deadly in his voice. He was getting ready to go all the way. Dykstra was sure of it.

*I'll testify in court. And when they ask me what I did to stop it, I'll say nothing. I'll say that I listened. That I remembered. That I was a witness. And then I will explain that that is what writers do when they're not actually writing.*

Dykstra thought of running back to his Jag — quietly! — and using the phone in the console to call the state police. *99 was all it took. The signs saying so were posted every ten miles or so: IN CASE OF ACCIDENT DIAL *99 ON CELLULAR. Except there was never a cop around when you needed one. The closest tonight would turn out to be in Bradenton or maybe Ybor City, and by the time the trooper got here, this little red rodeo would be over.

From the women's room there now came a series of thick hiccuping sounds, interspersed with low gagging noises. One of the stall doors banged. The woman knew that Lee meant it just as surely as Dykstra knew it. Just vomiting again would likely be enough to set him off. He would go crazy on her and finish the job. And if they caught him? Second degree. No premeditation. He could be out in fifteen months and dating this one's kid sister.

*Go back to your car, John. Go back to your car, get in behind the wheel, and drive away from here. Start working on the idea that this never happened. And make sure you don't read the paper or watch the TV news for the next couple of days. That'll help. Do it. Do it now. You're a writer, not a fighter. You stand five-nine, you weigh 162 pounds, you've got a bad shoulder, and the only thing you can do here is make things worse. So get back in your car and send up a little prayer to whatever God looks out for women like Ellen.*

And he actually turned away before an idea occurred to him.

The Dog wasn't real, but Rick Hardin *was.*

Ellen Whitlow of Nokomis had fallen into one of the toilets and landed on the hopper with her legs spread and her skirt up, just like the hoor she was, and Lee started in there after her, meaning to grab her by the ears and start slamming her dumb head against the tiles. He'd had enough. He was going to teach her a lesson she'd never forget.

Not that these thoughts went through his mind in any coherent fashion. What was in his mind now was mostly red. Under it, over it, seeping through it was a chanting voice that sounded like Steven Tyler of Aerosmith: *Ain't my baby anyway, ain't mine, ain't mine, you ain't pinning it on me, you fuckin' hoor.*

He took three steps, and that was when a car horn began to blat rhythmically somewhere close by, spoiling his own rhythm, spoiling his concentration, taking him out of his head, making him look around: *Bamp! Bamp! Bamp! Bamp!*

*Car alarm,* he thought, and looked from the entrance to the women's room back to the woman sitting in the stall. From the door to the hoor. His fists began to clench in indecision. Suddenly he pointed at her with his right index finger, the nail long and dirty.

"Move and you're dead, bitch," he told her, and started for the door.

It was brightly lit in the shithouse and

almost as brightly lit in the rest-area parking lot, but in the notch between the two wings it was dark. For a moment he was blind, and that was when something hit him high up on the back, driving him forward in a stumbling run that took him only two steps forward before he tripped over something else — a leg — and went sprawling on the concrete.

There was no pause, no hesitation. A boot kicked him in the thigh, freezing the big muscle there, and then high up on his blue-jeaned ass, almost to the small of his back. He started to scramble —

A voice above him said, "Don't roll over, Lee. I've got a tire iron in my hand. Stay on your stomach or I'll beat your head in."

Lee lay where he was with his hands out in front of him, almost touching.

"Come out of there, Ellen," said the man who had hit him. "We have no time to fool around. Come out right now."

There was a pause. Then the hoor's voice, trembling and thick: "Did you hurt him? Don't you hurt him!"

"He's okay, but if you don't come out right now, I'm going to hurt him bad. I'll have to." A pause, then: "And it'll be your fault."

Meanwhile, the car horn, beating monotonously into the night — *Bamp! Bamp! Bamp! Bamp!*

Lee started to turn his head on the pavement. It hurt. What had the fucker hit him

185

with? Had he said a tire iron? He couldn't remember.

The boot slammed into his ass again. Lee yelled and turned his face back to the pavement.

"Come out, lady, or I'm going to open up his head! I have no choice here!"

When she spoke again, she was closer. Her voice was unsteady, but now tending toward outrage: "Why did you *do* that? You didn't have to do that!"

"I called the police on my cell," the man standing above him said. "There was a trooper at mile 140. So we've got ten minutes, maybe a little less. Mr. Lee-Lee, do you have the car keys or does she?"

Lee had to think about it.

"She does," he said at last. "She said I was too drunk to drive."

"All right. Ellen, you go down there and get in that PT Cruiser, and you drive away. You keep going until you get to Lake City, and if you've got the brains God gave a duck, you won't turn around there, either."

"I ain't leaving him with you!" She sounded very angry now. "Not when you got that thing!"

"Yes, you are. You do it right now or I'll fuck him up royally."

"You bully!"

The man laughed, and the sound frightened Lee more than the fellow's speaking voice.

"I'll count to thirty. If you're not driving southbound out of the rest area by then, I'll take his head right off his shoulders. I'll drive it like a golf ball."

"You can't —"

"Do it, Ellie. Do it, honey."

"You heard him," the man said. "Your big old teddy bear wants you to go. If you want to let him finish beating the shit out of you tomorrow night — and the baby — that's fine with me. I won't be around tomorrow night. But right now I'm done fucking with you; *so you put your dumb ass in gear.*"

This was a command she understood, delivered in language familiar to her, and Lee saw her bare legs and sandals moving past his lowered line of vision. The man who'd sandbagged him started counting loudly: *"One, two, three, four . . ."*

"Hurry the hell *up!*" Lee shouted, and the boot was on his ass, but more gently now, rocking him rather than whacking him. But it still hurt. Meanwhile, *Bamp! Bamp! Bamp!* into the night. "Get your ass in *gear!*"

At that her sandals began to run. Her shadow ran beside them. The man had reached twenty when the PT Cruiser's little sewing-machine engine started up, had reached thirty when Lee saw its taillights backing into the parking area. Lee waited for the man to start whacking and was relieved when he didn't.

Then the PT Cruiser started down the exit lane and the engine sound began to fade, and then the man standing over him spoke with a kind of perplexity.

"Now," the man who'd sandbagged him said, "what am I going to do with *you?*"

"Don't hurt me," Lee said. "Don't hurt me, mister."

Once the PT Cruiser's taillights were out of sight, Hardin shifted the tire iron from one hand to the other. His palms were sweaty and he almost dropped it. That would have been bad. The tire iron would have clanged loudly on the concrete if he'd dropped it, and Lee would have been up in a flash. He wasn't as big as Dykstra had imagined, but he was dangerous. He'd already proved that.

*Sure, dangerous to pregnant women.*

But that was no way to think. If he let old Lee-Lee get up on his feet, this would be a whole new ball game. He could feel Dykstra trying to come back, wanting to discuss this and perhaps a few other points. Hardin pushed him away. This was not the time or place for a college English instructor.

"Now, what am I going to do with *you?*" he asked, the question one of honest perplexity.

"Don't hurt me," the man on the ground said. He was wearing glasses. That had been a major surprise. No way had either Hardin or Dykstra seen this man wearing glasses.

"Don't hurt me, mister."

"I got an idea." Dykstra would have said *I have an idea.* "Take your glasses off and put them beside you."

"Why —"

"Save the lip, just do it."

Lee, who was wearing faded Levi's and a Western-style shirt (now pulled out in the back and hanging over his butt), started to take off his wire-rimmed glasses with his right hand.

"No, do it with your other one."

"Why?"

"Don't ask me questions. Just do it. Take 'em off with your left hand."

Lee took off the queerly delicate spectacles and put them on the pavement. Hardin immediately stepped on them with the heel of one boot. There was a little snapping sound and the delicious grind of glass.

"Why'd you do that?" Lee cried.

"Why do you think? Have you got a gun or anything?"

"No! Jesus, *no!*"

And Hardin believed him. If there'd been one, it would have been a gator gun in the PT Cruiser's trunk. But he didn't think even that was likely. Standing outside the women's room, Dykstra had been imagining some big hulk of a construction worker. This guy looked like an accountant who worked out three times a week at Gold's Gym.

"I think I'll walk back to my car now," Hardin said. "Turn off the alarm and drive away."

"Yeah. Yeah, why don't you do th—"

Hardin put a warning foot on the man's butt again, this time rocking it back and forth a little more roughly.

"Why don't you just shut up? What did you think you were doing in there anyway?"

"Teaching her a fucking les—"

Hardin kicked him in the hip almost as hard as he could, pulling the blow a little bit at the last second. But only a little. Lee cried out in pain and fear. Hardin was dismayed at what he'd just done and how he'd done it, absolutely without thought. What dismayed him even more was that he wanted to do it again, and harder. He liked that cry of pain and fear, could do with hearing it again.

So how far was he from Shithouse Lee, lying out here with the shadow of the entryway running up his back on a crisp black diagonal? Not very, it seemed. But so what? It was a tiresome question, a movie-of-the-week question. A much more interesting one occurred to him. This question was how hard he could kick old Lee-Lee in the left ear without sacrificing accuracy for force. Square in the ear, *ka-pow*. He also wondered what kind of a sound it would make. A satisfying one, would be his guess. Of course he might kill the man doing that, but how much loss to the world would that be? And who would ever know? Ellen? Fuck her.

"You better shut up, my friend," Hardin said. "That would be your best course of action right about now. Just shut up. And when the state trooper gets here, you tell him whatever the fuck you want."

"Why don't you go? Just go and leave me alone. You broke my glasses, isn't that enough?"

"No," Hardin said truthfully. He thought a second. "You know what?"

Lee didn't ask him what.

"I'm going to walk slow to my car. You come on and come after me if you want. We'll do it face-to-face."

"Yeah, right!" Lee laughed tearfully. "I can't see shit without my glasses!"

Hardin pushed his own up on his nose. He didn't have to pee anymore. What a weird thing! "Look at you," he said. "Just look at you."

Lee must have heard something in his voice, because Hardin saw him start to tremble by the light of the silvery moon. But he didn't say anything, which was probably wise under the circumstances. And the man standing over him, who had never been in a fight in his whole life before this, not in high school, not even in *grammar* school, understood that this was really all over. If Lee had had a gun, he might have tried to shoot him in the back as he walked away. But otherwise, no. Lee was . . . what was the word?

Buffaloed.

Old Lee-Lee was buffaloed.

Hardin was struck by an inspiration. "I got your license number," he said. "And I know your name. Yours and hers. I'll be watching the papers, asshole."

Nothing from Lee. He just lay on his stomach with his broken glasses twinkling in the moonlight.

"Goodnight, asshole," Hardin said. He walked down to the parking lot and drove away. Shane in a Jaguar.

He was okay for ten minutes, maybe fifteen. Long enough to try the radio and then decide on the Lucinda Williams disc in the CD player instead. Then, all at once, his stomach was in his throat, still full of the chicken and potatoes he had eaten at the Pot o' Gold.

He pulled over into the breakdown lane, threw the Jag's transmission into park, started to get out, and realized there wasn't time for that. So he just leaned out instead with the seat belt still fastened and vomited onto the pavement beside the driver's-side door. He was shaking all over. His teeth were chattering.

Headlights appeared and swept toward him. They slowed down. Dykstra's first thought was that it was a state cop, finally a state cop. They always showed up when you didn't need them, didn't want them. His second one — a cold certainty — was that it was the PT Cruiser, Ellen at the wheel, Lee-Lee in the passenger seat, now with a tire iron of his own in his lap.

But it was just an old Dodge full of kids. One of them — a moronic-looking boy with what was probably red hair — poked his bepimpled moon of a face out the window and shouted, *"Throw it to your heeeels!"* This was followed by laughter, and the car accelerated away.

Dykstra closed the driver's-side door, put his head back, closed his eyes, and waited for the shakes to abate. After a while they did, and his stomach settled along the way. He realized he needed to pee again and took it as a good sign.

He thought of wanting to kick Lee-Lee in the ear — how hard? what sound? — and tried to force his mind away from it. Thinking about wanting to do that made him feel sick all over again.

Where his mind (his mostly obedient mind) went was to that missile-silo commander stationed out in Lonesome Crow, North Dakota (or maybe it was Dead Wolf, Montana). The one who was going quietly crazy. Seeing terrorists under every bush. Piling up badly written pamphlets in his locker, spending many a late night in front of the computer screen, exploring the paranoid back alleys of the Internet.

*And maybe the Dog's on his way to California to do a job . . . driving instead of flying because he's got a couple of special guns in the trunk of his Plymouth Road Runner . . . and he has car trouble . . .*

Sure. Sure, that was good. Or it could be, with a little more thought. Had he thought there was no place for the Dog out in the big empty of the American heartland? That was narrow thinking, wasn't it? Because under the right circumstances, anyone could end up anywhere, doing anything.

The shakes were gone. Dykstra put the Jag back in gear and got rolling. At Lake City he found an all-night gas station and convenience store, and there he stopped to empty his bladder and fill his gas tank (after checking the lot and the four pump islands for the PT Cruiser and not seeing it). Then he drove the rest of the way home, thinking his Rick Hardin thoughts, and let himself into his John Dykstra house by the canal. He always set the burglar alarm before leaving — it was the prudent thing to do — and he turned it off before setting it again for the rest of the night.

# STATIONARY BIKE

### I. METABOLIC WORKMEN

A week after the physical he had put off for a year (he'd actually been putting it off for three years, as his wife would have pointed out if she had still been alive), Richard Sifkitz was invited by Dr. Brady to view and discuss the results. Since the patient could detect nothing overtly ominous in his doctor's voice, he went willingly enough.

The results were rendered as numeric values on a sheet of paper headed METRO-POLITAN HOSPITAL, New York City. All the test names and numbers were in black except for one line. This one line was rendered in red, and Sifkitz was not very surprised to see that it was marked CHOLESTEROL. The number, which really stood out in that red ink (as was undoubtedly the intention), read 226.

Sifkitz started to enquire if that was a bad number, then asked himself if he wanted to start off this interview by asking something stupid. It would not have been printed in red, he reasoned, if it had been a good number. The rest of them were undoubtedly good numbers, or at least acceptable numbers, which was why they were printed in black. But he wasn't here to discuss them. Doctors were busy men, disinclined to waste time in head-patting. So instead of something stupid, he asked how bad a number two-twenty-six was.

Dr. Brady leaned back in his chair and laced his fingers together on his damnably skinny chest. "To tell you the truth," he said, "it's not a bad number at all." He raised a finger. "Considering what you eat, that is."

"I know I weigh too much," Sifkitz said humbly. "I've been meaning to do something about it." In fact, he had been meaning to do no such thing.

"To tell you more of the truth," Dr. Brady went on, "your weight is not so bad, either. Again, considering what you eat. And now I want you to listen closely, because this is a conversation I only have with my patients once. My male patients, that is; when it comes to weight, my female patients would talk my ear off, if I let them. Are you ready?"

"Yes," Sifkitz said, attempting to lace his fingers across his own chest and discovering he could not do it. What he discovered — or rediscovered, more properly put — was that he had a pretty good set of breasts. Not, so

196

far as he was aware, part of the standard equipment for men in their late thirties. He gave up his attempt to lace and folded, instead. In his lap. The sooner the lecture was begun, the sooner it would be done.

"You're six feet tall and thirty-eight years old," Dr. Brady said. "Your weight should be about a hundred and ninety, and your cholesterol should be just about the same. Once upon a time, back in the seventies, you could get away with a cholesterol reading of two-forty, but of course back in the seventies, you could still smoke in the waiting rooms at hospitals." He shook his head. "No, the correlation between high cholesterol and heart disease was simply too clear. The two-forty number consequently went by the boards.

"You are the sort of man who has been blessed with a good metabolism. Not a great one, mind you, but good? Yes. How many times do you eat at McDonald's or Wendy's, Richard? Twice a week?"

"Maybe once," Sifkitz said. He thought the average week actually brought four to six fast-food meals with it. Not counting the occasional weekend trip to Arby's.

Dr. Brady raised a hand as if to say Have it your way . . . which was, now that Sifkitz thought of it, the Burger King motto.

"Well, you're certainly eating somewhere, as the scales tell us. You weighed in on the day of your physical at two-twenty-three . . .

once again, and not coincidentally, very close to your cholesterol number."

He smiled a little at Sifkitz's wince, but at least it was not a smile devoid of sympathy.

"Here is what has happened so far in your adult life," Brady said. "In it, you have continued to eat as you did when you were a teenager, and to this point your body — thanks to that good-if-not-extraordinary metabolism — has pretty much kept up with you. It helps at this point to think of the metabolic process as a work-crew. Men in chinos and Doc Martens."

It may help you, Sifkitz thought, it doesn't do a thing for me. Meanwhile, his eyes kept being drawn back to that red number, that 226.

"Their job is to grab the stuff you send down the chute and dispose of it. Some they send on to the various production departments. The rest they burn. If you send them more than they can deal with, you put on weight. Which you have been doing, but at a relatively slow pace. But soon, if you don't make some changes, you're going to see that pace speed up. There are two reasons. The first is that your body's production facilities need less fuel than they used to. The second is that your metabolic crew — those fellows in the chinos with the tattoos on their arms — aren't getting any younger. They're not as efficient as they used to be. They're slower when it comes to separating the stuff to be sent on and the stuff that needs to be burned. And sometimes they bitch."

"Bitch?" Sifkitz asked.

Dr. Brady, hands still laced across his narrow chest (the chest of a consumptive, Sifkitz decided — certainly no breasts there), nodded his equally narrow head. Sifkitz thought it almost the head of a weasel, sleek and sharp-eyed. "Yes indeed. They say stuff like, 'Isn't he ever gonna slow down?' and 'Who does he think we are, the Marvel Comics superheroes?' and 'Cheezis, don't he ever give it a rest?' And one of them — the malingerer, every work-crew's got one — probably says, 'What the fuck does he care about us, anyway? He's on top, ain't he?'

"And sooner or later, they'll do what any bunch of working joes will do if they're forced to go on too long and do too much, without so much as a lousy weekend off, let alone a paid vacation: they'll get sloppy. Start goofing off and lying down on the job. One day one of 'em won't come in at all, and there'll come another — if you live long enough — when one of 'em can't come in, because he'll be lying home dead of a stroke or a heart attack."

"That's pleasant. Maybe you could take it on the road. Hit the lecture circuit. Oprah, even."

Dr. Brady unlaced his fingers and leaned forward across his desk. He looked at Richard Sifkitz, unsmiling. "You've got a choice to make and my job is to make you aware of it, that's all. Either you change your habits or you're going to find yourself in my office ten years from now with some serious problems — weight pushing three hundred pounds, maybe, Type Two diabetes, varicose veins, a stomach ulcer, and a cholesterol number to match your weight. At this point you can still turn around without crash-diets, tummy-tucks, or a heart attack to get your attention. Later on doing that'll get harder. Once you're past forty, it gets harder every year. After forty, Richard, the weight sticks to your ass like babyshit sticks to a bedroom wall."

"Elegant," Sifkitz said, and burst out laughing. He couldn't help it.

Brady didn't laugh, but he smiled, at least, and leaned back in his chair. "There's nothing elegant about where you're headed. Doctors don't usually talk about it any more than State Troopers talk about the severed head they found in a ditch near the car accident, or the blackened child they found in the closet the day after the Christmas tree lights caught the house on fire, but we know lots about the wonderful world of obesity, from women who grow mold in flaps of fat that haven't been washed all the way to the bottom in years to men who go everywhere in a cloud of stench because they haven't been able to wipe themselves properly in a decade

200

or more."

Sifkitz winced and made a waving-away gesture.

"I don't say you're going there, Richard — most people don't, they have a kind of built-in limiter, it seems — but there is some truth to that old saying about so-and-so digging his grave with a fork and spoon. Keep it in mind."

"I will."

"Good. That's the speech. Or sermon. Or whatever it is. I won't tell you to go your way and sin no more, I'll just say 'over to you.' "

Although he had filled in the OCCUPATION blank on his income tax return with the words FREELANCE ARTIST for the last twelve years, Sifkitz did not think of himself as a particularly imaginative man, and he hadn't done a painting (or even a drawing, really) just for himself since the year he graduated from DePaul. He did book jackets, some movie posters, a lot of magazine illustrations, the occasional cover for a trade-show brochure. He'd done one CD cover (for Slobberbone, a group he particularly admired) but would never do another one, he said, because you couldn't see the detail in the finished product without a magnifying glass. That was as close as he had ever come to what is called "artistic temperament."

If asked to name his favorite piece of work, he likely would have looked blank. If pressed, he might have said it was the painting of the young blond woman running through the grass that he had done for Downy Fabric Softener, but even that would have been a lie, something told just to make the question go away. In truth, he wasn't the kind of artist who had (or needed to have) favorites. It had been a long time since he'd picked up a brush to paint anything other than what someone commissioned him to paint, usually from a detailed ad agency memo or from a photograph (as had been the case with the woman running through the grass, evidently overjoyed that she had finally managed to beat static cling).

But, as surely as inspiration strikes the best of us — the Picassos, the Van Goghs, the Salvador Dalís — so it must eventually strike the rest of us, if only once or twice in a lifetime. Sifkitz took the crosstown bus home (he'd not owned a car since college), and as he sat looking out the window (the medical report with its one line of red type was folded into his back pocket), he found his eye again and again going to the various work-crews and construction gangs the bus rolled past: guys in hardhats tromping across a building site, some with buckets, some with boards balanced on their shoulders; Con Ed guys half-in and half-out of manholes surrounded by yellow tape stamped with the words WORK AREA; three guys erecting a scaffold in front of a department store display window while a fourth talked on his cell phone.

Little by little he realized a picture was forming in his mind, one which demanded its place in the world. When he was back to the SoHo loft that served as both his home and his studio, he crossed to the littered nest beneath the skylight without even bothering to pick the mail up off the floor. He dropped his jacket on top of it, as a matter of fact.

He paused only long enough to look at a number of blank canvases leaning in the corner, and dismiss them. He took a piece of plain white pressboard instead, and set to work with a charcoal pencil. The phone rang twice over the course of the next hour. He let the answering machine pick up both times.

He worked at this picture off and on — but rather more on than off, especially as time passed and he came to realize how good it was — over the next ten days, moving from the pressboard to a piece of canvas that was four feet long and three feet high when it seemed natural to do so. It was the biggest surface he'd worked on in over a decade.

The picture showed four men — workmen in jeans, poplin jackets, and big old work-boots — standing at the side of a country road which had just emerged from a deep stand of forest (this he rendered in shades of dark green and streaks of gray, working in a splashy, speedy, exuberant style). Two of the men had shovels; one had a bucket in each hand; the fourth was in the process of pushing his cap back from his forehead in a gesture that perfectly caught his end-of-the-day weariness and his growing realization that the job would never be done; that there was, in fact, more of the job needing to be done at the end of each day than there had been at the beginning. This fourth guy, wearing a battered old gimme-cap with the word LIPID printed above the bill, was the foreman. He was talking to his wife on his cell phone. Coming home, honey, nah, don't want to go out, not tonight, too tired, want to get an early start in the morning. The guys bitched about that but I brought 'em around. Sifkitz didn't know how he knew all this, but he did. Just as he knew that the man with the buckets was Freddy, and he owned the truck in which the men had come. It was parked just outside the picture on the right; you could see the top of its shadow. One of the shovel guys, Carlos, had a bad back and was seeing a chiropractor.

There was no sign of what job the men had been doing in the picture, that was a little beyond the left side, but you could see how exhausted they were. Sifkitz had always been a detail-man (that green-gray blur of forest was very unlike him), and you could read how weary these men were in every feature of their faces. It was even in the sweat-stains on the collars of their shirts.

Above them, the sky was a queer organic red.

Of course he knew what the picture represented and understood that queer sky perfectly. This was the work-crew of which his doctor had spoken, at the end of their day. In the real world beyond that organic red sky, Richard Sifkitz, their employer, had just eaten his bed-time snack (a left-over piece of cake, maybe, or a carefully hoarded Krispy Kreme) and laid his head down on his pillow. Which meant they were finally free to go home for the day. And would they eat? Yes, but not as much as he did. They would be too tired to eat much, it was on their faces. Instead of eating a big meal they'd put their feet up, these guys who worked for The Lipid Company, and watch TV for a little while. Maybe fall asleep in front of it and then wake up a couple of hours later, with the regular shows gone and Ron Popeil on, showing his latest invention to an adoring studio audience. And they'd turn it off with the remote and shuffle away to bed, shedding clothes as they went without so much as a backward look.

All of this was in the picture, although none of it was in the picture. Sifkitz was not obsessed with it, it did not become his life, but he understood it was something *new* in his life, something good. He had no idea what he could do with such a thing once it was

205

finished, and didn't really care. For the time being he just liked getting up in the morning and looking at it with one eye open as he picked the cloth of his Big Dog boxers out of the crack of his ass. He supposed when it was done, he would have to name it. So far he had considered and rejected "Quittin' Time," "The Boys Call It a Day," and "Berkowitz Calls It a Day." Berkowitz being the boss, the foreman, the one with the Motorola cell phone, the guy in the LIPID cap. None of those names were quite right, and that was okay. He'd know the right name for the picture when it finally occurred to him. It would make a *cling!* sound in his head. In the meantime there was no hurry. He wasn't even sure the picture was the point. While painting it, he had lost fifteen pounds. Maybe that was the point.

Or maybe it wasn't.

## II. STATIONARY BIKE

Somewhere — maybe at the end of a Salada tea-bag string — he had read that, for the person who aspires to lose weight, the most effective exercise is pushing back from the table. Sifkitz had no doubt this was true, but as time passed he more and more came to believe that losing weight wasn't his goal. Nor was getting buffed up his goal, although both of those things might be side-effects. He kept

206

thinking of Dr. Brady's metabolic working stiffs, ordinary joes who were really trying their best to do their job but getting no help from him. He could hardly not think of them when he was spending an hour or two every day painting them and their workaday world.

He fantasized quite a lot about them. There was Berkowitz, the foreman, who aspired to have his own construction company someday. Freddy, who owned the truck (a Dodge Ram) and fancied himself a fancy carpenter. Carlos, the one with the bad back. And Whelan, who was actually sort of a goldbrick. These were the guys whose job it was to keep him from having a heart attack or a stroke. They had to clean up the shit that kept bombing down from that queer red sky before it blocked the road into the woods.

A week after he began the painting (and about a week before he would finally decide it was done), Sifkitz went to The Fitness Boys on Twenty-ninth Street, and, after considering both a treadmill and a StairMaster (attractive but too expensive), bought a stationary bike. He paid an extra forty dollars to have it assembled and delivered.

"Use this every day for six months and your cholesterol number's down thirty points," said the salesman, a brawny young fellow in a Fitness Boys T-shirt. "I practically guarantee it."

The basement of the building where Sifkitz

lived was a rambling, multi-room affair, dark and shadowy, bellowing with furnace noise and crammed with tenants' possessions in stalls marked with the various apartment numbers. There was an alcove at the far end, however, that was almost magically empty. As if it had been waiting for him all along. Sifkitz had the deliverymen set up his new exercise machine on the concrete floor facing a bare beige wall.

"You gonna bring down a TV?" one of them asked.

"I haven't decided yet," Sifkitz said, although he had.

He rode the stationary bike in front of one bare beige wall for fifteen minutes or so every day until the painting was finished, knowing that fifteen minutes was probably not enough (although certainly better than nothing) but also knowing it was about all he could stand for the time being. Not because he got tired; fifteen minutes wasn't enough to tire him out. It was just boring in the basement. The whine of the wheels combined with the steady roar of the furnace quickly got on his nerves. He was all too aware of what he was doing, which was, basically, going nowhere in a basement under two bare lightbulbs that cast his double shadow on the wall in front of him. He also knew that things would improve once the picture upstairs was done and he could start on the one down here.

It was the same picture but he executed it much more quickly. He could do this because there was no need to put Berkowitz, Carlos, Freddy, and Whelan-the-goldbrick in this one. In this one they were gone for the day and he simply painted the country road on the beige wall, using forced perspective so that when he was mounted on the stationary bike, the track seemed to wind away from him and into that dark green and gray blur of forest. Riding the bike became less boring immediately, but after two or three sessions, he realized that he still wasn't done because what he was doing was still only exercise. He needed to put in the red sky, for one thing, but that was easy, nothing but slop work. He wanted to add more detail to both shoulders of the road "up front," and some litter, as well, but those things were also easy (and fun). The real problem had nothing to do with the picture at all. With either picture. The problem was that he had no goal, and that had always bugged him about exercise that existed for nothing more than its own sake. That kind of workout might tone you up and improve your health, but it was essentially meaningless while it was going on. Existential, even. That kind of workout was only about the next thing, for instance some pretty lady from some magazine's art department coming up to you at a party and asking if you'd lost weight. That wasn't even close to real motivation. He wasn't vain enough (or horny enough) for such possibilities to keep him going over the long haul. He'd eventually get bored, and lapse into his old Krispy Kreme ways. No, he had to decide where the road was, and where it was going. Then he could pretend to ride there. The idea excited him. Maybe it was silly — loony, even — but to Sifkitz that excitement, though mild, felt like the real deal. And he didn't have to tell anyone what he was up to, did he? Absolutely not. He could even get a Rand-McNally Road Atlas and mark his daily progress on one of the maps.

He was not an introspective man by nature, but on his walk back from Barnes & Noble with his new book of roadmaps under his arm, he found himself wondering exactly what had galvanized him so. A moderately high cholesterol number? He doubted it. Dr. Brady's solemn proclamation that he would find this battle much harder to fight once he was post-forty? That might have had something to do with it, but probably not all that much. Was he just ready for a change? That felt like getting warmer.

Trudy had died of a particularly ravenous blood-cancer, and Sifkitz had been with her, in her hospital room, when she passed on. He remembered how deep her last breath had been, how her sad and wasted bosom had heaved upward as she drew it in. As if she had known this was it, this was the one for the ages. He remembered how she'd let it out, and the sound it had made — *shaaaah!* And how after that her chest had just stayed where it was. In a way he had lived the last four years in just that sort of breathless hiatus. Only now the wind was blowing again, filling his sails.

Yet there was something else, something even more to the point: the work-crew Brady had summoned up and Sifkitz himself had named. There was Berkowitz, Whelan, Carlos, and Freddy. Dr. Brady hadn't cared about them; for Brady, the metabolic work-crew was just a metaphor. His job was to make Sifkitz care a little more about what was going on inside him, that was all, his metaphor not much different from the mommy who tells her toddler that "little men" are working to heal the skin on his scraped knee.

Sifkitz's focus, though . . .

Not on myself at all, he thought, shaking out the key that opened the lobby door. Never was. I cared about those guys, stuck doing a never-ending clean-up job. And the road. Why should they work so hard to keep it clear? Where did it go?

He decided it went to Herkimer, which was a small town up by the Canadian border. He found a skinny and unmarked blue line on the roadmap of upstate New York that rambled there all the way from Poughkeepsie, which was south of the state capital. Two, maybe three hundred miles. He got a more detailed plat map of upstate New York and thumbtacked the square where this road began on the wall beside his hasty . . . his hasty what-would-you-call-it? Mural wasn't right. He settled on "projection."

And that day when he mounted the stationary bike, he imagined that Poughkeepsie was behind him, not the stored television from 2-G, the stack of trunks from 3-F, the tarped dirt-bike from 4-A, but Po'-town. Ahead of him stretched the country road, just a blue squiggle to Monsieur Rand McNally, but the Old Rhinebeck Road according to the more detailed plat map. He zeroed the odometer on the bike, fixed his eyes firmly on the dirt that started where the concrete floor met the wall, and thought: It's really the road to good health. If you keep that somewhere in the back of your mind, you won't have to wonder if maybe a few of your screws got loose since Trudy died.

But his heart was beating a little too fast (as if he'd already started pedaling), and he felt the way he supposed most people did before setting out on a trip to a new place, where one might encounter new people and even new adventures. There was a can-holder above the stationary bike's rudimentary control panel, and into this he'd slipped a can of Red Bull, which purported to be a power drink. He was wearing an old Oxford shirt over his exercise shorts, because it had a pocket. Into this he'd placed two oatmeal-raisin cookies. Oatmeal and raisins were both supposed to be lipid-scrubbers.

And, speaking of them, The Lipid Company was gone for the day. Oh, they were still on duty in the painting upstairs — the useless, marketless painting that was so unlike him — but down here they'd piled back into Freddy's Dodge, had headed back to . . . to . . .

"Back to Poughkeepsie," he said. "They're listening to Kateem on WPDH and drinking beers out of paper bags. Today they . . . what did you do today, boys?"

Put in a couple of culverts, a voice whispered. Spring runoff damn near washed the road out near Priceville. Then we knocked off early.

Good. That was good. He wouldn't have to dismount his bike and walk around the washouts.

Richard Sifkitz fixed his eyes on the wall and began to pedal.

### III. On the Road to Herkimer

That was in the fall of 2002, a year after the Twin Towers had fallen into the streets of the Financial District, and life in New York City was returning to a slightly paranoid version of normal . . . except in New York, slightly paranoid *was* normal.

Richard Sifkitz had never felt saner or happier. His life fell into an orderly four-part harmony. In the morning he worked on whatever assignment was currently paying for his room and board, and there were more of these than ever, it seemed. The economy stank, all the newspapers said so, but for Richard Sifkitz, Freelance Commercial Artist, the economy was good.

He still ate lunch at Dugan's on the next block, but now usually a salad instead of a greasy double cheeseburger, and in the afternoon he worked on a new picture for himself: to begin with, a more detailed version of the projection on the wall of the basement alcove. The picture of Berkowitz and his crew had been set aside and covered with an old piece of sheet. He was done with it. Now he wanted a better image of what served him well enough downstairs, which was the road to Herkimer with the work-crew gone. And why shouldn't they be gone? Wasn't he maintaining the road himself these days? He was, and doing a damned good job. He'd gone back to Brady in late October to have his cholesterol re-tested, and the number this time had been written in black instead of red: 179. Brady had been more than respectful; he'd actually been a little jealous.

"This is better than mine," he said. "You really took it to heart, didn't you?"

"I guess I did," Sifkitz agreed.

"And that potbelly of yours is almost gone. Been working out?"

"As much as I can," Sifkitz agreed, and said no more on the subject. By then his workouts had gotten odd. Some people would consider them odd, anyway.

"Well," said Brady, "if you got it, flaunt it. That's my advice."

Sifkitz smiled at this, but it wasn't advice he took to heart.

His evenings — the fourth part of an Ordinary Sifkitz Day — he spent either watching TV or reading a book, usually sipping a tomato juice or a V-8 instead of a beer, feeling tired but contented. He was going to bed an hour earlier, too, and the extra rest agreed with him.

The heart of his days was part three, from four until six. Those were the two hours he spent on his stationary bike, riding the blue squiggle between Poughkeepsie and Herkimer. On the plat maps, it changed from the Old Rhinebeck Road to the Cascade Falls Road to the Woods Road; for awhile, north of Penniston, it was even the Dump Road. He could remember how, back at the beginning, even fifteen minutes on the stationary bike had seemed like an eternity. Now he sometimes had to force himself to quit after two hours. He finally got an alarm clock and started setting it for six p.m. The thing's aggressive bray was just about enough to . . . well . . .

It was just enough to wake him up.

Sifkitz found it hard to believe that he was falling asleep down in the alcove while riding the stationary bike at a steady fifteen miles per hour, but he didn't like the alternative, which was to think that he had gone a little crazy on the road to Herkimer. Or in his SoHo basement, if you liked that better. That he was having delusions.

One night while channel-surfing, he came across a program about hypnosis on A&E. The fellow being interviewed, a hypnotist who styled himself Joe Saturn, was saying that everyone practiced self-hypnosis every day. We used it to enter a work-oriented frame of mind in the morning; we used it to help us "get into the story" when reading novels or watching movies; we used it to get to sleep at night. This last was Joe Saturn's favorite example, and he talked at length about the patterns "successful sleepers" followed every night: checking the locks on the doors and windows, maybe, drawing a glass of water, maybe saying a little prayer or indulging in a spot of meditation. He likened these to the passes a hypnotist makes in front of his subject, and to his line of patter — counting back from ten to zero, for instance, or assuring the subject that he or she was "getting very sleepy." Sifkitz seized on this gratefully, deciding on the spot that he was spending his daily two hours on the stationary bike in a state of light to medium hypnosis.

Because, by the third week in front of the wall-projection, he was no longer spending those two hours in the basement alcove. By the third week, he was actually spending them on the road to Herkimer.

He would pedal contentedly enough along the packed dirt track that wound through the forest, smelling the odor of pine, hearing the cries of the crows or the crackle of leaves when he rolled through occasional drifts of them. The stationary bike became the three-speed Raleigh he'd owned as a twelve-year-old in suburban Manchester, New Hampshire. By no means the only bike he'd had before getting his driver's license at seventeen, but inarguably the best bike. The plastic cup-holder became a clumsily made but effective hand-welded ring of metal jutting over the bike-basket, and instead of Red Bull it contained a can of Lipton iced tea. Unsweetened.

On the road to Herkimer, it was always late October and just an hour before sunset. Although he rode two hours (both the alarm clock and the stationary bike's odometer confirmed this each time he finished), the sun never changed its position; it always laid the same long shadows across the dirt road

217

and flickered at him through the trees from the same quadrant of the sky as he traveled along with the manufactured wind of his passage blowing the hair back from his brow.

Sometimes there were signs nailed to trees where other roads crossed the one he was on. CASCADE ROAD, one said. HERKIMER, 120 MI., read another, this one pocked with old bullet-holes. The signs always corresponded to the information on the plat map currently tacked to the alcove wall. He had already decided that, once he reached Herkimer, he'd push on into the Canadian wilderness without even a stop to buy souvenirs. The road stopped there, but that was no problem; he'd already gotten a book titled *Plat Maps of Eastern Canada.* He would simply draw his own road on the plats, using a fine blue pencil and putting in lots of squiggles. Squiggles added miles.

He could go all the way to the Arctic Circle, if he wanted to.

One evening, after the alarm went off and startled him out of his trance, he approached the projection and looked at it for several long, considering moments, head cocked to one side. Anyone else would have seen very little; up that close the picture's trick of forced perspective ceased working and to the untrained eye the woodland scene collapsed into nothing but blobs of color — the light brown of the road's surface, the darker brown

that was a shallow drift of leaves, the blue-
and gray-streaked green of the firs, the bright
yellow-white of the westering sun to the far
left, perilously close to the door into the
furnace-room. Sifkitz, however, still saw the
picture perfectly. It was fixed firmly in his
mind now and never changed. Unless he was
riding, of course, but even then he was aware
of an underlying sameness. Which was good.
That essential sameness was a kind of touchstone, a way of assuring himself this was still
no more than an elaborate mind-game,
something plugged into his subconscious that
he could unplug whenever he wanted.

He had brought down a box of colors for
the occasional touch-up, and now, without
thinking too much about it, he added several
blobs of brown to the road, mixing them with
black to make them darker than the drifted
leaves. He stepped back, looked at the new
addition, and nodded. It was a small change
but in its way, perfect.

The following day, as he rode his three-
speed Raleigh through the woods (he was less
than sixty miles from Herkimer now and only
eighty from the Canadian border), he came
around a bend and there was a good-sized
buck deer standing in the middle of the road,
looking at him with startled dark velvet eyes.
It flipped up the white flag of its tail, dropped
a pile of scat, and was then off into the woods
again. Sifkitz saw another flip of its tail and

then the deer was gone. He rode on, giving the deer-shit a miss, not wanting it in the treads of his tires.

That night he silenced the alarm and approached the painting on the wall, wiping sweat from his forehead with a bandanna he took from the back pocket of his jeans. He looked at the projection critically, hands on hips. Then, moving with his usual confident speed — he'd been doing this sort of work for almost twenty years, after all — he painted the scat out of the picture, replacing it with a clutch of rusty beer cans undoubtedly left by some upstate hunter in search of pheasant or turkey.

"You missed those, Berkowitz," he said that night as he sat drinking a beer instead of a V-8 juice. "I'll pick 'em up myself tomorrow, but don't let it happen again."

Except when he went down the next day, there was no need to paint the beer cans out of the picture; they were already gone. For a moment he felt real fright prod his belly like a blunt stick — what had he done, sleep-walked down here in the middle of the night, picked up his trusty can of turp and a brush? — and then put it out of his mind. He mounted the stationary bike and was soon riding his old Raleigh, smelling the clean smells of the forest, relishing the way the wind blew his hair back from his forehead. And yet wasn't that the day things began to change? The day he sensed he might not be alone on the road to Herkimer? One thing was beyond doubt: it was the day after the disappearing beer cans that he had the really terrible dream and then drew the picture of Carlos's garage.

### IV. Man with Shotgun

It was the most vivid dream he'd had since the age of fourteen, when three or four brilliant wet-dreams had ushered him into physical manhood. It was the most horrible dream ever, hands down, nothing else even close. What made it horrible was the sense of impending doom that ran through it like a red thread. This was true even though the dream had a weird thinness: he knew he was dreaming but could not quite escape it. He felt as if he'd been wrapped in some terrible gauze. He knew his bed was near and he was in it — struggling — but he couldn't quite break through to the Richard Sifkitz who lay there, trembling and sweaty in his Big Dog sleep-shorts.

He saw a pillow and a beige telephone with a crack in the case. Then a hallway filled with pictures that he knew were of his wife and three daughters. Then a kitchen, the microwave oven flashing 4:16. A bowl of bananas (they filled him with grief and horror) on the Formica counter. A breezeway. And here lay

Pepe the dog with his muzzle on his paws, and Pepe did not raise his head but rolled his eyes up to look at him as he passed, revealing a gruesome, blood-threaded crescent of white, and that was when Sifkitz began to weep in the dream, understanding that all was lost.

Now he was in the garage. He could smell oil. He could smell old sweet grass. The LawnBoy stood in the corner like a suburban god. He could see the vise clamped to the work-table, old and dark and flecked with tiny splinters of wood. Next, a closet. His girls' ice-skates were piled on the floor, their laces as white as vanilla ice cream. His tools hung from pegs on the walls, arranged neatly, mostly yard-tools, a bear for working in his yard was

(Carlos. I am Carlos.)

On the top shelf, far out of the girls' reach, was a .410 shotgun, not used for years, nearly forgotten, and a box of shells so dark you could barely read the word Winchester on the side, only you could read it, just enough, and that was when Sifkitz came to understand that he was being carried along in the brain of a potential suicide. He struggled furiously to either stop Carlos or escape him and could do neither, even though he sensed his bed so near, just on the other side of the gauze that wrapped him from head to foot.

Now he was at the vise again, and the .410

was clamped in the vise, and the box of shells was on the work-table beside the vise, and here was a hacksaw, he was hacksawing off the barrel of the shotgun because that would make it easier to do what he had to do, and when he opened the box of shells there were two dozen of them, fat green buggers with brass bottoms, and the sound the gun made when Carlos snapped it closed wasn't cling! but CLACK! and the taste in his mouth was oily and dusty, oily on his tongue and dusty on the insides of his cheeks and his teeth, and his back hurt, it hurt LAMF, that was how they had tagged abandoned buildings (and sometimes ones that weren't abandoned) when he was a teenager and running with the Deacons in Po'-town, stood for LIKE A MOTHERFUCKER, and that was how his back hurt, but now that he was laid off the benefits were gone, Jimmy Berkowitz could no longer afford the bennies and so Carlos Martinez could no longer afford the drugs that made the pain a little less, could no longer afford the chiropractor that made the pain a little less, and the house-payments — ay, caramba, they used to say, joking, but he sure wasn't joking now, ay, caramba they were going to lose the house, less than five years from the finish-line but they were going to lose it, si-si, señor, and it was all that fuck Sifkitz's fault, him with his fucking road-maintenance hobby, and the curve of the trigger underneath his finger was like a crescent, like the unspeakable crescent of his dog's peering eye.

That was when Sifkitz woke up, sobbing and shaking, legs still in bed, head out and almost touching the floor, hair hanging. He crawled all the way out of the bedroom and started crawling across the main room to the easel under the skylight. Halfway there he found himself able to walk.

The picture of the empty road was still on the easel, the better and more complete version of the one downstairs on the alcove wall. He flung it away without a second look and set up a piece of two-foot-by-two pressboard in its place. He seized the nearest implement which would make a mark (this happened to be a UniBall Vision Elite pen) and began to draw. He drew for hours. At one point (he remembered this only vaguely) he needed to piss and could feel it running hot down his leg. The tears didn't stop until the picture was finished. Then, thankfully dry-eyed at last, he stood back and looked at what he had done.

It was Carlos's garage on an October afternoon. The dog, Pepe, stood in front of it with his ears raised. The dog had been drawn by the sound of the gunshot. There was no sign of Carlos in the picture, but Sifkitz knew exactly where the body lay, on the left, beside the work-table with the vise clamped to the edge. If his wife was home, she would have heard the shot. If she was out — perhaps shopping, more likely at work — it might be another hour or two before she came home and found him.

Beneath the image he had scrawled the words MAN WITH SHOTGUN. He couldn't remember doing this, but it was his printing and the right name for the picture. There was no man visible in it, no shotgun, either, but it was the right title.

Sifkitz went to his couch, sat down on it, and put his head in his hands. His right hand ached fiercely from clutching the unfamiliar, too-small drawing implement. He tried to tell himself he'd just had a bad dream, the picture the result of that dream. That there had never been any Carlos, never any Lipid Company, both of them were figments of his own imagination, drawn from Dr. Brady's careless metaphor.

But dreams faded, and these images — the phone with the crack in its beige case, the microwave, the bowl of bananas, the dog's eye — were as clear as ever. Clearer, even.

One thing was sure, he told himself. He was done with the goddam stationary bike. This was just a little too close to lunacy. If he kept on this way, soon he'd be cutting off his ear and mailing it not to his girlfriend (he didn't have one) but to Dr. Brady, who was surely responsible for this.

"Done with the bike," he said, with his head still in his hands. "Maybe I'll get a membership down at Fitness Boys, something like that, but I'm done with that fucking stationary bike."

Only he didn't get a membership at The Fitness Boys, and after a week without real exercise (he walked, but it wasn't the same — there were too many people on the sidewalks and he longed for the peace of the Herkimer Road), he could no longer stand it. He was behind on his latest project, which was an illustration a la Norman Rockwell for Fritos Corn Chips, and he'd had a call from both his agent and the guy in charge of the Fritos account at the ad agency. This had never happened to him before.

Worse, he wasn't sleeping.

The urgency of the dream had faded a little, and he decided it was only the picture of Carlos's garage, glaring at him from the corner of the room, that kept bringing it back, refreshing the dream the way a squirt of water from a mister may refresh a thirsty plant. He couldn't bring himself to destroy the picture (it was too damned good), but he turned it around so that the image faced nothing but the wall.

That afternoon he rode the elevator down to the basement and remounted the stationary bike. It turned into the old three-speed Raleigh almost as soon as he'd fixed his eyes on the wall-projection, and he resumed his ride north. He tried to tell himself that his sense of being followed was bogus, just something left over from his dream and the frenzied hours at the easel afterward. For a little while this actually did the job even though he knew better. He had reasons to make it do the job. The chief ones were that he was sleeping through the night again and had resumed working on his current assignment.

He finished the painting of the boys sharing a bag of Fritos on an idyllic suburban pitcher's mound, shipped it off by messenger, and the following day a check for ten thousand, two hundred dollars came with a note from Barry Casselman, his agent. *You scared me a little, hon,* the note said, and Sifkitz thought: *You're not the only one. Hon.*

Every now and then during the following week it occurred to him that he should tell someone about his adventures under the red sky, and each time he dismissed the idea. He could have told Trudy, but of course if Trudy had been around, things would never have gotten this far in the first place. The idea of telling Barry was laughable; the idea of telling Dr. Brady actually a little frightening. Dr. Brady would be recommending a good psychiatrist before you could say Minnesota Multiphasic.

The night he got the Fritos check, Sifkitz

noticed a change in the basement wall-mural. He paused in the act of setting his alarm and approached the projection (can of Diet Coke in one hand, reliable little Brookstone desk-clock in the other, oatmeal-raisin cookies tucked away safely in the old shirt pocket). Something was up in there, all right, something was different, but at first he was damned if he could tell what it was. He closed his eyes, counted to five (clearing his mind as he did so, an old trick), then sprang them open again, so wide that he looked like a man burlesquing fright. This time he saw the change at once. The bright yellow marquise shape over by the door to the furnace room was as gone as the clutch of beer cans. And the color of the sky above the trees was a deeper, darker red. The sun was either down or almost down. On the road to Herkimer, night was coming.

You have to stop this, Sifkitz thought, and then he thought: Tomorrow. Maybe tomorrow.

With that he mounted up and started riding. In the woods around him, he could hear the sound of birds settling down for the night.

## V. The Screwdriver Would Do
### for a Start

Over the next five or six days, the time Sifkitz spent on the stationary bike (and his childhood three-speed) was both wonderful and terrible. Wonderful because he had never felt better; his body was operating at absolute peak performance levels for a man his age, and he knew it. He supposed that there were pro athletes in better shape than he was, but by thirty-eight they would be approaching the end of their careers, and whatever joy they were able to take in the tuned condition of their bodies would necessarily be tainted by that knowledge. Sifkitz, on the other hand, might go on creating commercial art for another forty years, if he chose to. Hell, another fifty. Five full generations of football players and four of baseball players would come and go while he stood peacefully at his easel, painting book covers, automotive products, and Five New Logos for Pepsi-Cola.

Except . . .

Except that wasn't the ending folks familiar with this sort of story would expect, was it? Nor the sort of ending he expected himself.

The sense of being followed grew stronger with every ride, especially after he took down the last of the New York State plat maps and put up the first of the Canadian ones. Using a blue pen (the same one he'd used to create MAN WITH SHOTGUN), he drew an extension of the Herkimer Road on the previously roadless plat, adding lots of squiggles. By now he was pedaling faster, looking over his shoulder often, and finishing his rides covered with sweat, at first too out of breath to dismount the bike and turn off the braying alarm.

That looking-back-over-the-shoulder thing, now — that was interesting. At first when he did it he'd catch a glimpse of the basement alcove, and the doorway leading to the basement's larger rooms with its mazy arrangement of storage stalls. He'd see the Pomona Oranges crate by the door with the Brookstone desk alarm on it, marking off the minutes between four and six. Then a kind of red blur wiped across everything, and when it drained away he was looking at the road behind him, the autumn-bright trees on both sides (only not so bright now, not with twilight starting to thicken), and the darkening red sky overhead. Later, he didn't see the basement at all when he looked back, not even a flash of it. Just the road leading back to Herkimer, and eventually to Poughkeepsie.

He knew perfectly well what he was looking back over his shoulder for: headlights.

The headlights of Freddy's Dodge Ram, if you wanted to get specific about it. Because for Berkowitz and his crew, bewildered resentment had given way to anger. Carlos's suicide was what had tipped them over the edge. They blamed him and they were after him. And when they caught him, they'd —

What? They'd what?

Kill me, he thought, pedaling grimly on into the twilight. No need to be coy about it. They catch up, they'll kill me. I'm in the serious williwags now, not a town on that whole damn plat map, not so much as a village. I could scream my head off and no one would hear me except Barry the Bear, Debby the Doe, and Rudy the Raccoon. So if I see those headlights (or hear the motor, because Freddy might be running without lights), I would do well to get the hell back to SoHo, alarm or no alarm. I'm crazy to be here in the first place.

But he was having trouble getting back now. When the alarm went off the Raleigh would remain a Raleigh for thirty seconds or more, the road ahead would remain a road instead of reverting to blobs of color on cement, and the alarm itself sounded distant and strangely mellow. He had an idea that eventually he would hear it as the drone of a jet airplane high overhead, an American Airlines 767 out of Kennedy, perhaps, headed over the North Pole to the far side of the world.

He would stop, squeeze his eyes shut, then pop them wide open again. That did the trick, but he had an idea it might not work for long.

Then what? A hungry night spent in the woods, looking up at a full moon that looked like a bloodshot eye?

No, they'd catch up to him before then, he reckoned. The question was, did he intend to let that happen? Incredibly, part of him wanted to do just that. Part of him was angry at them. Part of him wanted to confront Berkowitz and the remaining members of his crew, ask them What did you expect me to do, anyway? Just go on the way things were, gobbling Krispy Kreme donuts, paying no attention to the washouts when the culverts plugged up and overflowed? Is that what you wanted?

But there was another part of him that knew such a confrontation would be madness. He was in tiptop shape, yes, but you were still talking three against one, and who was to say Mrs. Carlos hadn't loaned the boys her husband's shotgun, told them yeah, go get the bastard, and be sure to tell him the first one's from me and my girls.

Sifkitz had had a friend who'd beaten a bad cocaine addiction in the eighties, and he remembered this fellow saying the first thing you had to do was get it out of the house. You could always buy more, sure, that shit was everywhere now, on every streetcorner, but that was no excuse for keeping it where you could grab it any time your will weakened. So he'd gathered it all up and flushed it down the toilet. And once it was gone, he'd thrown his works out with the trash. That hadn't been the end of his problem, he'd said, but it had been the beginning of the end.

One night Sifkitz entered the alcove carrying a screwdriver. He had every intention of dismantling the stationary bike, and never mind the fact that he'd set the alarm for six p.m., as he always did, that was just habit. The alarm clock (like the oatmeal-raisin cookies) was part of his works, he supposed; the hypnotic passes he made, the machinery of his dream. And once he was done reducing the bike to unrideable components, he'd put the alarm clock out with the rest of the trash, just as his friend had done with his crack-pipe. He'd feel a pang, of course — the sturdy little Brookstone certainly wasn't to blame for the idiotic situation into which he'd gotten himself — but he would do it. Cowboy up, they'd told each other as kids; quit whining and just cowboy up.

He saw that the bike was comprised of four main sections, and that he'd also need an adjustable wrench to dismantle the thing completely. That was all right, though; the screwdriver would do for a start. He could use it to take off the pedals. Once that was done he'd borrow the adjustable wrench from the super's toolbox.

He dropped to one knee, slipped the tip of the borrowed tool into the slot of the first screw, and hesitated. He wondered if his friend had smoked one more rock before turning the rest of them down the toilet, just one more rock for old times' sake. He bet the guy had. Being a little stoned had probably stilled the cravings, made the disposal job a little easier. And if he had one more ride, then knelt here to take off the pedals with the endorphins flowing, wouldn't he feel a little less depressed about it? A little less likely to imagine Berkowitz, Freddy, and Whelan retiring to the nearest roadside bar, where they would buy first one pitcher of Rolling Rock and then another, toasting each other and Carlos's memory, congratulating each other on how they had beaten the bastard?

"You're crazy," he murmured to himself, and slipped the tip of the driver back into the notch of the screw. "Do it and be done."

He actually turned the screwdriver once (and it was easy; whoever had put this together in the back room of The Fitness Boys obviously hadn't had his heart in it), but when he did, the oatmeal-raisin cookies shifted a little in his pocket and he thought how good they always tasted when you were riding along. You just took your right hand off the handlebar, dipped it into your pocket, had a couple of bites, then chased it with a swallow of iced tea. It was the perfect combination. It just felt so good to be speeding along, having a little picnic as you went, and those sons of bitches wanted to take it away from him.

A dozen turns of the screw, maybe even less, and the pedal would drop off onto the concrete floor — clunk. Then he could move on to the other one, and then he could move on with his life.

This is not fair, he thought.

One more ride, just for old times' sake, he thought.

And, swinging his leg over the fork and settling his ass (firmer and harder by far than it had been on the day of the red cholesterol number) onto the seat, he thought: This is the way stories like this always go, isn't it? The way they always end, with the poor schmuck saying this is the last time, I'll never do this again.

Absolutely true, he thought, but I'll bet in real life, people get away with it. I bet they get away with it all the time.

Part of him was murmuring that real life had never been like this, what he was doing (and what he was experiencing) bore absolutely no resemblance whatever to real life as he understood it. He pushed the voice away, closed his ears to it.

It was a beautiful evening for a ride in the woods.

## VI. Not Quite the Ending
## Everyone Expected

And still, he got one more chance.

That was the night he heard the revving engine behind him clearly for the first time, and just before the alarm clock went off, the Raleigh he was riding suddenly grew an elongated shadow on the road ahead of him — the sort of shadow that could only have been created by headlights.

Then the alarm did go off, not a bray but a distant purring sound that was almost melodic.

The truck was closing in. He didn't need to turn his head to see it (nor does one ever want to turn and see the frightful fiend that close behind him treads, Sifkitz supposed later that night, lying awake in his bed and still wrapped in the cold-yet-hot sensation of disaster avoided by mere inches or seconds). He could see the shadow, growing longer and darker.

Hurry up, please, gentlemen, it's time, he thought, and squeezed his eyes closed. He could still hear the alarm, but it was still no more than that almost soothing purr, it was certainly no louder; what was louder was the engine, the one inside Freddy's truck. It was almost on him, and suppose they didn't want to waste so much as a New York minute in conversation? Suppose the one currently behind the wheel just mashed the pedal to the metal and ran him down? Turned him into roadkill?

He didn't bother to open his eyes, didn't waste time confirming that it was still the deserted road instead of the basement alcove. Instead he squeezed them even more tightly shut, focused all his attention on the sound of the alarm, and this time turned the polite voice of the barman into an impatient bellow:

HURRY UP PLEASE GENTLEMEN IT'S TIME!

And suddenly, thankfully, it was the sound of the engine that was fading and the sound of the Brookstone alarm that was swelling, taking on its old familiar rough get-up-get-up-get-up bray. And this time when he opened his eyes, he saw the projection of the road instead of the road itself.

But now the sky was black, its organic redness hidden by nightfall. The road was brilliantly lit, the shadow of the bike — a Raleigh — a clear black on the leaf-littered hardpack. He could tell himself he had dismounted the stationary bike and painted those changes while in his nightly trance, but he knew better, and not only because there was no paint on his hands.

This is my last chance, he thought. My last chance to avoid the ending everyone expects in stories like this.

But he was simply too tired, too shaky, to take care of the stationary bike now. He would take care of it tomorrow. Tomorrow morning, in fact, first thing. Right now all he wanted was to get out of this awful place where reality had worn so thin. And with that firmly in mind, Sifkitz staggered to the Pomona crate beside the doorway (rubber-legged, covered with a thin slime of sweat — the smelly kind that comes from fear rather than exertion) and shut the alarm off. Then he went upstairs and lay down on his bed. Some very long time later, sleep came.

The next morning he went down the cellar stairs, eschewing the elevator and walking firmly, with his head up and his lips pressed tightly together, A Man On A Mission. He went directly to the stationary bike, ignoring the alarm clock on the crate, dropped to one knee, picked up the screwdriver. He slipped it once more into the slot of a screw, one of the four that held the left-hand pedal . . .

. . . and the next thing he knew, he was speeding giddily along the road again, with the headlights brightening around him until he felt like a man on a stage that's dark save for one single spotlight. The truck's engine was too loud (something wrong with the muffler or the exhaust system), and it was out of tune, as well. He doubted if old Freddy had bothered with the last maintenance go-round. No, not with house-payments to make, groceries to buy, the kiddies still needing braces, and no weekly paycheck coming in.

He thought: I had my chance. I had my chance last night and I didn't take it.

He thought: Why did I do this? Why, when I knew better?

He thought: Because they made me, somehow. They made me.

He thought: They're going to run me down and I'll die in the woods.

But the truck did not run him down. It hurtled past him on the right instead, left-side wheels rumbling in the leaf-choked ditch, and then it swung across the road in front of him, blocking the way.

Panicked, Sifkitz forgot the first thing his father had taught him when he brought the three-speed home: When you stop, Richie, reverse the pedals. Brake the bike's rear wheel at the same time you squeeze the handbrake that controls the front wheel. Otherwise —

This was otherwise. In his panic he turned both hands into fists, squeezing the handbrake on the left, locking the front wheel. The bike bucked him off and sent him flying at the truck with LIPID COMPANY printed on the driver's-side door. He threw his hands out and they struck the top of the truck's bed hard enough to numb them. Then he collapsed in a heap, wondering how many bones were broken.

The doors opened above him and he heard

the crackle of leaves as men in workboots got out. He didn't look up. He waited for them to grab him and make him get up, but no one did. The smell of the leaves was like old dry cinnamon. The footsteps passed him on either side, and then the crackle abruptly stopped.

Sifkitz sat up and looked at his hands. The palm of the right one was bleeding and the wrist of the left one was already swelling, but he didn't think it was broken. He looked around and the first thing he saw — red in the glow of the Dodge's taillights — was his Raleigh. It had been beautiful when his Dad brought it home from the bike-shop, but it wasn't beautiful any longer. The front wheel was warped out of true, and the rear tire had come partly off the rim. For the first time he felt something other than fear. This new emotion was anger.

He got shakily to his feet. Beyond the Raleigh, back the way he'd come, was a hole in reality. It was strangely organic, as if he were looking through the hole at the end of some duct in his own body. The edges wavered and bulged and flexed. Beyond it, three men were standing around the stationary bike in the basement alcove, standing in postures he recognized from every work-crew he'd ever seen in his life. These were men with a job to do. They were deciding how to do it.

And suddenly he knew why he'd named

them as he had. It was really idiotically simple. The one in the Lipid cap, Berkowitz, was David Berkowitz, the so-called Son of Sam and a New York *Post* staple the year Sifkitz had come to Manhattan. Freddy was Freddy Albemarle, this kid he'd known in high school — they'd been in a band together, and had become friends for a simple enough reason: they both hated school. And Whelan? An artist he'd met at a conference somewhere. Michael Whelan? Mitchell Whelan? Sifkitz couldn't quite remember, but he knew the guy specialized in fantasy art, dragons and such. They had spent a night in the hotel bar, telling stories about the comic-horrible world of movie-poster art.

Then there was Carlos, who'd committed suicide in his garage. Why, he had been a version of Carlos Delgado, also known as the Big Cat. For years Sifkitz had followed the fortunes of the Toronto Blue Jays, simply because he didn't want to be like every other American League baseball fan in New York and root for the Yankees. The Cat had been one of Toronto's very few stars.

"I made you all," he said in a voice that was little more than a croak. "I created you out of memories and spare parts." Of course he had. Nor had it been for the first time. The boys on the Norman Rockwell pitcher's mound in the Fritos ad, for instance — the ad agency had, at his request, provided him

241

with photographs of four boys of the correct age, and Sifkitz had simply painted them in. Their mothers had signed the necessary waivers; it had been business as usual.

If they heard him speak, Berkowitz, Freddy, and Whelan gave no sign. They spoke a few words among themselves that Sifkitz could hear but not make out; they seemed to come from a great distance. Whatever they were, they got Whelan moving out of the alcove while Berkowitz knelt by the stationary bike, just as Sifkitz himself had done. Berkowitz picked up the screwdriver and in no time at all the left-hand pedal dropped off onto the concrete — clunk. Sifkitz, still on the deserted road, watched through the queer organic hole as Berkowitz handed the screwdriver to Freddy Albemarle — who, with Richard Sifkitz, had played lousy trumpet in the equally lousy high school band. They had played a hell of a lot better when they were rocking. Somewhere in the Canadian woods an owl hooted, the sound inexpressibly lonely. Freddy went to work unscrewing the other pedal. Whelan, meanwhile, returned with the adjustable wrench in his hand. Sifkitz felt a pang at the sight of it.

Watching them, the thought that went through Sifkitz's mind was: If you want something done right, hire a professional. Certainly Berkowitz and his boys wasted no time. In less than four minutes the stationary bike was nothing but two wheels and three disconnected sections of frame laid on the concrete, and so neatly that the parts looked like one of those diagrams called "exploded schematics."

Berkowitz himself dropped the screws and bolts into the front pockets of his Dickies, where they bulged like handfuls of spare change. He gave Sifkitz a meaningful look as he did this, one that made Sifkitz angry all over again. By the time the work-crew came back through the odd, ductlike hole (dropping their heads as they did so, like men passing through a low doorway), Sifkitz's fists were clenched again, even though doing that made the wrist of the left one throb like hell.

"You know what?" he asked Berkowitz. "I don't think you can hurt me. I don't think you can hurt me, because then what happens to you? You're nothing but a . . . a sub-contractor!"

Berkowitz looked at him levelly from beneath the bent bill of his LIPID cap.

"I made you up!" Sifkitz said, and counted them off, poking the index finger out of his right fist and pointing it at each one in turn like the barrel of a gun. "You're the Son of Sam! You're nothing but a grown-up version of this kid I played the horn with at Sisters of Mercy High! You couldn't play E-flat to save your life! And you're an artist specializing in dragons and enchanted maidens!"

The remaining members of The Lipid Company were singularly unimpressed.

"What does that make you?" Berkowitz asked. "Did you ever think of that? Are you going to tell me there might not be a larger world out there someplace? For all you know, you're nothing but a random thought going through some unemployed Certified Public Accountant's head while he sits on the jakes, reading the paper and taking his morning dump."

Sifkitz opened his mouth to say that was ridiculous, but something in Berkowitz's eyes made him shut it again. Go on, his eyes said. Ask a question. I'll tell you more than you ever wanted to know.

What Sifkitz said instead was, "Who are you to tell me I can't get fit? Do you want me to die at fifty? Jesus Christ, what's wrong with you?"

Freddy said, "I ain't no philosopher, Mac. All I know is that my truck needs a tune-up I can't afford."

"And I've got one kid who needs orthopedic shoes and another one who needs speech therapy," Whelan added.

"The guys working on the Big Dig in Boston have got a saying," Berkowitz said. " 'Don't kill the job, let it die on its own.' That's all we're asking, Sifkitz. Let us dip our beaks. Let us earn our living."

"This is crazy," Sifkitz muttered. "Totally
—"

"I don't give a shit how you feel about it,
you motherfucker!" Freddy shouted, and Sifkitz realized the man was almost crying. This
confrontation was as stressful for them as it
was for him. Somehow realizing that was the
worst shock of all. "I don't give a shit about
you, you ain't nothing, you don't work, you
just piddle around and make your little pitch-
ers, but don't you take the bread out of my
kids' mouths, you hear? Don't you do it!"

He started forward, hands rolling into fists
and coming up in front of his face: an absurd
John L. Sullivan boxing pose. Berkowitz put
a hand on Freddy's arm and pulled him back.

"Don't be a hardass about it, man," Whelan
said. "Live and let live, all right?"

"Let us dip our beaks," Berkowitz repeated,
and of course Sifkitz recognized the phrase;
he'd read *The Godfather* and seen all the movies. Could any of these guys use a word or a
slang phrase that wasn't in his own vocabu-
lary? He doubted it. "Let us keep our dignity,
man. You think we can go to work drawing
pictures, like you?" He laughed. "Yeah, right.
If I draw a cat, I gotta write CAT underneath
so people know what it is."

"You killed Carlos," Whelan said, and if
there had been accusation in his voice, Sifkitz
had an idea he might have been angry all over
again. But all he heard was sorrow. "We told

245

him, 'Hold on, man, it'll get better,' but he wasn't strong. He could never, you know, look ahead. He lost all his hope." Whelan paused, looked up at the dark sky. Not far off, Freddy's Dodge rumbled roughly. "He never had much to start with. Some people don't, you know."

Sifkitz turned to Berkowitz. "Let me get this straight. What you want —"

"Just don't kill the job," Berkowitz said. "That's all we want. Let the job die on its own."

Sifkitz realized he could probably do as this man was asking. It might even be easy. Some people, if they ate one Krispy Kreme, they had to go and finish the whole box. If he'd been that type of man, they would have a serious problem here . . . but he wasn't.

"Okay," he said. "Why don't we give it a try." And then an idea struck him. "Do you think I could have a company hat?" He pointed to the one Berkowitz was wearing.

Berkowitz gave a smile. It was brief, but more genuine than the laugh when he'd said he couldn't draw a cat without having to write the word under it. "That could be arranged."

Sifkitz had an idea Berkowitz would stick out his hand then, but Berkowitz didn't. He just gave Sifkitz a final measuring glance from beneath the bill of his cap and then started toward the cab of the truck. The other two

246

followed.

"How long before I decide none of this happened?" Sifkitz asked. "That I took the stationary bike apart myself because I just . . . I don't know . . . just got tired of it?"

Berkowitz paused, hand on the doorhandle, and looked back. "How long do you want it to be?" he asked.

"I don't know," Sifkitz said. "Hey, it's beautiful out here, isn't it?"

"It always was," Berkowitz said. "We always kept it nice." There was an undertone of defensiveness in his voice that Sifkitz chose to ignore. It occurred to him that even a figment of one's imagination could have its pride.

For a few moments they stood there on the road, which Sifkitz had lately come to think of as The Great Trans-Canadian Lost Highway, a pretty grand name for a no-name dirt track through the woods, but also pretty nice. None of them said anything. Somewhere the owl hooted again.

"Indoors, outdoors, it's all the same to us," Berkowitz said. Then he opened the door and swung up behind the wheel.

"Take care of yourself," Freddy said.

"But not too much," Whelan added.

Sifkitz stood there while the truck made an artful three-point turn on the narrow road and started back the way it came. The duct-like opening was gone, but Sifkitz didn't worry about that. He didn't think he'd have any trouble getting back when the time came. Berkowitz made no effort to avoid the Raleigh but ran directly over it, finishing a job that was already finished. There were sproinks and goinks as the spokes in the wheels broke. The taillights dwindled, then disappeared around a curve. Sifkitz could hear the thump of the motor for quite awhile, but that faded, too.

He sat down on the road, then lay down on his back, cradling his throbbing left wrist against his chest. There were no stars in the sky. He was very tired. Better not go to sleep, he advised himself, something's likely to come out of the woods — a bear, maybe — and eat you. Then he fell asleep anyway.

When he woke up, he was on the cement floor of the alcove. The dismantled pieces of the stationary bike, now screwless and bolt-less, lay all around him. The Brookstone alarm clock on the crate read 8:43 p.m. One of them had apparently turned off the alarm.

I took this thing apart myself, he thought. That's my story, and if I stick to it I'll believe it soon enough.

He climbed the stairs to the building's lobby and decided he was hungry. He thought maybe he'd go out to Dugan's and get a piece of apple pie. Apple pie wasn't the world's most unhealthy snack, was it? And when he got there, he decided to have it a la mode.

"What the hell," he told the waitress. "You

only live once, don't you?"

"Well," she replied, "that's not what the Hindus say, but whatever floats your boat."

Two months later, Sifkitz got a package.

It was waiting for him in the lobby of his building when he got back from having dinner with his agent (Sifkitz had fish and steamed vegetables, but followed it with a crème brûlée). There was no postage on it, no Federal Express, Airborne Express, or UPS logo, no stamps. Just his name, printed in ragged block letters: RICHARD SIF-KITZ. That's a man who'd have to print CAT underneath his drawing of one, he thought, and had no idea at all why he'd thought it. He took the box upstairs and used an X-Acto knife from his work-table to slice it open. Inside, beneath a big wad of tissue paper, was a brand-new gimme cap, the kind with the plastic adjustable band in back. The tag inside read Made In Bangladesh. Printed above the bill in a dark red that made him think of arterial blood was one word: LIPID.

"What's that?" he asked the empty studio, turning the cap over and over in his hands. "Some kind of blood component, isn't it?"

He tried the hat on. At first it was too small, but when he adjusted the band at the back, the fit was perfect. He looked at it in his bedroom mirror and still didn't quite like it. He took it off, bent the bill into a curve, and tried it again. Now it was almost right. It would look better still when he got out of his going-to-lunch clothes and into a pair of paint-splattered jeans. He'd look like a real working stiff . . . which he was, in spite of what some people might think.

Wearing the LIPID cap while he painted eventually became a habit with him, like allowing himself seconds on days of the week that started with S, and having pie a la mode at Dugan's on Thursday nights. Despite whatever the Hindu philosophy might be, Richard Sifkitz believed you only went around once. That being the case, maybe you should allow yourself a little bit of everything.

# THE THINGS THEY
# LEFT BEHIND

The things I want to tell you about — the ones they left behind — showed up in my apartment in August of 2002. I'm sure of that, because I found most of them not long after I helped Paula Robeson with her air conditioner. Memory always needs a marker, and that's mine. She was a children's book illustrator, good-looking (hell, *fine*-looking), husband in import-export. A man has a way of remembering occasions when he's actually able to help a good-looking lady in distress (even one who keeps assuring you she's "very married"); such occasions are all too few. These days the would-be knight errant usually just makes matters worse.

She was in the lobby, looking frustrated, when I came down for an afternoon walk. I said *Hi, howya doin',* the way you do to other folks who share your building, and she asked me in an exasperated tone that stopped just short of querulousness why the super had to be on vacation *now.* I pointed out that even

251

cowgirls get the blues and even supers go on vacation; that August, furthermore, was an extremely logical month to take time off. August in New York (and in Paris, *mon ami*) finds psychoanalysts, trendy artists, and building superintendents mighty thin on the ground.

She didn't smile. I'm not sure she even got the Tom Robbins reference (obliqueness is the curse of the reading class). She said it might be true about August being a good month to take off and go to the Cape or Fire Island, but her damned apartment was just about burning *up* and the damned air conditioner wouldn't so much as burp. I asked her if she'd like me to take a look, and I remember the glance she gave me — those cool, assessing gray eyes. I remember thinking that eyes like that probably saw quite a lot. And I remember smiling at what she asked me: *Are you safe?* It reminded me of that movie, not *Lolita* (thinking about *Lolita,* sometimes at two in the morning, came later) but the one where Laurence Olivier does the impromptu dental work on Dustin Hoffman, asking him over and over again, *Is it safe?*

*I'm safe,* I said. *Haven't attacked a woman in over a year. I used to attack two or three a week, but the meetings are helping.*

A giddy thing to say, but I was in a fairly giddy mood. A *summer* mood. She gave me another look, and then *she* smiled. Put out her hand. *Paula Robeson,* she said. It was the left hand she put out — not normal, but the one with the plain gold band on it. I think that was probably on purpose, don't you? But it was later that she told me about her husband being in import-export. On the day when it was my turn to ask *her* for help.

In the elevator, I told her not to expect too much. Now, if she'd wanted a man to find out the underlying causes of the New York City Draft Riots, or to supply a few amusing anecdotes about the creation of the small-pox vaccine, or even to dig up quotes on the sociological ramifications of the TV remote control (the most important invention of the last fifty years, in my 'umble opinion), I was the guy.

*Research is your game, Mr. Staley?* she asked as we went up in the slow and clattery elevator.

I admitted that it was, although I didn't add that I was still quite new to it. Nor did I ask her to call me Scott — that would have spooked her all over again. And I certainly didn't tell her that I was trying to forget all I'd once known about rural insurance. That I was, in fact, trying to forget quite a lot of things, including about two dozen faces.

You see, I may be trying to forget, but I still remember quite a lot. I think we all do when we put our minds to it (and sometimes, rather more nastily, when we don't). I even remember something one of those South American novelists said — you know, the ones they call the Magical Realists? Not the guy's name, that's not important, but this quote: *As infants, our first victory comes in grasping some bit of the world, usually our mothers' fingers. Later we discover that the world, and the things of the world, are grasping us, and have been all along.* Borges? Yes, it might have been Borges. Or it might have been Márquez. That I *don't* remember. I just know I got her air conditioner running, and when cool air started blowing out of the convector, it lit up her whole face. I also know it's true, that thing about how perception switches around and we come to realize that the things we thought we were holding are actually holding us. Keeping us prisoner, perhaps — Thoreau certainly thought so — but also holding us in place. That's the trade-off. And no matter what Thoreau might have thought, I believe the trade is mostly a fair one. Or I did then; now, I'm not so sure.

And I know these things happened in late August of 2002, not quite a year after a piece of the sky fell down and everything changed for all of us.

On an afternoon about a week after Sir Scott Staley donned his Good Samaritan armor and successfully battled the fearsome air conditioner, I took my afternoon walk to the Staples on 83rd Street to get a box of Zip discs and a ream of paper. I owed a fellow forty pages of background on the development of the Polaroid camera (which is more interesting a story than you might think). When I got back to my apartment, there was a pair of sunglasses with red frames and very distinctive lenses on the little table in the foyer where I keep bills that need to be paid, claim checks, overdue-book notices, and things of that nature. I recognized the glasses at once, and all the strength went out of me. I didn't fall, but I dropped my packages on the floor and leaned against the side of the door, trying to catch my breath and staring at those sunglasses. If there had been nothing to lean against, I believe I would have swooned like a miss in a Victorian novel — one of those where the lustful vampire appears at the stroke of midnight.

Two related but distinct emotional waves struck me. The first was that sense of horrified shame you feel when you know you're about to be caught in some act you will never be able to explain. The memory that comes to mind in this regard is of a thing that happened to me — or almost happened — when I was sixteen.

My mother and sister had gone shopping in Portland and I supposedly had the house to myself until evening. I was reclining naked on my bed with a pair of my sister's under-pants wrapped around my cock. The bed was scattered with pictures I'd clipped from magazines I'd found in the back of the garage — the previous owner's stash of *Penthouse* and *Gallery* magazines, very likely. I heard a car come crunching into the driveway. No mistaking the sound of that motor; it was my mother and sister. Peg had come down with some sort of flu bug and started vomiting out the window. They'd gotten as far as Poland Springs and turned around.

I looked at the pictures scattered all over the bed, my clothes scattered all over the floor, and the foam of pink rayon in my left hand. I remember how the strength flowed out of my body, and the terrible sense of lassitude that came in its place. My mother was yelling for me — "Scott, Scott, come down and help me with your sister, she's sick" — and I remember thinking, "What's the use? I'm caught. I might as well accept it, I'm caught and this is the first thing they'll think of when they think about me for the rest of my life: Scott, the jerk-off artist."

But more often than not a kind of survival overdrive kicks in at such moments. That's what happened to me. I might go down, I decided, but I wouldn't do so without at least an effort to save my dignity. I threw the pictures and the panties under the bed. Then I jumped into my clothes, moving with numb but sure-fingered speed, all the time thinking of this crazy old game show I used to watch, *Beat the Clock.*

I can remember how my mother touched my flushed cheek when I got downstairs, and the thoughtful concern in her eyes. "Maybe you're getting sick, too," she said.

"Maybe I am," I said, and gladly enough. It was half an hour before I discovered I'd forgotten to zip my fly. Luckily, neither Peg nor my mother noticed, although on any other occasion one or both of them would have asked me if I had a license to sell hot dogs (this was what passed for wit in the house where I grew up). That day one of them was too sick and the other was too worried to be witty. So I got a total pass.

Lucky me.

What followed the first emotional wave that August day in my apartment was much simpler: I thought I was going out of my mind. Because those glasses couldn't be there. Absolutely could not. No way.

Then I raised my eyes and saw something else that had most certainly not been in my apartment when I left for Staples half an hour before (locking the door behind me, as I always did). Leaning in the corner between the kitchenette and the living room was a baseball bat. Hillerich & Bradsby, according to the label. And while I couldn't see the other side, I knew what was printed there well enough: CLAIMS ADJUSTOR, the words burned into the ash with the tip of a soldering iron and then colored deep blue.

Another sensation rushed through me: a third wave. This was a species of surreal dismay. I don't believe in ghosts, but I'm sure that at that moment I looked as though I had just seen one.

I felt that way, too. Yes indeed. Because those sunglasses had to be gone — long-time gone, as the Dixie Chicks say. Ditto Cleve Farrell's Claims Adjustor. ("Besboll been bery-bery good to mee," Cleve would sometimes say, waving the bat over his head as he sat at his desk. "In-SHOO-rance been bery-bery bad.")

I did the only thing I could think of, which was to grab up Sonja D'Amico's shades and trot back down to the elevator with them, holding them out in front of me the way you might hold out something nasty you found on your apartment floor after a week away on vacation — a piece of decaying food, or the body of a poisoned mouse. I found myself remembering a conversation I'd had about Sonja with a fellow named Warren Anderson. *She must have looked like she thought she was going to pop back up and ask somebody for a Coca-Cola,* I had thought when he told me what he'd seen. Over drinks in the Blarney Stone Pub on Third Avenue, this had been, about six weeks after the sky fell down. After we'd toasted each other on not being dead.

Things like that have a way of sticking, whether you want them to or not. Like a musical phrase or the nonsense chorus to a pop song that you just can't get out of your head. You wake up at three in the morning, needing to take a leak, and as you stand there in front of the bowl, your cock in your hand and your mind about ten percent awake, it comes back to you: *Like she thought she was going to pop back up. Pop back up and ask for a Coke.* At some point during that conversation Warren had asked me if I remembered her funny sunglasses, and I said I did. Sure I did.

Four floors down, Pedro the doorman was standing in the shade of the awning and talking with Rafe the FedEx man. Pedro was a serious hardboy when it came to letting deliverymen stand in front of the building — he had a seven-minute rule, a pocket watch with which to enforce it, and all the beat cops were his buddies — but he got on with Rafe, and sometimes the two of them would stand there for twenty minutes or more with their heads together, doing the old New York Yak. Politics? Besboll? The Gospel According to Henry David Thoreau? I didn't know and never cared less than on that day. They'd been there when I went up with my office supplies, and were still there when a far less carefree Scott Staley came back down. A Scott Staley who had discovered a small but noticeable hole in the column of reality. Just the two of them being there was enough for me. I walked up and held my right hand, the one with the sunglasses in it, out to Pedro.

"What would you call these?" I asked, not bothering to excuse myself or anything, just butting in headfirst.

He gave me a considering stare that said, "I am surprised at your rudeness, Mr. Staley, truly I am," then looked down at my hand. For a long moment he said nothing, and a horrible idea took possession of me: he saw nothing because there was nothing to see. Only my hand outstretched, as if this were Turnabout Tuesday and I expected *him* to tip *me.* My hand was empty. Sure it was, had to be, because Sonja D'Amico's sunglasses no longer existed. Sonja's joke shades were a long time gone.

"I call them sunglasses, Mr. Staley," Pedro said at last. "What else would I call them? Or is this some sort of trick question?"

Rafe the FedEx man, clearly more interested, took them from me. The relief of seeing him holding the sunglasses and looking at them, almost *studying* them, was like having someone scratch that exact place between your shoulder blades that itches. He stepped out from beneath the awning and held them up to the day, making a sun-star flash off each of the heart-shaped lenses.

"They're like the ones the little girl wore in that porno movie with Jeremy Irons," he said at last.

I had to grin in spite of my distress. In New York, even the deliverymen are film critics. It's one of the things to love about the place.

"That's right, *Lolita*," I said, taking the glasses back. "Only the heart-shaped sunglasses were in the version Stanley Kubrick directed. Back when Jeremy Irons was still nothing but a putter." That one hardly made sense (even to me), but I didn't give Shit One. Once again I was feeling giddy . . . but not in a good way. Not this time.

"Who played the pervo in that one?" Rafe asked.

I shook my head. "I'll be damned if I can remember right now."

"If you don't mind me saying," Pedro said, "you look rather pale, Mr. Staley. Are you coming down with something? The flu, perhaps?"

*No, that was my sister,* I thought of saying. *The day I came within about twenty seconds of getting caught masturbating into her panties while I looked at a picture of Miss April.* But I hadn't been caught. Not then, not on 9/11, either. Fooled ya, beat the clock again. I couldn't speak for Warren Anderson, who told me in the Blarney Stone that he'd stopped on the third floor that morning to talk about the Yankees with a friend, but not getting caught had become quite a specialty of mine.

"I'm all right," I told Pedro, and while that wasn't true, knowing I wasn't the only one who saw Sonja's joke shades as a thing that actually existed in the world made me feel better, at least. If the sunglasses were in the world, probably Cleve Farrell's Hillerich & Bradsby was, too.

"Are those *the* glasses?" Rafe suddenly asked in a respectful, ready-to-be-awestruck voice. "The ones from the first *Lolita?*"

"Nope," I said, folding the bows behind the heart-shaped lenses, and as I did, the name of the girl in the Kubrick version of the film came to me: Sue Lyon. I still couldn't remember who played the pervo. "Just a knock-off."

"Is there something special about them?" Rafe asked. "Is that why you came rushing down here?"

"I don't know," I said. "Someone left them behind in my apartment."

I went upstairs before they could ask any more questions and looked around, hoping there was nothing else. But there was. In addition to the sunglasses and the baseball bat with CLAIMS ADJUSTOR burned into the side, there was a Howie's Laff-Riot Farting Cushion, a conch shell, a steel penny suspended in a Lucite cube, and a ceramic mushroom (red with white spots) that came with a ceramic Alice sitting on top of it. The Tarting Cushion had belonged to Jimmy Eagleton and got a certain amount of play every year at the Christmas party. The ceramic Alice had been on Maureen Hannon's desk — a gift from her granddaughter, she'd told me once. Maureen had the most beautiful white hair, which she wore long, to her waist. You rarely see that in a business situation, but she'd been with the company for almost forty years and felt she could wear her hair any way she liked. I remembered both the conch shell and the steel penny, but not in whose cubicles (or offices) they had been. It might come to me; it might not. There had been lots of cubicles (and offices) at Light and Bell, Insurers.

The shell, the mushroom, and the Lucite cube were on the coffee table in my living room, gathered in a neat pile. The Farting Cushion was — quite rightly, I thought — lying on top of my toilet tank, beside the current issue of Spenck's Rural Insurance Newsletter. Rural insurance used to be my specialty, as I think I told you. I knew all the odds.

What were the odds on this?

When something goes wrong in your life and you need to talk about it, I think that the first impulse for most people is to call a family member. This wasn't much of an option for me. My father put an egg in his shoe and beat it when I was two and my sister was four. My mother, no quitter she, hit the ground running and raised the two of us, managing a mail-order clearinghouse out of our home while she did so. I believe this was a business she actually created, and she made an adequate living at it (only the first year was really scary, she told me later). She smoked like a chimney, however, and died of lung cancer at the age of forty-eight, six or eight years before the Internet might have made her a dot-com millionaire.

My sister Peg was currently living in Cleveland, where she had embraced Mary Kay cosmetics, the Indians, and fundamentalist Christianity, not necessarily in that order. If I called and told Peg about the things I'd found in my apartment, she would suggest I get down on my knees and ask Jesus to come into my life. Rightly or wrongly, I did not feel Jesus could help me with my current problem.

I was equipped with the standard number of aunts, uncles, and cousins, but most lived west of the Mississippi, and I hadn't seen any of them in years. The Killians (my mother's side of the family) have never been a reuning bunch. A card on one's birthday and at Christmas were considered sufficient to fulfill all familial obligations. A card on Valentine's

Day or at Easter was a bonus. I called my sister on Christmas or she called me, we muttered the standard crap about getting together "sometime soon," and hung up with what I imagine was mutual relief.

The next option when in trouble would probably be to invite a good friend out for a drink, explain the situation, and then ask for advice. But I was a shy boy who grew into a shy man, and in my current research job I work alone (out of preference) and thus have no colleagues apt to mature into friends. I made a few in my last job — Sonja and Cleve Farrell, to name two — but they're dead, of course.

I reasoned that if you don't have a friend you can talk to, the next-best thing would be to rent one. I could certainly afford a little therapy, and it seemed to me that a few sessions on some psychiatrist's couch (four might do the trick) would be enough for me to explain what had happened and to articulate how it made me feel. How much could four sessions set me back? Six hundred dollars? Maybe eight? That seemed a fair price for a little relief. And I thought there might be a bonus. A disinterested outsider might be able to see some simple and reasonable explanation I was just missing. To my mind the locked door between my apartment and the outside world seemed to do away with most of those, but it was *my* mind, after all; wasn't that the point? And perhaps the problem?

I had it all mapped out. During the first session I'd explain what had happened. When I came to the second one, I'd bring the items in question — sunglasses, Lucite cube, conch shell, baseball bat, ceramic mushroom, the ever-popular Farting Cushion. A little show-and-tell, just like in grammar school. That left two more during which my rent-a-pal and I could figure out the cause of this disturbing tilt in the axis of my life and set things straight again.

A single afternoon spent riffling the Yellow Pages and dialing the telephone was enough to prove to me that the idea of psychiatry was unworkable in fact, no matter how good it might be in theory. The closest I came to an actual appointment was a receptionist who told me that Dr. Jauss might be able to work me in the following January. She intimated even that would take some inspired shoehorning. The others held out no hope whatsoever. I tried half a dozen therapists in Newark and four in White Plains, even a hypnotist in Queens, with the same result. Mohammed Atta and his Suicide Patrol might have been very bery-bery bad for the city of New York (not to mention for the in-SHOO-rance business), but it was clear to me from that single fruitless afternoon on the telephone that they had been a boon to the psychiatric profession, much as the psychiatrists themselves might wish otherwise. If you wanted to lie on some professional's couch in the summer of 2002, you had to take a number and wait in line.

I could sleep with those things in my apartment, but not well. They whispered to me. I lay awake in my bed, sometimes until two, thinking about Maureen Hannon, who felt she had reached an age (not to mention a level of indispensability) at which she could wear her amazingly long hair any way she damn well liked. Or I'd recall the various people who'd gone running around at the Christmas party, waving Jimmy Eagleton's famous Farting Cushion. It was, as I may have said, a great favorite once people got two or three drinks closer to New Year's. I remembered Bruce Mason asking me if it didn't look like an enema bag for elfs — "elfs," he said — and by a process of association remembered that the conch shell had been his. Of course. Bruce Mason, Lord of the Flies. And a step further down the associative food chain I found the name and face of James Mason, who had played Humbert Humbert back when Jeremy Irons was still just a putter. The mind is a wily monkey; sometime him take-a de banana, sometime him don't. Which is why I'd brought the

267

sunglasses downstairs, although I'd been aware of no deductive process at the time. I'd only wanted confirmation. There's a George Seferis poem that asks, *Are these the voices of our dead friends, or is it just the gramophone?* Sometimes it's a good question, one you have to ask someone else. Or . . . listen to this.

Once, in the late eighties, near the end of a bitter two-year romance with alcohol, I woke up in my study after dozing off at my desk in the middle of the night. I staggered off to my bedroom, where, as I reached for the light switch, I saw someone moving around. I flashed on the idea (the near *certainty*) of a junkie burglar with a cheap pawnshop .32 in his trembling hand, and my heart almost came out of my chest. I turned on the light with one hand and was grabbing for something heavy off the top of my bureau with the other — anything, even the silver frame holding the picture of my mother, would have done — when I saw the prowler was me. I was staring wild-eyed back at myself from the mirror on the other side of the room, my shirt half-untucked and my hair standing up in the back. I was disgusted with myself, but I was also relieved.

I wanted this to be like that. I wanted it to be the mirror, the gramophone, even someone playing a nasty practical joke (maybe someone who knew why I hadn't been at the office on that day in September). But I knew it was none of those things. The Farting Cushion was there, an actual guest in my apartment. I could run my thumb over the buckles on Alice's ceramic shoes, slide my finger down the part in her yellow ceramic hair. I could read the date on the penny inside the Lucite cube.

Bruce Mason, alias Conch Man, alias Lord of the Flies, took his big pink shell to the company shindig at Jones Beach one July and blew it, summoning people to a jolly picnic lunch of hotdogs and hamburgers. Then he tried to show Freddy Lounds how to do it. The best Freddy had been able to muster was a series of weak honking sounds like . . . well, like Jimmy Eagleton's Farting Cushion. Around and around it goes. Ultimately, every associative chain forms a necklace.

In late September I had a brainstorm, one of those ideas so simple you can't believe you didn't think of it sooner. Why was I holding onto this unwelcome crap, anyway? Why not just get rid of it? It wasn't as if the items were in trust; the people who owned them weren't going to come back at some later date and ask for them to be returned. The last time I'd seen Cleve Farrell's face it had been on a poster, and the last of those had been torn down by November of '01. The general (if unspoken) feeling was that such homemade homages were bumming out the tourists, who'd begun to creep back to Fun City. What had happened was horrible, most New Yorkers opined, but America was still here and Matthew Broderick would only be in *The Producers* for so long.

I'd gotten Chinese that night, from a place I like two blocks over. My plan was to eat it as I usually ate my evening meal, watching Chuck Scarborough explain the world to me. I was turning on the television when the epiphany came. They *weren't* in trust, these unwelcome souvenirs of the last safe day, nor were they evidence. There had been a crime, yes — everyone agreed to that — but the perpetrators were dead and the ones who'd set them on their crazy course were on the run. There might be trials at some future date, but Scott Staley would never be called to the stand, and Jimmy Eagleton's Farting Cushion would never be marked Exhibit A.

I left my General Tso's chicken sitting on the kitchen counter with the cover still on the aluminum dish, got a laundry bag from the shelf above my seldom-used washing machine, put the things into it (sacking them up, I couldn't believe how light they were, or how long I'd waited to do such a simple thing), and rode down in the elevator with the bag sitting between my feet. I walked to the corner of 75th and Park, looked around to make sure I wasn't being watched (God knows why I felt so furtive, but I did), then put litter in its place. I took one look back over my shoulder as I walked away. The handle of the bat poked out of the basket invitingly. Someone would come along and take it, I had no doubt. Probably before Chuck Scarborough gave way to John Seigenthaler or whoever else was sitting in for Tom Brokaw that evening.

On my way back to my apartment, I stopped at Fun Choy for a fresh order of General Tso's. "Last one no good?" asked Rose Ming, at the cash register. She spoke with some concern. "You tell why."

"No, the last one was fine," I said. "Tonight I just felt like two."

She laughed as though this were the funniest thing she'd ever heard, and I laughed, too. Hard. The kind of laughter that goes well beyond giddy. I couldn't remember the last time I'd laughed like that, so loudly and so naturally. Certainly not since Light and Bell, Insurers, fell into West Street.

I rode the elevator up to my floor and walked the twelve steps to 4-B. I felt the way seriously ill people must when they awaken one day, assess themselves by the sane light of morning, and discover that the fever has broken. I tucked my takeout bag under my left arm (an awkward maneuver but workable in the short run) and then unlocked my door. I turned on the light. There, on the table where I leave bills that need to be paid, claim checks, and overdue-book notices, were Sonja D'Amico's joke sunglasses, the ones with the red frames and the heart-shaped Lolita lenses. Sonja D'Amico who had, according to Warren Anderson (who was, so far as I knew, the only other surviving employee of Light and Bell's home office), jumped from the one hundred and tenth floor of the stricken building.

He claimed to have seen a photo that caught her as she dropped, Sonja with her hands placed primly on her skirt to keep it from skating up her thighs, her hair standing up against the smoke and blue of that day's sky, the tips of her shoes pointed down. The description made me think of "Falling," the poem James Dickey wrote about the stewardess who tries to aim the plummeting stone of her body for water, as if she could come up smiling, shaking beads of water from her hair and asking for a Coca-Cola.

"I vomited," Warren told me that day in the Blarney Stone. "I never want to look at a picture like that again, Scott, but I know I'll never forget it. You could see her face, and I think she believed that somehow . . . yeah, that somehow she was going to be all right."

I've never screamed as an adult, but I almost did so when I looked from Sonja's sunglasses to Cleve Farrell's CLAIMS ADJUSTOR, the latter once more leaning nonchalantly in the

272

corner by the entry to the living room. Some part of my mind must have remembered that the door to the hallway was open and both of my fourth-floor neighbors would hear me if I did scream; then, as the saying is, I would have some 'splainin to do.

I clapped my hand over my mouth to hold it in. The bag with the General Tso's chicken inside fell to the hardwood floor of the foyer and split open. I could barely bring myself to look at the resulting mess. Those dark chunks of cooked meat could have been anything.

I plopped into the single chair I keep in the foyer and put my face in my hands. I didn't scream and I didn't cry, and after a while I was able to clean up the mess. My mind kept trying to go toward the things that had beaten me back from the corner of 75th and Park, but I wouldn't let it. Each time it tried to lunge in that direction, I grabbed its leash and forced it away again.

That night, lying in bed, I listened to conversations. First the things talked (in low voices), and then the people who had owned the things replied (in slightly louder ones). Sometimes they talked about the picnic at Jones Beach — the coconut odor of suntan lotion and Lou Bega singing "Mambo No. 5" over and over from Misha Bryzinski's boom box. Or they talked about Frisbees sailing under the sky while dogs chased them. Sometimes they discussed children puddling along the wet sand with the seats of their shorts and their bathing suits sagging. Mothers in swimsuits ordered from the Lands' End catalogue walking beside them with white gloop on their noses. How many of the kids that day had lost a guardian Mom or a Frisbee-throwing Dad? Man, that was a math problem I didn't want to do. But the voices I heard in my apartment *did* want to do it. They did it over and over.

I remembered Bruce Mason blowing his conch shell and proclaiming himself the Lord of the Flies. I remembered Maureen Hannon once telling me (not at Jones Beach, not this conversation) that *Alice in Wonderland* was the first psychedelic novel. Jimmy Eagleton telling me one afternoon that his son had a learning disability to go along with his stutter, two for the price of one, and the kid was going to need a tutor in math and another one in French if he was going to get out of high school in the foreseeable future. "Before he's eligible for the AARP discount on textbooks" was how Jimmy had put it. His cheeks pale and a bit stubbly in the long afternoon light, as if that morning the razor had been dull.

I'd been drifting toward sleep, but this last one brought me fully awake again with a start, because I realized the conversation must have taken place not long before September Eleventh. Maybe only days. Perhaps even the Friday before, which would make it the last day I'd ever seen Jimmy alive. And the l'il putter with the stutter and the learning disability: had his name actually been Jeremy, as in Jeremy Irons? Surely not, surely that was just my mind (sometime him take-a de banana) playing its little games, but it had been *close* to that, by God. Jason, maybe. Or Justin. In the wee hours everything grows, and I remember thinking that if the kid's name *did* turn out to be Jeremy, I'd probably go crazy. Straw that broke the camel's back, baby.

Around three in the morning I remembered who had owned the Lucite cube with the steel penny in it: Roland Abelson, in Liability. He called it his retirement fund. It was Roland who had a habit of saying "Lucy, you got some 'splainin to do." One night in the fall of '01, I had seen his widow on the six o'clock news. I had talked with her at one of the company picnics (very likely the one at Jones Beach) and thought then that she was pretty, but widowhood had refined that prettiness, winnowed it into severe beauty. On the news report she kept referring to her husband as "missing." She would not call him "dead." And if he *was* alive — if he ever turned up — he would have some 'splainin to do. You bet. But of course, so would she. A woman who has gone from pretty to beautiful as the result of a mass murder would certainly have some 'splainin to do.

Lying in bed and thinking of this stuff — remembering the crash of the surf at Jones Beach and the Frisbees flying under the sky — filled me with an awful sadness that finally emptied in tears. But I have to admit it was a learning experience. That was the night I came to understand that *things* — even little ones, like a penny in a Lucite cube — can get heavier as time passes. But because it's a weight of the mind, there's no mathematical formula for it, like the ones you can find in an insurance company's Blue Books, where the rate on your whole life policy goes up $x$ if you smoke and coverage on your crops goes up $y$ if your farm's in a tornado zone. You see what I'm saying?

It's a weight of the mind.

The following morning I gathered up all the items again, and found a seventh, this one under the couch. The guy in the cubicle next to mine, Misha Bryzinski, had kept a small pair of Punch and Judy dolls on his desk. The one I spied under my sofa with my little eye was Punch. Judy was nowhere to be found, but Punch was enough for me. Those black eyes, staring out from amid the ghost bunnies, gave me a terrible sinking feeling of dismay. I fished the doll out, hating the streak of dust it left behind. A thing that leaves a trail is a real thing, a thing with weight. No question about it.

I put Punch and all the other stuff in the little utility closet just off the kitchenette, and there they stayed. At first I wasn't sure they would, but they did.

My mother once told me that if a man wiped his ass and saw blood on the toilet tissue, his response would be to shit in the dark for the next thirty days and hope for the best. She used this example to illustrate her belief that the cornerstone of male philosophy was "If you ignore it, maybe it'll go away."

I ignored the things I'd found in my apartment, I hoped for the best, and things actually got a little better. I rarely heard those voices whispering in the utility closet (except late at night), although I was more and more apt to take my research chores out of the house. By the middle of November, I was spending most of my days in the New York Public Library. I'm sure the lions got used to seeing me there with my PowerBook.

Then, just before Thanksgiving, I happened to be going out of my building one day and met Paula Robeson, the maiden fair whom I'd rescued by pushing the reset button on her air conditioner, coming in.

With absolutely no forethought whatsoever — if I'd had time to think about it, I'm convinced I never would have said a word — I asked her if I could buy her lunch and talk

277

to her about something.

"The fact is," I said, "I have a problem. Maybe you could push my reset button."

We were in the lobby. Pedro the doorman was sitting in the corner, reading the *Post* (and listening to every word, I have no doubt — to Pedro, his tenants were the world's most interesting daytime drama). She gave me a smile both pleasant and nervous. "I guess I owe you one," she said, "but . . . you know I'm married, don't you?"

"Yes," I said, not adding that she'd shaken with me wrong-handed so I could hardly fail to notice the ring.

She nodded. "Sure, you must've seen us together at least a couple of times, but he was in Europe when I had all that trouble with the air conditioner, and he's in Europe now. Edward, that's his name. Over the last two years he's been in Europe more than he's here, and although I don't like it, I'm very married in spite of it." Then, as a kind of afterthought, she added: "Edward is in import-export."

*I used to be in insurance, but then one day the company exploded,* I thought of saying. In the end, I managed something a little more sane.

"I don't want a date, Ms. Robeson," no more than I wanted to be on a first-name basis with her, and was that a wink of disappointment I saw in her eyes? By God, I

278

thought it was. But at least it convinced her. I was still *safe.*

She put her hands on her hips and looked at me with mock exasperation. Or maybe not so mock. "Then what *do* you want?"

"Just someone to talk to. I tried several shrinks, but they're . . . busy."

"*All* of them?"

"It would appear so."

"If you're having problems with your sex life or feeling the urge to race around town killing men in turbans, I don't want to know about it."

"It's nothing like that. I'm not going to make you blush, I promise." Which wasn't quite the same as saying *I promise not to shock you* or *You won't think I'm crazy.* "Just lunch and a little advice, that's all I'm asking. What do you say?"

I was surprised — almost flabbergasted — by my own persuasiveness. If I'd planned the conversation in advance, I almost certainly would have blown the whole deal. I suppose she was curious, and I'm sure she heard a degree of sincerity in my voice. She may also have surmised that if I was the sort of man who liked to try his hand picking up women, I would have had a go on that day in August when I'd actually been alone with her in her apartment, the elusive Edward in France or Germany. And I have to wonder how much actual desperation she saw in my face.

In any case, she agreed to have lunch with me on Friday at Donald's Grill down the street. Donald's may be the least romantic restaurant in all of Manhattan — good food, fluorescent lights, waiters who make it clear they'd like you to hurry. She did so with the air of a woman paying an overdue debt about which she's nearly forgotten. This was not exactly flattering, but it was good enough for me. Noon would be fine for her, she said. If I'd meet her in the lobby, we could walk down there together. I told her that would be fine for me, too.

That night was a good one for me. I went to sleep almost immediately, and there were no dreams of Sonja D'Amico going down beside the burning building with her hands on her thighs, like a stewardess looking for water.

As we strolled down 86th Street the following day, I asked Paula where she'd been when she heard.

"San Francisco," she said. "Fast asleep in a Wradling Hotel suite with Edward beside me, undoubtedly snoring as usual. I was coming back here on September twelfth and Edward was going on to Los Angeles for meetings. The hotel management actually rang the fire alarm."

"That must have scared the hell out of you."

"It did, although my first thought wasn't

fire but earthquake. Then this disembodied voice came through the speakers, telling us that there was no fire in the hotel, but a hell of a big one in New York."

"Jesus."

"Hearing it like that, in bed in a strange room . . . hearing it come down from the ceiling like the voice of God . . ." She shook her head. Her lips were pressed so tightly together that her lipstick almost disappeared. "That was very frightening. I suppose I understand the urge to pass on news like that, and immediately, but I still haven't entirely forgiven the management of the Wradling for doing it that way. I don't think I'll be staying there again."

"Did your husband go on to his meetings?"

"They were canceled. I imagine a lot of meetings were canceled that day. We stayed in bed with the TV on until the sun came up, trying to get our heads around it. Do you know what I mean?"

"Yes."

"We talked about who might have been there that we knew. I suppose we weren't the only ones doing that, either."

"Did you come up with anyone?"

"A broker from Shearson Lehman and the assistant manager of the Borders book store in the mall," she said. "One of them was all right. One of them . . . well, you know, one of them wasn't. What about you?"

So I didn't have to sneak up on it, after all. We weren't even at the restaurant yet and here it was.

"*I* would have been there," I said. "I *should* have been there. It's where I worked. In an insurance company on the hundred and tenth floor."

She stopped dead on the sidewalk, looking up at me, eyes wide. I suppose to the people who had to veer around us, we must have looked like lovers. "Scott, *no!*"

"Scott, yes," I said. And finally told someone about how I woke up on September Eleventh expecting to do all the things I usually did on weekdays, from the cup of black coffee while I shaved all the way to the cup of cocoa in front of the midnight news summary on Channel Thirteen. A day like any other day, that was what I had in mind. I think that is what Americans had come to expect as their right. Well, guess what? That's an airplane! Flying into the side of a skyscraper! Ha-ha, asshole, the joke's on you, and half the goddam world's laughing!

I told her about looking out my apartment window and seeing the seven a.m. sky was perfectly cloudless, the sort of blue so deep you think you can almost see through it to the stars beyond. Then I told her about the voice. I think everyone has various voices in their heads and we get used to them. When I was sixteen, one of mine spoke up and suggested it might be quite a kick to masturbate into a pair of my sister's underpants. *She has about a thousand pairs and surely won't miss one, y'all,* the voice opined. (I did not tell Paula Robeson about this particular adolescent adventure.) I'd have to call that the voice of utter irresponsibility, more familiarily known as Mr. Yow, Git Down.

"Mr. Yow, Git Down?" Paula asked doubtfully.

"In honor of James Brown, the King of Soul."

"If you say so."

Mr. Yow, Git Down had had less and less to say to me, especially since I'd pretty much given up drinking, and on that day he awoke from his doze just long enough to speak a dozen words, but they were life-changers. Life-*savers.*

The first five (that's me, sitting on the edge of the bed): *Yow, call in sick, y'all!* The next seven (that's me, plodding toward the shower and scratching my left buttock as I go): *Yow, spend the day in Central Park!* There was no premonition involved. It was clearly Mr. Yow, Git Down, not the voice of God. It was just a version of my very own voice (as they all are), in other words, telling me to play hooky. *Do a little suffin fo' yo'self, Gre't God!* The last time I could recall hearing this version of my voice, the subject had been a karaoke contest at a bar on Amsterdam Avenue: *Yow, sing along wit' Neil Diamond, fool — git up on stage and git ya bad self down!*

"I guess I know what you mean," she said, smiling a little.

"Do you?"

"Well . . . I once took off my shirt in a Key West bar and won ten dollars dancing to 'Honky Tonk Women.' " She paused. "Edward doesn't know, and if you ever tell him, I'll be forced to stab you in the eye with one of his tie tacks."

"Yow, you go, girl," I said, and her smile became a rather wistful grin. It made her look younger. I thought this had a chance of working.

We walked into Donald's. There was a cardboard turkey on the door, cardboard Pilgrims on the green tile wall above the steam table.

"I listened to Mr. Yow, Git Down and I'm here," I said. "But some other things are here, too, and he can't help with them. They're things I can't seem to get rid of. Those are what I want to talk to you about."

"Let me repeat that I'm no shrink," she said, and with more than a trace of uneasiness. The grin was gone. "I majored in German and minored in European history."

*You and your husband must have a lot to talk about,* I thought. What I said out loud was that it didn't have to be her, necessarily, just someone.

"All right. Just as long as you know."

A waiter took our drink orders, decaf for her, regular for me. Once he went away she asked me what things I was talking about.

"This is one of them." From my pocket I withdrew the Lucite cube with the steel penny suspended inside it and put it on the table. Then I told her about the other things, and to whom they had belonged. Cleve "Besboll been bery-bery good to me" Farrell. Maureen Hannon, who wore her hair long to her waist as a sign of her corporate indispensability. Jimmy Eagleton, who had a divine nose for phony accident claims, a son with learning disabilities, and a Farting Cushion he kept safely tucked away in his desk until the Christmas party rolled around each year. Sonja D'Amico, Light and Bell's best accountant, who had gotten the Lolita sunglasses as a bitter divorce present from her first husband. Bruce "Lord of the Flies" Mason, who would always stand shirtless in my mind's eye, blowing his conch on Jones Beach while the waves rolled up and expired around his bare feet. Last of all, Misha Bryzinski, with whom I'd gone to at least a dozen Mets games. I told her about putting everything but Misha's Punch doll in a trash basket on the corner of Park and 75th, and how they had beaten me back to my apartment, possibly because I had stopped for a second order of General Tso's chicken. During all of this, the Lucite cube stood on the table between us. We managed to eat at least some of our meal in spite of his stern profile.

When I was finished talking, I felt better than I'd dared to hope. But there was a silence from her side of the table that felt terribly heavy.

"So," I said, to break it. "What do you think?"

She took a moment to consider that, and I didn't blame her. "I think that we're not the strangers we were," she said finally, "and making a new friend is never a bad thing. I think I'm glad I know about Mr. Yow, Git Down and that I told you what I did."

"I am, too." And it was true.

"Now may I ask you two questions?"

"Of course."

"How much of what they call 'survivor guilt' are you feeling?"

"I thought you said you weren't a shrink."

"I'm not, but I read the magazines and have even been known to watch *Oprah*. That my husband *does* know, although I prefer not to rub his nose in it. So . . . how much, Scott?"

I considered the question. It was a good one — and, of course, it was one I'd asked myself on more than one of those sleepless nights. "Quite a lot," I said. "Also, quite a lot of relief, I won't lie about that. If Mr. Yow, Git Down was a real person, he'd never have to pick up another restaurant tab. Not when I was with him, at least." I paused. "Does that shock you?"

She reached across the table and briefly touched my hand. "Not even a little."

Hearing her say that made me feel better than I would have believed. I gave her hand a brief squeeze and then let it go. "What's your other question?"

"How important to you is it that I believe your story about these things coming back?"

I thought this was an excellent question, even though the Lucite cube was right there next to the sugar bowl. Such items are not exactly rare, after all. And I thought that if she *had* majored in psychology rather than German, she probably would have done fine.

"Not as important as I thought an hour ago," I said. "Just telling it has been a help."

She nodded and smiled. "Good. Now here's my best guess: someone is very likely playing a game with you. Not a nice one."

"Trickin' on me," I said. I tried not to show it, but I'd rarely been so disappointed. Maybe a layer of disbelief settles over people in certain circumstances, protecting them. Or maybe — probably — I hadn't conveyed my own sense that this thing was just . . . happening. *Still* happening. The way avalanches do.

"Trickin' on you," she agreed, and then: "But you don't believe it."

More points for perception. I nodded. "I locked the door when I went out, and it was locked when I came back from Staples. I heard the clunk the tumblers make when they turn. They're loud. You can't miss them."

"Still . . . survivor guilt is a funny thing. And powerful, at least according to the magazines."

"This . . ." *This isn't survivor guilt* was what I meant to say, but it would have been the wrong thing. I had a fighting chance to make a new friend here, and having a new friend would be good, no matter how the rest of this came out. So I amended it. "I don't think this is survivor guilt." I pointed to the Lucite cube. "It's right there, isn't it? Like Sonja's sunglasses. You see it. I do, too. I suppose I could have bought it myself, but . . ." I shrugged, trying to convey what we both surely knew: *anything* is possible.

"I don't think you did that. But neither can I accept the idea that a trapdoor opened between reality and the twilight zone and these things fell out."

Yes, that was the problem. For Paula the idea that the Lucite cube and the other things which had appeared in my apartment had some supernatural origin was automatically off-limits, no matter how much the facts might seem to support the idea. What I needed to do was to decide if I needed to argue the point more than I needed to make a friend.

I decided I did not.

"All right," I said. I caught the waiter's eye and made a check-writing gesture in the air. "I can accept your inability to accept."

"Can you?" she asked, looking at me closely.

"Yes." And I thought it was true. "If, that is, we could have a cup of coffee from time to time. Or just say hi in the lobby."

"Absolutely." But she sounded absent, not really in the conversation. She was looking at the Lucite cube with the steel penny inside it. Then she looked up at me. I could almost see a lightbulb appearing over her head, like in a cartoon. She reached out and grasped the cube with one hand. I could never convey the depth of the dread I felt when she did that, but what could I say? We were New Yorkers in a clean, well-lighted place. For her part, she'd already laid down the ground rules, and they pretty firmly excluded the supernatural. The supernatural was out of bounds. Anything hit there was a do-over.

And there was a light in Paula's eyes. One that suggested Ms. Yow, Git Down was in the house, and I know from personal experience that's a hard voice to resist.

"Give it to me," she proposed, smiling into my eyes. When she did that I could see — for the first time, really — that she was sexy as well as pretty.

"Why?" As if I didn't know.

"Call it my fee for listening to your story."

"I don't know if that's such a good —"

"It is, though," she said. She was warming to her own inspiration, and when people do that, they rarely take no for an answer. "It's a *great* idea. I'll make sure this piece of memorabilia at least doesn't come back to you, wagging its tail behind it. We've got a safe in the apartment." She made a charming little pantomime gesture of shutting a safe door, twirling the combination, and then throwing the key back over her shoulder.

"All right," I said. "It's my gift to you." And I felt something that might have been mean-spirited gladness. Call it the voice of Mr. Yow, You'll Find Out. Apparently just getting it off my chest wasn't enough, after all. She hadn't believed me, and at least part of me *did* want to be believed and resented Paula for not getting what it wanted. That part knew that letting her take the Lucite cube was an absolutely terrible idea, but was glad to see her tuck it away in her purse, just the same.

"There," she said briskly. "Mama say bye-bye, make all gone. Maybe when it doesn't come back in a week — or two, I guess it all depends on how stubborn your subconscious wants to be — you can start giving the rest of the things away." And her saying that was her real gift to me that day, although I didn't know it then.

"Maybe so," I said, and smiled. Big smile

for the new friend. Big smile for pretty Mama. All the time thinking, You'll find out.

Yow.

She did.

Three nights later, while I was watching Chuck Scarborough explain the city's latest transit woes on the six o'clock news, my doorbell rang. Since no one had been announced, I assumed it was a package, maybe even Rafe with something from FedEx. I opened the door and there stood Paula Robeson.

This was not the woman with whom I'd had lunch. Call this version of Paula Ms. Yow, Ain't That Chemotherapy *Nasty*. She was wearing a little lipstick but nothing else in the way of makeup, and her complexion was a sickly shade of yellow-white. There were dark brownish purple arcs under her eyes. She might have given her hair a token swipe with the brush before coming down from the fifth floor, but it hadn't done much good. It looked like straw and stuck out on either side of her head in a way that would have been comic-strip funny under other circumstances. She was holding the Lucite cube up in front of her breasts, allowing me to note that the well-kept nails on that hand were gone. She'd chewed them away, right down to the quick. And my first thought, God help me, was *yep, she found out.*

She held it out to me. "Take it back," she said.

I did so without a word.

"His name was Roland Abelson," she said. "Wasn't it?"

"Yes."

"He had red hair."

"Yes."

"Not married but paying child support to a woman in Rahway."

I hadn't known that — didn't believe *anyone* at Light and Bell had known that — but I nodded again, and not just to keep her rolling. I was sure she was right. "What was her name, Paula?" Not knowing why I was asking, not yet, just knowing I had to know.

"Tonya Gregson." It was as if she was in a trance. There was something in her eyes, though, something so terrible I could hardly stand to look at it. Nevertheless, I stored the name away. *Tonya Gregson, Rahway.* And then, like some guy doing stockroom inventory: *One Lucite cube with penny inside.*

"He tried to crawl under his desk, did you know that? No, I can see you didn't. His hair was on fire and he was crying. Because in that instant he understood he was never going to own a catamaran or even mow his lawn again." She reached out and put a hand on my cheek, a gesture so intimate it would have been shocking even if her hand had not been so cold. "At the end, he would have given every cent he had, and every stock option he held, just to be able to mow his lawn again. Do you believe that?"

"Yes."

"The place was full of screams, he could smell jet fuel, and *he understood it was his dying hour.* Do you understand that? Do you understand the *enormity* of that?"

I nodded. I couldn't speak. You could have put a gun to my head and I still wouldn't have been able to speak.

"The politicians talk about memorials and courage and wars to end terrorism, but burning hair is apolitical." She bared her teeth in an unspeakable grin. A moment later it was gone. "He was trying to crawl under his desk with his hair on fire. There was a plastic thing under his desk, a what-do-you-call it —"

"Mat —"

"Yes, a mat, a plastic mat, and his hands were on that and he could feel the ridges in the plastic and smell his own burning hair. Do you understand that?"

I nodded. I started to cry. It was Roland Abelson we were talking about, this guy I used to work with. He was in Liability and I didn't know him very well. To say hi to is all; how was I supposed to know he had a kid in Rahway? And if I hadn't played hooky that day, my hair probably would have burned, too. I'd never really understood that before.

"I don't want to see you again," she said.

She flashed her gruesome grin once more, but now she was crying, too. "I don't care about your problems. I don't care about any of the shit you found. We're quits. From now on you leave me alone." She started to turn away, then turned back. She said: "They did it in the name of God, but there is no God. If there was a God, Mr. Staley, He would have struck all eighteen of them dead in their boarding lounges with their boarding passes in their hands, but no God did. They called for passengers to get on and those fucks just got on."

I watched her walk back to the elevator. Her back was very stiff. Her hair stuck out on either side of her head, making her look like a girl in a Sunday funnies cartoon. She didn't want to see me anymore, and I didn't blame her. I closed the door and looked at the steel Abe Lincoln in the Lucite cube. I looked at him for quite a long time. I thought about how the hair of his beard would have smelled if U.S. Grant had stuck one of his everlasting cigars in it. That unpleasant frying aroma. On TV, someone was saying that there was a mattress blowout going on at Sleepy's. After that, Len Berman came on and talked about the Jets.

That night I woke up at two in the morning, listening to the voices whisper. I hadn't had any dreams or visions of the people who owned the objects, hadn't seen anyone with their hair on fire or jumping from the windows to escape the burning jet fuel, but why would I? I knew who they were, and the things they left behind had been left for me. Letting Paula Robeson take the Lucite cube had been wrong, but only because she was the wrong person.

And speaking of Paula, one of the voices was hers. *You can start giving the rest of the things away,* it said. And it said, *I guess it all depends on how stubborn your subconscious wants to be.*

I lay back down and after a while I was able to go to sleep. I dreamed I was in Central Park, feeding the ducks, when all at once there was a loud noise like a sonic boom and smoke filled the sky. In my dream, the smoke smelled like burning hair.

I thought about Tonya Gregson in Rahway — Tonya and the child who might or might not have Roland Abelson's eyes — and thought I'd have to work up to that one. I decided to start with Bruce Mason's widow.

I took the train to Dobbs Ferry and called a taxi from the station. The cabbie took me to a Cape Cod house on a residential street. I gave him some money, told him to wait — I wouldn't be long — and rang the doorbell. I had a box under one arm. It looked like the kind that contains a bakery cake.

I only had to ring once because I'd called ahead and Janice Mason was expecting me. I had my story carefully prepared and told it with some confidence, knowing that the taxi sitting in the driveway, its meter running, would forestall any detailed cross-examination.

On September seventh, I said — the Friday before — I had tried to blow a note from the conch Bruce kept on his desk, as I had heard Bruce himself do at the Jones Beach picnic. (Janice, Mrs. Lord of the Flies, nodding; she had been there, of course.) Well, I said, to make a long story short, I had persuaded Bruce to let me have the conch shell over the weekend so I could practice. Then, on Tuesday morning, I'd awakened with a raging sinus infection and a horrible headache to go with it. (This was a story I had already told several people.) I'd been drinking a cup of tea when I heard the boom and saw the rising smoke. I hadn't thought of the conch shell again until just this week. I'd been cleaning out my little utility closet and by damn, there it was. And I just thought . . . well, it's not much of a keepsake, but I just thought maybe you'd like to . . . you know . . .

Her eyes filled up with tears just as mine had when Paula brought back Roland Abelson's "retirement fund," only these weren't accompanied by the look of fright that I'm sure was on my own face as Paula stood there with her stiff hair sticking out on either side of her head. Janice told me she would be glad to have any keepsake of Bruce.

"I can't get over the way we said good-bye," she said, holding the box in her arms. "He always left very early because he took the train. He kissed me on the cheek and I opened one eye and asked him if he'd bring back a pint of half-and-half. He said he would. That's the last thing he ever said to me. When he asked me to marry him, I felt like Helen of Troy — stupid but absolutely true — and I wish I'd said something better than 'Bring home a pint of half-and-half.' But we'd been married a long time, and it seemed like business as usual that day, and . . . we don't know, do we?"

"No."

"Yes. Any parting could be forever, and we don't know. Thank you, Mr. Staley. For coming out and bringing me this. That was very kind." She smiled a little then. "Do you remember how he stood on the beach with his shirt off and blew it?"

"Yes," I said, and looked at the way she held the box. Later she would sit down and take the shell out and hold it on her lap and cry. I knew that the conch, at least, would never come back to my apartment. It was home.

I returned to the station and caught the train

back to New York. The cars were almost empty at that time of day, early afternoon, and I sat by a rain- and dirt-streaked window, looking out at the river and the approaching skyline. On cloudy and rainy days, you almost seem to be creating that skyline out of your own imagination, a piece at a time.

Tomorrow I'd go to Rahway, with the penny in the Lucite cube. Perhaps the child would take it in his or her chubby hand and look at it curiously. In any case, it would be out of my life. I thought the only difficult thing to get rid of would be Jimmy Eagleton's Farting Cushion — I could hardly tell Mrs. Eagleton I'd brought it home for the weekend in order to practice using it, could I? But necessity is the mother of invention, and I was confident that I would eventually think of some halfway plausible story.

It occurred to me that other things might show up, in time. And I'd be lying if I told you I found that possibility entirely unpleasant. When it comes to returning things which people believe have been lost forever, things that have *weight,* there are compensations. Even if they're only little things, like a pair of joke sunglasses or a steel penny in a Lucite cube . . . yeah. I'd have to say there are compensations.

# GRADUATION
## AFTERNOON

Janice has never settled on the right word for
the place where Buddy lives. It's too big to
be called a house, too small to be an estate,
and the name on the post at the foot of the
driveway, Harborlights, gags her. It sounds
like the name of a restaurant in New London,
the kind where the special is always fish. She
usually winds up just calling it "your place,"
as in "Let's go to your place and play tennis"
or "Let's go to your place and go swimming."

It's pretty much the same deal with Buddy
himself, she thinks, watching him trudge up
the lawn toward the sound of shouts on the
other side of the house, where the pool is.
You didn't want to call your boyfriend Buddy,
but when reverting to his real name meant
Bruce, it left you with no real ground to stand
on.

Or expressing feelings, that was that. She
knew he wanted to hear her say she loved
him, especially on his graduation day —
surely a better present than the silver medal-

lion she'd given him, although the medallion had set her back a teeth-clenching amount — but she couldn't do it. She couldn't bring herself to say, "I love you, Bruce." The best she could manage (and again with that interior clench) was "I'm awfully fond of you, Buddy." And even that sounded like a line out of a British musical comedy.

"You don't mind what she said, do you?" That was the last thing he'd asked her before heading up the lawn to change into his swim trunks. "That isn't why you're staying behind, is it?"

"No, just want to hit a few more. And look at the view." The house did have that going for it, and she could never get enough. Because you could see the whole New York cityscape from this side of the house, the buildings reduced to blue toys with sun gleaming on the highest windows. Janice thought that when it came to NYC, you could only get that sense of exquisite stillness from a distance. It was a lie she loved.

"Because she's just my gran," he went on. "You know her by now. If it enters her head, it exits her mouth."

"I know," Janice said. And she liked Buddy's gran, who made no effort to hide her snobbery. There it was, out and beating time to the music. They were the Hopes, came to Connecticut along with the rest of the Heavenly Host, thank you so much. She is Janice

Gandolewski, who will have her own graduation day — from Fairhaven High — two weeks from now, after Buddy has left with his three best buddies to hike the Appalachian Trail.

She turns to the basket of balls, a slender girl of good height in denim shorts, sneakers, and a shell top. Her legs flex as she rises on tiptoe with each serve. She's good-looking and knows it, her knowing of the functional and non-fussy sort. She's smart, and knows it. Very few Fairhaven girls manage relationships with boys from the Academy — other than the usual we-all-know-where-we-are, quick-and-dirty Winter Carnival or Spring Fling weekends, that is — and she has done so in spite of the *ski* that trails after her wherever she goes, like a tin can tied to the bumper of a family sedan. She has managed this social hat-trick with Bruce Hope, also known as Buddy.

And when they were coming up from the basement media room after playing video games — most of the others still down there, and still with their mortarboards cocked back on their heads — they had overheard his gran, in the parlor with the other adults (because this was really *their* party; the kids would have their own tonight, first at Holy Now! out on Route 219, which had been fourwalled for the occasion by Jimmy Frederick's dad and mom, pursuant to the mandatory designated-driver rule, and then later, at the beach, under a full June moon, could you give me spoon, do I hear swoon, is there a swoon in the house).

"That was Janice-Something-Unpronounceable," Gran was saying in her oddly piercing, oddly toneless deaf-lady voice. "She's very pretty, isn't she? A townie. Bruce's friend for now." She didn't quite call Janice Bruce's starter-model, but of course it was all in the tone.

She shrugs and hits a few more balls, legs flexing, racket reaching. The balls fly hard and true across the net, each touching down deep in the receiver's box on the far side.

They have in fact learned from each other, and she suspects that's what these things are about. What they are for. And Buddy has not, in truth, been that hard to teach. He respected her from the first — maybe a little too much. She had to teach him out of that — the pedestal-worship part of that. And she thinks he hasn't been that bad a lover, given the fact that kids are denied the finest of accommodations and the luxury of time when it comes to giving their bodies the food they come to want.

"We did the best we could," she says, and decides to go and swim with the others, let him show her off one final time. He thinks they'll have all summer before he goes off to Princeton and she goes to State, but she thinks not; she thinks part of the purpose of the upcoming Appalachian hike is to separate them as painlessly but as completely as possible. In this Janice senses not the hand of the hale-and-hearty, good-fellows-every-one father, or the somehow endearing snobbery of the grandmother — *a townie, Bruce's friend for now* — but the smiling and subtle practicality of the mother, whose one fear (it might as well be stamped on her lovely, unlined forehead) is that the townie girl with the tin can tied to the end of her name will get pregnant and trap her boy into the wrong marriage.

"It would be wrong, too," she murmurs as she wheels the basket of balls into the shed and flips the latch. Her friend Marcy keeps asking her what she sees in him at all — *Buddy,* she all but sneers, wrinkling her nose. *What do you do all weekend? Go to garden parties? To polo matches?*

In fact, they have been to a couple of polo matches, because Tom Hope still rides — although, Buddy confided, this was apt to be his last year if he didn't stop putting on weight. But they have also made love, some of it sweaty and intense. Sometimes, too, he makes her laugh. Less often, now — she has an idea that his capacity to surprise and amuse is far from infinite — but yes, he still does. He's a lean and narrow-headed boy who breaks the rich-kid-geek mold in interesting and sometimes very unexpected ways. Also he thinks the world of her, and that isn't entirely bad for a girl's self-image.

Still, she doesn't think he will resist the call of his essential nature forever. By the age of thirty-five or so, she guesses he will have lost most or all of his enthusiasm for eating pussy and will be more interested in collecting coins. Or refinishing Colonial rockers, like his father does out in the — ahem — carriage-house.

She walks slowly up the long acre of green grass, looking out toward the blue toys of the city dreaming in the far distance. Closer at hand are the sounds of shouts and splashing from the pool. Inside, Bruce's mother and father and gran and closest friends will be celebrating the one chick's high school graduation in their own way, at a formal tea. Tonight the kids will go out and party down in a more righteous mode. Alcohol and not a few tabs of X will be ingested. Club music will throb through big speakers. No one will play the country stuff Janice grew up with, but that's all right; she still knows where to find it.

When she graduates there will be a much smaller party, probably at Aunt Kay's restaurant, and of course she is bound for educational halls far less grand or traditional, but she has plans to go farther than she suspects Buddy goes even in his dreams. She will be a journalist. She will begin on the campus newspaper, and then will see where that takes her. One rung at a time, that's the way to do it. There are plenty of rungs on the ladder. She has talent to go along with her looks and unshowy self-confidence. She doesn't know how much, but she will find out. And there's luck. That, too. She knows enough not to count on it, but also enough to know it tends to come down on the side of the young.

She reaches the stone-flagged patio and looks down the rolling acre of lawn to the double tennis court. It all looks very big and very rich, very *special,* but she is wise enough to know she is only eighteen. There may come a time when it all looks quite ordinary to her, even in the eye of her memory. Quite small. It is this sense of perspective before the fact that makes it all right for her to be Janice-Something-Unpronounceable, and a townie, and Bruce's friend for now. Buddy, with his narrow head and fragile ability to make her laugh at unexpected times. *He* has never made her feel small, probably knows she'd leave him the first time he ever tried.

She can go directly through the house to the pool and the changing rooms on the far side, but first she turns slightly to her left to once again look at the city across all those miles of blue afternoon distance. She has time to think, *It could be my city someday, I could call it home,* before an enormous spark

305

lights up there, as if some God deep in the machinery had suddenly flicked His Bic.

She winces from the brilliance, which is at first like a thick, isolated stroke of lightning. And then the entire southern sky lights up a soundless lurid red. Formless bloodglare obliterates the buildings. Then for a moment they are there again, but ghostlike, as if seen through an interposing lens. A second or a tenth of a second after that they are gone forever, and the red begins to take on the shape of a thousand newsreels, climbing and boiling.

It is silent, silent.

Bruce's mother comes out on the patio and stands next to her, shading her eyes. She is wearing a new blue dress. A tea-dress. Her shoulder brushes Janice's and they look south at the crimson mushroom climbing, eating up the blue. Smoke is rising from around the edges — dark purple in the sunshine — and then being pulled back in. The red of the fireball is too intense to look at, it will blind her, but Janice cannot look away. Water is gushing down her cheeks in broad warm streams, but she cannot look away.

"What's that?" Bruce's mother asks. "If it's some kind of advertising, it's in very poor taste!"

"It's a bomb," Janice says. Her voice seems to be coming from somewhere else. On a live feed from Hartford, maybe. Now huge black blisters are erupting in the red mushroom, giving it hideous features that shift and change — now a cat, now a dog, now Bobo the Demon Clown — grimacing across the miles above what used to be New York and is now a smelting furnace. "A nuke. And an almighty big one. No little dirty backpack model, or —"

Whap! Heat spreads upward and downward on the side of her face, and water flies from both of her eyes, and her head rocks. Bruce's Mom has just slapped her. And hard.

"Don't you even joke about that!" Bruce's mother commands. "There's nothing funny about that!"

Other people are joining them on the patio now, but they are little more than shades; Janice's vision has either been stolen by the brightness of the fireball, or the cloud has blotted out the sun. Maybe both.

"That's in very . . . poor . . . *TASTE!*" Each word rising. *Taste* comes out in a scream.

Someone says, "It's some kind of special effect, it has to be, or else we'd hear —"

But then the sound reaches them. It's like a boulder running down an endless stone flume. It shivers the glass along the south side of the house and sends birds up from the trees in whirling squadrons. It fills the day. And it doesn't stop. It's like an endless sonic boom. Janice sees Bruce's gran go walking slowly down the path that leads to the multi-car garage with her hands to her ears. She walks with her head down and her back bent and her butt sticking out, like a dispossessed warhag starting down a long refugee road. Something hangs down on the back of her dress, swinging from side to side, and Janice isn't surprised to note (with what vision she has left) that it's Gran's hearing aid.

"I want to wake up," a man says from behind Janice. He speaks in a querulous, pestering tone. "I want to wake up. Enough is enough."

Now the red cloud has grown to its full height and stands in boiling triumph where New York was ninety seconds ago, a dark red and purple toadstool that has burned a hole straight through this afternoon and all the afternoons to follow.

A breeze begins to push through. It is a hot breeze. It lifts the hair from the sides of her head, freeing her ears to hear that endless grinding boom even better. Janice stands watching, and thinks about hitting tennis balls, one after the other, all of them landing so close together you could have caught them in a roasting pan. That is pretty much how she writes. It is her talent. Or was.

She thinks about the hike Bruce and his friends won't be taking. She thinks about the party at Holy Now! they won't be attending tonight. She thinks about the records by Jay-Z and Beyoncé and The Fray they won't be listening to — no loss there. And she thinks of the country music her dad listens to in his pickup truck on his way to and from work. That's better, somehow. She will think of Patsy Cline or Skeeter Davis and in a little while she may be able to teach what is left of her eyes not to look.

# N.

## 1. THE LETTER

*May 28, 2008*

Dear Charlie,

It seems both strange and perfectly natural to call you that, although when I last saw you I was nearly half the age I am now. I was sixteen and had a terrible crush on you. (Did you know? Of course you did.) Now I'm a happily married woman with a little boy, and I see you all the time on CNN, talking about Things Medical. You are as handsome now (well, almost!) as you were "back in the day," when the three of us used to go fishing and to movies at The Railroad in Freeport.

Those summers seem like a long time ago — you and Johnny inseparable, me tagging along whenever you'd let me. Which was probably more often than I deserved! Yet your note of condolence brought it all back to me, and how I cried. Not just for Johnny, but for all three of us. And, I suppose, for how simple and uncomplicated life seemed. How golden we were!

You saw his obituary, of course. "Accidental death" can cover such a multitude of sins, can't it? In the news story, Johnny's death was reported as the result of a fall, and of course he *did* fall — at a spot we all knew well, one he had asked me about only last Christmas — but it was no accident. There was a good deal of sedative in his bloodstream. Not nearly enough to kill him, but according to the coroner it could have been enough to disorient him, especially if he was looking over the railing. Hence, "accidental death."

But I know it was suicide.

There was no note at home or on his body, but that might have been Johnny's idea of a kindness. And you, as a doctor yourself, will know that psychiatrists have an extremely high rate of suicide. It's as if the patients' woes are a kind of acid, eating away at the psychic defenses of their therapists. In the majority of cases, those defenses are thick enough to remain intact. In Johnny's? I think not . . . thanks to one unusual patient. And he wasn't sleeping much during the last two or three months of his life; such terrible dark circles under his eyes! Also, he was canceling appointments right & left. Going on long drives. He would not say where, but I think I may know.

That brings me to the enclosure, which I

hope you will look at when you finish this letter. I know you are busy, but — if it will help! — think of me as the love-struck girl I was, with my hair tied back in a ponytail that was always coming loose, forever tagging along!

Although Johnny was on his own, he had formed a loose affiliation with two other "shrinks" in the last four years of his life. His current case files (not many, due to his cutting back) went to one of these Drs. following his death. Those files were in his office. But when I was cleaning out his study at home, I came upon the little manuscript I have enclosed. They are case notes for a patient he calls "N.," but I have seen his more formal case notes on a few occasions (not to snoop, but only because a folder happened to be open on his desk), and I know this is not like those. For one thing, they weren't done in his office, because there is no heading, as on the other case notes I have seen, and there is no red CONFIDENTIAL stamp at the bottom. Also, you will notice a faint vertical line on the pages. His home printer does this.

But there was something else, which you will see when you unwrap the box. He has printed two words on the cover in thick black strokes: BURN THIS. I almost did, without looking inside. I thought, God help me, it might be his private stash of drugs or printouts of some weird strain of Internet pornography. In the end, daughter of Pandora that I am, my curiosity got the best of me. I wish it hadn't.

Charlie, I have an idea my brother may have been planning a book, something popular in the style of Oliver Sacks. Judging by this piece of manuscript, it was obsessive-compulsive behavior he was initially focused on, and when I add in his suicide (if it *was* suicide!), I wonder if his interest didn't spring from that old adage "Physician, Heal Thyself!"

In any case, I found the account of N., and my brother's increasingly fragmentary notes, disturbing. How disturbing? Enough so I'm forwarding the manuscript — which I have not copied, by the way, this is the only one — to a friend he hadn't seen in ten years and I haven't seen in fourteen. Originally I thought, "Perhaps this could be published. It could serve as a kind of living memorial to my brother."

But I no longer think that. The thing is, the manuscript seems *alive,* and not in a good way. I know the places that are mentioned, you see (I'll bet you know some of them, too — the field N. speaks of, as Johnny notes, must have been close to where we went to school as children), and since reading the pages, I feel a strong desire to see if I can find it. Not in spite of the manuscript's disturbing nature but because of it — and if *that* isn't obsessional, what is?!?

I don't think finding it would be a good idea.

But Johnny's death haunts me, and not just because he was my brother. So does the enclosed manuscript. Would you read it? Read it and tell me what you think? Thank you, Charlie. I hope this isn't too much of an intrusion. And . . . if *you* should decide to honor Johnny's request and burn it, you would never hear a murmur of protest from me.

Fondly,
From Johnny Bonsaint's "little sis,"
Sheila Bonsaint LeClaire
964 Lisbon Street
Lewiston, Maine 04240

PS — Oy, such a crush I had on you!

## 2. The Case Notes

*June 1, 2007*

N. is 48 years old, a partner in a large Portland accounting firm, divorced, the father of two daughters. One is doing postgraduate work in California, the other is a junior at a college here in Maine. He describes his current relationship with his ex-wife as "distant but amicable."

He says, "I know I look older than 48. It's because I haven't been sleeping. I've tried Ambien and the other one, the green moth one, but they only make me feel groggy."

When I ask how long he's been suffering from insomnia, he needs no time to think it over.

"Ten months."

I ask him if it's the insomnia that brought him to me. He smiles up at the ceiling. Most patients choose the chair, at least on their first visit — one woman told me that lying on the couch would make her feel like "a joke neurotic in a *New Yorker* cartoon" — but N. has gone directly to the couch. He lies there with his hands laced tightly together on his chest.

"I think we both know better than that, Dr. Bonsaint," he says.

I ask him what he means.

"If I only wanted to get rid of the bags under my eyes, I'd either see a plastic surgeon or go to my family doctor — who recommended you, by the way, he says you're very good — and ask for something stronger than Ambien or the green moth pills. There must be stronger stuff, right?"

I say nothing to this.

"As I understand it, insomnia's always a symptom of something else."

I tell him that isn't always so, but in most cases it is. And, I add, if there is another problem, insomnia is rarely the only symptom.

"Oh, I have others," he says. "Tons. For instance, look at my shoes."

I look at his shoes. They are lace-up brogans. The left one is tied at the top, but the right has been tied at the bottom. I tell him that's very interesting.

"Yes," he says. "When I was in high school, it was the fashion of girls to tie their sneakers at the bottom if they were going steady. Or if there was a boy they liked and they *wanted* to go steady."

I ask him if he's going steady, thinking this may break the tension I see in his posture — the knuckles of his laced-together hands are white, as if he fears they might fly away unless he exerts a certain amount of pressure to keep them where they are — but he doesn't laugh. He doesn't even smile.

"I'm a little past the going-steady stage of life," he says, "but there *is* something I want."

He considers.

"I tried tying *both* of my shoes at the bottom. It didn't help. But one up and one down — that actually seems to do some good." He frees his right hand from the deathgrip his left has on it and holds it up with the thumb and forefinger almost touching. "About this much."

I ask him what he wants.

"For my mind to be right again. But trying to cure one's mind by tying one's shoelaces according to some high school code of communication . . . slightly adjusted to fit the current situation . . . that's crazy, wouldn't you say? And crazy people should seek help. If they have any sanity left at all — which I flatter myself I do — they know that. So here I am."

He slides his hands together again and looks at me with defiance and fright. Also, I think, with some relief. He's lain awake trying to imagine what it will be like to tell a psychiatrist that he fears for his sanity, and when he did it, I neither ran shrieking from the room nor called for the men in the white coats. Some patients imagine I have a posse of such white-coated men in the very next room, equipped with butterfly nets and straitjackets.

I ask him to give me some instances of his current mental wrongness, and he shrugs.

"The usual OCD shit. You've heard it all a hundred times before. It's the underlying cause I came here to deal with. What happened in August of last year. I thought maybe you could hypnotize me and make me forget it." He looks at me hopefully.

I tell him that, while nothing is impossible, hypnotism works better when it's employed as an aid to memory rather than as a block.

"Ah," he says. "I didn't know that. Shit." He looks up at the ceiling again. The muscles in the side of his face are working, and I think he has something more to say. "It could be dangerous, you know." He stops, but this is only a pause; the muscles along his jaw are still flexing and relaxing. "What's wrong with me could be very dangerous." Another pause. "To me." Another pause. "Possibly to others."

Every therapy session is a series of choices; branching roads with no signposts. Here I could ask him what *it* is — the dangerous thing — but I elect not to. Instead I ask him what sort of OCD shit he's talking about. Other than the one-up, one-down tying thing, which is a pretty damn good example. (I do not say this.)

"You know it all," he says, and gives me a sly look that makes me a bit uncomfortable. I don't show it; he isn't the first patient who has made me uncomfortable. Psychiatrists are spelunkers, really, and any spelunker will tell you that caves are full of bats and bugs. Not nice, but most are essentially harmless.

I ask him to humor me. And to remember that we are still just getting to know each other.

"Not going steady just yet, eh?"

No, I tell him, not quite yet.

"Well, we better be soon," he says, "because I'm at Condition Orange here, Dr. Bonsaint. Edging into Condition Red."

I ask him if he counts things.

"Of course I do," he says. "The number of clues in the New York *Times* crossword puzzles . . . and on Sundays I count twice, because those puzzles are bigger and double-checking seems in order. Necessary, in fact. My own footsteps. Number of telephone rings when I call someone. I eat at the Colonial Diner on most workdays, it's three blocks from the office, and on my way there I'll count black shoes. On my way back, I'll count brown ones. I tried red once, but that was ridiculous. Only women wear red shoes, and not many, at that. Not in the daytime. I only counted three pair, so I went back to the Colonial and started again, only the second time I counted brown shoes."

I ask him if he has to count a certain number of shoes in order to achieve satisfaction.

"Thirty's good," he says. "Fifteen pair. Most days, that's no problem."

And why is it necessary to reach a certain number?

He considers, then looks at me. "If I say 'you know,' will you just ask me to explain what it is you're supposed to know? I mean, you've dealt with OCD before and I've researched it — exhaustively — both in my own head and on the Internet, so can't we just cut to the chase?"

I say that most counters feel that reaching a certain total, known as "the goal number," is necessary to maintain order. To keep the world spinning on its axis, so to speak.

He nods, satisfied, and the floodgates break.

"One day, when I was counting my way

back to the office, I passed a man with one leg cut off at the knee. He was on crutches, with a sock on his stump. If he'd been wearing a black shoe, it would have been no problem. Because I was on my way *back,* you see. But it was brown. That threw me off for the whole day, and that night I couldn't sleep at all. Because odd numbers are bad." He taps the side of his head. "At least up here they are. There's a rational part of my mind that knows it's all bullshit, but there's another part that knows it absolutely isn't, and that part rules. You'd think that when nothing bad happened — in fact something *good* happened that day, an IRS audit we were worried about was canceled for absolutely no reason — the spell would break, but it didn't. I'd counted thirty-seven brown shoes instead of thirty-eight, and when the world didn't end, that irrational part of my mind said it was because I not only got above thirty, I got *well* above thirty.

"When I load the dishwasher, I count plates. If there's an even number above ten in there, all is well. If not, I add the correct number of clean ones to make it right. Same with forks and spoons. There has to be at least twelve pieces in the little plastic caddy at the front of the dishwasher. Which, since I live alone now, usually means adding clean ones."

What about knives, I ask, and he shakes his

head at once.

"Never knives. Not in the dishwasher."

When I ask why not, he says he doesn't know. Then, after a pause, he gives me a guilty sideways look. "I always wash the knives by hand, in the sink."

Knives in the silverware caddy would disturb the order of the world, I suggest.

"No!" he exclaims. "You understand, Dr. Bonsaint, but you don't understand *completely.*"

Then you have to help me, I say.

"The order of the world is already disturbed. *I* disturbed it last summer, when I went to Ackerman's Field. Only I didn't understand. Not then."

But you do now? I ask.

"Yes. Not everything, but enough."

I ask him if he is trying to fix things or only trying to keep the situation from getting worse.

A look of unutterable relief fills his face, relaxing all the muscles there. Something that has been crying out for articulation has finally been spoken aloud. These are the moments I live for. It's not a cure, far from it, but for the time being N. has gotten some relief. I doubt if he expected it. Most patients do not.

"I can't fix it," he whispers. "But I can keep things from getting worse. Yes. I *have* been."

Again I have come to one of those branching points. I could ask him what happened last summer — last August, I presume — in Ackerman's Field, but it is probably still too early. Better to loosen the roots of this infected tooth a little more first. And I really doubt that the source of the infection can be so recent. More likely, whatever happened to him last summer was only a kind of firing pin.

I ask him to tell me about his other symptoms.

He laughs. "That would take all day, and we only have . . ." He glances at his wrist. ". . . twenty-two minutes left. Twenty-two is a good number, by the way."

Because it's even? I ask.

His nod suggests I am wasting time with the obvious.

"My . . . my *symptoms,* as you call them . . . come in clusters." Now he's looking up at the ceiling. "There are three of these clusters. They poke out of me . . . the sane part of me . . . like rocks . . . rocks, you know . . . oh God, dear God . . . like the fucking *rocks* in that fucking *field* . . ."

Tears are coursing down his cheeks. At first he doesn't seem to notice, only lies on the couch with his fingers laced together, looking up at the ceiling. But then he reaches for the table beside him, where sits what Sandy, my receptionist, calls The Eternal Box of Kleenex. He takes two, wipes his cheeks, then crumples the tissue. It disappears into the

323

lace of his fingers.

"There are three clusters," he resumes, speaking in a voice that isn't quite steady. "Counting is the first. It's important, but not so important as touching. There are certain things I need to touch. Stove-burners, for instance. Before leaving the house in the morning or going to bed at night. I might be able to see they're off — all the dials pointing straight up, all the burners dark — but I still have to touch them to be absolutely sure. And the front of the oven door, of course. Then I started touching the light switches before leaving the house or the office. Just a quick double-tap. Before I get into my car, I have to tap four times on the roof. And six times when I get to where I'm going. Four's a good number, and six is an *okay* number, but ten . . . ten is like . . ." I can see one tear-track he's missed, running a zigzag course from the corner of his right eye to the lobe of his ear.

Like going steady with the girl of your dreams? I suggest.

He smiles. He has a lovely, weary smile — a smile that's finding it increasingly hard to get up in the morning.

"That's right," he says. "And she's got her sneaker laces tied at the bottom so everyone knows it."

You touch other things? I ask, knowing the answer to this. I have seen many cases like N.

during the five years I've been in practice. I sometimes picture these unfortunates as men and women being pecked to death by predatory birds. The birds are invisible — at least until a psychiatrist who is good, or lucky, or both, sprays them with his version of Luminol and shines the right light on them — but they are nevertheless very real. The wonder is that so many OCDs manage to live productive lives, just the same. They work, they eat (often not enough or too much, it's true), they go to movies, they make love to their girlfriends and boyfriends, their wives and husbands . . . and all the time those birds are there, clinging to them and pecking away little bits of flesh.

"I touch many things," he says, and again favors the ceiling with his weary, charming smile. "You name it, I touch it."

So counting is important, I say, but touching is more important. What is above touching?

*"Placing,"* he says, and suddenly begins to shiver all over, like a dog that's been left out in a cold rain. "Oh God."

He suddenly sits up and swings his legs over the edge of the couch. On the table beside him there is a vase of flowers in addition to The Eternal Box of Kleenex. Moving very quickly, he shifts the box and the vase so they are diagonal to each other. Then he takes two of the tulips from the vase and lays them stem to stem so that one blossom touches the Kleenex box and the other the vase.

"That makes it safe," he says. He hesitates, then nods as if he's confirmed in his mind that what he's thinking is the right thing. "It preserves the world." He hesitates again. "For now."

I glance down at my watch. Time is up, and we've done quite enough for one day.

"Next week," I say. "Same bat-time, same bat-station." Sometimes I turn this little joke into a question, but not with N. He needs to come back, and knows it.

"No magical cure, huh?" he asks. This time the smile is almost too sad to look at.

I tell him that he may feel better. (This sort of positive suggestion never hurts, as all psychiatrists know.) Then I tell him to throw away his Ambien and "the green moth pills" — Lunesta, I assume. If they don't work at night, all they can do is cause trouble for him during his waking hours. Falling asleep on the 295 Connector won't solve any of his problems.

"No," he says. "I suppose not. Doc, we never discussed the root cause. I know what it is —"

Next week we may get to that, I tell him. In the meantime, I want him to keep a chart divided into three sections: counting, touching, and placing. Will he do that?

"Yes," he says.

I ask him, almost casually, if he feels suicidal.

"The thought has crossed my mind, but I have a great deal to do."

This is an interesting and rather troubling response.

I give him my card and tell him to call — day or night — if the idea of suicide begins to seem more attractive. He says he will. But then, almost all of them promise.

"In the meantime," I say at the door, putting my hand on his shoulder, "keep going steady with life."

He looks at me, pale and not smiling now, a man being pecked to pieces by invisible birds. "Have you ever read 'The Great God Pan,' by Arthur Machen?"

I shake my head.

"It's the most terrifying story ever written," he says. "In it, one of the characters says 'lust always prevails.' But lust isn't what he means. What he means is compulsion."

Paxil? Perhaps Prozac. But neither until I get a better fix on this interesting patient.

*June 7, 2007*
*June 14, 2007*
*June 28, 2007*

N. brings his "homework" to our next session, as I fully expected he would. There are many things in this world you can't depend on, and many people you can't trust, but

OCDs, unless they are dying, almost always complete their tasks.

In a way his charts are comical; in another way, sad; in another, frankly horrible. He is an accountant, after all, and I assume he's used one of his accounting programs to create the contents of the folder he hands me before proceeding to the couch. They are spreadsheets. Only instead of investments and income-flow, these charts detail the complex terrain of N.'s obsessions. The top two sheets are headed COUNTING; the next two TOUCH-ING; the final six PLACING. Thumbing through them, I'm hard put to understand how he finds time for any other activities. Yet OCDs almost always find a way. The idea of invisible birds recurs to me; I see them roosting all over N., pecking away his flesh in bloody nibbles.

When I look up, he's on the couch, once more with his hands laced together tightly on his chest. And he's rearranged the vase and the tissue-box so they are again connected on a diagonal. The flowers are white lilies today. Seeing them that way, laid out on the table, makes me think of funerals.

"Please don't ask me to put them back," he says, apologetic but firm. "I'll leave before I do that."

I tell him I have no intention of asking him to put them back. I hold up the spreadsheets and compliment him on how professional they look. He shrugs. I then ask him if they represent an overview or if they only cover the last week.

"Just the last week," he says. As if the matter is of no interest to him. I suppose it is not. A man being pecked to death by birds can have little interest in last year's insults and injuries, or even last week's; he's got today on his mind. And, God help him, the future.

"There must be two or three thousand items here," I say.

"Call them events. That's what I call them. There are six hundred and four counting events, eight hundred and seventy-eight touching events, and twenty-two hundred and forty-six placing events. All even numbers, you'll notice. They add up to thirty-seven hundred and twenty-eight, also an even number. If you add the individual numbers in that total — 3728 — you come out with twenty, also even. A good number." He nods, as if confirming this to himself. "Divide 3728 by two and you come out with eighteen-hundred and sixty-four. 1864 adds up to nineteen, a powerful odd number. Powerful and *bad*." He actually shivers a little.

"You must be very tired," I say.

To this he makes no verbal reply, nor does he nod, but he answers, all the same. Tears trickle down his cheeks toward his ears. I am reluctant to add to his burden, but I recognize

one fact: if we don't begin this work soon —
"no ditzing around," as Sister Sheila would
say — he won't be capable of the work at all.
I can already see a deterioration in his appearance (wrinkled shirt, indifferent shave,
hair badly in need of a trim), and if I asked
his colleagues about him, I would almost
surely see those quick exchanged glances that
tell so much. The spreadsheets are amazing
in their way, but N. is clearly running out of
strength. It seems to me that there is no
choice but to fly directly to the heart of the
matter, and until that heart is reached, there
will be no Paxil or Prozac or anything else.

I ask if he is ready to tell me what happened
last August.

"Yes," he says. "It's what I came to do." He
takes some tissues from the Eternal Box and
wipes his cheeks. Wearily. "But Doc . . . are
you sure?"

I have never had a patient ask me that, or
speak to me in quite that tone of reluctant
sympathy. But I tell him yes, I'm sure. My
job is to help him, but in order for me to do
that, he must be willing to help himself.

"Even if it puts you at risk of winding up
like I am now? Because it could happen. I'm
lost, but I think — I hope — that I haven't
gotten to the drowning-man state, so panicky
I'd be willing to pull down anyone who was
trying to save me."

I tell him I don't quite understand.

"I'm here because all this may be in my head," he says, and knocks his knuckles against his temple, as if he wants to make sure I know where his head is at. "But it might not be. I can't really tell. That's what I mean when I say I'm lost. And if it's not mental — if what I saw and sensed in Ackerman's Field is real — then I'm carrying a kind of infection. Which I could pass on to you."

*Ackerman's Field.* I make a note of it, although everything will be on the tapes. When we were children, my sister and I went to Ackerman School, in the little town of Harlow, on the banks of the Androscoggin. Which is not far from here; thirty miles at most.

I tell him I'll take my chances, and say that in the end — more positive reinforcement — I'm sure we'll both be fine.

He utters a hollow, lonely laugh. "Wouldn't that be nice," he says.

"Tell me about Ackerman's Field."

He sighs and says, "It's in Motton. On the east side of the Androscoggin."

Motton. One town over from Chester's Mill. Our mother used to buy milk and eggs at Boy Hill Farm in Motton. N. is talking about a place that cannot be more than seven miles from the farmhouse where I grew up. I almost say, *I knew it!*

I don't, but he looks over at me sharply,

almost as if he caught my thought. Perhaps he did. I don't believe in ESP, but I don't entirely discount it, either.

"Don't ever go there, Doc," he says. "Don't even look for it. Promise me."

I give my promise. In fact, I haven't been back to that broken-down part of Maine in over fifteen years. It's close in miles, distant in desire. Thomas Wolfe made a characteristically sweeping statement when he titled his magnum opus *You Can't Go Home Again;* it's not true for everyone (Sister Sheila often goes back; she's still close to several of her childhood friends), but it's true for me. Although I suppose I'd title my own book *I Won't Go Home Again.* What I remember are bullies with harelips dominating the playground, empty houses with staring glassless windows, junked-out cars, and skies that always seemed white and cold and full of fleeing crows.

"All right," N. says, and bares his teeth for a moment at the ceiling. Not in aggression; it is, I'm quite sure, the expression of a man preparing to do a piece of heavy lifting that will leave him aching the next day. "I don't know if I can express it very well, but I'll do my best. The important thing to remember is that up til that day in August, the closest thing to OCD behavior I exhibited was popping back into the bathroom before going to work to make sure I'd gotten all the nose hairs."

Maybe this is true; more likely it isn't. I don't pursue the subject. Instead, I ask him to tell me what happened that day. And he does.

For the next three sessions, he does. At the second of those sessions — June 15th — he brings me a calendar. It is, as the saying goes, Exhibit A.

### 3. N.'s Story

I'm an accountant by trade, a photographer by inclination. After my divorce — and the children growing up, which is a divorce of a different kind, and almost as painful — I spent most of my weekends rambling around, taking landscape shots with my Nikon. It's a film camera, not a digital. Toward the end of every year, I took the twelve best pix and turned them into a calendar. I had them printed at a little place in Freeport called The Windhover Press. It's pricey, but they do good work. I gave the calendars to my friends and business associates for Christmas. A few clients, too, but not many — clients who bill five or six figures usually appreciate something that's silver-plated. Myself, I prefer a good landscape photo every time. I have no pictures of Ackerman's Field. I took some, but they never came out. Later on I borrowed a digital camera. Not only did the pictures not come out, I fried the camera's insides. I had to buy a new one for the guy I borrowed it from. Which was all right. By then I think I would have destroyed any pictures I took of *that* place, anyway. If *it* allowed me, that is.

{*I ask him what he means by "it." N. ignores the question as if he hasn't heard it.*}

I've taken pictures all over Maine and New Hampshire, but tend to stick pretty much to my own patch. I live in Castle Rock — up on the View, actually — but I grew up in Harlow, like you. And don't look so surprised, Doc, I Googled you after my GP suggested you — everybody Googles everybody these days, don't they?

Anyway, that part of central Maine is where I've done my best work: Harlow, Motton, Chester's Mill, St. Ives, Castle-St.-Ives, Canton, Lisbon Falls. All along the banks of the mighty Androscoggin, in other words. Those pictures look more . . . *real,* somehow. The '05 calendar's a good example. I'll bring you one and you can decide for yourself. January through April and September through December were all taken close to home. May through August are . . . let's see . . . Old Orchard Beach . . . Pemnaquid Point, the lighthouse, of course . . . Harrison State Park . . . and Thunder Hole in Bar Harbor. I thought I was really getting something at Thunder Hole, I was excited, but when I saw the proofs, reality came crashing back down. It was just another tourist-snap.

Good composition, but so what, right? You can find good composition in any shitshop tourist calendar.

Want my opinion, just as an amateur? I think photography's a much artier art than most people believe. It's logical to think that, if you've got an eye for composition — plus a few technical skills you can learn in any photography class — one pretty place should photograph as well as any other, especially if you're just into landscapes. Harlow, Maine or Sarasota, Florida, just make sure you've got the right filter, then point and shoot. Only it's not like that. Place matters in photography just like it does in painting or writing stories or poetry. I don't know *why* it does, but . . .

{*There is a long pause.*}

Actually I do. Because an artist, even an amateur one like me, puts his soul into the things he creates. For some people — ones with the vagabond spirit, I imagine — the soul is portable. But for me, it never seemed to travel even as far as Bar Harbor. The snaps I've taken along the Androscoggin, though . . . those speak to me. And they do to others, too. The guy I do business with at Windhover said I could probably get a book deal out of New York, end up getting paid for my calendars rather than paying for them myself, but that never interested me. It seemed a little too . . . I don't know . . . public? Pretentious?

I don't know, something like that. The calendars are little things, just between friends. Besides, I've got a job. I'm happy crunching numbers. But my life sure would have been dimmer without my hobby. I was happy just knowing a few friends had my calendars hung in their kitchens or living rooms. Even in their damn mudrooms. The irony is I haven't taken many pictures since the ones I took in Ackerman's Field. I think that part of my life may be over, and it leaves a hole. One that whistles in the middle of the night, as if there was a wind way down inside. A wind trying to fill up what's no longer there. Sometimes I think life is a sad, bad business, Doc. I really do.

On one of my rambles last August, I came to a dirt road in Motton that I didn't remember ever seeing before. I'd just been riding, listening to tunes on the radio, and I'd lost track of the river, but I knew it couldn't be far, because it has a smell. It's kind of dank and fresh at the same time. You know what I'm talking about, I'm sure. It's an *old* smell. Anyway, I turned up that road.

It was bumpy, almost washed out in a couple of places. Also, it was getting late. It must have been around seven in the evening, and I hadn't stopped anywhere for supper. I was hungry. I almost turned around, but then the road smoothed out and started going uphill instead of down. That smell was stronger, too. When I turned off the radio, I could hear the river as well as smell it — not loud, not close, but it was there.

Then I came to a tree down across the road, and I almost went back. I could have, even though there was no place to turn around. I was only a mile or so in from Route 117, and I could have backed out in five minutes. I think now that something, some force that exists on the bright side of our lives, was giving me that opportunity. I think the last year would have been a lot different if I'd just thrown the transmission in reverse. But I didn't. Because that smell . . . it's always reminded me of childhood. Also, I could see a lot more sky at the crest of the hill. The trees — some pine, mostly junk birch — drew back up there, and I thought, "There's a field." It occurred to me that if there was, it probably looked down on the river. It also occurred to me that there might be a good spot to turn around up there, but that was very secondary to the idea that I might be able to take a picture of the Androscoggin at sunset. I don't know if you remember that we had some spectacular sunsets last August, but we did.

So I got out and moved the tree. It was one of those junk birches, so rotted it almost came apart in my hands. But when I got back into my car, I still almost went back instead of forward. There really is a force on the bright side of things; I believe that. But it seemed like the sound of the river was clearer with the tree out of the way — stupid, I know, but it really seemed that way — so I threw the transmission into low and drove my little Toyota 4Runner the rest of the way up.

I passed a little sign tacked to a tree. ACKERMAN'S FIELD, NO HUNTING, KEEP OUT, it said. Then the trees drew back, first on the left, then on the right, and there it was. It took my breath away. I barely remember turning off the car and getting out, and I don't remember grabbing my camera, but I must have, because I had it in my hand when I got to the edge of the field, with the strap and lens-bag knocking against my leg. I was struck to my heart and through my heart, knocked clean out of my ordinary life.

Reality is a mystery, Dr. Bonsaint, and the everyday texture of things is the cloth we draw over it to mask its brightness and darkness. I think we cover the faces of corpses for the same reason. We see the faces of the dead as a kind of gate. It's shut against us . . . but we know it won't *always* be shut. Someday it will swing open for each of us, and each of us will go through.

But there are places where the cloth gets ragged and reality is thin. The face beneath peeps through . . . but not the face of a corpse. It would almost be better if it was. Ackerman's Field is one of those places, and no damn wonder whoever owns it put up a

KEEP OUT sign.

The day was fading. The sun was a ball of red gas, flattened at the top and bottom, sitting above the western horizon. The river was a long, bloody snake in its reflected glow, eight or ten miles distant, but the sound of it carrying to me on the still evening air. Blue-gray woods rose behind it in a series of ridges to the far horizon. I couldn't see a single house or road. Not a bird sang. It was as if I'd been tumbled back four hundred years in time. Or four million. The first white streamers of groundmist were rising out of the hay — which was high. Nobody had been in there to cut it, although that was a big field, and good graze. The mist came out of the darkening green like breath. As if the earth itself was alive.

I think I staggered a little. It wasn't the beauty, although it was beautiful; it was how everything that lay before me seemed *thin,* almost to the point of hallucination. And then I saw those damned rocks rising out of the uncut hay.

There were seven, or so I thought — the tallest two about five feet high, the shortest only three or so, the rest in between. I remember walking down to the closest of them, but it's like remembering a dream after it starts to decompose in the morning light — you know how they do that? Of course you do, dreams must be a big part of your workday. Only this was no dream. I could hear the hay whickering against my pants, could feel the khaki getting damp from the mist and starting to stick to my skin below the knees. Every now and then a bush — clumps of sumac were growing here and there — would pull my lens-bag back and then drop it again so it would thump harder than usual against my thigh.

I got to the nearest of the rocks and stopped. It was one of the five-footers. At first I thought there were faces carved in it — not human faces, either; the faces of beasts and monsters — but then I shifted my position a little and saw it was just a trick of the evening light, which thickens shadows and makes them look like . . . well, like anything. In fact, after I stood in my new position for awhile, I saw new faces. Some of these looked human, but they were just as horrible. *More* horrible, really, because human is always more horrible, don't you think? Because we *know* human, we *understand* human. Or think we do. And these looked like they were either screaming or laughing. Maybe both at the same time.

I thought it was the quiet screwing with my imagination, and the isolation, and the *bigness* of it — how much of the world I could see laid out in front of me. And how time seemed to be holding its breath. As if everything would stay the way it was forever, with sunset not more than forty minutes away and the sun sitting red over the horizon and that faded clarity in the air. I thought it was those things that were making me see faces where there was nothing but coincidence. I think differently now, but now it's too late.

I snapped some pictures. Five, I think. A bad number, although I didn't know that yet. Then I stood back, wanting to get all seven of them in one picture, and when I framed the shot, I saw that there were really eight, standing in a kind of rough ring. You could tell — when you really looked, you could — that they were part of some underlying geological formation that had either poked out of the ground eons ago, or had maybe been exposed more recently by flooding (the field had a fairly steep downward slope, so I thought that was very possible), but they also looked *planned,* like stones in a Druid's circle. There was no carving in them, though. Except for what the elements had done. I know, because I went back in daylight and made sure of it. Chips and folds in the stone. No more than that.

I took another four shots — which makes a total of nine, another bad number, although slightly better than five — and when I lowered the camera and looked again with my naked eye, I saw the faces, leering and grinning and grunting. Some human, some bestial. And I counted seven stones.

But when I looked into the viewfinder again, there were eight.

I started to feel dizzy and scared. I wanted to be out of there before full dark came — away from that field and back on Route 117, with loud rock and roll on the radio. But I couldn't just leave. Something deep inside me — as deep as the instinct that keeps us drawing in breaths and letting them out — insisted on that. I felt that if I left, something terrible would happen, and perhaps not just to me. That sense of *thinness* swept over me again, as if the world was fragile at this particular place, and one person would be enough to cause an unimaginable cataclysm. If he weren't very, very careful.

That's when my OCD shit started. I went from stone to stone, touching each one, counting each one, and marking each in its place. I wanted to be gone — desperately wanted to be gone — but I did it and I didn't skimp the job. Because I *had* to. I knew that the way I know I have to keep breathing if I want to stay alive. By the time I got back to where I'd started, I was trembling and wet with sweat as well as mist and dew. Because touching those stones . . . it wasn't nice. It caused . . . ideas. And raised images. Ugly ones. One was of chopping up my ex-wife with an axe and laughing while she screamed and raised her bloody hands to ward off the blows.

But there were eight. Eight stones in Ackerman's Field. A good number. A *safe* number. I knew that. And it no longer mattered if I looked at them through the camera's viewfinder or with my naked eyes; after touching them, they were *fixed.* It was getting darker, the sun was halfway over the horizon (I must have spent twenty minutes or more going around that rough circle, which was maybe forty yards across), but I could see well enough — the air was weirdly clear. I still felt afraid — there was something wrong there, everything screamed it, the very silence of the birds screamed it — but I felt relieved, too. The wrong had been put at least partly right by touching the stones . . . and *looking* at them again. Getting their places in the field set into my mind. That was as important as the touching.

{*A pause to think.*}

No, *more* important. Because it's how we see the world that keeps the darkness beyond the world at bay. Keeps it from pouring through and drowning us. I think all of us might know that, way down deep. So I turned to go, and I was most of the way back to my car — I might even have been touching the doorhandle — when something turned me around again. And that was when I *saw.*

{*He is silent for a long time. I notice he is trembling. He has broken out in a sweat. It gleams on his forehead like dew.*}

343

There was something in the *middle* of the stones. In the middle of the circle they made, either by chance or design. It was black, like the sky in the east, and green like the hay. It was turning very slowly, but it never took its eyes off me. It *did* have eyes. Sick pink ones. I knew — my *rational* mind knew — that it was just light in the sky I was seeing, but at the same time I knew it was something more. That something was *using* that light. Something was using the sunset to see with, and what it was seeing was *me*.

{*He's crying again. I don't offer him the Kleenex, because I don't want to break the spell. Although I'm not sure I could have offered them in any case, because he's cast a spell over me, too. What he's articulating is a delusion, and part of him knows it — "shadows that looked like faces," etc. — but it's very strong, and strong delusions travel like cold germs on a sneeze.*}

I must have kept backing up. I don't remember doing it; I just remember thinking that I was looking at the head of some grotesque monster from the outer darkness. And thinking that where there was one, there would be more. Eight stones would keep them captive — barely — but if there were only seven, they'd come flooding through from the darkness on the other side of reality and overwhelm the world. For all I knew, I was looking at the least and smallest of them.

For all I knew, that flattened snakehead with the pink eyes and what looked like great long quills growing out of its snout was only a *baby.*

It saw me looking.

The fucking thing *grinned* at me, and its teeth were heads. Living human heads.

Then I stepped on a dead branch. It snapped with a sound like a firecracker, and the paralysis broke. I don't think it's impossible that that thing floating inside the circle of stones was hypnotizing me, the way a snake is supposed to be able to do with a bird.

I turned and ran. My lens-bag kept smacking my leg, and each smack seemed to be saying *Wake up! Wake up! Get out! Get out!* I pulled open the door of my 4Runner, and I heard the little bell dinging, the one that means you left your key in the ignition. I thought of some old movie where William Powell and Myrna Loy are at the desk of a fancy hotel and Powell rings the bell for service. Funny what goes through your mind at moments like that, isn't it? There's a gate in our heads, too — that's what I think. One that keeps the insanity in all of us from flooding our intellects. And at critical moments, it swings open and all kinds of weird shit comes flooding through.

I started the engine. I turned on the radio, turned it up loud, and rock music came roaring out of the speakers. It was The Who, I remember that. And I remember popping on the headlights. When I did, those stones seemed to *jump toward me.* I almost screamed. But there were eight, I counted them, and eight is safe.

{*There's another long pause here. Almost a full minute.*}

The next thing I remember, I was back on Route 117. I don't know how I got there, if I turned around or backed out. I don't know how long it took me, but The Who song was over and I was listening to The Doors. God help me, it was "Break On Through to the Other Side." I turned the radio off.

I don't think I can tell you any more, Doc, not today. I'm exhausted.

{*And he looks it.*}

{*Next Session*}

I thought the effect the place had had on me would dissipate on the drive home — just a bad moment out in the woods, right? — and surely by the time I was in my own living room, with the lights and TV on, I'd be okay again. But I wasn't. If anything, that feeling of dislocation — of having touched some other universe that was inimical to ours — seemed to be stronger. The conviction remained that I'd seen a face — worse, the suggestion of some huge reptilian body — in that circle of stones. I felt . . . *infected.* Infected by

346

the thoughts in my own head. I felt *danger-ous,* too — as if I could summon that thing just by thinking about it too much. And it wouldn't be alone. That whole other cosmos would come spilling through, like vomit through the bottom of a wet paper bag.

I went around and locked all the doors. Then I was sure that I'd forgotten a couple, so I went around and checked them all again. This time I counted: front door, back door, pantry door, bulkhead door, garage overhead door, back garage door. That was six, and it came to me that six was a good number. Like eight is a good number. They're friendly numbers. Warm. Not cold, like five or . . . you know, seven. I relaxed a little, but I still went around one last time. Still six. "Six is a fix," I remember saying. After that I thought I'd be able to sleep, but I couldn't. Not even with an Ambien. I kept seeing the setting sun on the Androscoggin, turning it into a red snake. The mist coming out of the hay like tongues. And the thing in the stones. That most of all.

I got up and counted all the books in my bedroom bookcase. There were ninety-three. That's a bad number, and not just because it's odd. Divide ninety-three by three and you come out with thirty-one: thirteen backwards. So I got a book from the little bookcase in the hall. But ninety-four is only a little better, because nine and four add up to thirteen.

There are thirteens everywhere in this world of ours, Doc. You don't know. Anyway, I added six more books to the bedroom case. I had to cram, but I got them in. A hundred is okay. Fine, in fact.

I was heading back to bed, then started wondering about the hall bookcase. If I'd, you know, robbed Peter to pay Paul. So I counted those, and that was all right: fifty-six. The numbers add to eleven, which is odd but not the *worst* odd, and fifty-six divides to twenty-eight — a good number. After that I could sleep. I think I had bad dreams, but I don't remember them.

Days went by, and my mind kept going back to Ackerman's Field. It was like a shadow had fallen over my life. I was counting lots of things by then, and touching things — to make sure I understood their places in the world, the real world, *my* world — and I'd started to place things, too. Always even numbers of things, and usually in a circle or on a diagonal line. Because circles and diagonals keep things out.

Usually, that is. And never permanently. One small accident and fourteen becomes thirteen, or eight becomes seven.

In early September, my younger daughter visited and commented on how tired I looked. She wanted to know if I was overworking. She also noticed that all the living-room knickknacks — stuff her mom hadn't taken after the divorce — had been placed in what she called "crop circles." She said, "You're getting a little wiggy in your old age, aren't you, Dad?" And that was when I decided I had to go back to Ackerman's Field, this time in full daylight. I thought if I saw it in daylight, saw just a few meaningless rocks standing around in an uncut hayfield, I'd realize how foolish the whole thing was, and my obsessions would blow away like a dandelion puff in a strong breeze. I wanted that. Because counting, touching, and placing — those things are a lot of work. A lot of responsibility.

On my way, I stopped at the place where I got my pictures developed and saw the ones I'd taken that evening in Ackerman's Field hadn't come out. They were just gray squares, as if they'd been fogged by some strong radiation. That gave me pause, but it didn't stop me. I borrowed a digital camera from one of the guys at the photo shop — that's the one I fried — and drove out to Motton again, and fast. You want to hear something stupid? I felt like a man with a bad case of poison ivy going to the drugstore for a bottle of Calamine Lotion. Because that was what it was like — an itch. Counting and touching and placing could scratch it, but scratching affords only temporary relief at best. It's more likely to spread whatever's causing the itch. What I wanted was a cure. Going back to

349

Ackerman's Field wasn't it, but I didn't know that, did I? Like the man said, we learn by doing. And we learn even more by trying and failing.

It was a beautiful day, not a cloud in the sky. The leaves were still green, but the air had that brilliant clarity you only get when the seasons change. My ex-wife used to say that early fall days like that are our reward for putting up with the tourists and summer people for three months, standing in line while they use their credit cards to buy beer. I felt good, I remember that. I felt certain I was going to put all the crazy shit to rest. I was listening to a greatest-hits compilation by Queen and thinking how fine Freddie Mercury sounded, how *pure.* I sang along. I drove over the Androscoggin in Harlow — the water on either side of the old Bale Road Bridge bright enough to knock your eyes out — and I saw a fish jump. It made me laugh out loud. I hadn't laughed like that since the evening in Ackerman's Field, and it sounded so good I did it again.

Then up over Boy Hill — I bet you know where that is — and past the Serenity Ridge Cemetery. I've taken some good photos in there, although I never put one in a calendar. I came to the dirt byroad not five minutes later. I started to turn in, then jammed on the brakes. Just in time, too. If I'd been any slower, I would have ripped my 4Runner's grille in two. There was a chain across the road, and a new sign hanging from it: ABSOLUTELY NO TRESPASSING.

Now I could have told myself it was just a coincidence, that the person who owned those woods and that field — not necessarily a guy named Ackerman, but maybe — put up that chain and that sign every fall, to discourage hunters. But deer season doesn't start until November first. Even bird season doesn't start til October. I think someone watches that field. With binocs, maybe, but maybe with some less normal form of sight. Someone knew I'd been there, and that I might be back.

"Leave it alone, then!" I told myself. "Unless you want to risk getting arrested for trespassing, maybe get your picture in the Castle Rock *Call.* That would be good for business, wouldn't it?"

But there was no way I was going to stop, not if there was a chance I could go up to that field, see nothing, and consequently feel better. Because — dig this — at the same time I was telling myself that if someone wanted me off his property I ought to respect that person's wishes, I was counting the letters in that sign and coming out with twenty-three, which is a *terrible* number, far worse than thirteen. I knew it was crazy to think that way, but I *was* thinking that way, and some part of me knew it wasn't a bit crazy.

I stashed my 4Runner in the Serenity Ridge parking lot, then walked back to the dirt road with the borrowed camera slung over my shoulder in its little zippered case. I went around the chain — it was easy — and walked up the road to the field. Turned out I would've had to walk even if the chain *hadn't* been there, because there were half a dozen trees lying across the road this time, and not just trashwood birches. Five were good-sized pines, and the last one was a mature oak. They hadn't just fallen over, either; those babies had been dropped with a chainsaw. They didn't even slow me down. I climbed over the pines and detoured around the oak. Then I was on the hill climbing to the field. I barely gave the other sign — ACKERMAN'S FIELD, NO HUNTING, KEEP OUT — a glance. I could see the trees drawing back at the crest of the hill, I could see dusty beams of sun shining between the ones nearest the top, and I could see acres and acres of blue sky up there, looking jolly and optimistic. It was midday. There would be no giant river-snake bleeding in the distance, only the Androscoggin I grew up with and have always loved — blue and beautiful, the way ordinary things can be when we see them at their best. I broke into a run. My feeling of crazy optimism lasted all the way to the top, but the minute I saw those stones standing there like fangs, my good feelings fell away. What replaced them was dread and horror.

There were seven stones again. Just seven. And in the middle of them — I don't know just how to explain this so you'll understand — there was a *faded* place. It wasn't like a shadow, exactly, but more like . . . you know how the blue will fade out of your favorite jeans over time? Especially at stress-points like the knees? It was like that. The color of the hay was washed to a greasy lime color, and instead of blue, the sky above that circle of stones looked *grayish.* I felt that if I walked in there — and part of me wanted to — I could punch out with one fist and tear right through the fabric of reality. And if I did, something would grab me. Something on the other side. I was sure of it.

Still, something in me *wanted to do it.* It wanted to . . . I don't know . . . quit the foreplay and get right to the fucking.

I could see — or thought I could, I'm still not sure about this part — the place where the eighth stone belonged, and I could see that . . . that *fadedness . . .* bulging toward it, trying to get through where the protection of the stones was thin. I was terrified! Because if it got out, every unnamable thing on the other side would be born into our world. The sky would turn black, and it would be full of new stars and insane constellations.

I unslung the camera, but dropped it on the ground when I tried to unzip the bag it was in. My hands were shaking as if I was having some kind of seizure. I picked up the camera case and unzipped it, and when I looked at the stones again, I saw that the space inside them wasn't just faded anymore. It was turning black. And I could see *eyes* again. Peering out of the darkness. This time they were yellow, with narrow black pupils. Like cat's eyes. Or snake eyes.

I tried to lift the camera, but I dropped it again. And when I reached for it, the hay closed over it, and I had to tug it free. No, I had to *rip* it free. I was on my knees by then, yanking on the strap with both hands. And a breeze started to blow out of the gap where the eighth stone should have been. It blew the hair off my forehead. It stank. It smelled of carrion. I raised the camera to my face, but at first I could see nothing. I thought, *It's blinded the camera, it's somehow blinded the camera,* and then I remembered it was a digital Nikon, and you have to turn it on. I did that — I heard the beep — but I still could see nothing.

The breeze was a wind by then. It sent the hay rippling down the length of the field in big waves of shadow. The smell was worse. And the day was darkening. There wasn't a cloud in the sky, it was pure blue, but the day was darkening, just the same. As if some great invisible planet was eclipsing the sun.

Something spoke. Not English. Something

that sounded like "Cthun, cthun, deeyanna, deyanna." But then . . . Christ, then it said my *name*. It said, "Cthun, N., deeyanna, N." I think I screamed, but I'm not sure, because by then the wind had become a gale that was roaring in my ears. I *should* have screamed. I had every right to scream. Because *it knew my name!* That grotesque, unnamable thing *knew my name.* And then . . . the camera . . . do you know what I realized?

{*I ask him if he left the lens cap on, and he utters a shrill laugh that runs up my nerves and makes me think of rats scampering over broken glass.*}

Yes! Right! The lens cap! The fucking lens cap! I tore it off and raised the camera to my eye — it's a wonder I didn't drop it again, my hands were shaking so badly, and the hay never would have let it go again, no, never, because the second time it would have been ready. But I didn't drop it, and I could see through the viewfinder, and there were eight stones. Eight. Eight keeps things straight. That darkness was still swirling in the middle, but it was retreating. And the wind blowing around me was diminishing.

I lowered the camera and there were seven. Something was bulging out of the darkness, something I can't describe to you. I can see it — I see it in my dreams — but there are no words for that kind of blasphemy. A pulsing leather helmet, that's as close as I can get. One with yellow goggles on each side. Only the goggles . . . I think they were eyes, and I know they were looking at me.

I raised the camera again, and saw eight stones. I snapped off six or eight shots as if to mark them, to fix them in place forever, but of course that didn't work, I only fried the camera. Lenses can see those stones, Doc — I'm pretty sure a person could see them in a mirror, too, maybe even through a plain pane of glass — but they can't record them. The only thing that can record them, hold them in place, is the human mind, the human memory. And even that's undependable, as I've found out. Counting, touching, and placing works for awhile — it's ironic to think that behaviors we consider neurotic are actually holding the world in place — but sooner or later whatever protection they offer decays. And it's so much work.

So damn much work.

I wonder if we could be done for today. I know it's early, but I'm very tired.

{*I tell him I will prescribe a sedative, if he wants — mild, but more reliable than Ambien or Lunesta. It will work if he doesn't overdo it. He gives me a grateful smile.*}

That would be good, very good. But can I ask you a favor?

{*I tell him that of course he can.*}

Prescribe either twenty, forty, or sixty.

Those are all good numbers.

*{Next Session}*
*{I tell him he looks better, although this is far from true. What he looks like is a man who will be institutionalized soon, if he doesn't find a way to get back to his personal Highway 117. Turn around or back up, it doesn't matter which, but he has to get away from that field. So do I, actually. I've been dreaming about N.'s field, which I'm sure I could find if I wanted to. Not that I do — that would be too much like sharing my patient's delusion — but I'm sure I could find it. One night this weekend (while I was having trouble finding sleep myself), it occurred to me that I must have driven past it, not just once but hundreds of times. Because I've been over the Bale Road Bridge hundreds of times, and past Serenity Ridge Cemetery thousands of times; that was on the schoolbus route to James Lowell Elementary, where Sheila and I went. So sure, I could find it. If I wanted to. If it exists.*

*{I ask if the prescription helps, if he's been sleeping. The dark circles under his eyes tell me he hasn't been, but I'm curious to hear how he responds.}*

Much better. Thanks. And the OCD's a little better, too.

*{As he says this, his hands — more prone to tell the truth — are stealthily placing the vase*

*and the Kleenex box at opposing corners of the table by the couch. Today Sandy has put out roses. He arranges them so they link the box and the vase. I ask him what happened after he went up to to Ackerman's Field with the borrowed camera. He shrugs.*}

Nothing. Except of course I paid for the photo-shop guy's Nikon. Pretty soon it really *was* hunting season, and those woods get dangerous, even if you're wearing blaze orange from head to toe. Although I somehow doubt if there are many deer in that area; I imagine they steer clear.

The OCD shit smoothed out, and I started sleeping through the night again.

Well . . . some of the nights. There were dreams, of course. In the dreams I was always in that field, trying to pull the camera out of the hay, but the hay wouldn't let go. The blackness spilled out of the circle like oil, and when I looked up I saw the sky had cracked open from east to west and a terrible black light was pouring out . . . light that was alive. And hungry. That's when I'd wake up, drenched with sweat. Sometimes screaming.

Then, in early December, I got a letter at the office. It was marked PERSONAL with a small object inside. I tore it open and what fell out onto my desk was a little key with a tag on it. The tag said A.F. I knew what it was, and what it meant. If there'd been a letter, it would have said, "I tried to keep you out. It's not my fault, and maybe not yours, but either way this key, and all it opens, is yours now. Take good care of it."

That weekend I drove back out to Motton, but I didn't bother parking in the lot at Serenity Ridge. I didn't need to anymore, you see. The Christmas decorations were up in Portland and the other small towns I passed along the way. It was bitterly cold, but there wasn't any snow yet. You know how it's always colder just before the snow comes? That's how it was that day. But the sky was overcast, and the snow *did* come, a blizzard that very night. It was a big one. Do you remember?

{*I tell him I do. I have reason to remember (although I don't tell him this). Sheila and I were snowed in at the home place, where we'd gone to check on some repair work. We got squiffy and danced to old Beatles and Rolling Stones records. It was pleasant.*}

The chain was still across the road, but the A.F. key fit the lock. And the downed trees had been hauled to one side. As I'd known they would be. It was no good blocking the road anymore, because that field is now *my* field, those stones are now *my* stones, and whatever it is they're keeping in is my responsibility.

{*I ask him if he was frightened, sure the answer must be yes. But N. surprises me.*}

Not much, no. Because the place was different. I knew it even from the end of the road, where it **T**'s into 117. I could feel it. And I could hear crows cawing as I opened the lock with my new key. Ordinarily I think that's an ugly sound, but that day it sounded very sweet. At the risk of sounding pretentious, it sounded like redemption.

I knew there'd be eight stones in Ackerman's Field, and I was right. I knew they wouldn't look so much like a circle, and I was right about that, too; they looked like random outcroppings again, part of the underlying bedrock that had been exposed by a tectonic shift, or a withdrawing glacier eighty thousand years ago, or a flood of more recent vintage.

I understood other things, too. One was that I had activated the place *just by looking at it.* Human eyes take away the eighth stone. A camera lens will put it back, but won't lock it in place. I had to keep renewing the protection with symbolic acts.

{*He pauses, thinking, and when he speaks again he seems to have changed the subject.*}

Did you know that Stonehenge may have been a combination clock and calendar?

{*I tell him I've read this somewhere.*}

The people who built that place, and others like it, must have known they could tell time with no more than a sundial, and as for the calendar — we know that prehistoric people in Europe and Asia told the days simply by making marks on sheltered rock walls. So what does that make Stonehenge, if it *is* a gigantic clock/calendar? A monument to OCD behavior, that's what I think — a gigantic neurosis standing in a Salisbury field.

Unless it's protecting something as well as keeping track of hours and months. Locking out an insane universe that happens to lie right next door to ours. I have days — many of them, especially last winter, when I felt pretty much like my old self again — when I'm sure that's bullshit, that everything I thought I saw in Ackerman's Field was in my own head. That all this OCD crap is just a mental stutter.

Then I have other days — they started again this spring — when I'm sure it's all true: I activated something. And in so doing, I became the latest baton carrier in a long, long line of them, maybe going all the way back to prehistoric times. I know that sounds crazy — why else would I be telling it to a psychiatrist? — and I have whole days when I'm sure it *is* crazy . . . even when I'm counting things, going around my house at night touching light switches and stove burners, I'm sure it's all just . . . you know . . . bad chemicals in my head that a few of the right pills will fix.

I especially thought that last winter, when

things were good. Or at least better. Then, in April of this year, things started getting bad again. I was counting more, touching more, and placing just about everything that wasn't nailed down in circles or diagonals. My daughter — the one who's going to school near here — again expressed concerns about how I looked and how jumpy I seemed. She asked if it was the divorce, and when I said it wasn't, she looked as if she didn't believe me. She asked if I'd consider "seeing someone," and by God, here I am.

I started having nightmares again. One night in early May I woke on my bedroom floor, screaming. In my dream I'd seen a huge gray-black monstrosity, a winged gargoyle-thing with a leathery head like a helmet. It was standing in the ruins of Portland, a thing a mile high at least — I could see wisps of cloud floating around its plated arms. There were screaming people struggling in its taloned fists. And I knew — *knew* — it had escaped from the standing stones in Ackerman's Field, that it was only the first and least of the abominations to be released from that other world, and it was my fault. Because I had failed in my responsibilities.

I stumbled through the house, putting things in circles and then counting them to make sure the circles contained only even numbers, and it came to me that I wasn't too late, that it had only started to come awake.

{*I ask him what he means by "it."*}

The force! Remember *Star Wars?* "Use the force, Luke"?

{*He laughs wildly.*}

Except this is a case of *don't* use the force! *Stop* the force! *Imprison* the force! The chaotic something that keeps driving at that thin place — and all the thin places of the world, I imagine. Sometimes I think there's a whole chain of ruined universes behind that force, stretching back untold eons in time like monstrous footprints . . .

{*He says something under his breath that I don't catch. I ask him to repeat, but he shakes his head.*}

Hand me your pad, Doc. I'll write it. If what I'm telling you is true and not just in my fucked-up head, it's not safe to say the name aloud.

{*He prints CTHUN in large capital letters. He shows it to me, and when I nod, he tears the sheet to shreds, counts the shreds — to make sure the number is even, I suppose — and then deposits them in the wastebasket near the couch.*}

The key, the one I got in the mail, was in my home safe. I got it out and drove back to Motton — over the bridge, past the cemetery, up that damned dirt track. I didn't think about it, because it wasn't the sort of decision you have to consider. It would be like sitting down to consider whether or not you should put out the drapes in your living room if you came in and saw them on fire. No — I just went.

But I took my camera. You better believe *that*.

My nightmare woke me at five or so, and it was still early morning when I got to Ackerman's Field. The Androscoggin was beautiful — it looked like a long silver mirror instead of a snake, with fine tendrils of mist rising from its surface and then spreading above it in a, I don't know, temperature inversion, or something. That spreading cloud exactly mimicked the river's bends and turns, so it looked like a ghost-river in the sky.

The hay was growing up in the field again, and most of the sumac bushes were turning green, but I saw a scary thing. And no matter how much of this other stuff is in my head (and I'm perfectly willing to acknowledge it might be), this was real. I've got pictures that show it. They're foggy, but in a couple you can see the mutations in the sumac bushes closest to the stones. The leaves are black instead of green, and the branches are *twisted* . . . they seem to make letters, and the letters seem to spell . . . you know . . . *its* name.

{*He gestures to the wastebasket where the shreds of paper lie.*}

The darkness was back inside the stones —

there were only seven, of course, that's why I'd been drawn out there — but I saw no eyes. Thank God, I was still in time. There was just the darkness, turning and turning, seeming to mock the beauty of that silent spring morning, seeming to exult in the fragility of our world. I could see the Androscoggin through it, but the darkness — it was almost Biblical, a pillar of smoke — turned the river to a filthy gray smear.

I raised my camera — I had the strap around my neck, so even if I dropped it, it wouldn't fall into the clutch of the hay — and looked through the viewfinder. Eight stones. I lowered it and there were seven again. Looked through the viewfinder and saw eight. The second time I lowered the camera, it stayed eight. But that wasn't enough, and I knew it. I knew what I had to do.

Forcing myself to go down to that ring of stones was the hardest thing I've ever done. The sound of the hay brushing against the cuffs of my pants was like a voice — low, harsh, protesting. Warning me to keep away. The air began to taste diseased. Full of cancer and things that are maybe even worse, germs that don't exist in our world. My skin began to thrum, and I had an idea — truth is, I *still* have this idea — that if I stepped between two of those stones and into the circle, my flesh would liquefy and go dripping off my bones. I could hear the wind that sometimes blows out of there, turning in its own private cyclone. And I knew *it* was coming. The thing with the helmet-head.

{*He gestures again to the scraps in the waste-basket.*}

It was coming, and if I saw it this close up, it would drive me mad. I'd end my life inside that circle, taking pictures that would show nothing but clouds of gray. But something drove me onward. And when I got there, I . . .

{*N. stands up and walks slowly around the couch in a deliberate circle. His steps — both grave and prancing, like the steps of a child playing ring-a-rosie — are somehow awful. As he circles, he reaches out to touch stones I cannot see. One . . . two . . . three . . . four . . . five . . . six . . . seven . . . eight. Because eight keeps things straight. Then he stops and looks at me. I have had patients in crisis — many — but I have never seen such a haunted stare. I see horror, but not insanity; I see clarity rather than confusion. It must all be a delusion, of course, but there can be no doubt that he understands it completely.*}

{*I say, "When you got there, you touched them."*}

Yes, I touched them, one after the other. And I can't say I felt the world grow safer — more solid, more *there* — with every stone I touched, because that wouldn't be true. It

366

was every *two* stones. Just the even numbers, do you see? That turning darkness began to recede with each pair, and by the time I got to eight, it was gone. The hay inside the stones was yellow and dead, but the darkness was gone. And somewhere — far off — I heard a bird sing.

I stepped back. The sun was fully up by then, and the ghost-river over the real one had entirely disappeared. The stones looked like stones again. Eight granite outcroppings in a field, not even a circle, unless you worked to imagine one. And I felt myself *divide.* One part of my mind knew the whole thing was just a product of my imagination, and that my imagination had some kind of disease. The other part knew it was all true. That part even understood why things had gotten better for awhile.

It's the solstice, do you see? You see the same patterns repeated all over the world — not just at Stonehenge, but in South America and Africa, even the Arctic! You see it in the American midwest — my daughter even saw it, and she knows nothing about this! *Crop circles,* she said! It *is* a calendar — Stonehenge and all the others, marking not just days and months but times of greater and lesser danger.

That split in my mind was tearing me apart. *Is* tearing me apart. I've been out there a dozen more times since that day, and on the twenty-first — the day of the appointment with you I had to cancel, do you remember?

{*I tell him I do, of course I do.*}

I spent that whole day in Ackerman's Field, watching and counting. Because the twenty-first was the summer solstice. The day of *highest* danger. Just as the winter solstice in December is the day when the danger is lowest. It was last year, it will be again this year, it has been every year since the beginning of time. And in the months ahead — until fall, at least — I've got my work cut out for me. The twenty-first . . . I can't tell you how awful it was out there. The way that eighth stone kept shimmering out of existence. How hard it was to concentrate it back into the world. The way the darkness would gather and recede . . . gather and recede . . . like the tide. Once I dozed off and when I looked up there was an inhuman eye — a hideous three-lobed eye — looking back at me. I screamed, but I didn't run. Because the world was depending on me. Depending on me and not even knowing it. Instead of running, I raised my camera and looked through the viewfinder. Eight stones. No eye. But after that I stayed awake.

Finally the circle steadied, and I knew I could go. At least for that day. By then the sun was setting again, as it had on the first evening; a ball of fire sitting on the horizon, turning the Androscoggin into a bleeding snake.

And Doc — whether it's real or just a delusion, the work is just as hard. And the responsibility! I'm so tired. Talk about having the weight of the world on your shoulders . . .

{*He's back on the couch again. He is a big man, but now he looks small and shriveled. Then he smiles.*}

At least I'll get a break come winter. If I make it that far. And you know what? I think we've finished, you and I. As they used to say on the radio, "This concludes today's program." Although . . . who knows? You may see me again. Or at least hear from me.

{*I tell him on the contrary, we have a lot more work to do. I tell him he is carrying a weight; an invisible eight-hundred-pound gorilla on his back, and that together we can persuade it to climb down. I say we can do it, but it will take time. I say all these things, and I write him two prescriptions, but in my heart I fear that he means it; he's done. He takes the prescriptions, but he's done. Perhaps only with me; perhaps with life itself.*}

Thank you, Doc. For everything. For *listening*. And those?

{*He points to the table beside the couch, with its careful arrangement.*}

I wouldn't move them, if I were you.

{*I give him an appointment card, and he tucks*

*it carefully away in his pocket. And when he pats the pocket with his hand to make sure it's safe, I think perhaps I am wrong, and I will actually see him on July 5th. I have been wrong before. I have come to like N., and I don't want him to step into that ring of stones for good. It only exists in his mind, but that doesn't mean it's not real.}*

*{Final Session Ends}*

### 4. Dr. Bonsaint's Manuscript (Fragmentary)

*July 5, 2007*

I called his home phone number when I saw the obituary. Got C., the daughter who goes to school here in Maine. She was remarkably composed, saying that in her heart she was not surprised. She told me she was the first to arrive at N.'s Portland home (her summer job is in Camden, not that far distant), but I could hear others in the house. That's good. The family exists for many reasons, but its most basic function may be to draw together when a member dies, and that is particularly important when the death is violent and unexpected — murder or suicide.

She knew who I was. Talked freely. Yes, it was suicide. His car. The garage. Towels laid along the bottoms of the doors, and I am sure an even number of them. Ten or twenty; both good numbers, according to N. Thirty not so good, but do people — especially men living on their own — have as many as thirty towels in their homes? I'm pretty sure they don't. I know I don't.

There will be an inquest, she said. They will find drugs — the very ones I prescribed, I have no doubt — in his system, but probably not in lethal amounts. Not that it matters, I suppose; N. is just as dead, no matter what the cause.

She asked me if I would come to the funeral. I was touched. To the point of tears, in fact. I said I would, if the family would have me. Sounding surprised, she said of course they would . . . why not?

"Because in the end I couldn't help him," I said.

"You tried," she said. "That's the important thing." And I felt the stinging in my eyes again. Her kindness.

Before hanging up, I asked her if he left a note. She said yes. Three words. *Am so tired.*

He should have added his name. That would have made four.

*July 7, 2007*

At both the church and cemetery, N.'s people — especially C. — took me in and made me welcome. The miracle of family, which can open its circle even at such critical times. Even to take in a stranger. There were close to a hundred people, many from the extended family of his professional life. I wept at the graveside. Am neither surprised nor ashamed: identification between analyst and patient can be a powerful thing. C. took my hand, hugged me, and thanked me for trying to help her father. I told her she was welcome, but I felt like an imposter, a failure.

Beautiful summer day. What mockery.

Tonight I have been playing the tapes of our sessions. I think I will transcribe them. There is surely at least an article in N.'s story — a small addition to the literature of obsessive-compulsive disorder — and perhaps something larger. A book. Yet I am hesitant. What holds me back is knowing I'd have to visit that field, and compare N.'s fantasy to the reality. His world to mine. That the field exists I am quite sure. And the stones? Yes, probably there are stones. With no meaning beyond those his compulsions lent them.

Beautiful red sunset this evening.

*July 17, 2007*
I took the day off and went out to Motton. It has been on my mind, and in the end I saw no reason not to go. I was "dither-dathering," our mother would have said. If I intend to write up N.'s case, such dither-dathering must stop. No excuses. With markers from my childhood to guide me — the Bale Road Bridge (which Sheila and I used to call, for

reasons I can no longer remember, the Fail Road Bridge), Boy Hill, and especially the Serenity Ridge Cemetery — I thought I would find N.'s road without too much trouble, and I did. There could be little question, because it was the only dirt track with a chain across it and a NO TRESPASSING sign.

I parked in the cemetery lot, as N. had done before me. Although it was a bright hot summer midday, I could hear only a few birds singing, and those very distant. No cars passed on Route 117, only one overloaded pulp-truck that went droning past at seventy miles an hour, blowing my hair back from my forehead in a blast of hot air and oily exhaust. After that it was just me. I thought of childhood walks taken to the Fail Road Bridge with my little Zebco fishing rod propped on my shoulder like a soldier's carbine. I was never afraid then, and told myself I wasn't afraid on this day.

But I was. Nor do I count that fear as completely irrational. Backtrailing a patient's mental illness to its source is never comfortable.

I stood at the chain, asking myself if I really wanted to do this — if I wanted to trespass, not just on land that wasn't mine, but on an obsessive-compulsive fantasy that had very likely killed its possessor. (Or — this is probably closer — its possessed.) The choice didn't seem as clear as it had in the morning, when I put on my jeans and old red hiking boots. This morning it seemed simple: "Go out and compare the reality to N.'s fantasy, or give up the idea of the article (or book)." But what is reality? Who am I to insist that the world perceived by Dr. B.'s senses is more "real" than that which was perceived by those of the late Accountant N.?

The answer to that seemed clear enough: Dr. B. is a man who has not committed suicide, a man who does not count, touch, or place, a man who believes that numbers, whether odd or even, are just numbers. Dr. B. is a man who is able to cope with the world. Ultimately, Accountant N. was not. Therefore, Dr. B.'s perception of reality is more viable than Accountant N.'s.

But once I was there, and sensed the quiet power of the place (even at the foot of the road, while still outside the chain), it occurred to me that the choice was really much simpler: walk up that deserted road to Ackerman's Field or turn around and walk back down the blacktop to my car. Drive away. Forget the possible book, forget the rather more probable article. Forget N. and get on with my own life.

Except. Except.

Driving away might (I only say *might*) mean that on some level, one deep in my subconscious, where all the old superstitions still live (going hand in hand with all the old red urges), I had accepted N.'s belief that Ackerman's Field contains a thin place protected by magic ringstones, and that if I were to go there, I might re-activate some terrible process, some terrible *struggle,* which N. felt his suicide could halt (at least temporarily). It would mean I had accepted (in that same deep part of me where we are all nearly as similar as ants toiling in an underground nest) the idea that I was to be the next guardian. That I had been called. And if I gave in to such notions . . .

"My life would never be the same." I said that aloud. "I could never look at the world in the same way."

All at once the business seemed very serious. Sometimes we drift, do we not? Into places where the choices are no longer simple, and the consequences of picking the wrong option become grave. Perhaps life-or sanity-threatening.

Or . . . what if they aren't choices at all? What if they only *look* like choices?

I pushed the idea aside and squeezed past one of the posts holding the chains. I have been called a witch-doctor both by patients and (jokingly, I assume) by my peers, but I had no wish to think of myself that way; to look at myself in the shaving-mirror and think, *There is a man who was influenced at a critical moment not by his own thought-processes but by a dead patient's delusion.*

There were no trees across the road, but I saw several — birches and pines, mostly — lying in the ditch on the uphill side. They might have fallen this year and been dragged aside, or last year, or the year before. It was impossible for me to tell. I'm no woodsman.

I came to a rising hill and saw the woods pull away on either side, opening a vast stretch of hot summer sky. It was like walking into N.'s head. I stopped halfway up the hill, not because I was out of breath, but to ask myself one final time if this was what I wanted. Then I continued on.

I wish I hadn't.

The field was there, and the view opening to the west was every bit as spectacular as N. had suggested — breathtaking, really. Even with the sun high and yellow instead of sitting red above the horizon. The stones were there, too, about forty yards down the slope. And yes, they *do* suggest circularity, although they are in no sense the sort of circle one sees at Stonehenge. I counted them. There were eight, just as N. said.

(Except when he said there were seven.)

The grass inside that rough grouping did look a bit patchy and yellow compared to the thigh-high greenery in the rest of the field (it stretches down to a wide acreage of mixed oaks, firs, and birches), but it was by no means dead. What caught my attention closer by was a little cluster of sumac bushes. Those weren't dead, either — at least I don't think so, but the leaves were black instead of green-streaked-with-red, and they had no shape. They were ill-formed things, somehow hard to look at. They offended the order the eye expected. I can't put it any better than that.

About ten yards down from where I stood, I saw something white caught in one of those bushes. I walked toward it, saw it was an envelope, and knew N. had left it for me. If not on the day of his suicide, then not long before. I felt a terrible sinking in my stomach. A clear sense that in deciding to come here (if I *did* decide), I had made the wrong choice. That I had been certain to make the wrong choice, in fact, having been educated to trust my intellect over my instincts.

Rubbish. I know I shouldn't be thinking this way.

Of course (here's a point!), N. knew, too, and went on thinking that way just the same. No doubt counting the towels even as he prepared for his own . . .

To make sure it was an even number.

Shit. The mind gets up to funny tricks, doesn't it? Shadows grow faces.

The envelope was wrapped in a clear plastic Baggie to keep it dry. The printing on the front was perfectly firm, perfectly clear: **DR. JOHN BONSAINT.**

I took it out of the Baggie, then looked down the slope at the stones again. Still eight.

Of course there were. But not a bird sang, not a cricket creaked. The day held its breath. Every shadow was carved. I know now what N. meant about feeling cast back in time.

There was something in the envelope; I could feel it sliding back and forth, and my fingers knew it for what it was even before I tore off the end of the envelope and dumped it into the palm of my hand. A key.

Also a note. Just two words. *Sorry, Doc.* And his name, of course. First name only. That makes three words, in all. Not a good number. At least according to N.

I put the key in my pocket and stood beside a sumac bush that didn't look like a sumac bush — black leaves, branches twisted until they almost looked like runes, or letters . . .

Not *CTHUN!*

. . . and decided, *Time to leave. That's enough. If something has mutated the bushes, some environmental condition that's poisoned the ground, so be it. The bushes are not the important part of this landscape; the stones are the important part. There are eight. You have tested the world and found it as you hoped it would be, as you knew it would be, as it always was. If this field seems too quiet — fraught, somehow — that is undoubtedly the lingering effect of N.'s story on your own mind. Not to mention his suicide. Now go back to your life. Never mind the silence, or the sense — in your mind like a thundercloud — that something is lurking in that silence. Go back to your life, Dr. B.*

*Go back while you still can.*

I returned to the end of the road. The high green hay whickering against my jeans like a low, gasping voice. The sun beating on my neck and shoulders.

I felt an urge to turn and look again. Strong urge. I fought it and lost.

When I turned around I saw seven stones. Not eight, but seven. I counted them twice to make sure. And it *did* seem darker inside the stones, as if a cloud had passed over the sun. One so small it made shade only in that place. Only it didn't look like a shadow. It looked like *a particular* darkness, one that was moving over the yellow, matted grass, circling in on itself and then belling out again toward the gap where, I was sure (*almost* sure; that's the hell of it) an eighth stone had been standing when I arrived.

I thought, *I have no camera to look through and make it come back.*

I thought, *I have to make this stop while I can still tell myself nothing is happening.* Right or wrong, I was less concerned with the fate of the world than with losing hold of my own perceptions; losing hold of my *idea* of the world. I did not believe in N.'s delusion for even a moment, but that darkness . . .

I didn't want it to get a foothold, do you

see? Not even a *toehold.*

I had put the key back into the torn envelope and tucked the envelope into my hip pocket, but I was still holding the Baggie. Without really thinking about what I was doing, I raised it in front of my eyes and looked at the stones through it. They were a little distorted, a little bleary even when I pulled the plastic tight, but still clear enough. There were eight again, right enough, and that perceived darkness . . .

That funnel

Or tunnel

. . . was gone. (Of course it was never there to begin with.) I lowered the Baggie — not without some trepidation, I admit it — and looked at the stones dead-on. Eight. Solid as the foundation of the Taj Mahal. Eight.

I walked back down the road, successfully fighting the compulsion to take one more look. Why look again? Eight is eight. Let's get that straight. (My little joke.)

I have decided against the article. Best to put the whole business of N. behind me. The important thing is that I actually *went* there, and faced — I am quite sure this is true — the insanity that is in all of us, the Dr. B.'s of the world as well as the N.'s. What did they call it in WWI? "Going to see the elephant." I went to see the elephant, but that does not mean I have to *draw* the elephant. Or in my case write a description of the elephant.

And if I thought I saw more? If for a few seconds . . .

Well, yes. But wait. That only shows the strength of the delusion that captured poor N. Explains his suicide in a way no note can. Yet some things are best left alone. This is probably just such a case. That darkness . . .

That funnel-tunnel, that *perceived* —

In any case, I'm done with N. No book, no article. "Turn the page." The key undoubtedly opens the lock on the chain at the end of the road, but I'll never use it. I threw it away.

"And so to bed," as the late great Sammy Pepys used to say.

Red sun tonight, sailor's delight shining over that field. Mist rising from the hay? Perhaps. From the green hay. Not the yellow.

The Androscoggin will be red tonight, a long snake bleeding in a dead birth canal. (Fancy!) I would like to see that. For whatever reason. I admit it.

This is just tiredness. It will be gone tomorrow morning. Tomorrow morning I may even want to reconsider the article. Or the book. But not tonight.

And so to bed.


*July 18, 2007*
Fished the key out of the trash this morning and put it in my desk drawer. Throwing it away seems too much like admitting some-

thing might be. You know.

Well. And anyway: it's just a key.

*July 27, 2007*

All right, yes, I admit it. I have been counting a few things and making sure there are even numbers around me. Paper clips. Pencils in the jar. Things of that nature. Doing this is strangely soothing. I have caught N.'s cold for sure. (My little joke, but not a joke.)

My mentor-psychiatrist is Dr. J. in Augusta, now Chief of Staff at Serenity Hill. I called him and we had a general discussion — which I framed as research for a paper I might deliver this winter at the Chicago convention — a lie, of course, but sometimes, you know, it's easier to — about the transitive nature of OCD symptoms, from patient to analyst. J. confirmed my own researches. The phenomena isn't common, but it's not a complete rarity, either.

He said, "This doesn't have any personal concern for you, Johnny, does it?"

Keen. Perceptive. Always was. And has lots of info about yours truly!

"No," I said. "I've just gotten interested in the subject. In fact, it's become something of a compulsion."

We ended the conversation laughing and then I went to the coffee table and counted the books there. Six. That's good. Six is a fix. (N.'s little rhyme.) I checked my desk to make sure the key was there and of course it is, where else would it be? One key. Is one good or bad? "The cheese stands alone," you know. Probably not germane, but something to think about!

I started out of the room, then remembered there were magazines on the coffee table as well as books and counted those, as well. Seven! I took the *People* with Brad Pitt on the cover and threw it in the trash.

Look, if it makes me feel better, what harm? And it was only Brad Pitt!

And if this gets worse, I *will* come clean with J. This is a promise I make to myself.

I think a Neurontin scrip might help. Although it's an anti-seizure medication, strictly speaking, in cases like mine it's been known to help. Of course . . .

*August 3, 2007*

Who am I kidding? There *are* no cases like this, and Neurontin doesn't help. Tits on a bull.

But counting helps. Strangely soothing. And something else. *The key was on the wrong side of the drawer I put it in!* That was intuition but intuition is not to be SNEEZED AT. I moved it. Better. Then put another key (safe-deposit box) on the other side. Seems to balance it. Six is a fix but two is true (joke). Good sleep last night.

Well, no. Nightmares. The Androscoggin at sunset. A red wound. A birth canal. But dead.

*August 10, 2007*
Something is wrong out there. The eighth stone is weakening. There is no sense telling myself this isn't so, because every nerve in my body — *every cell in my skin!!* — proclaims it's true. Counting books (and shoes, yes, that's true, N.'s intuition and not to be "sneezed at") helps, but does not fix THE BASIC PROBLEM. Not even Placing Diagonals helps too much, although it certainly . . .

Toast crumbs on the kitchen counter, for instance. You line them up with the blade of a knife. Line of sugar on the table, HA! But who knows how many crumbs? How many grains of sugar? Too many to count!!

This must end. I'm going out there.

I will take a camera.

*August 11, 2007*
The darkness. Dear Christ. It *was almost complete.* And something else.

*The darkness had an eye.*

*August 12*
Did I see anything? Actually?

I don't know. I think I did, but I don't know.

There are 23 words in this entry.

26 is better.

*August 19*

I picked up the phone to call J., tell him what's going on with me, then put it down. What would I tell him? Besides: 1-207-555-1863=11. A bad number.

Valium helps more than Neurontin. I think. As long as I don't overdue it

*Sept 16*

Back from Motown. Covered with sweat. Shaking. But eight again. I fixed it. I! Fixed it! IT! Thank God. But . . .

But!

*I cannot live my life this way.*

No, but — I WAS JUST IN TIME. *IT WAS ON THE VERGE OF GETTING OUT.* The protections only hold so long and then a house-call is necessary! (My little joke.)

I saw the 3-lobed eye N. spoke of. It belongs to nothing from this world or this universe.

*It is trying to eat its way thru.*

Except I don't accept this. I let N.'s obsession get a finger in my psyche (it's playing stinkyfinger with me if you get my little joke) and it has continued to widen the gap, slipping in a second finger, a third, a whole pulling hand. Opening me up. Opening up my

But!

*I saw with my own eyes.* There is a world behind this world, filled with monsters

Gods
*HATEFUL GODS!*

One thing. If I kill myself, what? If it's not real, the torment still ends. If it is real, the eighth stone out there solidifies again. At least until someone else — the next "CARE-TAKER" — goes heedlessly prospecting up that road and sees . . .

Makes suicide almost look good!

*October 9, 2007*

Better lately. My ideas seem more my own. And when I last went out to Ackerman's Field (2 days ago), my worries were all for naught. There were 8 stones there. I looked at them — solid as houses — and saw a crow in the sky. It swerved to avoid the airspace over the stones, "ziss is true," (joke) but it was there. And as I stood at the end of the road with my camera hung over my neck (nix pix in Motton stix, those stones don't photo-graph, N. was right about that much, anyway; possibly radon??), I wondered how I ever could have thought there were only 7. I admit that I counted my steps back to my car (and then paced around a little when an odd number brought me to the driver's door), but these things do not let go all at once. They are CRAMPS in the MIND! Yet maybe . . .

Do I dare hope I'm getting better?

*October 10, 2007*

Of course there is another possibility, loath as I am to admit it: that N. was right about the solstices. We are moving away from one and toward the other now. Summer gone; winter ahead. Which, if true, is good news only in the short term. If I should have to deal with such wracking mental spasms next spring . . . and the spring after that . . .

I couldn't, that's all.

How that eye haunts me. Floating in the gathering darkness.

Other things behind it

*CTHUN!*


*November 16, 2007*

Eight. Always were. I'm sure now. Today the field was silent, the hay dead, the trees at the foot of the slope bare, the Androscoggin gray steel beneath an iron sky. The world waiting for snow.

And my God, best of all: a bird roosting on one of those stones!

A BIRD!

Realized only when I was driving back to Lewiston that I didn't bother counting my steps when going back to the car.

Here is the truth. What must be the truth. I caught a cold from one of my patients, but now I'm getting better. Cough gone, sniffles drying up.

The little **joke** was on me all along.

*December 25, 2007*

I shared Christmas dinner and the ritual exchange of presents with Sheila and her family. When Don took Seth to the candle-light ritual at the church (I'm sure the good Methodists would be shocked if they knew the pagan roots of such rites), Sheila squeezed my hand and said, "You're back. That's good. I was worried."

Well, you can't fool your own flesh and blood, it seems. Dr. J. may only have suspected something was wrong, but Sheila knew. Dear Sheila.

"I had a sort of crisis this summer and fall," I said. "A crisis of the spirit, you might call it."

Although it was more a crisis of the psyche. When a man begins to think the only purpose served by his perceptions is to mask the knowledge of terrible other worlds — that is a crisis of the psyche.

Sheila, always practical, said: "As long as it wasn't cancer, Johnny. That's what I was afraid of."

Dear Sheila! I laughed and hugged her.

Later on, while we were doing a final polish on the kitchen (and sipping eggnog), I asked her if she remembered why we used to call the Bale Road Bridge the *Fail* Road Bridge. She cocked her head and laughed.

"It was your old friend who thought that up. The one I had such a crush on."

388

"Charlie Keen," I said. "I haven't seen him in a dog's age. Except on TV. The poor man's Sanjay Gupta."

She whacked my arm. "Jealousy doesn't become you, dear. Anyway, we were fishing from the bridge one day — you know, with those little poles we all had — and Charlie peered over the side and said, 'You know, anyone who fell off this thing could not fail to kill themselves.' It just struck us funny, and we laughed like maniacs. You don't remember that?"

But then I did. Bale Road Bridge became Fail Road Bridge from that day on. And what old Charlie said was true enough. Bale Stream is very shallow at that point. Of course it flows into the Androscoggin (probably you can see the merging-point from Ackerman's Field, although I never noticed), which is a lot deeper. And the Androscoggin flows to the sea. World leads onto world, doesn't it? Each deeper than the last; this is a design all the earth proclaims.

Don and Seth came back in, Sheila's big guy and her little guy, all dusted with snow. We had a group hug, very New Age, and then I drove home listening to Christmas carols. Really happy for the first time in ever so long.

I believe these notes . . . this diary . . . this chronicle of madness avoided (perhaps by bare inches, I think I really did almost "go over the bridge") . . . can end now.

Thank God, and merry Christmas to me.

*April 1, 2008*
It's April Fool's, and the fool is me. I woke from a dream of Ackerman's Field.

In it the sky was blue, the river was a darker blue in its valley, the snow was melting, the first green grass was poking through the remaining ribbons of white, and once more there were only seven stones. Once more there was darkness in the circle. Only a smudge for now, but it will deepen unless I take care of it.

I counted books after waking (sixty-four, a good number, even and divisible all the way down to 1 — think about it), and when that didn't turn the trick I spilled coffee onto the kitchen counter and made a diagonal. That fixed things — for now — but I will have to go out there and make another "house call." Must not dither-dather.

Because it's starting again.

The snow is almost gone, the summer solstice is approaching (still over the horizon but approaching), and it has started again.

I feel

God help me, I feel like a cancer patient who has been in remission and wakes one morning to discover a big fat lump in his armpit.

I can't do this.

I must do this.

*{Later}*

There was still snow on the road, but I got up to "AF" all right. Left my car in the cemetery parking lot and walked. There were indeed only seven stones, as in my dream. Looked thru the viewfinder of my camera. 8 again. 8 is fate and keeps the world strait. Good deal.

For the world!

*Not* such a good deal for Dr. Bonsaint.

That this should be happening again; my mind groans at the prospect.

Please God don't let it be happening again.


*April 6, 2008*

Took longer today to make 7 into 8, and I know I have much "long distance" work ahead of me, i.e. counting things and making diagonals and — not placing, N. was wrong about that — it's *balancing* that needs to be done. It's simbolic, like the break and whine in communion.

I'm tired, though. And the solstitch is so far away.

Its still gathering its power and the solstit is so far away.

I wish N. had dyed before coming into my office. That selfish bastyard.


*May 2, 2008*

I thought it would kill me this time. Or break

my mind. *Is* my mind broken? My God how can I tell? There is no God, there can be no God in the face of that darkness, and the EYE that peers from it. And something else.

*THE THING WITH THE HELMET HEAD. BORN OUT OF LIVING UNSANE DARKNESS.*

There was chanting. Chanting from deep inside the ringstones, deep inside the darkness. But I made 7 into 8 once again, although it took a long long long lung long time. Many loox thru the vufinder, also making circles and counting paces, widening the circle to 64 paces and that did it, thank god. "The widening gyre" — Yeets! Then I looked up. Looked around. And saw *its* name woven into every sumac bush and every tree at the foot of that hellish field: *Cthun, Cthun, Cthun, Cthun.* I looked into the sky for releef and saw the clods spelling it out as they traversed the blue: *CTHUN* in the sky. Looked at the river and saw its curves spell out a giant **C.** C for Cthun.

How can I be responsible for the world? How can this be?

Its not fare!!!!!!!!

*May 4, 2008*
If I can close the door by killing myself

And the peace, even if it is only the peece of oblitsion

I am going out there again, but this time

392

not all the way. Just to the Fail Road Bridge. The water there is shallow, the bed lined with rocks.

The drop must be 30 feet.

Not the best number but still

Anyone who falls off that thing cannot fail to

Cannot fail

I cant stop thinking about that hideous 3-lobe eye

The thing with the helmet head

The screaming faces in the stones

*CTHUN!*

*{Dr. Bonsaint's manuscript ends here.}*

### 5. THE SECOND LETTER

*June 8, 2008*

Dear Charlie,

I haven't heard from you about Johnny's manuscript, and that is good. Please ignore my last letter, and if you still have the pages, burn them. That was Johnny's request, and I should have honored it myself.

I told myself I was only going out as far as the Fail Road Bridge — to see the place where we all had so many happy times as kids, the place where he ended his life when the happy times ran out. I told myself it might bring closure (that's the word Johnny would have used). But of course the mind under my mind — where, I'm sure Johnny would claim, we are all pretty much alike — knew better. Why else did I take the key?

Because it was there, in his study. Not in the same drawer where I found the manuscript, but in the top one — the one above the kneehole. With another key to "balance it," just as he said.

Would I have sent you the key with the manuscript, if I'd found them both in the same place? I don't know. I don't. But I'm glad, on the whole, at the way things turned out. Because you might've been tempted to go out there. Simple curiosity might have drawn you, or possibly something else. Something stronger.

Or possibly that's so much bullshit. Possibly I only took the key and went out to Motton and found that road because I am what I said I was in my first letter: a daughter of Pandora. How can I tell for sure? N. couldn't. Neither could my brother, not even at the very end, and as he used to say, "I'm a professional, don't try this at home."

In any case, don't worry about me. I'm fine. And even if I'm not, I can do the math. Sheila LeClaire has 1 husband and 1 child. Charlie Keen — according to what I read in Wikipedia — has 1 wife and 3 children. Hence, you have more to lose. And besides, maybe I never got over that crush I had on you.

*Under no circumstances come back here.*

Keep doing your reports on obesity and prescription drug abuse and heart attacks in men under 50 and things like that. Normal things like that.

And if you haven't read that manuscript (I can hope for this, but doubt it; I'm sure Pandora also had sons), ignore that, too. Put all this down to a woman hysterical over the unexpected loss of her brother.

There's nothing out there.

Just some rocks.

I saw with my own eyes.

I swear there's nothing out there, *so stay away.*

### 6. THE NEWSPAPER ARTICLE

[From the Chester's Mill *Democrat:*
June 1, 2008]

## WOMAN JUMPS FROM BRIDGE, MIMICS BROTHER'S SUICIDE

**By Julia Shumway**

MOTTON — After prominent psychiatrist John Bonsaint committed suicide by jumping from the Bale River Bridge in this little central Maine town a little over a month ago, friends said that his sister, Sheila LeClaire, was confused and depressed. Her husband, Donald LeClaire, said she was "totally devastated." No one, he went on, thought she was contemplating suicide.

But she was.

"Although there was no note," County Coroner Richard Chapman said, "all the signs are there. Her car was parked neatly and considerately off the road on the Harlow side of the bridge. It had been locked, and her purse was on the passenger seat, with her driver's license laid on top." He went on to say that LeClaire's shoes were found on the railing itself, placed carefully side by side. Chapman said only an inquest would show if she drowned or died on impact.

In addition to her husband, Sheila Le-Claire leaves a seven-year-old son. Services have not yet been set.

### 7. The E-Mail

*keen1981*
*3:44 PM*
*June 5 '08*


Chrissy —

Please cancel all appointments for the next week. I know this is short notice, and I know how much flak you are going to catch, but it cannot be helped. There is a matter I have to tend to back home in Maine. Two old friends, brother and sister, have committed suicide under peculiar circumstances . . . and in the same f — king place! Given the extremely odd manuscript the sister sent me before copying (*apparently* copying) her brother's suicide, I believe this bears investigation. The brother, John Bonsaint, was my best friend when I was growing up; we saved each other from more than a few schoolyard beatings!

Hayden can do the blood-sugar story. I know he thinks he can't, but he can. And even if he can't, I have to go. Johnny and Sheila were close to family.

And besides: I don't mean to be a Philistine about it, but there might be a story in this. On obsessive-compulsive disorder. Not as big a blip on the radar as cancer, maybe, but sufferers will tell you it's still some mighty scary shit.

Thanx, Chrissy —
Charlie

# THE CAT FROM HELL

Halston thought the old man in the wheel-chair looked sick, terrified, and ready to die. He had experience in seeing such things. Death was Halston's business; he had brought it to eighteen men and six women in his career as an independent hitter. He knew the death look.

The house — mansion, actually — was cold and quiet. The only sounds were the low snap of the fire on the big stone hearth and the low whine of the November wind outside.

"I want you to make a kill," the old man said. His voice was quavery and high, peevish. "I understand that is what you do."

"Who did you talk to?" Halston asked.

"With a man named Saul Loggia. He says you know him."

Halston nodded. If Loggia was the go-between, it was all right. And if there was a bug in the room, anything the old man — Drogan — said was entrapment.

"Who do you want hit?"

Drogan pressed a button on the console built into the arm of his wheelchair and it buzzed forward. Close-up, Halston could smell the yellow odors of fear, age, and urine all mixed. They disgusted him, but he made no sign. His face was still and smooth.

"Your victim is right behind you," Drogan said softly.

Halston moved quickly. His reflexes were his life and they were always set on a filed pin. He was off the couch, falling to one knee, turning, hand inside his specially tailored sport coat, gripping the handle of the short-barrelled .45 hybrid that hung below his armpit in a spring-loaded holster that laid it in his palm at a touch. A moment later it was out and pointed at . . . a cat.

For a moment Halston and the cat stared at each other. It was a strange moment for Halston, who was an unimaginative man with no superstitions. For that one moment as he knelt on the floor with the gun pointed, he felt that he knew this cat, although if he had ever seen one with such unusual markings he surely would have remembered.

Its face was an even split: half black, half white. The dividing line ran from the top of its flat skull and down its nose to its mouth, straight-arrow. Its eyes were huge in the gloom, and caught in each nearly circular black pupil was a prism of firelight, like a sullen coal of hate.

And the thought echoed back to Halston: *We know each other, you and I.*

Then it passed. He put the gun away and stood up. "I ought to kill you for that, old man. I don't take a joke."

"And I don't make them," Drogan said. "Sit down. Look in here." He had taken a fat envelope out from beneath the blanket that covered his legs.

Halston sat. The cat, which had been crouched on the back of the sofa, jumped lightly down into his lap. It looked up at Halston for a moment with those huge dark eyes, the pupils surrounded by thin green-gold rings, and then it settled down and began to purr.

Halston looked at Drogan questioningly.

"He's very friendly," Drogan said. "At first. Nice friendly pussy has killed three people in this household. That leaves only me. I am old, I am sick . . . but I prefer to die in my own time."

"I can't believe this," Halston said. "You hired me to hit a cat?"

"Look in the envelope, please."

Halston did. It was filled with hundreds and fifties, all of them old. "How much is it?"

"Six thousand dollars. There will be another six when you bring me proof that the cat is dead. Mr. Loggia said twelve thousand was your usual fee?"

Halston nodded, his hand automatically

stroking the cat in his lap. It was asleep, still purring. Halston liked cats. They were the only animals he did like, as a matter of fact. They got along on their own. God — if there was one — had made them into perfect, aloof killing machines. Cats were the hitters of the animal world, and Halston gave them his respect.

"I need not explain anything, but I will," Drogan said. "Forewarned is forearmed, they say, and I would not want you to go into this lightly. And I seem to need to justify myself. So you'll not think I'm insane."

Halston nodded again. He had already decided to make this peculiar hit, and no further talk was needed. But if Drogan wanted to talk, he would listen.

"First of all, you know who I am? Where the money comes from?"

"Drogan Pharmaceuticals."

"Yes. One of the biggest drug companies in the world. And the cornerstone of our financial success has been this." From the pocket of his robe he handed Halston a small, unmarked vial of pills. "Tri-Dormal-phenobarbin, compound G. Prescribed almost exclusively for the terminally ill. It's extremely habit-forming, you see. It's a combination pain-killer, tranquilizer, and mild hallucinogen. It is remarkable in helping the terminally ill face their conditions and adjust to them."

"Do you take it?" Halston asked.

Drogan ignored the question. "It is widely prescribed throughout the world. It's a synthetic, was developed in the fifties at our New Jersey labs. Our testing was confined almost solely to cats, because of the unique quality of the feline nervous system."

"How many did you wipe out?"

Drogan stiffened. "That is an unfair and prejudicial way to put it."

Halston shrugged.

"In the four-year testing period which led to FDA approval of Tri-Dormal-G, about fifteen thousand cats . . . uh, expired."

Halston whistled. About four thousand cats a year. "And now you think this one's back to get you, huh?"

"I don't feel guilty in the slightest," Drogan said, but that quavering, petulant note was back in his voice. "Fifteen thousand test animals died so that hundreds of thousands of human beings —"

"Never mind that," Halston said. Justifications bored him.

"That cat came here seven months ago. I've never liked cats. Nasty, disease-bearing animals . . . always out in the fields . . . crawling around in barns . . . picking up God knows what germs in their fur . . . always trying to bring something with its insides falling out into the house for you to look at . . . it was my sister who wanted to take it in. She found out. She paid." He looked at the cat sleeping on Halston's lap with dead hate.

"You said the cat killed three people."

Drogan began to speak. The cat dozed and purred on Halston's lap under the soft, scratching strokes of Halston's strong and expert killer's fingers. Occasionally a pine knot would explode on the hearth, making it tense like a series of steel springs covered with hide and muscle. Outside the wind whined around the big stone house far out in the Connecticut countryside. There was winter in that wind's throat. The old man's voice droned on and on.

Seven months ago there had been four of them here — Drogan, his sister Amanda, who at seventy-four was two years Drogan's elder, her lifelong friend Carolyn Broadmoor ("of the Westchester Broadmoors," Drogan said), who was badly afflicted with emphysema, and Dick Gage, a hired man who had been with the Drogan family for twenty years. Gage, who was past sixty himself, drove the big Lincoln Mark IV, cooked, served the evening sherry. A day-maid came in. The four of them had lived this way for nearly two years, a dull collection of old people and their family retainer. Their only pleasures were *The Hollywood Squares* and waiting to see who would outlive whom.

Then the cat had come.

"It was Gage who saw it first, whining and

skulking around the house. He tried to drive it away. He threw sticks and small rocks at it, and hit it several times. But it wouldn't go. It smelled the food, of course. It was little more than a bag of bones. People put them out beside the road to die at the end of the summer season, you know. A terrible, inhumane thing."

"Better to fry their nerves?" Halston asked.

Drogan ignored that and went on. He hated cats. He always had. When the cat refused to be driven away, he had instructed Gage to put out poisoned food. Large, tempting dishes of Calo cat food spiked with Tri-Dormal-G, as a matter of fact. The cat ignored the food. At that point Amanda Drogan had noticed the cat and had insisted they take it in. Drogan had protested vehemently, but Amanda had gotten her way. She always did, apparently.

"But she found out," Drogan said. "She brought it inside herself, in her arms. It was purring, just as it is now. But it wouldn't come near me. It never has . . . yet. She poured it a saucer of milk. 'Oh, look at the poor thing, it's starving,' she cooed. She and Carolyn both cooed over it. Disgusting. It was their way of getting back at me, of course. They knew the way I've felt about felines ever since the Tri-Dormal-G testing program twenty years ago. They enjoyed teasing me, baiting me with it." He looked at Halston grimly. "But they paid."

In mid-May, Gage had gotten up to set breakfast and had found Amanda Drogan lying at the foot of the main stairs in a litter of broken crockery and Little Friskies. Her eyes bulged sightlessly up at the ceiling. She had bled a great deal from the mouth and nose. Her back was broken, both legs were broken, and her neck had been literally shattered like glass.

"It slept in her room," Drogan said. "She treated it like a baby . . . 'Is oo hungry, darwing? Does oo need to go out and do poopoos?' Obscene, coming from an old battle-axe like my sister. I think it woke her up, meowing. She got his dish. She used to say that Sam didn't really like his Friskies unless they were wetted down with a little milk. So she was planning to go downstairs. The cat was rubbing against her legs. She was old, not too steady on her feet. Half-asleep. They got to the head of the stairs and the cat got in front of her . . . tripped her . . ."

Yes, it could have happened that way, Halston thought. In his mind's eye he saw the old woman falling forward and outward, too shocked to scream. The Friskies spraying out as she tumbled head over heels to the bottom, the bowl smashing. At last she comes to rest at the bottom, the old bones shattered, the eyes glaring, the nose and ears trickling blood. And the purring cat begins to work its way down the stairs, contentedly munching Little Friskies . . .

"What did the coroner say?" he asked Drogan.

"Death by accident, of course. But I knew."

"Why didn't you get rid of the cat then? With Amanda gone?"

Because Carolyn Broadmoor had threatened to leave if he did, apparently. She was hysterical, obsessed with the subject. She was a sick woman, and she was nutty on the subject of spiritualism. A Hartford medium had told her (for a mere twenty dollars) that Amanda's soul had entered Sam's feline body. Sam had been Amanda's, she told Drogan, and if Sam went, *she* went.

Halston, who had become something of an expert at reading between the lines of human lives, suspected that Drogan and the old Broadmoor bird had been lovers long ago, and the old dude was reluctant to let her go over a cat.

"It would have been the same as suicide," Drogan said. "In her mind she was still a wealthy woman, perfectly capable of packing up that cat and going to New York or London or even Monte Carlo with it. In fact she was the last of a great family, living on a pittance as a result of a number of bad investments in the sixties. She lived on the second floor here in a specially controlled, super-humidified room. The woman was seventy, Mr. Halston.

She was a heavy smoker until the last two years of her life, and the emphysema was very bad. I wanted her here, and if the cat had to stay . . ."

Halston nodded and then glanced meaningfully at his watch.

"Near the end of June, she died in the night. The doctor seemed to take it as a matter of course . . . just came and wrote out the death certificate and that was the end of it. But the cat was in the room. Gage told me."

"We all have to go sometime, man," Halston said.

"Of course. That's what the doctor said. But I knew. I remembered. Cats like to get babies and old people when they're asleep. And steal their breath."

"An old wives' tale."

"Based on fact, like most so-called old wives' tales," Drogan replied. "Cats like to knead soft things with their paws, you see. A pillow, a thick shag rug . . . or a blanket. A crib blanket or an old person's blanket. The extra weight on a person who's weak to start with . . ."

Drogan trailed off, and Halston thought about it. Carolyn Broadmoor asleep in her bedroom, the breath rasping in and out of her damaged lungs, the sound nearly lost in the whisper of special humidifiers and air conditioners. The cat with the queer black-and-white markings leaps silently onto her spinster's bed and stares at her old and wrinkle-grooved face with those lambent, black-and-green eyes. It creeps onto her thin chest and settles its weight there, purring . . . and the breathing slows . . . and the cat purrs as the old woman slowly smothers beneath its weight on her chest.

He was not an imaginative man, but Halston shivered a little.

"Drogan," he said, continuing to stroke the purring cat. "Why don't you just have it put away? A vet would give it the gas for twenty dollars."

Drogan said, "The funeral was on the first of July. I had Carolyn buried in our cemetery plot next to my sister. The way she would have wanted it. Only July third I called Gage to this room and handed him a wicker basket . . . a picnic hamper sort of thing. Do you know what I mean?"

Halston nodded.

"I told him to put the cat in it and take it to a vet in Milford and have it put to sleep. He said, 'Yes, sir,' took the basket, and went out. Very like him. I never saw him alive again. There was an accident on the turnpike. The Lincoln was driven into a bridge abutment at better than sixty miles an hour. Dick Gage was killed instantly. When they found him there were scratches on his face."

Halston was silent as the picture of how it might have been formed in his brain again.

No sound in the room but the peaceful crackle of the fire and the peaceful purr of the cat in his lap. He and the cat together before the fire would make a good illustration for that Edgar Guest poem, the one that goes: "The cat on my lap, the hearth's good fire / . . . A happy man, should you enquire."

Dick Gage moving the Lincoln down the turnpike toward Milford, beating the speed limit by maybe five miles an hour. The wicker basket beside him — a picnic hamper sort of thing. The chauffeur is watching traffic, maybe he's passing a big cab-over Jimmy and he doesn't notice the peculiar black-on-one-side, white-on-the-other face that pokes out of one side of the basket. Out of the driver's side. He doesn't notice because he's passing the big trailer truck and that's when the cat jumps onto his face, spitting and clawing, its talons raking into one eye, puncturing it, deflating it, blinding it. Sixty and the hum of the Lincoln's big motor and the other paw is hooked over the bridge of the nose, digging in with exquisite, damning pain — maybe the Lincoln starts to veer right, into the path of the Jimmy, and its airhorn blares ear-shatteringly, but Gage can't hear it because the cat is yowling, the cat is spread-eagled over his face like some huge furry black spider, ears laid back, green eyes glaring like spotlights from hell, back legs jittering and digging into the soft flesh of the old man's neck. The car veers wildly back the other way. The bridge abutment looms. The cat jumps down and the Lincoln, a shiny black torpedo, hits the cement and goes up like a bomb.

Halston swallowed hard and heard a dry click in his throat.

"And the cat came back?"

Drogan nodded. "A week later. On the day Dick Gage was buried, as a matter of fact. Just like the old song says. The cat came back."

"It survived a car crash at sixty? Hard to believe."

"They say each one has nine lives. When it comes back . . . that's when I started to wonder if it might not be a . . . a . . ."

"Hellcat?" Halston suggested softly.

"For want of a better word, yes. A sort of demon sent . . ."

"To punish you."

"I don't know. But I'm afraid of it. I feed it, or rather, the woman who comes in to do for me feeds it. She doesn't like it either. She says that face is a curse of God. Of course, she's local." The old man tried to smile and failed. "I want you to kill it. I've lived with it for the last four months. It skulks around in the shadows. It looks at me. It seems to be . . . waiting. I lock myself in my room every night and still I wonder if I'm going to wake up one early morning and find it . . . curled up on my chest . . . and purring."

The wind whined lonesomely outside and made a strange hooting noise in the stone chimney.

"At last I got in touch with Saul Loggia. He recommended you. He called you a stick, I believe."

"A one-stick. That means I work on my own."

"Yes. He said you'd never been busted, or even suspected. He said you always seem to land on your feet . . . like a cat."

Halston looked at the old man in the wheelchair. And suddenly his long-fingered, muscular hands were lingering just above the cat's neck.

"I'll do it now, if you want me to," he said softly. "I'll snap its neck. It won't even know —"

"No!" Drogan cried. He drew in a long, shuddering breath. Color had come up in his sallow cheeks. "Not . . . not here. Take it away."

Halston smiled humorlessly. He began to stroke the sleeping cat's head and shoulders and back very gently again. "All right," he said. "I accept the contract. Do you want the body?"

"No. Kill it. Bury it." He paused. He hunched forward in the wheelchair like some ancient buzzard. "Bring me the tail," he said. "So I can throw it in the fire and watch it burn."

■ ■ ■ ■

Halston drove a 1973 Plymouth with a custom Cyclone Spoiler engine. The car was jacked and blocked, and rode with the hood pointing down at the road at a twenty-degree angle. He had rebuilt the differential and the rear end himself. The shift was a Pensy, the linkage was Hearst. It sat on huge Bobby Unser Wide Ovals and had a top end of a little past one-sixty.

He left the Drogan house at a little past 9:30. A cold rind of crescent moon rode overhead through the tattering November clouds. He rode with all the windows open, because that yellow stench of age and terror seemed to have settled into his clothes and he didn't like it. The cold was hard and sharp, eventually numbing, but it was good. It was blowing that yellow stench away.

He got off the turnpike at Placer's Glen and drove through the silent town, which was guarded by a single yellow blinker at the intersection, at a thoroughly respectable thirty-five. Out of town, moving up S.R. 35, he opened the Plymouth up a little, letting her walk. The tuned Spoiler engine purred like the cat had purred on his lap earlier this evening. Halston grinned at the simile. They moved between frost-white November fields full of skeleton cornstalks at a little over seventy.

The cat was in a double-thickness shopping bag, tied at the top with heavy twine. The bag was in the passenger bucket seat. The cat had been sleepy and purring when Halston put it in, and it had purred through the entire ride. It sensed, perhaps, that Halston liked it and felt at home with it. Like himself, the cat was a one-stick.

Strange hit, Halston thought, and was surprised to find that he was taking it seriously *as* a hit. Maybe the strangest thing about it was that he actually liked the cat, felt a kinship with it. If it had managed to get rid of those three old crocks, more power to it . . . especially Gage, who had been taking it to Milford for a terminal date with a crewcut veterinarian who would have been more than happy to bundle it into a ceramic-lined gas chamber the size of a microwave oven. He felt a kinship, but no urge to renege on the hit. He would do it the courtesy of killing it quickly and well. He would park off the road beside one of these November-barren fields and take it out of the bag and stroke it and then snap its neck and sever its tail with his pocket knife. And, he thought, the body I'll bury honorably, saving it from the scavengers. I can't save it from the worms, but I can save it from the maggots.

He was thinking these things as the car moved through the night like a dark blue ghost and that was when the cat walked in front of his eyes, up on the dashboard, tail raised arrogantly, its black-and-white face turned toward him, its mouth seeming to grin at him.

"Ssssshhhh —" Halston hissed. He glanced to his right and caught a glimpse of the double-thickness shopping bag, a hole chewed — or clawed — in its side. Looked ahead again . . . and the cat lifted a paw and batted playfully at him. The paw skidded across Halston's forehead. He jerked away from it and the Plymouth's big tires wailed on the road as it swung erratically from one side of the narrow blacktop to the other.

Halston batted at the cat on the dashboard with his fist. It was blocking his field of vision. It spat at him, arching its back, but it didn't move. Halston swung again, and instead of shrinking away, it leaped at him.

*Gage,* he thought. *Just like Gage —*

He stamped the brake. The cat was on his head, blocking his vision with its furry belly, clawing at him, gouging at him. Halston held the wheel grimly. He struck the cat once, twice, a third time. And suddenly the road was gone, the Plymouth was running down into the ditch, thudding up and down on its shocks. Then, impact, throwing him forward against his seat belt, and the last sound he heard was the cat yowling inhumanly, the voice of a woman in pain or in the throes of sexual climax.

He struck it with his closed fist and felt only the springy, yielding flex of its muscles.

Then, second impact. And darkness.

The moon was down. It was an hour before dawn.

The Plymouth lay in a ravine curdled with groundmist. Tangled in its grille was a snarled length of barbed wire. The hood had come unlatched, and tendrils of steam from the breached radiator drifted out of the opening to mingle with the mist.

No feeling in his legs.

He looked down and saw that the Plymouth's firewall had caved in with the impact. The back of that big Cyclone Spoiler engine block had smashed into his legs, pinning them.

Outside, in the distance, the predatory squawk of an owl dropping onto some small, scurrying animal.

Inside, close, the steady purr of the cat.

It seemed to be grinning, like Alice's Cheshire had in Wonderland.

As Halston watched it stood up, arched its back, and stretched. In a sudden limber movement like rippled silk, it leaped to his shoulder. Halston tried to lift his hands to push it off.

His arms wouldn't move.

*Spinal shock,* he thought. *Paralyzed. Maybe*

*temporary. More likely permanent.*

The cat purred in his ear like thunder.

"Get off me," Halston said. His voice was hoarse and dry. The cat tensed for a moment and then settled back. Suddenly its paw batted Halston's cheek, and the claws were out this time. Hot lines of pain down to his throat. And the warm trickle of blood.

Pain.

*Feeling.*

He ordered his head to move to the right, and it complied. For a moment his face was buried in smooth, dry fur. Halston snapped at the cat. It made a startled, disgruntled sound in its throat — *yowk!* — and leaped onto the seat. It stared up at him angrily, ears laid back.

"Wasn't supposed to do that, was I?" Halston croaked.

The cat opened its mouth and hissed at him. Looking at that strange, schizophrenic face, Halston could understand how Drogan might have thought it was a hellcat. It —

His thoughts broke off as he became aware of a dull, tingling feeling in both hands and forearms.

*Feeling. Coming back. Pins and needles.*

The cat leaped at his face, claws out, spitting.

Halston shut his eyes and opened his mouth. He bit at the cat's belly and got nothing but fur. The cat's front claws were clasped

417

on his ears, digging in. The pain was enormous, brightly excruciating. Halston tried to raise his hands. They twitched but would not quite come out of his lap.

He bent his head forward and began to shake it back and forth, like a man shaking soap out of his eyes. Hissing and squalling, the cat held on. Halston could feel blood trickling down his cheeks. It was hard to get his breath. The cat's chest was pressed over his nose. It was possible to get some air in by mouth, but not much. What he did get came through fur. His ears felt as if they had been doused with lighter fluid and then set on fire.

He snapped his head back, and cried out in agony — he must have sustained a whiplash when the Plymouth hit. But the cat hadn't been expecting the reverse and it flew off. Halston heard it thud down in the backseat.

A trickle of blood ran in his eye. He tried again to move his hands, to raise one of them and wipe the blood away.

They trembled in his lap, but he was still unable to actually move them. He thought of the .45 special in its holster under his left arm.

*If I can get to my piece, kitty, the rest of your nine lives are going in a lump sum.*

More tingles now. Dull throbs of pain from his feet, buried and surely shattered under the engine block, zips and tingles from his legs — it felt exactly the way a limb that

418

you've slept on does when it's starting to wake up. At that moment Halston didn't care about his feet. It was enough to know that his spine wasn't severed, that he wasn't going to finish out his life as a dead lump of body attached to a talking head.

*Maybe I had a few lives left myself.*

Take care of the cat. That was the first thing. *Then get out of the wreck* — maybe someone would come along, that would solve both problems at once. Not likely at 4:30 in the morning on a back road like this one, but barely possible. And —

And what was the cat doing back there?

He didn't like having it on his face, but he didn't like having it behind him and out of sight, either. He tried the rear-view mirror, but that was useless. The crash had knocked it awry and all it reflected was the grassy ravine he had finished up in.

A sound from behind him, like low, ripping cloth.

Purring.

*Hellcat my ass. It's gone to sleep back there.*

And even if it hadn't, even if it was somehow planning murder, what could it do? It was a skinny little thing, probably weighed all of four pounds soaking wet. And soon . . . soon he would be able to move his hands enough to get his gun. He was sure of it.

Halston sat and waited. Feeling continued to flood back into his body in a series of pins-

and-needles incursions. Absurdly (or maybe in instinctive reaction to his close brush with death) he got an erection for a minute or so. *Be kind of hard to beat off under present circumstances,* he thought.

A dawn-line was appearing in the eastern sky. Somewhere a bird sang.

Halston tried his hands again and got them to move an eighth of an inch before they fell back.

*Not yet. But soon.*

A soft thud on the seatback beside him. Halston turned his head and looked into the black-white face, the glowing eyes with their huge dark pupils.

Halston spoke to it.

"I have never blown a hit once I took it on, kitty. This could be a first. I'm getting my hands back. Five minutes, ten at most. You want my advice? Go out the window. They're all open. Go out and take your tail with you."

The cat stared at him.

Halston tried his hands again. They came up, trembling wildly. Half an inch. An inch. He let them fall back limply. They slipped off his lap and thudded to the Plymouth's seat. They glimmered there palely, like large tropical spiders.

The cat was grinning at him.

*Did I make a mistake?* he wondered confusedly. He was a creature of hunch, and the feeling that he had made one was suddenly overwhelming. Then the cat's body tensed, and even as it leaped, Halston knew what it was going to do and he opened his mouth to scream.

The cat landed on Halston's crotch, claws out, digging.

At that moment, Halston wished he *had* been paralyzed. The pain was gigantic, terrible. He had never suspected that there could be such pain in the world. The cat was a spitting coiled spring of fury, clawing at his balls.

Halston *did* scream, his mouth yawning open, and that was when the cat changed direction and leaped at his face, leaped at his mouth. And at that moment Halston knew that it was something more than a cat. It was something possessed of a malign, murderous intent.

He caught one last glimpse of that black-and-white face below the flattened ears, its eyes enormous and filled with lunatic hate. It had gotten rid of the three old people and now it was going to get rid of John Halston.

It rammed into his mouth, a furry projectile. He gagged on it. Its front claws pinwheeled, tattering his tongue like a piece of liver. His stomach recoiled and he vomited. The vomit ran down into his windpipe, clogging it, and he began to choke.

In this extremity, his will to survive overcame the last of the impact paralysis. He brought his hands up slowly to grasp the cat. *Oh my God,* he thought.

The cat was forcing its way into his mouth, flattening its body, squirming, working itself further and further in. He could feel his jaws creaking wider and wider to admit it.

He reached to grab it, yank it out, destroy it . . . and his hands clasped only the cat's tail.

Somehow it had gotten its entire body into his mouth. Its strange, black-and-white face must be crammed into his very throat.

A terrible thick gagging sound came from Halston's throat, which was swelling like a flexible length of garden hose.

His body twitched. His hands fell back into his lap and the fingers drummed senselessly on his thighs. His eyes sheened over, then glazed. They stared out through the Plymouth's windshield blankly at the coming dawn.

Protruding from his open mouth was two inches of bushy tail . . . half-black, half-white. It switched lazily back and forth.

It disappeared.

A bird cried somewhere again. Dawn came in breathless silence then, over the frost-rimmed fields of rural Connecticut.

The farmer's name was Will Reuss.

He was on his way to Placer's Glen to get the inspection sticker renewed on his farm truck when he saw the late morning sun twinkle on something in the ravine beside the road. He pulled over and saw the Plymouth lying at a drunken, canted angle in the ditch, barbed wire tangled in its grille like a snarl of steel knitting.

He worked his way down, and then sucked in his breath sharply. "Holy moley," he muttered to the bright November day. There was a guy sitting bolt upright behind the wheel, eyes open and glaring emptily into eternity. The Roper organization was never going to include him in its presidential poll again. His face was smeared with blood. He was still wearing his seat belt.

The driver's door had been crimped shut, but Reuss managed to get it open by yanking with both hands. He leaned in and unstrapped the seat belt, planning to check for ID. He was reaching for the coat when he noticed that the dead guy's shirt was rippling, just above the belt buckle. Rippling . . . and bulging. Splotches of blood began to bloom there like sinister roses.

"What the Christ?" He reached out, grasped the dead man's shirt, and pulled it up.

Will Reuss looked — and screamed.

Above Halston's navel, a ragged hole had been clawed in his flesh. Looking out was the gore-streaked black-and-white face of a cat, its eyes huge and glaring.

Reuss staggered back, shrieking, hands clapped to his face. A score of crows took cawing wing from a nearby field.

The cat forced its body out and stretched in obscene languor.

Then it leaped out the open window. Reuss caught sight of it moving through the high dead grass and then it was gone.

It seemed to be in a hurry, he later told a reporter from the local paper.

As if it had unfinished business.

# The New York Times AT SPECIAL BARGAIN RATES

She's fresh out of the shower when the phone begins to ring, but although the house is still full of relatives — she can hear them downstairs, it seems they will never go away, it seems she never had so many — no one picks up. Nor does the answering machine, as James programmed it to do after the fifth ring.

Anne goes to the extension on the bedtable, wrapping a towel around her, her wet hair thwacking unpleasantly on the back of her neck and bare shoulders. She picks it up, she says hello, and then he says her name. It's James. They had thirty years together, and one word is all she needs. He says *Annie* like no one else, always did.

For a moment she can't speak or even breathe. He has caught her on the exhale and her lungs feel as flat as sheets of paper. Then, as he says her name again (sounding uncharacteristically hesitant and unsure of himself), the strength slips from her legs. They turn to sand and she sits on the bed, the towel falling off her, her wet bottom dampening the sheet beneath her. If the bed hadn't been there, she would have gone to the floor.

Her teeth click together and that starts her breathing again.

"James? Where *are* you? *What happened?*" In her normal voice, this might have come out sounding shrewish — a mother scolding her wayward eleven-year-old who's come late to the supper-table yet again — but now it emerges in a kind of horrified growl. The murmuring relatives below her are, after all, planning his funeral.

James chuckles. It is a bewildered sound. "Well, I tell you what," he says. "I don't exactly know where I am."

Her first confused thought is that he must have missed the plane in London, even though he called her from Heathrow not long before it took off. Then a clearer idea comes: although both the *Times* and the TV news say there were no survivors, there was at least one. Her husband crawled from the wreckage of the burning plane (and the burning apartment building the plane hit, don't forget that, twenty-four more dead on the ground and the number apt to rise before the world moved on to the next tragedy) and has been wandering around Brooklyn ever since, in a state of shock.

"Jimmy, are you all right? Are you . . . are

you burned?" The truth of what that would mean occurs after the question, thumping down with the heavy weight of a dropped book on a bare foot, and she begins to cry. "Are you in the hospital?"

"Hush," he says, and at his old kindness — and at that old word, just one small piece of their marriage's furniture — she begins to cry harder. "Honey, hush."

"But I don't *understand!*"

"I'm all right," he says. "Most of us are."

"Most — ? There are *others?*"

"Not the pilot," he says. "He's not so good. Or maybe it's the co-pilot. He keeps screaming. 'We're going down, there's no power, oh my God.' Also 'This isn't my fault, don't let them blame it on me.' He says that, too."

She's cold all over. "Who is this really? Why are you being so horrible? I just lost my husband, you asshole!"

"Honey —"

"Don't call me that!" There's a clear strand of mucus hanging from one of her nostrils. She wipes it away with the back of her hand and then flings it into the wherever, a thing she hasn't done since she was a child. "Listen, mister — I'm going to star-sixty-nine this call and the police will come and slam your ass . . . your ignorant, unfeeling *ass* . . ."

But she can go no farther. It's his voice. There's no denying it. The way the call rang right through — no pickup downstairs, no

427

answering machine — suggests this call was just for her. And . . . *honey, hush.* Like in the old Carl Perkins song.

He has remained quiet, as if letting her work these things through for herself. But before she can speak again, there's a beep on the line.

"James? *Jimmy?* Are you still there?"

"Yeah, but I can't talk long. I was trying to call you when we went down, and I guess that's the only reason I was able to get through at all. Lots of others have been trying, we're lousy with cell phones, but no luck." That beep again. "Only now my phone's almost out of juice."

"Jimmy, did you know?" This idea has been the hardest and most terrible part for her — that he might have known, if only for an endless minute or two. Others might picture burned bodies or dismembered heads with grinning teeth; even light-fingered first responders filching wedding rings and diamond ear-clips, but what has robbed Annie Driscoll's sleep is the image of Jimmy looking out his window as the streets and cars and the brown apartment buildings of Brooklyn swell closer. The useless masks flopping down like the corpses of small yellow animals. The overhead bins popping open, carry-ons starting to fly, someone's Norelco razor rolling up the tilted aisle.

"Did you know you were going down?"

"Not really," he says. "Everything seemed all right until the very end — maybe the last thirty seconds. Although it's hard to keep track of time in situations like that, I always think."

*Situations like that.* And even more telling: *I always think.* As if he has been aboard half a dozen crashing 767s instead of just the one.

"In any case," he goes on, "I was just calling to say we'd be early, so be sure to get the FedEx man out of bed before I got there."

Her absurd attraction for the FedEx man has been a joke between them for years. She begins to cry again. His cell utters another of those beeps, as if scolding her for it.

"I think I died just a second or two before it rang the first time. I think that's why I was able to get through to you. But this thing's gonna give up the ghost pretty soon."

He chuckles as if this is funny. She supposes that in a way it is. She may see the humor in it herself, eventually. *Give me ten years or so,* she thinks.

Then, in that just-talking-to-myself voice she knows so well: "Why didn't I put the tiresome motherfucker on charge last night? Just forgot, that's all. Just forgot."

"James . . . honey . . . the plane crashed two days ago."

A pause. Mercifully with no beep to fill it. Then: "Really? Mrs. Corey *said* time was funny here. Some of us agreed, some of us disagreed. I was a disagreer, but looks like she was right."

"Hearts?" Annie asks. She feels now as if she is floating outside and slightly above her plump damp middle-aged body, but she hasn't forgotten Jimmy's old habits. On a long flight he was always looking for a game. Cribbage or canasta would do, but hearts was his true love.

"Hearts," he agrees. The phone beeps again, as if seconding that.

"Jimmy . . ." She hesitates long enough to ask herself if this is information she really wants, then plunges with that question still unanswered. "Where *are* you, exactly?"

"Looks like Grand Central Station," he says. "Only bigger. And emptier. As if it wasn't really Grand Central at all but only . . . mmm . . . a movie-set of Grand Central. Do you know what I'm trying to say?"

"I . . . I think so . . ."

"There certainly aren't any trains . . . and we can't hear any in the distance . . . but there are doors going everywhere. Oh, and there's an escalator, but it's broken. All dusty, and some of the treads are broken." He pauses, and when he speaks again he does so in a lower voice, as if afraid of being overheard. "People are leaving. Some climbed the escalator — I saw them — but most are using the doors. I guess I'll have to leave, too. For one thing, there's nothing to eat. There's a candy machine, but that's broken, too."

"Are you . . . honey, are you hungry?"

"A little. Mostly what I'd like is some water. I'd *kill* for a cold bottle of Dasani."

Annie looks guiltily down at her own legs, still beaded with water. She imagines him licking off those beads and is horrified to feel a sexual stirring.

"I'm all right, though," he adds hastily. "For now, anyway. But there's no sense staying here. Only . . ."

"What? What, Jimmy?"

"I don't know which door to use."

Another beep.

"I wish I knew which one Mrs. Corey took. She's got my damn cards."

"Are you . . ." She wipes her face with the towel she wore out of the shower; then she was fresh, now she's all tears and snot. "Are you scared?"

"Scared?" he asks thoughtfully. "No. A little worried, that's all. Mostly about which door to use."

*Find your way home,* she almost says. *Find the right door and find your way home.* But if he did, would she want to see him? A ghost might be all right, but what if she opened the door on a smoking cinder with red eyes and the remains of jeans (he always traveled in jeans) melted into his legs? And what if Mrs. Corey was with him, his baked deck of cards

431

in one twisted hand?

*Beep.*

"I don't need to tell you to be careful about the FedEx man anymore," he says. "If you really want him, he's all yours."

She shocks herself by laughing.

"But I did want to say I love you —"

"Oh honey I love you t —"

"— and not to let the McCormack kid do the gutters this fall, he works hard but he's a risk-taker, last year he almost broke his fucking neck. And don't go to the bakery anymore on Sundays. Something's going to happen there, and I know it's going to be on a Sunday, but I don't know which Sunday. Time really *is* funny here."

The McCormack kid he's talking about must be the son of the guy who used to be their caretaker in Vermont . . . only they sold that place ten years ago, and the kid must be in his mid-twenties by now. And the bakery? She supposes he's talking about Zoltan's, but what on *earth* —

*Beep.*

"Some of the people here were on the ground, I guess. That's very tough, because they don't have a clue how they got here. And the pilot keeps screaming. Or maybe it's the co-pilot. I think he's going to be here for quite awhile. He just wanders around. He's very confused."

The beeps are coming closer together now.

"I have to go, Annie. I can't stay here, and the phone's going to shit the bed any second now, anyway." Once more in that I'm-scolding-myself voice (impossible to believe she will never hear it again after today; impossible *not* to believe) he mutters, "It would have been so simple just to . . . well, never mind. I love you, sweetheart."

"Wait! Don't go!"

"I c —"

"I love you, too! Don't go!"

But he already has. In her ear there is only black silence.

She sits there with the dead phone to her ear for a minute or more, then breaks the connection. The non-connection. When she opens the line again and gets a perfectly normal dial tone, she touches star-sixty-nine after all. According to the robot who answers her page, the last incoming call was at nine o'clock that morning. She knows who that one was: her sister Nell, calling from New Mexico. Nell called to tell Annie that her plane had been delayed and she wouldn't be in until tonight. Nell told her to be strong.

All the relatives who live at a distance — James's, Annie's — flew in. Apparently they feel that James used up all the family's Destruction Points, at least for the time being.

There is no record of an incoming call at — she glances at the bedside clock and sees it's now 3:17 p.m. — at about ten past three, on the third afternoon of her widowhood.

Someone raps briefly on the door and her brother calls, "Anne? Annie?"

"Dressing!" she calls back. Her voice sounds like she's been crying, but unfortunately, no one in this house would find that strange. "Privacy, please!"

"You okay?" he calls through the door. "We thought we heard you talking. And Ellie thought she heard you call out."

"Fine!" she calls, then wipes her face again with the towel. "Down in a few!"

"Okay. Take your time." Pause. "We're here for you." Then he clumps away.

"Beep," she whispers, then covers her mouth to hold in laughter that is some emotion even more complicated than grief finding the only way out it has. "Beep, beep. Beep, beep, beep." She lies back on the bed, laughing, and above her cupped hands her eyes are large and awash with tears that overspill down her cheeks and run all the way to her ears. "Beep-fucking-beepity-beep."

She laughs for quite awhile, then dresses and goes downstairs to be with her relatives, who have come to share their grief with hers. Only they feel apart from her, because he didn't call any of them. He called her. For better or worse, he called her.

During the autumn of that year, with the

blackened remains of the apartment building the jet crashed into still closed off from the rest of the world by yellow police tape (although the taggers have been inside, one leaving a spray-painted message reading CRISPY CRITTERS STOP HERE), Annie receives the sort of e-blast computer-addicts like to send to a wide circle of acquaintances. This one comes from Gert Fisher, the town librarian in Tilton, Vermont. When Annie and James summered there, Annie used to volunteer at the library, and although the two women never got on especially well, Gert has included Annie in her quarterly updates ever since. They are usually not very interesting, but halfway through the weddings, funerals, and 4-H winners in this one, Annie comes across a bit of news that makes her catch her breath. Jason McCormack, the son of old Hughie McCormack, was killed in an accident on Labor Day. He fell from the roof of a summer cottage while cleaning the gutters and broke his neck.

"He was only doing a favor for his dad, who as you may remember had a stroke the year before last," Gert wrote before going on to how it rained on the library's end-of-summer lawn sale, and how disappointed they all were.

Gert doesn't say in her three-page compendium of breaking news, but Annie is quite sure Jason fell from the roof of what used to be their cottage. In fact, she is positive.

■ ■ ■ ■

Five years after the death of her husband (and the death of Jason McCormack not long after), Annie remarries. And although they relocate to Boca Raton, she gets back to the old neighborhood often. Craig, the new husband, is only semi-retired, and his business takes him to New York every three or four months. Annie almost always goes with him, because she still has family in Brooklyn and on Long Island. More than she knows what to do with, it sometimes seems. But she loves them with that exasperated affection that seems to belong, she thinks, only to people in their fifties and sixties. She never forgets how they drew together for her after James's plane went down, and made the best cushion for her that they could. So she wouldn't crash, too.

When she and Craig go back to New York, they fly. About this she never has a qualm, but she stops going to Zoltan's Family Bakery on Sundays when she's home, even though their raisin bagels are, she is sure, served in heaven's waiting room. She goes to Froger's instead. She is actually there, buying doughnuts (the doughnuts are at least passable), when she hears the blast. She hears it clearly even though Zoltan's is eleven blocks away. LP gas explosion. Four killed, including the woman who always passed Annie her bagels with the top of the bag rolled down, saying, "Keep it that way until you get home or you lose the freshness."

People stand on the sidewalks, looking east toward the sound of the explosion and the rising smoke, shading their eyes with their hands. Annie hurries past them, not looking. She doesn't want to see a plume of rising smoke after a big bang; she thinks of James enough as it is, especially on the nights when she can't sleep. When she gets home she can hear the phone ringing inside. Either everyone has gone down the block to where the local school is having a sidewalk art sale, or no one can hear that ringing phone. Except for her, that is. And by the time she gets her key turned in the lock, the ringing has stopped.

Sarah, the only one of her sisters who never married, *is* there, it turns out, but there is no need to ask her why she didn't answer the phone; Sarah Bernicke, the one-time disco queen, is in the kitchen with the Village People turned up, dancing around with the O-Cedar in one hand, looking like a chick in a TV ad. She missed the bakery explosion, too, although their building is even closer to Zoltan's than Froger's.

Annie checks the answering machine, but there's a big red zero in the MESSAGES WAITING window. That means nothing in itself, lots of people call without leaving a message, but —

Star-sixty-nine reports the last call at eight-forty last night. Annie dials it anyway, hoping against hope that somewhere outside the big room that looks like a Grand Central Station movie-set he found a place to re-charge his phone. To him it might seem he last spoke to her yesterday. Or only minutes ago. *Time is funny here,* he said. She has dreamed of that call so many times it now almost seems like a dream itself, but she has never told anyone about it. Not Craig, not even her own mother, now almost ninety but alert and with a firmly held belief in the afterlife.

In the kitchen, the Village People advise that there is no need to feel down. There isn't, and she doesn't. She nevertheless holds the phone very tightly as the number she has star-sixty-nined rings once, then twice. Annie stands in the living room with the phone to her ear and her free hand touching the brooch above her left breast, as if touching the brooch could still the pounding heart beneath it. Then the ringing stops and a recorded voice offers to sell her the *New York Times* at special bargain rates that will not be repeated.

# MUTE

There were three confession booths. The light over the door of the middle one was on. No one was waiting. The church was empty. Colored light came in through the windows and made squares on the central aisle. Monette thought about leaving and didn't. Instead he walked to the booth that was open for business and went inside. When he closed the door and sat down, the little slider on his right opened. In front of him, tacked to the wall with a blue pushpin, was a file card. Typed on it was FOR ALL HAVE SINNED AND FALLEN SHORT OF GOD'S GLORY. It had been a long time, but Monette didn't think that was standard equipment. He didn't even think it was Baltimore Catechism.

From the other side of the mesh screen, the priest spoke. "How you doing, my son?"

Monette didn't think that was standard, either. But it was all right. Just the same, he couldn't reply at first. Not a word. And that was sort of funny, considering what he had to say.

"Son? Cat got your tongue?"

Still nothing. The words were there, but they were all blocked up. Absurd or not, Monette had a sudden image of a clogged toilet.

The blur beyond the screen shifted. "Been a while?"

"Yes," Monette said. It was something.

"Want me to give you a hint?"

"No, I remember. Bless me, Father, for I have sinned."

"Uh-huh, and how long has it been since your last confession?"

"I don't remember. A long time. Not since I was a kid."

"Well, take it easy — it's like riding a bike."

But for a moment he could still say nothing. He looked at the typed message on the pushpin and his throat worked. His hands were kneading themselves, tighter and tighter, until they made a big fist that was rocking back and forth between his thighs.

"Son? The day is rolling by, and I have company coming for lunch. Actually, my company is *bringing* lu—"

"Father, I may have committed a terrible sin."

Now the priest was silent for a while. *Mute,* Monette thought. There was a white word if there ever was one. Type it on a file card and it ought to disappear.

When the priest on the other side of the screen spoke again, his voice was still friendly but more grave. "What's your sin, my son?"

And Monette said, "I don't know. You'll have to tell me."

-2-

It was starting to rain when Monette came up on the northbound entrance ramp to the turnpike. His suitcase was in the trunk, and his sample cases — big boxy things, the kind lawyers tote when they're taking evidence into court — were in the backseat. One was brown, one black. Both were embossed with the Wolfe & Sons logo: a timber wolf with a book in its mouth. Monette was a salesman. He covered all of northern New England. It was Monday morning. It had been a bad weekend, very bad. His wife had moved out to a motel, where she was probably not alone. Soon she might go to jail. Certainly there would be a scandal, and infidelity was going to be the least of it.

On the lapel of his jacket, he wore a button reading, ASK ME ABOUT THE BEST FALL LIST EVER!!

There was a man standing at the foot of the ramp. He was wearing old clothes and holding up a sign as Monette approached and the rain grew stronger. There was a battered brown knapsack between feet dressed in dirty sneakers. The Velcro closure of one sneaker had come loose and stuck up like a cockeyed tongue. The hitchhiker had no cap, let alone an umbrella.

At first all Monette could make out of the sign were crudely drawn red lips with a black slash drawn diagonally through them. When he got a little closer, he saw the words above the slashed mouth read I AM MUTE! Below the slashed mouth was this: WILL YOU GIVE ME A RIDE???

Monette put on his blinker to make his turn onto the ramp. The hitchhiker flipped the sign over. On the other side was an ear, just as crudely drawn, with a slash through it. Above the ear: I AM DEAF! Below it: PLEASE MAY I HAVE A RIDE???

Monette had driven millions of miles since he was sixteen, most of them in the dozen years he had been repping for Wolfe & Sons, selling one best fall list ever after another, and during that time he had never picked up a single hitchhiker. Today he swerved over at the edge of the ramp with no hesitation and came to a stop. The St. Christopher's medal looped over the rearview mirror was still swinging back and forth when he used the button on his door to pop open the locks. Today he felt he had nothing to lose.

The hitchhiker slid in and put his battered little pack between his damp and dirty sneakers. Monette had thought, looking at him, that the fellow would smell bad, and he wasn't wrong. He said, "How far you going?"

The hitchhiker shrugged and pointed up the ramp. Then he bent and carefully put his sign on top of his pack. His hair was stringy and thin. There was some gray in it.

"I know which way, but . . ." Monette realized the man wasn't hearing him. He waited for him to straighten up. A car blew past and up the ramp, honking even though Monette had left him plenty of room to get by. Monette gave him the finger. This he *had* done before, but never for such minor annoyances.

The hitchhiker fastened his seat belt and looked at Monette, as if to ask what the holdup was. There were lines on his face, and stubble. Monette couldn't even begin to guess his age. Somewhere between old and not old, that was all he knew.

"How far are you going?" Monette asked, this time enunciating each word, and when the guy still only looked at him — average height, skinny, no more than a hundred and fifty pounds — he said, "Can you read lips?" He touched his own.

The hitchhiker shook his head and made some hand gestures.

Monette kept a pad in the console. While he wrote *How far?* on it, another car cruised past, now pulling up a fine rooster tail of moisture. Monette was going all the way to

443

Derry, a hundred and sixty miles, and these were the kind of driving conditions he usually loathed, second only to heavy snow. But today he reckoned it would be all right. Today the weather — and the big rigs, pulling up their secondary storms of flying water as they droned past — would keep him occupied.

Not to mention this guy. His new passenger. Who looked at the note, then back at Monette. It occurred to Monette later that maybe the guy couldn't read, either — learning to read when you're a deaf-mute had to be damn hard — but understood the question mark. The man pointed through the windshield and up the ramp. Then he opened and closed his hands eight times. Or maybe it was ten. Eighty miles. Or a hundred. If he knew at all.

"Waterville?" Monette guessed.

The hitchhiker looked at him blankly.

"Okay," Monette said. "Whatever. Just tap me on the shoulder when we get where you're going."

The hitchhiker looked at him blankly.

"Well, I guess you will," Monette said. "Assuming you've even got a destination in mind, that is." He checked his rearview, then got rolling. "You're pretty much cut off, aren't you?"

The guy was still looking at him. He shrugged and put his palms over his ears.

"I know," Monette said, and merged.

"Pretty much cut off. Phone lines down. But today I almost wish I was you and you were me." He paused. "Almost. Mind some music?"

And when the hitchhiker just turned his head away and looked out the window, Monette had to laugh at himself. Debussy, AC/DC, or Rush Limbaugh, it was all the same to this guy.

He had bought the new Josh Ritter CD for his daughter — it was her birthday in a week — but hadn't remembered to send it to her yet. Too many other things going on just lately. He set the cruise control once they'd cleared Portland, slit the wrapping with his thumb, and stuck the CD in the player. He supposed it was now technically a used CD, not the kind of thing you give your beloved only child. Well, he could always buy her another one. Assuming, that was, he still had money to buy one with.

Josh Ritter turned out to be pretty good. Kind of like early Dylan, only with a better attitude. As he listened, he mused on money. Affording a new CD for Kelsie's birthday was the least of his problems. The fact that what she really wanted — and needed — was a new laptop wasn't very high on the list either. If Barb had done what she said she had done — what the SAD office *confirmed* that she'd done — he didn't know how he was going to afford the kid's last year at Case Western.

Even assuming he still had a job himself. *That* was a problem.

He turned the music up to drown the problem out and partially succeeded, but by the time they reached Gardiner, the last chord had died out. The hitchhiker's face and body were turned away to the passenger window. Monette could see only the back of his stained and faded duffle coat, with too-thin hair straggling down over the collar in bunches. It looked like there had been something printed on the back of the coat once, but now it was too faded to make out.

*That's the story of this poor schmo's life,* Monette thought.

At first Monette couldn't decide if the hitchhiker was dozing or looking at the scenery. Then he noted the slight downward tilt of the man's head and the way his breath was fogging the glass of the passenger window, and decided dozing was more likely. And why not? The only thing more boring than the Maine Turnpike south of Augusta was the Maine Turnpike south of Augusta in a cold spring rain.

Monette had other CDs in the center console, but instead of rummaging through them, he turned off the car's sound system. And after he'd passed through the Gardiner toll station — not stopping, only slowing, the wonders of E-ZPass — he began to talk.

Monette stopped talking and checked his watch. It was quarter to noon, and the priest had said he had company coming for lunch. That the company was bringing lunch, actually.

"Father, I'm sorry this is taking so long. I'd speed it up if I knew how, but I don't."

"That's all right, son. I'm interested now."

"Your company —"

"Will wait while I'm doing the Lord's work. Son, did this man rob you?"

"No," Monette said. "Unless you count my peace of mind. Does that count?"

"Most assuredly. What *did* he do?"

"Nothing. Looked out the window. I thought he was dozing, but later I had reasons to think I was wrong about that."

"What did *you* do?"

"Talked about my wife," Monette said. Then he stopped and considered. "No, I didn't. I *vented* about my wife. I *ranted* about my wife. I *spewed* about my wife. I . . . you see . . ." He struggled with it, lips pressed tightly together, looking down at that big twisting fist of hands between his thighs. Finally he burst out, "He was a *deaf-mute,* don't you see? I could say anything and not have to listen to him make an analysis, give an opinion, or offer me sage advice. He was *deaf,* he was *mute,* hell, I thought he was probably *asleep,* and I could say any fucking thing I wanted to!"

In the booth with the file card pinned to the wall, Monette winced.

"Sorry, Father."

"What exactly did you say about her?" the priest asked.

"I told him she was fifty-four," Monette said. "That was how I started. Because that was the part . . . you know, that was the part I just couldn't swallow."

### -4-

After the Gardiner tolls, the Maine Turnpike becomes a free road again, running through three hundred miles of fuck-all: woods, fields, the occasional house trailer with a satellite dish on the roof and a truck on blocks in the side yard. Except in the summer, it is sparsely traveled. Each car becomes its own little world. It occurred to Monette even then (perhaps it was the St. Christopher's medal swinging from the rearview, a gift from Barb in better, saner days) that it was like being in a rolling confessional. Still, he started slowly, as so many confessors do.

"I'm married," he said. "I'm fifty-five and my wife is fifty-four."

He considered this while the windshield wipers ticked back and forth.

"Fifty-four, Barbara's fifty-four. We've been

married twenty-six years. One kid. A daughter. A lovely daughter. Kelsie Ann. She goes to school in Cleveland, and I don't know how I'm going to keep her there, because two weeks ago, with no warning, my wife turned into Mount St. Helens. Turns out she's got a boyfriend. Has had a boyfriend for almost two years. He's a teacher — well, of course he is, what else would he be? — but she calls him Cowboy Bob. Turns out a lot of those nights I thought she was at Cooperative Extension or Book Circle, she was drinking tequila shooters and line dancing with Cowboy Fucking Bob."

It was funny. Anyone could see that. It was sitcom shit if there had ever been sitcom shit. But his eyes — although tearless — were stinging as if they were full of poison ivy. He glanced to his right, but the hitchhiker was still mostly turned away, and now his forehead was leaning against the glass of the passenger window. Sleeping for sure.

*Almost* for sure.

Monette hadn't spoken of her betrayal aloud. Kelsie still didn't know, although the bubble of her ignorance would pop soon. The straws were flying in the wind — he'd hung up on three different reporters before leaving on this trip — but there was nothing they could print or broadcast yet. That would change soon, but Monette would go on getting by with *No comment* for as long as possible, mostly to spare himself embarrassment. In the meantime, though, he was commenting plenty, and doing so brought a great, angry relief. In a way it was like singing in the shower. Or vomiting there.

"She's fifty-four," he said. "That's what I can't get over. It means she started up with this guy, whose real name is Robert Yandowsky — how's that for a cowboy name — when she was fifty-two. Fifty-*two!* Would you say that's old enough to know better, my friend? Old enough to have sowed your wild oats, then ripped them up again and planted a more useful crop? My God, she wears *bifocals!* She's had her gallbladder out! And she's boffing this guy! In the Grove Motel, where the two of them have set up housekeeping! I gave her a nice house in Buxton, a two-car garage, she's got an Audi on long lease, and she threw it all away to get drunk on Thursday nights in Range Riders, then shag this guy until the dawn's early light — or however long they can manage — and she's fifty-four! Not to mention Cowboy Bob, *who is fucking sixty!*"

He heard himself ranting, told himself to stop, saw the hitchhiker hadn't moved (unless he'd sunk a little deeper into the collar of his duffle coat — that might have happened), and realized he didn't *have* to stop. He was in a car. He was on I-95, somewhere east of the sun and west of Augusta. His passenger was a deaf-mute. He could rant if he wanted to rant.

He ranted.

"Barb spilled everything. She wasn't defiant about it, and she wasn't ashamed. She seemed . . . serene. Shell-shocked, maybe. Or still living in a fantasy world."

And she'd said it was partly his fault.

"I'm on the road a lot, that much is true. Over three hundred days last year. She was on her own — we only had the one chick, you know, and that one finished with high school and flown the coop. So it was my fault. Cowboy Bob and all the rest of it."

His temples were throbbing, and his nose was almost shut. He sniffed back hard enough to make black dots fly before his eyes and got no relief. Not in his nose, anyway. In his head he finally felt better. He was very glad he'd picked the hitchhiker up. He could have spoken these things aloud in the empty car, but —

### -5-

"But it wouldn't have been the same," he told the shape on the other side of the confessional wall. He looked straight ahead as he said it, right at FOR ALL HAVE SINNED AND FALLEN SHORT OF GOD'S GLORY. "Do you understand that, Father?"

"Of course I do," the priest replied — and

rather cheerfully. "Even though you've clearly fallen away from Mother Church — except for a few superstitious remnants like your St. Christopher's medal — you shouldn't even have to ask. Confession is good for the soul. We've known that for two thousand years."

Monette had taken to wearing the St. Christopher's medal that had once upon a time swung from his rearview mirror. Perhaps it was just superstition, but he had driven millions of miles in all kinds of shit weather with that medal for company and had never so much as dented a fender.

"Son, what else did she do, your wife? Besides sinning with Cowboy Bob?"

Monette surprised himself by laughing. And on the other side of the screen, the priest laughed, too. The difference was the quality of the laughter. The priest saw the funny side. Monette supposed he was still trying to ward off insanity.

"Well, there was the underwear," he said.

### -6-

"She bought underwear," he told the hitch-hiker, who still sat slumped and mostly turned away, with his forehead against the window and his breath fogging the glass. Pack between his feet, sign resting on top with the side reading I AM MUTE! facing up. "She showed me. It was in the guest room closet.

It damn near *filled* the guest room closet. Bustiers and camisoles and bras and silk stockings still in their packages, dozens of pairs. What looked like about a thousand garter belts. But mostly there were panties, panties, panties. She said Cowboy Bob was 'a real panty man.' I think she would have gone on, told me just how that worked, but I got the picture. I got it a lot better than I wanted to. I said, 'Of course he's a panty man, he grew up jerking off to PLAYBOY, he's fucking *sixty*.' "

They were passing the Fairfield sign now. Green and smeary through the windshield, with a wet crow hunched on top.

"It was the good stuff, too," Monette said. "A lot was Victoria's Secret from the mall, but there was also stuff from a high-priced underwear boutique called Sweets. In Boston. I didn't even know there *were* underwear boutiques, but I have since been educated. Had to've been thousands of dollars' worth piled up in that closet. Also shoes. High heels, for the most part. You know, stilettos. She had that hot-babe thing down pat. Although I imagine she took off her bifocals when she put on her latest Wonderbra and tap pants. But —"

A semi droned by. Monette had his headlights on and automatically flicked his high beams for a moment when the rig was past. The driver flicked a thank-you with his taillights. Sign language of the road.

"But a lot of it hadn't even been *worn*. That was the thing. It was just . . . just pack-ratted away. I asked her why she'd bought so goddam much, and she either didn't know or couldn't explain. 'We just got into the habit,' she said. 'It was like foreplay, I guess.' Not ashamed. Not defiant. Like she was thinking, *This is all a dream I'll wake up from soon.* The two of us standing there are looking at that rummage sale of slips and skivvies and shoes and God knows what else piled in the back. Then I asked her where she got the money — I mean, I see the credit-card slips at the end of each month, and there weren't any from Sweets of Boston — and we got to the real problem. Which was embezzlement."

### -7-

"Embezzlement," the priest said. Monette wondered if the word had ever been spoken in this confessional before and decided it probably had been. *Theft* for sure.

"She worked for MSAD 19," Monette said. "MSAD stands for Maine School Administrative District. It's one of the big ones, just south of Portland. Based in Dowrie, as a matter of fact, home of both Range Riders — the line-dancing joint — and the historic Grove Motel, just down the road from there. Convenient. Get your dancing and your fuh . . .

your lovemaking all in the same area. Why, you wouldn't even have to drive your car if you happened to have a snootful. Which on most evenings they did have. Tequila shooters for her, whiskey for him. Jack, naturally. She told me. She told me everything."

"Was she a teacher?"

"Oh no — teachers don't have access to that kind of money; she never could have embezzled over a hundred and twenty thousand dollars if she'd been a teacher. We've had the district superintendent and his wife over to the house for dinner, and of course I saw him at all the end-of-school-year picnics, usually at the Dowrie Country Club. Victor McCrea. University of Maine graduate. Played football. Majored in phys ed. Crew cut. Probably floated through on gift Cs, but a nice man, the kind who knows fifty different guy-walks-into-a-bar jokes. In charge of a dozen schools, from the five elementaries to Muskie High. Very large annual budget, might be able to add four and four on his own in a pinch. Barb was his executive secretary for twelve years."

Monette paused.

"Barb had the checkbook."

-8-

The rain was getting heavier. Now it was just short of a downpour. Monette slowed to fifty

455

without even thinking about it, while other cars buzzed blithely past him in the left lane, each dragging up its own cloud of water. Let them buzz. He himself had had a long and accident-free career selling the best fall list ever (not to mention the best spring list ever and a few Summer Surprise lists, which mostly consisted of cookbooks, diet books, and *Harry Potter* knockoffs), and he wanted to keep it that way.

On his right, the hitchhiker stirred a little.

"You awake, buddy?" Monette asked. A useless question, but natural.

The hitchhiker uttered a comment from the end of him that apparently wasn't mute: *Ph-weeet.* Small, polite, and — best of all — odorless.

"I take that as a yes," Monette said, returning his attention to his driving. "Where was I?"

The underwear, that's where he was. He could still see it. Piled up in the closet like a teenager's wet dream. Then the confession of the embezzlement: that staggering figure. After he'd taken time to consider the possibility that she might be lying for some crazy reason (but of course it was *all* crazy), he had asked her how much was left, and she said — in that same calm and dazed manner — that there was nothing left, really, although she supposed she could get more. For a while, at least.

" 'But they're going to find out soon now,' she said. 'If it was just poor old clueless Vic, I suppose I could go on forever, but the state auditors were in last week. They asked too many questions, and they took copies of the records. It won't be long now.'

"So I asked her how she could spend well over a hundred thousand dollars on knickers and garter belts," Monette told his silent companion. "I didn't feel angry — at least not then, I guess I was too shocked — but I was honestly curious. And she said — in that same way, not ashamed, not defiant, like she was sleep-walking: 'Well, we got interested in the lottery. I suppose we thought we could make it back that way.' "

Monette paused. He watched the windshield wipers go back and forth. He briefly considered the idea of twisting the wheel to the right and sending the car into one of the concrete overpass supports just ahead. He rejected the idea. He would later tell the priest part of the reason was that ancient childhood prohibition against suicide, but mostly he was thinking he'd like to hear the Josh Ritter album at least one more time before he died.

Plus, he was no longer alone.

Instead of committing suicide (and taking his passenger with him), he drove beneath the overpass at that steady, moderate fifty (for maybe two seconds the windshield was clear, then the wipers once more found work to do) and resumed his story.

"They must have bought more lottery tickets than anyone in history." He thought it over, then shook his head. "Well . . . probably not. But they bought ten thousand for sure. She said that last November — I was in New Hampshire and Massachusetts almost that whole month, plus the sales conference in Delaware — they bought over two thousand. Powerball, Megabucks, Paycheck, Pick 3, Pick 4, Triple Play, they hit them all. At first they chose the numbers, but Barb said after a while that took too long and they went to the EZ Pick option."

Monette pointed to the white plastic box glued to his windshield, just below the stem of the rearview mirror.

"All these gadgets speed up the world. Maybe that's a good thing, but I sort of doubt it. She said, 'We went the EZ Pick route because the people standing in line behind you get impatient if you take too long to pick your own numbers, especially when the jackpot's over a hundred million.' She said sometimes she and Yandowsky split up and hit different stores, as many as two dozen in an evening. And of course they sold them right there at the place where they went to line dance.

"She said, 'The first time Bob played, we won five hundred dollars on a Pick 3. It was so romantic.' " Monette shook his head. "After that, the romance stayed, but the winning pretty much stopped. That was what she said. She said once they won a thousand, but by then they were already thirty thousand in the bucket. *In the bucket* is what she called it.

"One time — this was in January, while I was out on the road trying to earn back the price of the cashmere coat I got her for Christmas — she said they went up to Derry and spent a couple of days. I don't know if they've got line dancing up there or not, I never checked, but they've got a place called Hollywood Slots. They stayed in a suite, ate high off the hog — she said *high off the hog* — and dropped seventy-five hundred playing video poker. But, she said, they didn't like that so much. Mostly they just stuck to the lottery, plugging in more and more of the SAD's dough, trying to get even before the state auditors came and the roof fell in. And every now and then, of course, she'd buy some new underwear. A girl wants to be fresh when she's buying Powerball tix at the local 7-Eleven.

"You all right, buddy?"

There was no response from his passenger — of course not — so Monette reached out and shook the man's shoulder. The hitcher lifted his head from the window (his forehead had left a greasy mark on the glass) and looked around, blinking his red-rimmed eyes as if he had been asleep. Monette didn't think he'd been asleep. No reason why, just a feeling.

He made a thumb-and-forefinger circle at the hitchhiker, then raised his eyebrows.

For a moment the hitcher only looked blank, giving Monette time to think the guy was bull-stupid as well as deaf-mute. Then he smiled and nodded and returned the circle.

"Okay," Monette said. "Just checking."

The man leaned his head back against the window again. In the meantime, the guy's presumed destination, Waterville, had slid behind them and into the rain. Monette didn't notice. He was still living in the past.

"If it had been just lingerie and the kind of lottery games where you pick a bunch of numbers, the damage might have been limited," he said. "Because playing the lottery that way takes time. It gives you a chance to come to your senses, always presuming you have any to come to. You have to stand in line and collect the slips and save them in your wallet. Then you have to watch TV or check the paper for the results. It might still have been okay. If, that is, you can call anything okay about your wife catting around with a stoneboat-dumb history teacher and flushing thirty or forty thousand dollars' worth of the school district's money down the shitter. But thirty grand I might have been able to cover. I could have taken out a second mortgage on the house. Not for Barb, no way, but for Kelsie Ann. A kid just starting out in life doesn't need a stinking fish like that around her neck. Restitution is what they call it. I would have made restitution even if it meant living in a two-bedroom apartment. You know?"

The hitchhiker obviously *didn't* know — not about beautiful young daughters just starting out in life, or second mortgages, or restitution. He was warm and dry in his dead-silent world, and that was probably better.

Monette plowed forward nonetheless.

"Thing is, there are quicker ways to chuck your money, and it's as legal as . . . as buying underwear."

### -9-

"They moved on to scratch tickets, didn't they?" the priest asked. "What the Lottery Commission calls instant winners."

"You speak like a man who's had a flutter himself," Monette said.

"From time to time," the priest agreed, and with an admirable lack of hesitation. "I always tell myself that if I should ever get a real golden ticket, I'd put all the money into the church. But I never risk more than five dollars a week." This time there *was* hesitation. "Sometimes ten." Another pause. "And once I bought a twenty-dollar scratch, back when

461

they were new. But that was a momentary madness. I never did it again."

"At least not so far," Monette said.

The priest chuckled. "The words of a man who has truly had his fingers burned, son." He sighed. "I'm fascinated by your story, but I wonder if we could move it along a bit faster? My company will wait while I do the Lord's work, but not forever. And I believe we're having chicken salad, heavy on the mayo. A favorite of mine."

"There's not much more," Monette said. "If you've played, you've got the gist of it. You can buy the scratch tickets at all the same places you can buy the Powerball and Megabucks tickets, but you can also buy them at a lot of other places, including turnpike rest stops. You don't even need to do business with a clerk; you can get them from a machine. The machines are always green, the color of money. By the time Barb came clean —"

"By the time she confessed," the priest said, with what might have been a touch of actual slyness.

"Yes, by the time she *confessed,* they'd pretty much settled on the twenty-dollar scratch-offs. Barb said she never bought any when she was on her own, but when she was with Cowboy Bob, they'd buy a lot. Hoping for that big score, you know. Once she said they bought a hundred of those puppies in a single night. That's two thousand dollars' worth. They got back eighty. They each had their own little plastic ticket scratcher. They look like snow scrapers for elves and have MAINE STATE LOTTERY written on the handle. They're green, like the vending machines that sell the tickets. She showed me hers — it was under the guest room bed. You couldn't make out anything except TERY on it. Could have been MYSTERY instead of LOTTERY. The sweat from her palm had wiped out all the rest."

"Son, did you strike her? Is that why you're here?"

"No," Monette said. "I wanted to *kill* her for it — the money, not the cheating, the cheating part just seemed unreal, even with all that fuh . . . all that underwear right in front of my eyes. But I didn't lay so much as a finger on her. I think it was because I was too tired. All that information had just tired me out. What I wanted to do was take a nap. A long one. Maybe a couple of days long. Is that strange?"

"No," the priest said.

"I asked her how she could do something like that to me. Did she care so little? And *she* asked —"

"She asked me how come I didn't know," Monette told the hitchhiker. "And before I could say anything, she answered herself, so I guess it was a whatchacallit, a rhetorical question. She said, 'You didn't know because you didn't care. You were almost always on the road, and when you weren't on the road, you *wanted* to be on the road. It's been ten years since you cared what underwear I have on — why would you, when you don't care about the woman inside it? But you care now, don't you? You do now.'

"Man, I just looked at her. I was too tired to kill her — or even slap her — but I was mad, all right. Even through the shock, I was mad. She was trying to make it my fault. You see that, don't you? Trying to lay it all off on my fucking *job,* as if I could get another one that paid even half as much. I mean, at my age what else am I qualified for? I guess I could get a job as school crossing guard — I don't have any morals busts in my past — but that would be about it."

He paused. Far down the road, still mostly hidden by a shifting camisole of rain, was a blue sign.

He considered, then said, "But even that wasn't the real point. You want to know the point? Her point? I was supposed to feel guilty for *liking* my job. For not drudging through my days until I found the right person to go *absolutely fucking bombers* with!"

The hitcher stirred a little, probably only because they'd hit a bump (or run over some roadkill), but it made Monette realize he was shouting. And hey, the guy might not be completely deaf. Even if he was, he might feel vibrations in the bones of his face once sounds passed a certain decibel level. Who the fuck knew?

"I didn't get into it with her," Monette said in a lower voice. "I *refused* to get into it with her. I think I knew that if I did, if we really started to argue, anything might happen. I wanted to get out of there while I was still in shock . . . because that was protecting her, see?"

The hitchhiker said nothing, but Monette saw for both of them.

"I said, 'What happens now?' and she said, 'I suppose I'll go to jail.' And you know what? If she'd started to cry then, I might have held her. Because after twenty-six years of marriage, things like that get to be a reflex. Even when most of the feeling's gone. But she didn't cry, so I walked out. Just turned around and walked out. And when I came back, there was a note saying she'd *moved* out. That was almost two weeks ago, and I haven't seen her since. Talked to her on the phone a few times, that's all. Talked to a lawyer, too. Froze all our accounts, not that it'll do any good once the legal wheels start turning. Which will be soon. The caca is going to clog the air-cooling system, if you take my meaning. Then I suppose I'll see her again. In court. Her and Cowboy Fucking Bob."

Now he could read the blue sign: PITTS-FIELD REST AREA 2 MI.

"Ah, shit!" he cried. "Waterville's fifteen miles back thataway, partner." And when the deaf-mute didn't stir (of course not), Monette realized he didn't know the guy had been going to the Ville anyway. Not for sure. In any case, it was time to get this straightened out. The rest area would do for that, but for a minute or two longer they would remain enclosed in this rolling confessional, and he felt he had one more thing to say.

"It's true that I haven't felt much for her in a very long time," he said. "Sometimes love just runs out. And it's also true that I haven't been entirely faithful — I've taken a little road comfort from time to time. But does *that* warrant *this?* Does it justify a woman blowing up a life the way a kid would blow up a rotten apple with a firecracker?"

He pulled into the rest area. There were maybe four cars in the lot, huddled up against the brown building with the vending machines in the front. To Monette the cars looked like cold children left out in the rain. He parked. The hitchhiker looked at him questioningly.

"Where are you going?" Monette asked, knowing it was hopeless.

The deaf-mute considered. He looked around and saw where they were. He looked back at Monette as if to say, *Not here.*

Monette pointed back south and raised his eyebrows. The deaf-mute shook his head, then pointed north. Opened and closed his fists, showing his fingers six times . . . eight . . . ten. Same as before, basically. But this time Monette got it. He thought life might have been simpler for this guy if someone had taught him the sideways figure-eight symbol that means *infinity.*

"You're basically just rambling, aren't you?" Monette asked.

The deaf-mute only looked at him.

"Yeah you are," Monette said. "Well, I tell you what. You listened to my story — even though you didn't know you were listening to it — and I'll get you as far as Derry." An idea struck him. "In fact, I'll drop you at the Derry Shelter. You can get a hot and a cot, at least for one night. I have to take a leak. You need to take a leak?"

The deaf-mute looked at him with patient blankness.

"A leak," Monette said. "A *piss.*" He started to point at his crotch, realized where they were, and decided a road bum would think he was signing for a blowjob right here beside the Hav-A-Bite machines. He pointed toward the silhouettes on the side of the building instead — black cutout man, black cutout woman. The man had his legs apart, the woman had hers together. Pretty much the story of the human race in sign language.

This his passenger got. He shook his head decisively, then made another thumb-and-forefinger circle for good measure. Which left Monette with a delicate problem: leave Mr. Silent Vagabond in the car while he did his business or turn him out into the rain to wait . . . in which case the guy would almost certainly know why he was being put out.

Only it wasn't a problem at all, he decided. There was no money in the car, and his personal luggage was locked in the trunk. There were his sample cases in the backseat, but he somehow didn't think the guy was going to steal two seventy-pound cases and go trotting down the rest area's exit ramp with them. For one thing, how would he hold up his I AM MUTE! sign?

"I'll be right back," Monette said, and when the hitchhiker only looked at him with those red-rimmed eyes, Monette pointed to himself, to the restroom icons, then back to himself. This time the hitchhiker nodded and made another thumb-and-forefinger circle.

Monette went to the toilet and pissed for what felt like twenty minutes. The relief was exquisite. He felt better than he had since

Barb had dropped her bombshell. It occurred to him for the first time that he was going to get through this. And he would help Kelsie get through it. He remembered a quote from some old German (or maybe a Russian, it certainly sounded like the Russian view of life): Whatever does not kill me makes me stronger.

He went back to his car, whistling. He even gave the coin-op lottery-ticket machine a comradely slap as he went by. At first he thought maybe he couldn't see his passenger because the guy was lying down . . . in which case, Monette would have to shoo him up-right again so he could get behind the wheel. But the hitchhiker wasn't lying down. The hitchhiker was gone. Had taken his pack and his sign and decamped.

Monette checked the backseat and saw his Wolfe & Sons cases undisturbed. Looked into the glove compartment and saw the paltry identification kept within — registration, insurance card, AAA card — was still there. All that was left of the bum was a lingering smell, not entirely unpleasant: sweat and faint pine, as if the guy had been sleeping rough.

He thought he'd see the guy at the foot of the ramp, holding up his sign and patiently switching it from side to side so that potential Good Samaritans got the complete lowdown on his defects. If so, Monette would stop and pick him up again. The job didn't feel done,

469

somehow. Delivering the guy to the Derry Shelter — that would make the job feel done. That would close the deal, and close the book. Whatever other failings he might have, he liked to finish things.

But the guy wasn't at the foot of the ramp; the guy was completely AWOL. And it wasn't until Monette was passing a sign reading DERRY 10 MI. that he looked up at the rear-view mirror and saw that his St. Christopher's medal, companion of all those millions of miles, was gone. The deaf-mute had stolen it. But not even that could break Monette's new optimism. Maybe the deaf-mute needed it more than he did. Monette hoped it would bring him good luck.

Two days later — by then he was selling the best fall list ever in Presque Isle — he got a call from the Maine State Police. His wife and Bob Yandowsky had been beaten to death in the Grove Motel. The killer had used a piece of pipe wrapped in a motel towel.

### -11-

"My . . . dear . . . *God!*" the priest breathed.

"Yes," Monette agreed, "that's pretty much what I thought."

"Your daughter . . . ?"

"Heartbroken, of course. She's with me, at home. We'll get through this, Father. She's tougher than I thought. And of course, she doesn't know about the other. The embezzlement. With luck, she never will. There's going to be a very large insurance payment, what they call double indemnity. Given everything that went on before, I think I would be in moderate to serious trouble with the police now if I didn't have a cast-iron alibi. And if there hadn't been . . . developments. As it is, I've been questioned several times."

"Son, you didn't pay someone to —"

"I've been asked that, too. The answer is no. I've thrown my bank accounts open to anyone who wants a look. Every penny is accounted for, both in my half of the wedded partnership and in Barb's. She was financially very responsible. At least in the sane part of her life.

"Father, can you open up on your side? I want to show you something."

Instead of replying, the priest opened his door. Monette slipped the St. Christopher's medal from around his neck, then reached around from his side. Their fingers touched briefly as the medal and its little pile of steel chain passed from hand to hand.

There was silence for five seconds as the priest considered it. Then he said, "This was returned to you when? Was it at the motel where —"

"No," Monette said. "Not the motel. The house in Buxton. On the dresser in what used to be our bedroom. Next to our wedding picture, actually."

"Dear God," the priest said.

"He could have gotten the address from my car registration when I was in the john."

"And of course you mentioned the name of the motel . . . and the town. . . ."

"Dowrie," Monette agreed.

For the third time the priest invoked the name of his Boss. Then he said, "The fellow wasn't deaf-mute at all, was he?"

"I'm almost positive he was mute," Monette said, "but he sure wasn't deaf. There was a note beside the medal, on a piece of paper he tore off the phone pad. All this must have happened while my daughter and I were at the funeral home, picking out a casket. The back door was open but not jimmied. He might have been smart enough to trig the lock, but I think I just forgot and left it open when we went out."

"The note said what?"

" 'Thank you for the ride,' " Monette said.

"I'll be damned." Thoughtful silence, then a soft knocking just outside the door of the confessional in which Monette sat, contemplating FOR ALL HAVE SINNED AND FALLEN SHORT OF GOD'S GLORY. Monette took back his medal.

"Have you told the police?"

"Yes, of course, the whole story. They think they know who the guy is. They're familiar with the sign. His name is Stanley Doucette.

He's spent years rambling around New England with that sign of his. Sort of like me, now that I think of it."

"Prior crimes of violence on his record?"

"A few," Monette said. "Fights, mostly. Once he beat a man pretty badly in a bar, and he's been in and out of mental institutions, including Serenity Hill, in Augusta. I don't think the police told me everything."

"Do you want to know everything?"

Monette considered, then said, "No."

"They haven't caught this fellow."

"They say it's only a matter of time. They say he's not bright. But he was bright enough to fool me."

"*Did* he fool you, son? Or did you know you were speaking to a listening ear? It seems to me that is the key question."

Monette was quiet for a long time. He didn't know if he had honestly searched his heart before, but he felt he was searching it now, and with a bright light. Not liking everything he found there but searching, yes. Not overlooking what he saw there. At least not on purpose.

"I did not," he said.

"And are you glad your wife and her lover are dead?"

In his heart, Monette instantly said *yes.* Aloud he said, "I'm relieved. I'm sorry to say that, Father, but considering the mess she made — and how it's apt to work out, with no trial and quiet restitution made out of the insurance money — I am relieved. Is that a sin?"

"Yes, my son. Sorry to break the news, but it is."

"Can you give me absolution?"

"Ten Our Fathers and ten Hail Marys," the priest said briskly. "The Our Fathers are for lack of charity — a serious sin but not mortal."

"And the Hail Marys?"

"Foul language in the confessional. At some point the adultery issue — yours, not hers — needs to be addressed, but now —"

"You have a lunch date. I understand."

"In truth, I've lost my appetite for lunch, although I should certainly greet my company. The main thing is, I think I'm a little too . . . too overwhelmed to go into your so-called road comfort just now."

"I understand."

"Good. Now son?"

"Yes?"

"Not to belabor the point, but are you *sure* you didn't give this man permission? Or encourage him in any way? Because then I think we'd be talking mortal sin instead of venial. I'd have to check with my own spiritual advisor to make sure, but —"

"No, Father. But do you think . . . is it possible that God put that guy in my car?"

In his heart, the priest instantly said *yes.*

474

Aloud he said, "That's blasphemy, good for ten more Our Fathers. I don't know how long you've been outside the doors, but even you should know better. Now do you want to say something else and try for more Hail Marys, or are we done here?"

"We're done, Father."

"Then you're shriven, as we say in the trade. Go your way and sin no more. And take care of your daughter, son. Children only have one mother, no matter how she may have behaved."

"Yes, Father."

Behind the screen, the form shifted. "Can I ask you one more question?"

Monette settled back, reluctantly. He wanted to be gone. "Yes."

"You say the police think they will catch this man."

"They tell me it's only a matter of time."

"My question is, do you *want* the police to catch this man?"

And because what he really wanted was to be gone and say his atonement in the even more private confessional of his car, Monette said, "Of course I do."

On his way back home, he added two extra Hail Marys and two extra Our Fathers.

# AYANA

I didn't think I would ever tell this story. My wife told me not to; she said no one would believe it and I'd only embarrass myself. What she meant, of course, was that it would embarrass her. "What about Ralph and Trudy?" I asked her. "They were there. They saw it, too."

"Trudy will tell him to keep his mouth shut," Ruth said, "and your brother won't need much persuading."

This was probably true. Ralph was at that time superintendent of New Hampshire School Administrative Unit 43, and the last thing a Department of Education bureaucrat from a small state wants is to wind up on one of the cable news outlets, in the end-of-the-hour slot reserved for UFOs over Phoenix and coyotes that can count to ten. Besides, a miracle story isn't much good without a miracle worker, and Ayana was gone.

But now my wife is dead — she had a heart attack while flying to Colorado to help out

477

with our first grandchild and died almost instantly. (Or so the airline people said, but you can't even trust them with your luggage these days.) My brother Ralph is also dead — a stroke while playing in a golden-ager golf tournament — and Trudy is gaga. My father is long gone; if he were still alive, he'd be a centenarian. I'm the last one standing, so I'll tell the story. It *is* unbelievable, Ruth was right about that, and it means nothing in any case — miracles never do, except to those lucky lunatics who see them everywhere. But it's interesting. And it *is* true. We all saw it.

My father was dying of pancreatic cancer. I think you can tell a lot about people by listening to how they speak about that sort of situation (and the fact that I describe cancer as "that sort of situation" probably tells you something about your narrator, who spent his life teaching English to boys and girls whose most serious health problems were acne and sports injuries).

Ralph said, "He's nearly finished his journey."

My sister-in-law Trudy said, "He's rife with it." At first I thought she said "He's ripe with it," which struck me as jarringly poetic. I knew it couldn't be right, not from her, but I wanted it to be right.

Ruth said, "He's down for the count."

I didn't say, "And may he stay down," but I

thought it. Because he suffered. This was twenty-five years ago — 1982 — and suffering was still an accepted part of end-stage cancer. I remember reading ten or twelve years later that most cancer patients go out silently only because they're too weak to scream. That brought back memories of my father's sickroom so strong that I went into the bathroom and knelt in front of the toilet bowl, sure I was going to vomit.

But my father actually died four years later, in 1986. He was in assisted living then, and it wasn't pancreatic cancer that got him, after all. He choked to death on a piece of steak.

Don "Doc" Gentry and his wife, Bernadette — my mother and father — retired to a suburban home in Ford City, not too far from Pittsburgh. After his wife died, Doc considered moving to Florida, decided he couldn't afford it, and stayed in Pennsylvania. When his cancer was diagnosed, he spent a brief time in the hospital, where he explained again and again that his nickname came from his years as a veterinarian. After he'd explained this to anyone who cared, they sent him home to die, and such family as he had left — Ralph, Trudy, Ruth, and me — came to Ford City to see him out.

I remember his back bedroom very well. On the wall was a picture of Christ suffering the little children to come unto him. On the floor was a rag rug my mother had made: shades of nauseous green, not one of her better ones. Beside the bed was an IV pole with a Pittsburgh Pirates decal on it. Each day I approached that room with increasing dread, and each day the hours I spent there stretched longer. I remembered Doc sitting on the porch glider when we were growing up in Derby, Connecticut — a can of beer in one hand, a cig in the other, the sleeves of a blinding white T-shirt always turned up twice to reveal the smooth curve of his biceps and the rose tattoo just above his left elbow. He was of a generation that did not feel strange going about in dark blue unfaded jeans — and who called jeans "dungarees." He combed his hair like Elvis and had a slightly dangerous look, like a sailor two drinks into a shore leave that will end badly. He was a tall man who walked like a cat. And I remember a summer street dance in Derby where he and my mother stopped the show, jitterbugging to "Rocket 88" by Ike Turner and the Kings of Rhythm. Ralph was sixteen then, I think, and I was eleven. We watched our parents with our mouths open, and for the first time I understood that they did it at night, did it with all their clothes off and never thought of us.

At eighty, turned loose from the hospital, my somehow dangerously graceful father had become just another skeleton in pajamas (his had the Pirates logo on them). His eyes lurked beneath wild and bushy brows. He sweated steadily in spite of two fans, and the smell that rose from his damp skin reminded me of old wallpaper in a deserted house. His breath was black with the perfume of decomposition.

Ralph and I were a long way from rich, but when we put a little of our money together with the remains of Doc's own savings, we had enough to hire a part-time private nurse and a housekeeper who came in five days a week. They did well at keeping the old man clean and changed, but by the day my sister-in-law said that Doc was ripe with it (I still prefer to think that was what she said), the Battle of the Smells was almost over. That scarred old pro shit was rounds ahead of the newcomer Johnson's baby powder; soon, I thought, the ref would stop the fight. Doc was no longer able to get to the toilet (which he invariably called "the can"), so he wore diapers and continence pants. He was still aware enough to know, and to be ashamed. Sometimes tears rolled from the corners of his eyes, and half-formed cries of desperate, disgusted amusement came from the throat that had once sent "Hey, Good Lookin' " out into the world.

The pain settled in, first in the midsection and then radiating outward until he would complain that even his eyelids and fingertips hurt. The painkillers stopped working. The nurse could have given him more, but that might have killed him and she refused. I wanted to give him more even if it did kill him. And I might have, with support from Ruth, but my wife wasn't the sort to provide that kind of prop.

"She'll know," Ruth said, meaning the nurse, "and then you'll be in trouble."

"He's my dad!"

"That won't stop her." Ruth had always been a glass-half-empty person. It wasn't the way she was raised; it was the way she was born. "She'll report it. You might go to jail."

So I didn't kill him. None of us killed him. What we did was mark time. We read to him, not knowing how much he understood. We changed him and kept the medication chart on the wall updated. The days were viciously hot and we periodically changed the location of the two fans, hoping to create a cross draft. We watched the Pirates games on a little color TV that made the grass look purple, and we told him that the Pirates looked great this year. We talked to each other above his ever-sharpening profile. We watched him suffer and waited for him to die. And one day while he was sleeping and rattling snores, I looked up from *Best American Poets of the Twentieth Century* and saw a tall, heavyset black woman and a black girl in dark glasses standing at the bedroom door.

That girl — I remember her as if it were this morning. I think she might have been seven, although extremely small for her age. Tiny, really. She was wearing a pink dress that stopped above her knobby knees. There was a Band-Aid printed with Warner Bros. cartoon characters on one equally knobby shin; I remember Yosemite Sam, with his long red mustache and a pistol in each hand. The dark glasses looked like a yard-sale consolation prize. They were far too big and had slid down to the end of the kid's snub nose, revealing eyes that were fixed, heavy-lidded, sheathed in blue-white film. Her hair was in cornrows. Over one arm was a pink plastic child's purse split down the side. On her feet were dirty sneakers. Her skin wasn't really black at all but a soapy gray. She was on her feet, but otherwise looked almost as sick as my father.

The woman I remember less clearly, because the child so drew my attention. The woman could have been forty or sixty. She had a close-cropped afro and a serene aspect. Beyond that, I recall nothing — not even the color of her dress, if she was wearing a dress. I think she was, but it might have been slacks.

"Who are you?" I asked. I sounded stupid, as if awakened from a doze rather than reading — although there is a similarity.

Trudy appeared from behind them and said the same thing. She sounded wide awake.

And from behind her, Ruth said in an oh-for-Pete's-sake voice: "The door must have come open, it won't ever stay on the latch. They must have walked right in."

Ralph, standing beside Trudy, looked back over his shoulder. "It's shut now. They must have closed it behind them." As if that were a mark in their favor.

"You can't come in here," Trudy told the woman. "We're busy. There's sickness here. I don't know what you want, but you have to go."

"You can't just walk into a place, you know," Ralph added. The three of them were crowded together in the sickroom doorway.

Ruth tapped the woman on the shoulder, and not gently. "Unless you want us to call the police, you have to go. Do you want us to do that?"

The woman took no notice. She pushed the little girl forward and said, "Straight on. Four steps. There's a poley thing, mind you don't trip. Let me hear you count."

The little girl counted like this: "One . . . two . . . free . . . four." She stepped over the metal feet of the IV pole on *free* without ever looking down — surely not looking at anything through the smeary lenses of her too-big yard-sale glasses. Not with those milky eyes. She passed close enough to me for the skirt of her dress to draw across my forearm like a thought. She smelled dirty and sweaty and — like Doc — sick. There were dark marks on both of her arms, not scabs but sores.

"Stop her!" my brother said to me, but I didn't. All this happened very quickly. The little girl bent over the stubbly hollow of my father's cheek and kissed it. A big kiss, not a little one. A smacky kiss.

Her little plastic purse swung lightly against the side of his head as she did it and my father opened his eyes. Later, both Trudy and Ruth said it was getting whacked with the purse that woke him. Ralph was less sure, and I didn't believe it at all. It didn't make a sound when it struck, not even a little one. There was nothing in that purse except maybe a Kleenex.

"Who are you, kiddo?" my father asked in his raspy fixing-to-die voice.

"Ayana," the child said.

"I'm Doc." He looked up at her from those dark caves where he now lived, but with more comprehension than I'd seen in the two weeks we'd been in Ford City. He'd reached a point where not even a ninth-inning walk-off home run could do much to crack his deepening glaze.

Trudy pushed past the woman and started to push past me, meaning to grab the child who had suddenly thrust herself into Doc's dying regard. I grabbed her wrist and stopped her. "Wait."

"What do you mean, wait? They're trespassers!"

"I'm sick, I have to go," the little girl said. Then she kissed him again and stepped back. This time she tripped over the feet of the IV pole, almost upending it and herself. Trudy grabbed the pole and I grabbed the child. There was nothing to her, only skin wrapped on a complex armature of bone. Her glasses fell off into my lap, and for a moment those milky eyes looked into mine.

"You be all right," Ayana said, and touched my mouth with her tiny palm. It burned me like an ember, but I didn't pull away. "You be all right."

"Ayana, come," the woman said. "We ought to leave these folks. Two steps. Let me hear you count."

"One . . . two," Ayana said, putting her glasses on and then poking them up her nose, where they would not stay for long. The woman took her hand.

"You folks have a blessed day, now," she said, and looked at me. "I'm sorry for you," she said, "but this child's dreams are over."

They walked back across the living room, the woman holding the girl's hand. Ralph trailed after them like a sheepdog, I think to make sure neither of them stole anything. Ruth and Trudy were bent over Doc, whose eyes were still open.

"Who was that child?" he asked.

"I don't know, Dad," Trudy said. "Don't let it concern you."

"I want her to come back," he said. "I want another kiss."

Ruth turned to me, her lips sucked into her mouth. This was an unlovely expression she had perfected over the years. "She pulled his IV line halfway out . . . he's bleeding . . . and you just sat there."

"I'll put it back," I said, and someone else seemed to be speaking. Inside myself was a man standing off to one side, silent and stunned. I could still feel the warm pressure of her palm on my mouth.

"Oh, don't bother! I already did."

Ralph came back. "They're gone," he said. "Walking down the street toward the bus stop." He turned to my wife. "Do you really want me to call the police, Ruth?"

"No. We'd just be all day filling out forms and answering questions." She paused. "We might even have to testify in court."

"Testify to what?" Ralph asked.

"I don't know what, how should I know what? Will one of you get the adhesive tape so we can keep this christing needle still? It's on the kitchen counter, I think."

"I want another kiss," my father said.

"I'll go," I said, but first I went to the front door — which Ralph had locked as well as closed — and looked out. The little green plastic bus shelter was only a block down, but no one was standing by the pole or under the shelter's plastic roof. And the sidewalk was empty. Ayana and the woman — whether mother or minder — were gone. All I had was the kid's touch on my mouth, still warm but starting to fade.

Now comes the miracle part. I'm not going to skimp it — if I'm going to tell this story, I'll try to tell it right — but I'm not going to dwell on it either. Miracle stories are always satisfying but rarely interesting, because they're all the same.

We were staying at one of the motels on Ford City's main road, a Ramada Inn with thin walls. Ralph annoyed my wife by calling it the Rammit Inn. "If you keep doing that, you'll eventually forget and say it in front of a stranger," my wife said. "Then you'll have a red face."

The walls were so thin that it was possible for us to hear Ralph and Trudy arguing next door about how long they could afford to stay. "He's my father," Ralph said, to which Trudy replied: "Try telling that to Connecticut Light and Power when the bill comes due. Or the state commissioner when your sick days run out."

It was a little past seven on a hot August evening. Soon Ralph would be leaving for my father's, where the part-time nurse was on duty until eight p.m. I found the Pirates on

TV and jacked the volume to drown out the depressing and predictable argument going on next door. Ruth was folding clothes and telling me the next time I bought cheap discount-store underwear, she was going to divorce me. Or shoot me for a stranger. The phone rang. It was Nurse Chloe. (This was what she called herself, as in "Drink a little more of this soup for Nurse Chloe.")

She wasted no time on pleasantries. "I think you should come right away," she said. "Not just Ralph for the night shift. All of you."

"Is he going?" I asked. Ruth stopped folding things and came over. She put a hand on my shoulder. We had been expecting this — hoping for it, really — but now that it was here, it was too absurd to hurt. Doc had taught me how to use a Bolo-Bouncer when I was a kid no older than that day's little blind intruder. He had caught me smoking under the grape arbor and had told me — not angrily but kindly — that it was a stupid habit, and I'd do well not to let it get a hold on me. The idea that he might not be alive when tomorrow's paper came? Absurd.

"I don't think so," Nurse Chloe said. "He seems better." She paused. "I've never seen anything like it in my life."

He was better. When we got there fifteen minutes later, he was sitting on the living-room sofa and watching the Pirates on the

489

house's larger TV — no technological marvel, but at least colorfast. He was sipping a protein shake through a straw. He had some color. His cheeks seemed plumper, perhaps because he was freshly shaved. He had regained himself. That was what I thought then; the impression has only grown stronger with the passage of time. And one other thing, which we all agreed on — even the doubting Thomasina to whom I was married: the yellow smell that had hung around him like ether ever since the doctors sent him home to die was gone.

He greeted us all by name, and told us that Willie Stargell had just hit a home run for the Buckos. Ralph and I looked at each other, as if to confirm we were actually there. Trudy sat on the couch beside Doc, only it was more of a whoomping down. Ruth went into the kitchen and got herself a beer. A miracle in itself.

"I wouldn't mind one of those, Ruthie-doo," my father said, and then — probably misinterpreting my slack and flabbergasted face for an expression of disapproval: "I feel better. Gut hardly hurts at all."

"No beer for you, I think," Nurse Chloe said. She was sitting in an easy chair across the room and showed no sign of gathering her things, a ritual that usually began twenty minutes before the end of her shift. Her annoying do-it-for-mommy authority seemed to have grown thin.

"When did this start?" I asked, not even sure what I meant by *this,* because the changes for the better seemed so general. But if I had any specific thing in mind, I suppose it was the departure of the smell.

"He was getting better when we left this afternoon," Trudy said. "I just didn't believe it."

"Bolsheveky," Ruth said. It was as close as she allowed herself to cursing.

Trudy paid no attention. "It was that little girl," she said.

"Bolsheveky!" Ruth cried.

"What little girl?" my father asked. It was between innings. On the television, a fellow with no hair, big teeth, and mad eyes was telling us the carpets at Juker's were so cheap they were almost free. And, dear God, no finance charges on layaway. Before any of us could reply to Ruth, Doc asked Nurse Chloe if he could have *half* a beer. She refused him. But Nurse Chloe's days of authority in that little house were almost over, and during the next four years — before a chunk of half-chewed meat stopped his throat forever — my father drank a great many beers. And enjoyed every one, I hope. Beer is a miracle in itself.

It was that night, while lying sleepless in our hard Rammit Inn bed and listening to the air conditioner rattle, that Ruth told me to keep my mouth shut about the blind girl, whom she called not Ayana but "the magic negro child," speaking in a tone of ugly sarcasm that was very unlike her.

"Besides," she said, "it won't last. Sometimes a light bulb will brighten up just before it burns out for good. I'm sure that happens to people too."

Maybe, but Doc Gentry's miracle took. By the end of the week he was walking in his backyard with me or Ralph supporting him. After that, we all went home. I got a call from Nurse Chloe on our first night back.

"We're not going, no matter how sick he is," Ruth said half-hysterically. "Tell her that."

But Nurse Chloe only wanted to say that she'd happened to see Doc coming out of the Ford City Veterinary Clinic, where he had gone to consult with the young head of practice about a horse with the staggers. He had his cane, she said, but wasn't using it. Nurse Chloe said she'd never seen a man "of his years" who looked any better. "Bright-eyed and ring-tailed," she said. "I still don't believe it." A month later he was walking (caneless) around the block, and that winter he was swimming every day at the local Y. He looked like a man of sixty-five. Everyone said so.

I talked to my father's entire medical team in

the wake of his recovery. I did it because what had happened to him reminded me of the so-called miracle plays that were big in the sticksville burgs of Europe in medieval times. I told myself if I changed Dad's name (or perhaps just called him Mr. G.) it could make an interesting article for some journal or other. It might have even been true — sort of — but I never did write the article.

It was Stan Sloan, Doc's family practice guy, who first raised the red flag. He had sent Doc to the University of Pittsburgh Cancer Institute and so was able to blame the consequent misdiagnosis on Drs. Retif and Zamachowski, who were my dad's oncologists there. They in turn blamed the radiologists for sloppy imaging. Retif said the chief of radiology was an incompetent who didn't know a pancreas from a liver. He asked not to be quoted, but after twenty-five years, I am assuming the statute of limitations on that one has run out.

Dr. Zamachowski said it was a simple case of organ malformation. "I was never comfortable with the original diagnosis," he confided. I talked to Retif on the phone, Zamachowski in person. He was wearing a white lab coat with a red T-shirt beneath that appeared to read I'D RATHER BE GOLFING. "I always thought it was Von Hippel-Lindau."

"Wouldn't that also have killed him?" I asked.

Zamachowski gave me the mysterious smile doctors reserve for clueless plumbers, housewives, and English teachers. Then he said he was late for an appointment.

When I talked to the chief of radiology, he spread his hands. "Here we are responsible for photography, not interpretation," he said. "In another ten years, we will be using equipment that will make such misinterpretations as this one all but impossible. In the meantime, why not just be glad your pop is alive? Enjoy him."

I did my best on that score. And during my brief investigation, which I of course called research, I learned an interesting thing: the medical definition of *miracle* is misdiagnosis.

Nineteen eighty-three was my sabbatical year. I had a contract with a scholarly press for a book called *Teaching the Unteachable: Strategies for Creative Writing,* but like my miracle-play article it never got written. In July, while Ruth and I were making plans for a camping trip, my urine abruptly turned pink. The pain came after that, first deep in my left buttock, then growing stronger as it migrated to my groin. By the time I started to piss actual blood — this was I think four days after the first twinges, and while I was still playing that famous game known the world over as Maybe It Will Go Away on Its Own — the pain had passed from serious into the realm of excruciating.

"I'm sure it's not cancer," Ruth said, which coming from her meant she was sure it was. The look in her eyes was even more alarming. She would deny this on her deathbed — her practicality was her pride — but I'm sure it occurred to her just then that the cancer that had left my father had battened on me.

It wasn't cancer. It was kidney stones. My miracle was called extracorporeal shock wave lithotripsy, which — in tandem with diuretic pills — dissolved them. I told my doctor I had never felt such pain in my life.

"I should think you never will again, even if you suffer a coronary," he said. "Women who've had stones compare the pain to that of childbirth. Difficult childbirth."

I was still in considerable pain but able to read a magazine while waiting for my follow-up doctor's appointment, and I considered this a great improvement. Someone sat down beside me and said, "Come on now, it's time."

I looked up. It wasn't the woman who had come into my father's sickroom; it was a man in a perfectly ordinary brown business suit. Nevertheless, I knew why he was there. It was never even a question. I also felt sure that if I didn't go with him, all the lithotripsy in the world would not help me.

We went out. The receptionist was away from her desk, so I didn't have to explain my sudden decampment. I'm not sure what I would have said, anyway. That my groin had suddenly stopped smoldering? That was absurd as well as untrue.

The man in the business suit looked a fit thirty-five: an ex-marine, maybe, who hadn't been able to part with the bristly gung-ho haircut. He didn't talk. We cut around the medical center where my doctor keeps his practice, then made our way down the block to Groves of Healing Hospital, me walking slightly bent over because of the pain, which no longer snarled but still glowered.

We went up to pedes and made our way down a corridor with Disney murals on the walls and "It's a Small World" drifting down from the overhead speakers. The ex-marine walked briskly, with his head up, as if he belonged there. I didn't, and I knew it. I had never felt so far from my home and the life I understood. If I had floated up to the ceiling like a child's Mylar GET WELL SOON balloon, I wouldn't have been surprised.

At the central nurses' station, the ex-marine squeezed my arm to make me stop until the two nurses there — one male, one female — were occupied. Then we crossed into another hall where a bald girl sitting in a wheelchair looked at us with starving eyes. She held out one hand.

"No," the ex-marine said, and simply led me on. But not before I got another look into those bright, dying eyes.

He took us into a room where a boy of about three was playing with blocks in a clear plastic tent that belled down over his bed. The boy stared at us with lively interest. He looked much healthier than the girl in the wheelchair — he had a full shock of red curls — but his skin was the color of lead, and when the ex-marine pushed me forward and then fell back into a position like parade rest, I sensed the kid was very ill indeed. When I unzipped the tent, taking no notice of the sign on the wall reading THIS IS A STERILE ENVIRONMENT, I thought his remaining time could have been measured in days rather than weeks.

I reached for him, registering my father's sick smell. The odor was a little lighter, but essentially the same. The kid lifted his own arms without reservation. When I kissed him on the corner of the mouth, he kissed back with a longing eagerness that suggested he hadn't been touched in a long time. At least not by something that didn't hurt.

No one came in to ask us what we were doing, or to threaten the police, as Ruth had that day in my father's sickroom. I zipped up the tent again. In the doorway I looked back and saw him sitting in his clear plastic tent with a block in his hands. He dropped it and waved to me — a child's wigwag, fingers opening and closing twice. I waved back the same way. He looked better already.

Once more the ex-marine squeezed my arm at the nurses' station, but this time we were spotted by the male nurse, a man with the kind of disapproving smile the head of my English department had raised to the level of art. He asked what we were doing there.

"Sorry, mate, wrong floor," the ex-marine said.

On the hospital steps a few minutes later, he said, "You can find your own way back, can't you?"

"Sure," I said, "but I'll have to make another appointment with my doctor."

"Yes, I suppose you will."

"Will I see you again?"

"Yes," he said, and walked off toward the hospital parking lot. He didn't look back.

He came again in 1987, while Ruth was at the market and I was cutting the grass and hoping the sick thud in the back of my head wasn't the beginning of a migraine but knowing it was. Since the little boy in Groves of Healing, I had been subject to them. But it was hardly ever him I thought of when I lay in the dark with a damp rag over my eyes. I thought of the little girl.

That time we went to see a woman at St. Jude's. When I kissed her, she put my hand on her left breast. It was the only one she had; the doctors had already taken the other.

"I love you, mister," she said, crying. I didn't know what to say. The ex-marine stood in the doorway, legs apart, hands behind his back. Parade rest.

Years passed before he came again: mid-December of 1997. That was the last time. By then my problem was arthritis, and it still is. The bristles standing up from the ex-marine's block of a head had gone mostly gray, and lines so deep they made him look a little like a ventriloquist's dummy had carved down from the corners of his lips. He took me out to an I-95 exit ramp north of town, where there had been a wreck. A panel truck had collided with a Ford Escort. The Escort was pretty well trashed. The paramedics had strapped the driver, a middle-aged man, to a stretcher. The cops were talking to the uniformed panel truck driver, who appeared shaken but unhurt.

The paramedics slammed the doors of the ambulance, and the ex-marine said, "Now. Shag your ass."

I shagged my elderly ass to the rear of the ambulance. The ex-marine hustled forward, pointing. "Yo! Yo! Is that one of those medical bracelets?"

The paramedics turned to look; one of them, and one of the cops who had been talking to the panel truck driver, went to where the ex-marine was pointing. I opened the rear door of the ambulance and crawled up to the

Escort driver's head. At the same time I clutched my father's pocket watch, which I had carried since he gave it to me as a wedding present. Its delicate gold chain was attached to one of my belt loops. There was no time to be gentle; I tore it free.

The man on the stretcher stared up at me from the gloom, his broken neck bulging in a shiny skin-covered doorknob at the nape. "I can't move my fucking toes," he said.

I kissed him on the corner of the mouth (it was my special place, I guess) and was backing out when one of the paramedics grabbed me. "What in the hell do you think you're doing?" he asked.

I pointed to the watch, which now lay beside the stretcher. "That was in the grass. I thought he'd want it." By the time the Escort driver was able to tell someone that it wasn't his watch and the initials engraved on the inside of the lid meant nothing to him, we would be gone. "Did you get his medical bracelet?"

The paramedic looked disgusted. "It was just a piece of chrome," he said. "Get out of here." Then, not quite grudgingly: "Thanks. You could have kept that."

It was true. I loved that watch. But . . . spur of the moment. It was all I had.

"You've got blood on the back of your hand," the ex-marine said as we drove back to my house. We were in his car, a nondescript Chevrolet sedan. There was a dog leash lying on the backseat and a St. Christopher's medal hanging from the rearview mirror on a silver chain. "You ought to wash it off when you get home."

I said I would.

"You won't be seeing me again," he said.

I thought of what the black woman had said about Ayana then. I hadn't thought of it in years. "Are my dreams over?" I asked.

He looked puzzled, then shrugged. "Your work is," he said. "I sure don't know anything about your dreams."

I asked him three more questions before he dropped me off for the last time and disappeared from my life. I didn't expect him to answer them, but he did.

"Those people I kiss — do they go on to other people? Kiss their boo-boos and make them all gone?"

"Some do," he said. "That's how it works. Others can't." He shrugged. "Or won't." He shrugged again. "It comes to the same."

"Do you know a little girl named Ayana? Although I suppose she'd be a big girl now."

"She's dead."

My heart dropped, but not too far. I suppose I had known. I thought again of the little girl in the wheelchair.

"She kissed my father," I said. "She only touched me. So why was I the one?"

"Because you were," he said, and pulled into my driveway. "Here we are."

An idea occurred to me. It seemed like a good one, God knows why. "Come for Christmas," I said. "Come for Christmas dinner. We have plenty. I'll tell Ruth you're my cousin from New Mexico." Because I had never told her about the ex-marine. Knowing about my father was enough for her. Too much, really.

The ex-marine smiled. That might not have been the only time I saw it, but it's the only time I remember. "Think I'll give it a miss, mate. Although I thank you. I don't celebrate Christmas. I'm an atheist."

That's really it, I guess — except for kissing Trudy. I told you she went gaga, remember? Alzheimer's. Ralph made good investments that left her well-off, and the kids saw that she went to a nice place when she was no longer okay to live at home. Ruth and I went to see her together until Ruth had her heart attack on the approach into Denver International. I went to see Trudy on my own not long after that, because I was lonely and sad and wanted some connection with the old days. But seeing Trudy as she had become, looking out the window instead of at me, munching at her lower lip while clear spit grizzled from the corners of her mouth, only made me feel worse. Like going back to your hometown to look at the house you grew up in and discovering a vacant lot.

I kissed the corner of her mouth before I left, but of course nothing happened. A miracle is no good without a miracle worker, and my miracle days are behind me now. Except late at night when I can't sleep. Then I can come downstairs and watch almost any movie I want. Even skin flicks. I have a satellite dish, you see, and something called Global Movies. I could even get the Pirates, if I wanted to order the MLB package. But I live on a fixed income these days, and while I'm comfortable, I also have to keep an eye on my discretionary spending. I can read about the Pirates on the Internet. All those movies are miracle enough for me.

# A Very Tight Place

Curtis Johnson rode his bike five miles every morning. He had stopped for a while after Betsy died, but found that without his morning exercise he was sadder than ever. So he took it up again. The only difference was that he stopped wearing his bike helmet. He rode two and a half miles down Gulf Boulevard, then turned around and rode back. He always kept to the bike lanes. He might not care if he lived or died, but he respected the rule of law.

Gulf Boulevard was the only road on Turtle Island. It ran past a lot of homes owned by millionaires. Curtis didn't notice them. For one thing, he was a millionaire himself. He had made his money the old-fashioned way, in the stock market. For another, he had no problem with any of the people living in the houses he passed. The only one he had a problem with was Tim Grunwald, alias The Motherfucker, and Grunwald lived in the other direction. Not the last lot on Turtle

Island before Daylight Channel, but the second-to-last. It was the last lot that was the problem between them (*one* of the problems). That lot was the biggest, with the best view of the Gulf, and the only one without a house on it. The only things on it were scrub grass, sea oats, stunted palms, and a few Australian pines.

The nicest thing, the very nicest, about his morning rides was no phone. He was officially off the grid. Once he got back, the phone would seldom leave his hand, especially while the market was open. He was athletic; he would stride around the house using the cordless, occasionally returning to his office, where his computer would be scrolling the numbers. Sometimes he left the house to walk out to the road, and then he took his cell phone. Usually he would turn right, toward the stub end of Gulf Boulevard. Toward The Motherfucker's house. But he wouldn't go so far that Grunwald could see him; Curtis wouldn't give the man that satisfaction. He just went far enough to make sure Grunwald wasn't trying to pull a fast one with the Vinton Lot. Of course there was no way The Motherfucker could get heavy machinery past him, not even at night — Curtis slept lightly since there was no Betsy lying beside him. But he still checked, usually standing behind the last palm in a shady stretch of two dozen. Just to be sure. Because destroying empty lots, burying them under tons of concrete, was Grunwald's goddam *business.*

And The Motherfucker was sly.

So far, though, all was well. If Grunwald *did* try to pull a fast one, Curtis was ready to empty the holes (legally speaking). Meanwhile, Grunwald had Betsy to answer for, and answer he would. Even if Curtis had largely lost his taste for the fray (he denied this to himself, but knew it was true), he would see that Grunwald answered for her. The Motherfucker would discover that Curtis Johnson had jaws of chrome . . . jaws of *chrome steel* . . . and when he took hold of a thing, he did not let go.

When he returned to his home on this particular Tuesday morning, with ten minutes still to go before the opening bell on Wall Street, Curtis checked his cell phone for messages, as he always did. Today there were two. One was from Circuit City, probably some salesman trying to sell him something under the guise of checking his satisfaction with the wall-hung flatscreen he'd purchased the month before.

When he scrolled down to the next message, he read this: *383-0910 TMF.*

The Motherfucker. Even his Nokia knew who Grunwald was, because Curtis had taught it to remember. The question was, what did The Motherfucker want with him on a Tuesday morning in June?

Maybe to settle, and on Curtis's terms.

He allowed himself a laugh at this idea, then played the message. He was stunned to hear that was exactly what Grunwald *did* want — or *appeared* to want. Curtis supposed it could be some sort of ploy, but he didn't understand what Grunwald stood to gain by such a thing. And then there was the tone: heavy, deliberate, almost plodding. Maybe it wasn't sorrow, but it surely *sounded* like sorrow. It was the way Curtis himself sounded all too often on the phone these days, as he tried to get his head back in the game.

"Johnson . . . Curtis," Grunwald said in his plodding voice. His recorded voice paused longer, as if debating the use of Curtis's given name, then moved on in the same dead and lightless way. "I can't fight a war on two fronts. Let's end this. I've lost my taste for it. If I ever had a taste for it. I'm in a very tight place, neighbor."

He sighed.

"I'm prepared to give up the lot, and for no financial consideration. I'll also compensate you for your . . . for Betsy. If you're interested, you can find me at Durkin Grove Village. I'll be there most of the day." A long pause. "I go out there a lot now. In a way I still can't believe the financing fell apart, and in a way I'm not surprised at all." Another long pause.

"Maybe you know what I mean."

Curtis thought he did. He seemed to have lost his nose for the market. More to the point, he didn't seem to care. He caught himself feeling something suspiciously like sympathy for The Motherfucker. That plodding voice.

"We used to be friends," Grunwald went on. "Do you remember that? I do. I don't think we can be friends again — things went too far for that, I guess — but maybe we could be neighbors again. Neighbor." Another of those pauses. "If I don't see you out at Grunwald's Folly, I'll just instruct my lawyer to settle. On your terms. But . . ."

Silence, except for the sound of The Motherfucker breathing. Curtis waited. He was sitting at the kitchen table now. He didn't know what he felt. In a little while he might, but for the time being, no.

"But I'd like to shake your hand and tell you I'm sorry about your damn dog." There was a choked sound that might have been — incredible! — the sound of a sob, and then a click, followed by the phone-robot telling him there were no more messages.

Curtis sat where he was for a moment longer, in a bright bar of Florida sun that the air conditioner couldn't quite cool out, not even at this hour. Then he went into his study. The market was open; on his computer screen, the numbers had begun their endless crawl. He realized they meant nothing to him. He left it running but wrote a brief note for Mrs. Wilson — *Had to go out* — before leaving the house.

There was a motor scooter parked in the garage beside his BMW, and on the spur of the moment he decided to take it. He would have to nip across the main highway on the other side of the bridge, but it wouldn't be the first time.

He felt a pang of hurt and grief as he took the scooter's key from the peg and the other attachment on the ring jingled. He supposed that feeling would pass in time, but now it was almost welcome. Almost like welcoming a friend.

The troubles between Curtis and Tim Grunwald had started with Ricky Vinton, who had once been old and rich and then progressed to old and senile. Before progressing to dead, he'd sold his undeveloped lot at the end of Turtle Island to Curtis Johnson for one-point-five million dollars, taking Curtis's personal check for a hundred and fifty thousand as earnest money and in return writing Curtis a bill of sale on the back of an advertising circular.

Curtis felt a little like a hound for taking advantage of the old fellow, but it wasn't as if Vinton — owner of Vinton Wire and Cable — was going away to starve. And while a million-five might be considered ridiculously low for such a prime piece of Gulfside real estate, it wasn't *insanely* low, given current market conditions.

Well . . . yes it was, but he and the old man had liked one another, and Curtis was one of those who believed all was fair in love and war, and that business was a subsidiary of the latter. The man's housekeeper — the same Mrs. Wilson who kept house for Curtis — witnessed the signatures. In retrospect Curtis realized he should have known better than that, but he was excited.

A month or so after selling the undeveloped lot to Curtis Johnson, Vinton sold it to Tim Grunwald, alias The Motherfucker. This time the price was a more lucid five-point-six million, and this time Vinton — perhaps not such a fool after all, perhaps actually sort of a con man, even if he was dying — got half a million in earnest money.

Grunwald's bill of sale had been witnessed by The Motherfucker's yardman (who also happened to be Vinton's yardman). Also pretty shaky, but Curtis supposed Grunwald had been as excited as he, Curtis, had been. Only Curtis's excitement proceeded from the idea that he would be able to keep the end of Turtle Island clean, pristine, and quiet. Exactly the way he liked it.

Grunwald, on the other hand, saw it as the perfect site for development: one condominium or perhaps even two (when Curtis thought of two, he thought of them as The Motherfucker Twin Towers). Curtis had seen such developments before — in Florida they popped up like dandelions on an indifferently maintained lawn — and he knew what The Motherfucker would be inviting in: idiots who mistook retirement funds for the keys to the kingdom of heaven. There would be four years of construction, followed by decades of old men on bicycles with pee bags strapped to their scrawny thighs. And old women who wore sun visors, smoked Parliaments, and didn't pick up the droppings after their designer dogs shat on the beach. Plus, of course, ice cream–slathered grandbrats with names like Lindsay and Jayson. If he let it happen, Curtis knew, he would die with their howls of discontent — *"You said we'd go to Disney World today!"* — in his ears.

He would not let it happen. And it turned out to be easy. Not pleasant, and the lot didn't belong to him, might *never* belong to him, but at least it wasn't Grunwald's. It didn't even belong to the relatives who had appeared (like roaches in a Dumpster when a bright light is suddenly turned on), disputing the signatures of the witnesses on both agreements. It belonged to the lawyers and the courts.

Which was like saying it belonged to nobody.

Curtis could work with nobody.

The wrangling had gone on for two years now, and Curtis's legal fees were approaching a quarter of a million dollars. He tried to think of the money as a contribution to some particularly nice environmental group — Johnsonpeace instead of Greenpeace — but of course he couldn't deduct *these* contributions on his income tax. And Grunwald pissed him off. Grunwald made it personal, partly because he hated to lose (Curtis hated it, too, in those days; not so much now), and partly because he had personal problems.

Grunwald's wife had divorced him; that was Personal Problem Number One. She was Mrs. Motherfucker no more. Then, Personal Problem Number Two, Grunwald had needed some sort of operation. Curtis didn't know for sure it was cancer, he only knew that The Motherfucker came out of Sarasota Memorial twenty or thirty pounds lighter, and in a wheelchair. He had eventually discarded the wheelchair, but hadn't been able to put the weight back on. Wattles hung from his formerly firm neck.

There were also problems with his once fearsomely healthy company. Curtis had seen that for himself at the site of The Motherfucker's current scorched-earth campaign. That would be Durkin Grove Village, located on the mainland twenty miles east of Turtle Island. The place was a half-constructed

513

ghost town. Curtis had parked on a knoll overlooking the silent suspension, feeling like a general surveying the ruins of an enemy encampment. Feeling that life was, all in all, his very own shiny red apple.

Betsy had changed everything. She was — had been — a Lowchen, elderly but still spry. When Curtis walked her on the beach, she always carried her little red rubber bone in her mouth. When Curtis wanted the TV remote, he only had to say "Fetch the idiot stick, Betsy," and she would pluck it from the coffee table and bring it to him in her mouth. It was her pride. And his, of course. She had been his best friend for seventeen years. The French lion-dogs usually lived to no more than fifteen.

Then Grunwald had put in an electric fence between his property and Curtis's.

That Motherfucker.

It wasn't especially high voltage, Grunwald said he could prove that and Curtis believed him, but it had been of a voltage high enough to do for a slightly overweight old dog with a bad heart. And why an electric fence in the first place? The Motherfucker had spouted a lot of bullshit having to do with discouraging potential home-breakers — presumably creeping from Curtis's property to that upon which *La Maison Motherfuckair* reared its purple stucco head — but Curtis didn't believe it. Dedicated home-breakers would come in a boat, from the Gulf side. What he believed was that Grunwald, disgruntled about the Vinton Lot, had put in the electric fence for the express purpose of annoying Curtis Johnson. And perhaps hurting his beloved dog. As for actually *killing* his beloved dog? Curtis believed that had been a bonus.

He was not a weeping man, but he had wept when, prior to her cremation, he had removed Betsy's dog tag from her collar.

Curtis sued The Motherfucker for the price of the dog — twelve hundred dollars. If he could have sued for ten million — that was roughly how much pain he felt when he looked at the idiot stick lying, innocent of dogspit now and forever, on the coffee table — he would have done so in a heartbeat, but his lawyer told him that pain and suffering wouldn't fly in a civil suit. Those things were for divorces, not dogs. He would have to settle for the twelve hundred, and he meant to have it.

The Motherfucker's lawyers responded that the electric fence had been strung a full ten yards on Grunwald's side of the property line, and the battle — the *second* battle — was on. It had been raging for eight months now. Curtis believed the delaying tactics being employed by The Motherfucker's lawyers suggested that they knew Curtis had a case. He also believed that their failure to propose a settlement, and Grunwald's failure to just cough up the twelve hundred, suggested that it had become as personal to Grunwald as it was to him. These lawyers were also costing them plenty. But of course, the matter was no longer about money.

Riding out along Route 17, through what had once been ranchland and was now just overgrown scrub ground (*Grunwald had been raving mad to build out here,* Curtis thought), Curtis only wished he felt happier about this turn of events. Victory was supposed to make your heart leap, and his wasn't. All he seemed to want was to see Grunwald, hear what he was actually proposing, and put all this shit behind them if the proposal wasn't too ridiculous. Of course that would probably mean the roach-relatives would get the Vinton Lot, and they might well decide to put up their own condo development, but did it even matter? It didn't seem to.

Curtis had his own problems to deal with, although his were mental rather than marital (God forbid), financial, or physical. They had begun not long after finding Betsy stiff and cold in the side yard. Others might have called these problems neuroses, but Curtis preferred to think of them as angst.

His current disenchantment with the stock market, which had fascinated him ceaselessly since he had discovered it at sixteen, was the most identifiable component of this angst, but by no means the only one. He had begun taking his pulse and counting his toothbrush strokes. He could no longer wear dark shirts, because he was plagued with dandruff for the first time since junior high school. Dead white crap plated up on his scalp and drifted down to his shoulders. If he scraped with the teeth of a comb, it came down in ghastly snow flurries. He hated this, but still sometimes found himself doing it while sitting at the computer, or while talking on the phone. Once or twice he'd scraped until he drew blood.

Scraping and scraping. Excavating that white deadness. Sometimes looking at the idiot stick on the coffee table and thinking (of course) of how happy Betsy was when she brought it to him. Human eyes hardly ever looked that happy, especially not when the humans in question were doing chores.

A midlife crisis, Sammy said (Sammy was his once-a-week masseur). You need to get laid, Sammy said, but he didn't offer his own services, Curtis noticed.

Still, the phrase rang true — as true as any twenty-first-century newspeak, he supposed. Whether the Vinton Lot fuck-a-monkey show had provoked the crisis or the crisis had provoked the Vinton mess, he didn't know. What he *did* know was that he had come to think *heart attack* instead of *indigestion* each time he felt a transient, stabbing pain in his chest, that he had become obsessed with the notion that his teeth were going to fall out (even though they had never given him any particular trouble), and that when he'd gotten a cold in April, he had diagnosed himself as being on the verge of a complete immunological breakdown.

Plus this other little problem. This compulsion, which he hadn't told his doctor about. Or even Sammy, and he told Sammy *everything.*

It was on him now, fifteen miles inland on seldom-traveled Route 17, which had never been particularly busy and had now been rendered all but obsolescent by the 375 Extension. Right here with the green scrub pressing in on both sides (the man had been *bonkers* to build out here), with the bugs singing in high grass no cows had grazed for ten years or more and the power lines buzzing and the sun beating down like a padded hammer on his helmetless head.

He knew just thinking of the compulsion summoned it, but that was of no particular help. None at all, in fact.

He pulled over where a track marked DURKIN GROVE VILLAGE ROAD shot off to the left (grass was now growing up the center hump, an arrow pointing the way to failure) and put the Vespa in neutral. Then, while it purred contentedly between his legs, he forked the first two fingers of his right hand into a V and stuck them down his throat. His gag reflex had grown numb over the last two or three months, and his hand was in almost all the way to the bracelets of fortune on his wrist before it finally happened.

Curtis leaned to one side and ejected his breakfast. It wasn't getting rid of the food that interested him; he was many things, but bulimic wasn't one of them. It wasn't even the vomiting part that he liked. What he liked was the *gagging:* that hard rejecting clench of the midsection, plus the accompanying yaw of the mouth and throat. The body was totally in gear, determined to oust the intruder.

The smells — green bushes, wild honeysuckle — were suddenly stronger. The light was brighter. The sun beat down more heavily than ever; the pad was off the hammer and he could feel the skin on the nape of his neck sizzling, the cells there maybe at this very moment turning outlaw and heading for the chaotic land of melanoma.

He didn't care. He was alive. He rammed his spread fingers down his throat again, scraping the sides. The rest of breakfast yurped up. The third time he produced only long strings of spittle, stained faintly pink with his throat's blood. Then he felt satisfied. Then he could go on toward Durkin Grove Village, The Motherfucker's half-built Xanadu out here in the silent bee-buzzing wilds of Charlotte County.

It occurred to him, as he putted modestly

along the overgrown lane in the right-hand wheelrut, that Grunwald might not be the only one who was in a tight place these days.

Durkin Grove Village was a mess.

There were puddles in the ruts of the not-yet-paved streets and in the cellar holes of unfinished (in some cases not yet even framed) buildings. What Curtis saw below — half-built shops, a few pieces of shabby-looking construction equipment here and there, sagging yellow caution tape — was surely a blueprint for deep financial trouble, perhaps even ruin. Curtis didn't know if The Motherfucker's preoccupation with the Vinton Lot — not to mention the decampment of his wife, his illness, and his legal problems concerning Curtis's dog — had been the cause of the man's current overextension or not, but he knew overextension was what it was. Even before continuing down to the open gate and seeing the sign posted there, he knew.

THIS SITE HAS BEEN CLOSED BY THE CHARLOTTE COUNTY DEPT OF BUILDING AND PLANNING
THE CHARLOTTE COUNTY BUREAU OF TAXATION THE FLORIDA BUREAU OF TAXATION UNITED STATES INTERNAL REVENUE
FOR FURTHER INFORMATION CALL

Below this, some exuberant wit had spray-painted: *DIAL EXTENSION 69 AND ASK FOR THE CUNT-LICKER GENERAL!*

The tar ended and the potholes began after the only three buildings that looked completed: two shops on one side of the street and a model home on the other. The model home was a faux Cape Cod that made Curtis's blood run cold. He didn't trust the Vespa on the unpaved surface, so he turned in beside a payloader that looked as if it had been parked there for a century or more — grass was growing in the dirt at the bottom of its partially raised scoop — put down the stand, and turned off the engine.

Silence poured in to fill the socket which had been occupied by the Vespa's fat purr. Then a crow cawed. It was answered by another. Curtis looked up and saw a trio of them poised on a scaffolding that enshrouded a partially finished brick building. Maybe it had been intended as a bank. *Now it's Grunwald's tombstone,* he thought, but the idea didn't even bring a smile to his lips. He felt like gagging himself again, and might even have done it, but farther down the deserted dirt street — at the far end, in fact — he saw a man standing beside a white sedan with a green palm tree on it. Above the palm tree:

GRUNWALD. Below it: CONTRACTORS & BUILDERS. The man was waving to him. Grunwald was for some reason driving a company car today instead of his Porsche. Curtis supposed it wasn't impossible that Grunwald had sold the Porsche. It wasn't impossible to think the IRS had seized it, and might even seize Grunwald's Turtle Island property. Then the Vinton Lot would be the least of his worries.

*I just hope they leave him enough to pay for my dog,* Curtis thought. He waved back to Grunwald, flicked the red alarm switch below the ignition after removing the key (these things were only reflex; he did not think the Vespa was in any danger of being stolen, not out here, but he had been taught to take care of his things), and put the key in his pocket with his cell phone. Then he started down the dirt street — a Main Street that never was, and, it now seemed certain, never would be — to meet his neighbor and settle the trouble between them once and for all, if that were possible. He was careful to avoid the puddles left from the previous night's shower.

"Yo, neighbor!" Grunwald said as Curtis approached. He was wearing khakis and a T-shirt with his company's palm-tree logo on it. The shirt bagged on him. Except for hectic blotches of red high on his cheekbones and dark — almost black — circles under his eyes, his face was pale. And although he sounded cheerful, he looked sicker than ever. *Whatever they tried to cut out of him,* Curtis thought, *they failed.* Grunwald had one hand behind him. Curtis assumed it was in his back pocket. This turned out not to be true.

A little farther down the rutted and puddled dirt road was a trailer up on blocks. The on-site office, Curtis supposed. There was a notice encased in a protective plastic sleeve, hanging from a little plastic suction cup. There was a lot printed on it, but all Curtis could read (all he needed to read) were the words at the top: NO ENTRY.

Yes, The Motherfucker had fallen on hard times. Hard cheese on Tony, as Evelyn Waugh might have said.

"Grunwald?" It was enough to start with; considering what had happened to Betsy, it was all The Motherfucker deserved. Curtis stopped about ten feet from him, his legs slightly spread to avoid a puddle. Grunwald's legs were spread, too. It occurred to Curtis that this was a classic pose: gunfighters about to do their deal on the only street of a ghost town.

"Yo, neighbor!" Grunwald repeated, and this time he actually laughed. There was something familiar about his laugh. And why not? Surely he had heard The Motherfucker laugh before. He couldn't remember just when, but surely he must have.

Behind Grunwald, across from the trailer

and not far from the company car Grunwald had driven out here, stood a line of four blue Port-O-Sans. Weeds and nodding wedelia sprouted around their bases. The runoff from frequent June thunderstorms (such afternoon tantrums were a Gulf Coast specialty) had undercut the ground in front of them and turned it into a ditch. Almost a creek. It was filled with standing water now, the surface dusty and bleared with pollen, so that it cast back only a vague blue intimation of sky. The quartet of shithouses leaned forward like frost-heaved old gravestones. There must have been quite a crew out here at one time, because there was also a fifth. That one had actually fallen over and lay door-down in the ditch. It was the final touch, underlining the fact that this project — crazy to begin with — was now a dead letter.

One of the crows took off from the scaffolding around the unfinished bank and flapped across the hazy blue sky, cawing at the two men facing each other below. The bugs buzzed unconcernedly in the high grass. Curtis realized he could smell the Port-O-Sans; they must not have been pumped out in some time.

"Grunwald?" he said again. And then (because now something more seemed to be required): "How can I help you? Do we have something to discuss?"

"Well, neighbor, it's how I can help *you.*

It's strictly down to that." He started to laugh again, then choked it off. And Curtis knew why the sound was familiar. He'd heard it on his cell phone, at the end of The Motherfucker's message. It hadn't been a choked-off sob, after all. And the man didn't look sick — or not *just* sick. He looked mad.

*Of course he's mad. He's lost everything. And you let him get you out here alone. Not wise, buddy. You didn't think it through.*

No. Since Betsy's death, he had neglected to think a great many things through. Hadn't seemed worth the trouble. But this time he should have taken the time.

Grunwald was smiling. Or at least showing his teeth. "I notice you didn't wear your helmet, neighbor." He shook his head, still smiling that cheery sick man's smile. His hair flapped against his ears. It looked as if it hadn't been washed in a while. "A wife wouldn't let you get away with careless shit like that, I bet, but of course guys like you don't have wives, do they? They have *dogs*." He stretched it out, turning it into something from *The Dukes of Hazzard: dawwwgs.*

"Fuck this, I'm taillights," Curtis said. His heart was hammering, but he didn't think it showed in his voice. He hoped not. All at once it seemed very important that Grunwald not know he was scared. He started to turn around, back the way he'd come.

"I thought the Vinton Lot *might* get you out

here," Grunwald said, "but I *knew* you'd come if I added in that butt-ugly dog of yours. I heard her yelp, you know. When she ran into the fence. Trespassing bitch."

Curtis turned back, unbelieving.

The Motherfucker was nodding, his lank hair framing his pale smiling face. "Yes," he said. "I went over and saw her lying on her side. Little ragbag with eyes. I watched her die."

"You said you were away," Curtis said. His voice sounded small in his own ears, a child's voice.

"Well, neighbor, I sure did lie about that. I was back early from my doctor's, and feeling sad that I had to turn him down after he'd worked so hard at persuading me to take the chemo, and then I saw that ragbag of yours lying in a puddle of her own puke, panting, flies all around her, and I cheered right up. I thought, 'Goddam, there *is* justice. There is justice after all.' It was only a low-voltage, low-current cattle fence — I was absolutely honest about that — but it certainly did the job, didn't it?"

Curtis Johnson got the full sense of this after a moment of utter, perhaps willful, incomprehension. Then he started forward, rolling his hands into fists. He hadn't hit anyone since a playground scuffle when he was in the third grade, but he meant to hit someone now. He meant to hit The Motherfucker. The bugs still buzzed obliviously in the grass, and the sun still hammered down — nothing in the essential world had changed except for him. The uncaring listlessness was gone. He cared about at least one thing: beating Grunwald until he cried and bled and crawfished. And he thought he could do it. Grunwald was twenty years older, and not well. And when The Motherfucker was on the ground — hopefully with his newly broken nose in one of those nasty puddles — Curtis would say, *That was for my ragbag. Neighbor.*

Grunwald took one compensatory step backward. Then he brought his hand out from behind his back. In it was a large handgun. "Stop right there, neighbor, or I'll put an extra hole in your head."

Curtis almost didn't stop. The gun seemed unreal. Death, out of that black eyehole? Surely not possible. But —

"It's a .45 AMT Hardballer," Grunwald said, "loaded with soft-point ammo. I got it the last time I was in Vegas. At a gun show. Just after Ginny left, that was. I thought I might shoot her, but I find I've lost all interest in Ginny. Basically, she's just another anorexic Suncoast cunt with Styrofoam tits. You, however — you're something different. You're *malevolent,* Johnson. You're a fucking gay witch."

Curtis stopped. He believed.

"But now you're in my power, as they say." The Motherfucker laughed, once more choking it off so it sounded strangely like a sob. "I don't even have to hit you dead on. This is a powerful gun, or so I was told. Even a hit in the hand would render you dead, because it would tear your hand right off. And in the midsection? Your guts'd fly forty feet. So do you want to try it? Do you feel lucky, punk?"

Curtis did not want to try it. He did not feel lucky. The truth was belated but obvious: he had been cozened out here by a complete barking lunatic.

"What do you want? I'll give you what you want." Curtis swallowed. There was an insectile click in his throat. "Do you want me to call off the suit about Betsy?"

"Don't call her Betsy," The Motherfucker said. He had the gun — the Hardballer, what a grotesque name — pointed at Curtis's face, and now the hole looked very big indeed. Curtis realized he would probably be dead before he heard the gun's report, although he might see flame — or the beginning of flame — spurt from the barrel. He also realized that he was perilously close to pissing himself. "Call her 'my ass-faced ragbag bitch.' "

"My ass-faced ragbag bitch," Curtis repeated at once, and didn't feel the slightest twinge of disloyalty to Betsy's memory.

"Now say, 'And how I loved to lick her smelly cunt,' " The Motherfucker further instructed.

Curtis was silent. He was relieved to discover there were still limits. Besides, if he said that, The Motherfucker would only want him to say something else.

Grunwald did not seem particularly disappointed. He waggled the gun. "Just joking about that one, anyway."

Curtis was silent. Part of his mind was roaring with panic and confusion, but another part seemed clearer than it had been since Betsy died. Maybe clearer than it had been in years. That part was musing on the fact that he really could die out here.

He thought, *What if I never get to eat another slice of bread?*, and for a moment his mind united — the confused part and the clear part — in a desire to live so strong it was terrible.

"What do you want, Grunwald?"

"For you to get into one of those Port-O-Sans. The one on the end." He waggled the gun again, this time to the left.

Curtis turned to look, feeling a small thread of hope. If Grunwald intended to lock him up . . . that was good, right? Maybe now that he'd scared Curtis and blown off a little steam, Grunwald intended to stash him and make his getaway. *Or maybe he'll go home and shoot himself,* Curtis thought. *Take that old .45 Hardballer cancer cure. A well-known folk remedy.*

He said, "All right. I can do that."

"But first I want you to empty your pockets. Dump them right out on the ground."

Curtis pulled out his wallet, then, reluctantly, his cell phone. A little sheaf of bills in a money clip. His dandruff-flecked comb.

"That it?"

"Yes."

"Turn those pocketses inside out, Precious. I want to see for myself."

Curtis turned out his left front pocket, then his right. A few coins and the key to his motor scooter fell to the ground, where they glittered in the hazy sun.

"Good," Grunwald said. "Now the back ones."

Curtis turned out his rear pockets. There was an old shopping list jotted on a scrap of paper. Nothing else.

Grunwald said, "Kick your cell phone over here."

Curtis tried, and missed completely.

"You asshole," Grunwald said, and laughed. The laugh ended in that same choking, sobbing sound, and for the first time in his life, Curtis completely understood murder. The clear part of his mind registered this as a wonderful thing, because murder — previously inconceivable to him — turned out to be as simple as reducing fractions.

"Hurry the fuck up," Grunwald said. "I want to go home and get in the hot tub.

Forget the painkillers, that hot tub is the only thing that works. I'd *live* in that baby if I could." But he did not look particularly anxious to be gone. His eyes were sparkling.

Curtis kicked at the phone again and this time connected, sending it skittering all the way to Grunwald's feet.

"He shoots, he scores!" The Motherfucker cried. He dropped to one knee, picked up the Nokia (never taking the gun off Curtis), then straightened up with a small, effortful grunt. He slipped Curtis's phone into the right pocket of his pants. He pointed the muzzle of the gun briefly at the litter lying on the road. "Now pick up the rest of your crap and put it back in your pockets. Get all the change. Who knows, you might find a snack machine in there."

Curtis did it silently, again feeling a little pang as he looked at the attachment on the Vespa's keyring. Some things didn't change even in extremis, it seemed.

"You forgot your shopping list, Fucko. You don't want to forget that. Everything back in your pockets. As for your phone, I'm going to put that back on its little charger in your little housie. After I delete the message I left you, that is."

Curtis picked up the scrap of paper — *OJ, Rolaids, pce of fish, Eng muffins,* it said — and stuffed it back into one of his rear pockets. "You can't do that," he said.

531

The Motherfucker raised his bushy old-man eyebrows. "Want to share?"

"The house alarm's set." Curtis couldn't remember if he had set it or not. "Also, Mrs. Wilson will be there by the time you get back to Turtle."

Grunwald gave him an indulgent look. The fact that it was *mad* indulgence made it terrifying instead of just infuriating. "It's *Thursday,* neighbor. Your housekeeper only comes in during the afternoons on Thursdays and Fridays. Did you think I wasn't keeping an eye on you? Just like you've been keeping one on me?"

"I don't —"

"Oh, I see you, peeking from behind your favorite palm tree on the road — did you think I didn't? — but you never saw *me,* did you? Because you're lazy. And lazy people are blind people. Lazy people get what they deserve." His voice lowered confidentially. "All gay people are lazy; it's been scientifically proven. The gay lobby tries to cover it up, but you can find the studies on the Internet."

In his mounting dismay, Curtis hardly noticed this last. *If he's been charting Mrs. Wilson . . . Christ, how long has he been brooding and planning?*

At least since Curtis had sued him over Betsy. Maybe even before.

"As for your alarm code . . ." The Mother-fucker loosed his sobbing laugh again. "I'll let you in on a little secret: your system was put in by Hearn Security, and I've been working with them for almost thirty years. I could have the security codes for any Hearn-serviced home on the Island, if I wanted. But, as it happens, the only one I wanted was yours." He sniffed, spat on the ground, then coughed a loose rumbling cough that came from deep in his chest. It sounded as if it hurt (Curtis hoped so), but the gun never wavered. "I don't think you set it, anyway. Got your mind on blowjobs and such."

"Grunwald, can't we —"

"No. We can't. You deserve this. You earned it, you bought it, you got it. Get in the fucking shithouse."

Curtis started toward the Port-O-Sans, but aimed for the one on the far right instead of the far left.

"Nope, nope," Grunwald said. Patiently, as if speaking to a child. "The one on the *other* end."

"That one's leaning too far," Curtis said. "If I get in, it might fall over."

"Nope," Grunwald said. "That thing's as solid as your beloved stock market. Special sides is why. But I'm sure you'll enjoy the smell. Guys like you spend a lot of time in crappers, you must like the smell. You must *love* the smell." Suddenly the gun poked into

Curtis's buttocks. Curtis gave a small, startled scream, and Grunwald laughed. That Motherfucker. "Now get in there before I decide to turn your old tan track into a brand-new superhighway."

Curtis had to lean across the ditch of still, scummy water, and because the Port-O-San was leaning, the door swung out and almost hit him in the face when it came off the latch. This occasioned another burst of laughter from Grunwald, and at the sound, Curtis was once more visited with thoughts of murder. All the same, it was amazing how engaged he felt. How suddenly in love with the green smells of the foliage and the hazy look of the blue Florida sky. How much he longed to eat a piece of bread — even a slice of Wonder Bread would be a gourmet treat; he would eat it with a napkin in his lap and choose a complementary vintage from his little wine closet. He had gained a whole new perspective on life. He only hoped he would live to enjoy it. And if The Motherfucker just intended to lock him in, maybe he would.

He thought (it was as random and as unprompted as his thought about the bread): *If I get out of this, I'm going to start giving money to Save the Children.*

"Get in there, Johnson."

"I tell you it'll fall over!"

"Who's the construction guy here? It won't fall over if you're careful. Get in."

"I don't understand why you're doing this!"

Grunwald laughed unbelievingly. Then he said, "You get your ass in there or I will blow it off, so help me God."

Curtis stepped across the ditch and into the Port-O-San. It rocked forward alarmingly under his weight. He cried out and leaned over the bench with the closed toilet seat in it, splaying his hands against the back wall. And while he was standing there like a suspect about to be frisked, the door slammed shut behind him. The sunlight was gone. He was suddenly in hot, deep shadows. He looked back over his shoulder and the Port-O-San rocked again, on the very edge of balance.

There was a knock on the door. Curtis could imagine The Motherfucker out there, leaning over the ditch, one hand braced on the blue siding, the other fisted up to knock with. "Comfy in there? Snug?"

Curtis made no reply. At least with Grunwald leaning on the Port-O-San's door, the damned thing had steadied.

"Sure you are. Snug as a bug in a whatever."

There was another thump, and then the toilet rocked forward again. Grunwald had removed his weight from it. Curtis once more assumed the position, standing on the balls of his feet, bending all his will to keeping the stinking cubicle more or less upright. Sweat was trickling down his face, stinging a shaving cut on the left jawline. This made him think of his own bathroom, usually taken for granted, with loving nostalgia. He would give every dollar in his retirement fund to be there, razor in his right hand, watching blood trickle through the shaving cream on the left-hand side while some stupid pop song played from the clock radio beside his bed. Something by The Carpenters or Don Ho.

*It's going over this time, going over for sure, that was his plan all along —*

But the Port-O-San steadied instead of tumbling over. All the same it was close to going, very close. Curtis stood on tiptoe with his hands braced against the wall and his midsection arched over the bench seat, becoming aware now of how badly the hot little cubicle smelled, even with the seat closed. There was the odor of disinfectant — it would be the blue stuff, of course — mingling with the stench of decaying human waste, and that made it somehow even worse.

When Grunwald spoke again, his voice came from beyond the rear wall. He had stepped over the ditch and circled around to the back of the Port-O-San. Curtis was so surprised he almost recoiled, but managed not to. Still, he couldn't suppress a jerk. His splayed hands momentarily left the wall. The Port-O-San tottered. He brought his hands back to the wall again, leaning forward as far as he could, and it steadied.

"How you doing, neighbor?"

"Scared to death," Curtis said. His hair had fallen onto his forehead, it was sticking in the sweat there, but he was afraid to flick it back. Even that much extra movement might send the Port-O-San tumbling. "Let me out. You've had your fun."

"If you think I'm having fun, you're very much mistaken," The Motherfucker said in a pedantic voice. "I've thought about this a long time, neighbor, and finally decided it was necessary — the only course of action. And it had to be now, because if I waited much longer, I'd no longer be able to trust my body to do what I needed it to do."

"Grunwald, we can settle this like men. I swear we can."

"Swear all you like, I would never take the word of a man like you," he said in that same pedantic voice. "Any man who takes the word of a faggot deserves what he gets." And then, yelling so loud his voice broke into splinters: *"YOU GUYS THINK YOU'RE SO SMART! HOW SMART DO YOU FEEL NOW?"*

Curtis said nothing. Each time he thought he was getting a handle on The Motherfucker's madness, new vistas opened before him.

At last, in a calmer tone, Grunwald went on.

"You want an explanation. You think you *deserve* one. Possibly you do."

Somewhere a crow cawed. To Curtis, in his

537

hot little box, it sounded like laughter.

"Did you think I was joking when I called you a gay witch? I was not. Does that mean you *know* you're a, well, a malevolent supernatural force sent to try me and test me? I don't know. I don't. I've spent many a sleepless night since my wife took her jewelry and left thinking about this question — among others — and I still don't. *You* probably don't."

"Grunwald, I assure you I'm not —"

"Shut up. I'm talking here. And of course, that's what you'd *say,* isn't it? Regardless of whether you knew or not, it's what you'd *say.* Look at the testimonies of various witches in Salem. Go on, look. I have. It's all on the Internet. They swore they weren't witches, and when they thought it would get them out of death's receiving room they swore they *were,* but very few of them actually *knew for sure themselves!* That becomes clear when you look at it with your enlightened . . . you know, enlightened . . . your enlightened whatever. Mind or whatever. Hey neighbor, how is it when I do this?"

Suddenly The Motherfucker — sick but apparently still quite strong — began to rock the Port-O-San. Curtis was almost thrown against the door, which would have resulted in disaster for sure.

*"Stop it!"* he roared. *"Stop doing that!"*

Grunwald laughed indulgently. The Port-

O-San stopped rocking. But Curtis thought the angle of the floor was steeper than it had been. "What a baby you are. It's as solid as the stock market, I tell you!"

A pause.

"Of course . . . there *is* this: all faggots are liars, but not all liars are faggots. It's not a balancing equation, if you see what I mean. I'm as straight as an arrow, always have been, I'd fuck the Virgin Mary and then go to a barn dance, but I lied to get you out here, I freely admit it, and I might be lying now."

That cough again — deep and dark and almost certainly painful.

"Let me out, Grunwald. I beg you. I am begging you."

A long pause, as if The Motherfucker were considering this. Then he resumed his previous scripture.

"In the end — when it comes to witches — we can't rely on confessions," he said. "We can't even rely on *testimony,* because it might be cocked. When you're dealing with witches, the subjective gets all . . . it gets all . . . you know. We can only rely on the *evidence.* So I considered the evidence in *my* case. Let's look at the facts. First, you fucked me on the Vinton Lot. That was the first thing."

"Grunwald, I never —"

"Shut up, neighbor. Unless you want me to tip over your happy little home, that is. In that case, you can talk all you want. Is that what you want?"

"No!"

"Good call. I don't know exactly *why* you fucked me, but I *believe* you did it because you were afraid I meant to stick a couple of condos out there on Turtle Point. In any case, the *evidence* — namely, your ridiculous so-called bill of sale — indicates that fuckery was what it was, pure and simple. You claim that Ricky Vinton meant to sell you that lot for one million, five hundred thousand dollars. Now, neighbor, I ask you. Would any judge and jury in the world believe that?"

Curtis didn't reply. He was afraid to even clear his throat now, and not just because it might set The Motherfucker off; it might tip the precariously balanced Port-O-San over. He was afraid it might go over if he so much as lifted a little finger from the back wall. Probably that was stupid, but maybe it wasn't.

"Then the relatives swooped in, complicating a situation that was already complicated enough — *by your gayboy meddling!* And you were the one who called them. You or your lawyer. That's obvious, a, you know, QED type of situation. Because you like things just the way they are."

Curtis remained silent, letting this go unchallenged.

"That's when you threw your curse. Must have been. Because the evidence bears it out.

'You don't need to see Pluto to deduce Pluto is there.' Some scientist said that. He figured out Pluto existed by observing the irregularities in some other planet's orbit, did you know that? Deducing witchcraft is like that, Johnson. You have to check the evidence and look for irregularities in the orbit of your, you know, your whatever. Life. Plus, your spirit darkens. It *darkens.* I felt that happening. Like an eclipse. It —"

He coughed some more. Curtis stood in the ready-to-be-frisked position, butt out, stomach arched over the toilet where Grunwald's carpenters had once sat down to take care of business after their morning coffee kicked in.

"Next, Ginny left me," The Motherfucker said. "She's currently living on Cape Cod. She says she's there by herself, of course she does, because she wants that alimony — they all do — but I know better. If that randy bitch didn't have a cock to pole-vault on twice a day, she'd eat chocolate truffles in front of *American Idol* until she exploded.

"Then the IRS. Those bastards came next, with their laptops and questions. 'Did you do this, did you do that, where's the paperwork on the other?' Was that witchcraft, Johnson? Or maybe fuckery of a more, I don't know, ordinary kind? Like you picking up the telephone and saying, 'Audit this guy, he's got a lot more cake in his pantry than he's letting on.' "

"Grunwald, I never called —"

The Port-O-San shook. Curtis rocked backward, sure that *this* time . . .

But once more the Port-O-San settled. Curtis was starting to feel woozy. Woozy and pukey. It wasn't just the smell; it was the *heat.* Or maybe it was both together. He could feel his shirt sticking to his chest.

"I'm laying out the evidence," Grunwald said. "You shut up when I'm laying out the evidence. Order in the fucking court."

*Why* was it so hot in here? Curtis looked up and saw no roof vents. Or — there were, but they were covered over. By what looked like a piece of sheet metal. Three or four holes had been punched into it, letting in some light but absolutely no breeze. The holes were bigger than quarters, smaller than silver dollars. He looked over his shoulder and saw another line of holes, but the two door vents were also almost completely covered.

"They've frozen my assets," Grunwald said in a heavy put-upon voice. "Did an audit first, said it was all just routine, but I know what they do, and I knew what was coming."

*Of course you did, because you were guilty as hell.*

"But even before the audit, I developed this cough. That was your work, too, of course. Went to the doctor. Lung cancer, neighbor, and it's spread to my liver and stomach and fuck knows what else. All the soft parts. Just what a witch would go for. I'm surprised you didn't put it in my balls and up my ass as well, although I'm sure it'll get there in good time. If I let it. But I won't. That's why, although I think I've got this business out here covered, my, you know, ass in diapers, it doesn't matter even if I don't. I'm going to put a bullet through my head pretty soon. From this very gun, neighbor. While I'm in my hot tub."

He sighed sentimentally.

"That's the only place I'm happy anymore. In my hot tub."

Curtis realized something. Maybe it was hearing The Motherfucker say *I think I've got this business out here covered,* but more likely he had known for some time now. The Motherfucker meant to tip the Port-O-San over. He was going to do that if Curtis blubbered and protested; he was going to do it if Curtis held his peace. It didn't really matter. But for the time being, he held his peace anyway. Because he wanted to stay upright as long as possible — yes, of course — but also out of dreadful fascination. Grunwald wasn't speaking metaphorically; Grunwald actually believed Curtis Johnson was some kind of sorcerer. His brain had to be rotting along with the rest of him.

*"LUNG CANCER!"* Grunwald proclaimed to his empty, deserted development — and then

began coughing again. Crows cawed in protest. "I quit smoking *thirty years ago, and I get lung cancer NOW?*"

"You're crazy," Curtis said.

"Sure, the world would say so. That was the plan, wasn't it? That was the fucking *PLAAAAN.* And then, on top of everything else, you sue me over your damn ass-faced *dog?* Your damn dog that was on *MY PROPERTY?* And what was the purpose of that? After you'd taken my lot, my wife, my business, and my life, what possible purpose? Humiliation, of course! Insult to injury! Coals to Newcastle! Witchcraft! And do you know what the Bible says? *Thou shalt not suffer a witch to live!* Everything that's happened to me is your fault, and *thou shalt not suffer a witch . . . TO LIVE!*"

Grunwald shoved the Port-O-San. He must have really put his shoulder into it, because there was no hesitation this time, no tottering. Curtis, momentarily weightless, fell backward. The latch should have broken under his weight, but didn't. The Motherfucker must have done something to that, too.

Then his weight returned and he crashed down on his back as the portable toilet hit the ground door-first. His teeth snapped shut on his tongue. The back of his head connected with the door and he saw stars. The

544

lid of the toilet opened like a mouth. Brown-black fluid, thick as syrup, vomited out. A decomposing turd landed on his crotch. Curtis gave a cry of revulsion, batted it aside, then wiped his hand on his shirt, leaving a brown stain. A vile creek was spilling out of the gaping toilet seat. It ran down the side of the bench seat and pooled around his sneakers. A Reese's Peanut Butter Cup wrapper floated in it. Streamers of toilet paper hung out of the toilet's mouth. It looked like New Year's Eve in hell. This absolutely could not be happening. It was a nightmare left over from childhood.

"How's the smell in there now, neighbor?" The Motherfucker called. He was laughing and coughing. "Just like home, isn't it? Think of it as a twenty-first-century gayboy ducking stool, why don't you? All you need is that gayboy Senator and a pile of Victoria's Secret undies and you could have a lingerie party!"

Curtis's back was wet, too. He realized the Port-O-San must have landed in or just bridged the water-filled ditch. Water was seeping in through the holes in the door.

"Mostly these portable toilets are just thin molded plastic — you know, the ones you see at truck stops or turnpike rest areas — and you could punch right through the walls or the roof, if you were dedicated. But at construction sites, we sheet-metal the sides. Cladding, it's called. Otherwise, people come along and punch holes through them. Vandals, just for fun, or gayboys like you. To make what they call 'glory holes.' Oh yes, I know about those things. I have all the information, neighbor. Or kids will come along and huck rocks through the roofs, just to hear the sound it makes. It's a popping sound, like popping a great big paper bag. So we sheet those, too. Of course it makes it hotter, but that's actually an efficiency thing. Nobody wants to spend fifteen minutes reading a magazine in a shithouse as hot as a Turkish prison cell."

Curtis turned over. He was lying in a brackish, smelly puddle. There was a piece of toilet paper wrapped around his wrist, and he stripped it away. He saw a brown smear — some long-since-laid-off construction worker's leavings — on the paper and began to cry. He was lying in shit and toilet paper, more water was bubbling in through the door, and it wasn't a dream. Somewhere not too far distant his Macintosh was scrolling up numbers from Wall Street, and here he lay in a puddle of pisswater with an old black turd curled in the corner and a gaping toilet seat not far above his heels, and it wasn't a dream. He would have sold his soul to wake up in his own bed, clean and cool.

*"Let me out! GRUNWALD, PLEASE!"*

"Can't. It's all arranged," The Motherfucker said in a businesslike voice. "You came out here to do a little sightseeing — a little gloating. You felt a call of nature, and there were the porta-potties. You stepped into the one on the end and it fell over. End of story. When you're found — when you're *finally* found — the cops will see they're all leaning, because the afternoon rains have undercut them. They'll have no way of knowing your current abode was leaning a little more than the others. Or that I took your cell phone. They'll just assume you left it at home, you silly sissy. The situation will look very clear to them. The *evidence,* you know — it always comes back to the evidence."

He laughed. No coughing this time, just the warm, self-satisfied laugh of a man who has covered all the bases. Curtis lay in filthy water that was now two inches deep, felt it soaking through his shirt and pants to his skin, and wished The Motherfucker would die of a sudden stroke or heart attack. Fuck the cancer; let him drop right out there on the unpaved street of his stupid bankrupt development. Preferably on his back, so the birds could peck out his eyes.

*If that happened, I'd die in here.*

True, but that was what Grunwald had planned from the first, so what difference?

"They'll see there was no robbery; your money is still in your pocket. So's the key to your motor scooter. Those things are very unsafe, by the way; almost as bad as ATVs.

And without a helmet! Shame on you, neighbor. I noticed you set the alarm, though, and that's fine. A nice touch, in fact. You don't even have a pen to write a note on the wall with. If you'd had one, I would have taken that, too, but you don't. It's going to look like a tragic accident."

He paused. Curtis could picture him out there with hellish clarity. Standing there in his too-big clothes with his hands stuffed in his pockets and his unwashed hair clumping over his ears. Ruminating. Talking to Curtis but also talking to himself, looking for loopholes even now, even after what must have been weeks of sleepless nights spent planning this.

"Of course, a person can't plan for everything. There are always wild cards in the deck. Deuces and jacks, man with the axe, natural sevens take all. That kind of thing. And chances of anyone coming out here and finding you? While you're still alive, that is? Low, I'd say. Very low. And what have I got to lose?" He laughed, sounding delighted with himself. "Are you lying in the shit, Johnson? I hope so."

Curtis looked at the coil of excrement he had shoved off his pants, but said nothing. There was a low buzzing. Flies. Only a few, but even a few was too many, in his opinion. They were escaping from the gaping toilet seat. They must have been trapped in the collection tank that should have been below him instead of lying at his feet.

"I'm going now, neighbor, but consider this: you are suffering a true, you know, witchly fate. And like the man said: in the shithouse, no one can hear you scream."

Grunwald started away. Curtis could track him by the diminishing sound of his coughing laughter.

"Grunwald! Grunwald, come back!"

Grunwald called: "Now *you're* the one in a tight place. A very tight place indeed."

Then — he should have expected it, *did* expect it, but it was still unbelievable — he heard the company car with the palm tree on the side starting up.

*"Come back, you Motherfucker!"*

But now it was the sound of the car that was diminishing, as Grunwald drove first up the unpaved street (Curtis could hear the wheels splashing through the puddles), then up the hill, past where a very different Curtis Johnson had parked his Vespa. The Motherfucker gave a single blip of his horn — cruel and cheery — and then the sound of the engine merged with the sound of the day, which was nothing but the buzz of the insects in the grass and the hum of the flies that had escaped from the waste tank and the drone of a far-off plane where the people in first class might be eating Brie on crackers.

A fly lit on Curtis's arm. He brushed it

away. It landed on the coil of turd and commenced its lunch. Suddenly the stench of the disturbed waste tank seemed like a living thing, like a brown-black hand crawling down Curtis's throat. But the smell of old decaying crap wasn't the worst; the worst was the smell of the disinfectant. It was the blue stuff. He knew it was the blue stuff.

He did a sit-up — there was just room — and vomited between his spread knees, into the puddled water and floating strands of toilet paper. After his earlier adventures in regurgitation there wasn't much left but bile. He sat bent over and panting, hands behind him and braced against the door he was now sitting on, the shaving cut by his jawline throbbing and stinging. Then he heaved again, this time producing only a belch that sounded like the buzz of a cicada.

And, oddly enough, he felt better. Somehow *honest.* That had been *earned* vomiting. No fingers down the throat needed. As far as his dandruff went, who knew? Perhaps he could gift the world with a new treatment: the Aged Urine Rinse. He would be sure to check his scalp for improvement when he got out of here. *If* he got out of here.

Sitting up, at least, was no problem. It was fearsomely hot, and the stench was terrible (he didn't want to think what might have been stirred up in the holding tank, and at the same time couldn't push such thoughts away), but at least there was headroom.

"Must count blessings," he muttered. "Must count those sons of bitches carefully."

Yes, and take stock. That would be good, too. The water he was sitting in wasn't getting any deeper, and that was probably another blessing. He wasn't going to drown. Not, that was, unless the afternoon showers turned into downpours. He had seen it happen. And it was no good telling himself he'd be out of here by afternoon, of *course* he would, because that kind of magical thinking would be playing right into The Motherfucker's hands. He couldn't just sit here, thanking God he at least had some headroom, and waiting for rescue.

*Maybe someone from the Charlotte County Department of Building and Planning will come out. Or a team of headhunters from the IRS.*

Nice to imagine, but he had an idea it wasn't going to happen. The Motherfucker would have taken those possibilities into consideration, too. Of course some bureaucrat or team of them might take an unscheduled swing by here, but counting on it would be as stupid as hoping that Grunwald would have a change of heart. And Mrs. Wilson would assume he'd gone to an afternoon movie in Sarasota, as he often did.

He rapped on the walls, first the left, then the right. On both sides he felt hard metal just beyond the thin and yielding plastic.

Cladding. He got up on his knees, and this time he did bump his head, but hardly noticed. What he saw was not encouraging: the flat ends of the screws holding the unit together. The heads were on the outside. This wasn't a shithouse; it was a coffin.

At this thought, his moment of clarity and calm vanished. Panic descended in its place. He began to hammer on the walls of the toilet, screaming to be let out. He threw himself from side to side like a child having a tantrum, trying to roll the Port-O-San over so he could at least free the door, but the fucking thing hardly moved at all. The fucking thing was heavy. The cladding that sheathed it made it heavy.

*Heavy like a coffin!* his mind shrieked. In his panic, every other thought had been banished. *Heavy like a coffin! Like a coffin! A coffin!*

He didn't know how long he went on like that, but at some point he tried to stand up, as if he could burst through the wall now facing the sky like Superman. He hit his head again, this time much harder. He fell forward on his stomach. His hand splutted into something gooey — something that smeared — and he wiped it on the seat of his jeans. He did this without looking. His eyes were squeezed shut. Tears trickled from the corners. In the blackness behind his lids, stars zoomed and exploded. He wasn't bleeding — he supposed that was good, one more goddam blessing to count — but he had almost knocked himself out.

"Calm down," he said. He got up on his knees again. His head was down, his hair hanging, his eyes closed. He looked like a man who was praying, and he supposed he was. A fly did a touch-and-go on the nape of his neck. "Going nuts won't help, he'd love it if he heard you screaming and carrying on, so calm down, don't give him what he'd love, just calm the fuck down and think about this."

What was there to think about? He was trapped.

Curtis sat back against the door and put his face in his hands.

Time passed and the world went on.

The world did its thing.

On Route 17, a few vehicles — mostly workhorses; farm trucks bound for either the markers in Sarasota or the whole-foods store in Nokomis, the occasional tractor, the postman's station wagon with the yellow lights on the roof — trundled by. None took the turnoff to Durkin Grove Village.

Mrs. Wilson arrived at Curtis's house, let herself in, read the note Mr. Johnson had left on the kitchen table, and began to vacuum. Then she ironed clothes in front of the afternoon soap operas. She made a macaroni casserole, stuck it in the fridge, then jotted simple instructions concerning its preparation — *Bake 350, 45 mins* — and left them on the table where Curtis's note had been. When thunder began to mutter out over the Gulf of Mexico, she left early. She often did this when it rained. Nobody down here knew how to drive in the rain, they treated every shower like a nor'easter in Vermont.

In Miami, the IRS agent assigned to the Grunwald case ate a Cuban sandwich. Instead of a suit, he wore a tropical shirt with parrots on it. He was sitting under an umbrella at a sidewalk restaurant. There was no rain in Miami. He was on vacation. The Grunwald case would still be there when he got back; the wheels of government ground slow but exceedingly fine.

Grunwald relaxed in his patio hot tub, dozing, until the approaching afternoon storm woke him with the sound of thunder. He hauled himself out and went inside. As he closed the sliding glass door between the patio and the living room, the rain began to fall. Grunwald smiled. "This'll cool you off, neighbor," he said.

The crows had once more taken up station on the scaffolding which clasped the half-finished bank on three sides, but when thunder cracked almost directly overhead and the rain began to fall they took wing and sought shelter in the woods, cawing their displeasure at being disturbed.

In the Port-O-San — it seemed he'd been locked in here for at least three years — Curtis listened to the rain on the roof of his prison. The roof that had been the rear side until The Motherfucker tipped it over. The rain tapped at first, then beat, then roared. At the height of the storm, it was like being in a telephone booth lined with stereo speakers. Thunder exploded overhead. He had a momentary vision of being struck by lightning and cooked like a capon in a microwave. He found this didn't disturb him much. It would be quick, at least, and what was happening now was slow.

The water began to rise again, but not fast. Curtis was actually glad about this, now that he had determined there was no actual risk of drowning like a rat that has tumbled into a toilet bowl. At least it *was* water, and he was very thirsty. He lowered his head to one of the holes in the steel cladding. Water from the overflowing ditch was bubbling up through it. He drank like a horse at a trough, sucking it up. The water was gritty, but he drank until his belly sloshed, constantly reminding himself that it *was* water, it *was*.

"There may be a certain piss content, but I'm sure it's low," he said, and began to laugh. The laughter turned to sobbing, then back to laughter again.

The rain ended around six p.m., as it usually did this time of year. The sky cleared in time to provide a grade-A Florida sunset. The few summer residents of Turtle Island gathered on the beach to watch it, as they usually did. No one commented on Curtis Johnson's absence. Sometimes he was there, sometimes he wasn't. Tim Grunwald was there, and several of the sunsetters remarked that he seemed exceptionally cheery that evening. Mrs. Peebles told her husband, as they walked home hand in hand along the beach, that she believed Mr. Grunwald was finally getting over the shock of losing his wife. Mr. Peebles told her she was a romantic. "Yes, dear," she said, momentarily putting her head on his shoulder, "that's why I married you."

When Curtis saw the light coming through the holes in the cladding — the few that weren't facedown in the ditch — fading from peach to gray, he realized he was actually going to spend the night in this stinking coffin with two inches of water on the floor and a half-closed toilet hole at his feet. He was probably going to *die* in here, but that seemed academic. To spend the *night* in here, however — hours stacked on more hours, piles of hours like piles of great black books — that was real and unavoidable.

The panic pounced again. He once more began to scream and pound the walls, this time turning around and around on his knees, first beating his right shoulder against one wall and then his left against the other.

*Like a bird caught in a church steeple,* he thought, but could not stop. One flailing foot splattered the escaped turd against the bottom of the bench seat. He tore his pants. He first bruised his knuckles, then split them. At last he stopped, weeping and sucking at his hands.

*Got to stop. Got to save my strength.*

Then he thought: *For what?*

By eight o'clock, the air had begun to cool. By ten o'clock, the puddle in which Curtis was lying had also cooled — seemed cold, in fact — and he began to tremble. He clutched his arms around himself and drew his knees up to his chest.

*I'll be all right as long as my teeth don't chatter,* he thought. *I can't bear to hear my teeth chatter.*

At eleven o'clock, Grunwald went to bed. He lay there in his pajamas under the revolving fan, looking up into the dark and smiling. He felt better than he had felt for months. He was gratified but not surprised. "Goodnight, neighbor," he said, and closed his eyes. He slept through the night without waking for the first time in six months.

At midnight, not far away from Curtis's makeshift cell, some animal — probably just a wild dog, but to Curtis it sounded like a hyena — let out a long, screaming howl. His teeth began to chatter. The sound was every bit as awful as he had feared.

Some unimaginable time later, he slept.

When he woke up, he was shivering all over. Even his feet were jerking, tapdancing like the feet of a junkie in withdrawal. *I'm getting sick, I'll have to go to the damn doctor, I ache all over,* he thought. Then he opened his eyes, saw where he was, *remembered* where he was, and gave a loud, desolate cry: *"Ohhhh . . . no! NO!"*

But it was oh yes. At least the Port-O-San wasn't entirely dark anymore. Light was coming through the circular holes: the pale rose glow of morning. It would soon strengthen as the day brightened and heated up. Before long he would be steam-cooking again.

*Grunwald will come back. He's had a night to think it over, he'll realize how insane this is, and he'll come back. He'll let me out.*

Curtis did not believe this. He wanted to, but didn't.

He needed to take a leak in the worst way, but he was damned if he was going to piss in the corner, even though there was crap and used toilet paper everywhere from yesterday's overturning. He felt somehow that if he did that — a nasty thing like that — it would be the same as announcing to himself that he had given up hope.

*I have given up hope.*

But he hadn't. Not completely. As tired and

achey as he was, as frightened and dispirited, part of him still hadn't given up hope. And there was a bright side: he felt no urge to gag himself, and he hadn't spent even a single minute of the night just gone by, nearly eternal though it had been, scourging his scalp with his comb.

There was no need to piss in the corner, anyway. He would just raise the toilet seat lid with one hand, aim with the other, and let fly. Of course, given the Port-O-San's new configuration, that would mean pissing horizontally instead of at a downward-pointing angle. The current throb in his bladder suggested that would be absolutely no problem. Of course the final squirt or two would probably go on the floor, but —

"But thems are the fortunes of war," he said, and surprised himself with a croaky laugh. "And as far as the toilet seat goes . . . fuck holding it up. I can do better than that."

He was no Mr. Hercules, but both the half-ajar toilet seat and the flanges holding it to the bench were plastic — the seat and ring black, the flanges white. This whole goddam box was really just a cheap plastic prefab job, you didn't have to be a big-time construction contractor to see that, and unlike the walls and the door, there was no cladding on the seat and its fastenings. He thought he could tear it off pretty easily, and if he could he would — if only to vent some of his anger and terror.

Curtis seized the seat and lifted it, meaning to grip the ring just beneath and pull sideways. Instead he paused, looking through the circular hole and into the tank beneath, trying to make sense of what he saw.

It looked like a thin seam of daylight.

He looked at this with perplexity into which hope came stealing slowly — not dawning, exactly, but seeming to rise through his sweaty, ordure-streaked skin. At first he thought it was either a swatch of fluorescent paint or an out-and-out optical illusion. This latter idea was reinforced when the line of light began to fade away. Little . . . less . . . least . . .

But then, just before it could disappear completely, it began to brighten again, a line of light so brilliant he could see it floating behind his lids when he closed his eyes.

*That's sunlight. The bottom of the toilet — what* was *the bottom before Grunwald tipped it over — is facing east, where the sun just rose.*

And when it faded?

"Sun went behind a cloud," he said, and shoved his sweat-clumped hair back from his forehead with the hand not holding the toilet seat. "Now it's out again."

He examined this idea for the deadly pollution of wishful thinking and found none. The evidence was before his eyes: sunlight shining through a thin crack in the bottom of the

Port-O-San's holding tank. Or perhaps it was a split. If he could get in there and widen that split, that glowing aperture into the outside world —

*Don't count on it.*

And to get to it, he would have to —

*Impossible,* he thought. *If you're thinking of wriggling into the holding tank through the toilet seat — like Alice into some shit-splattered Wonderland — think again. Maybe if you were the skinny kid you used to be, but that kid was thirty-five years ago.*

That was true. But he was still slim — he supposed his daily bicycle rides were mostly responsible for that — and the thing was, he thought he *could* wriggle in through the hole under the toilet seat's ring. It might not even be that tough.

*What about getting back out?*

Well . . . if he could do something about that seam of light, maybe he wouldn't have to leave the same way he went in.

"Assuming I can even *get* in," he said. His empty stomach was suddenly full of butterflies, and for the first time since arriving here at scenic Durkin Grove Village, he felt an urge to gag himself. He would be able to think more clearly about this if he just stuck his fingers down his throat and —

"No," he said curtly, and yanked the toilet seat and ring sideways with his left hand. The flanges creaked but didn't let go. He applied his other hand to the task. His hair fell back down on his forehead, and he gave an impatient snap of his head to flop it aside. He yanked again. The seat and ring held a moment longer, then tore free. One of the two white plastic dowels fell into the waste tank. The other, cracked down the middle, spun across the door Curtis was kneeling on.

He tossed the seat and ring aside and peered into the tank, hands braced on the bench. The first whiff of the poisoned atmosphere down there caused him to recoil, wincing. He thought he'd gotten used to the smell (or numbed to it), but that wasn't the case, at least not this close to the source. He wondered again when the damned thing had last been pumped.

*Look on the bright side; it's been a long time since it was used, too.*

Maybe, *probably,* but Curtis wasn't sure that made things any better. There was still a lot of stuff down there — a lot of *crap* down there, floating in whatever remained of the disinfected water. Dim as the light was, there was enough to be sure of that. Then there was the matter of getting back out again. He could probably do it — if he could go one way, he could almost certainly go the other — but it was all too easy to imagine how he'd look, a stinking creature being born from the ooze, not a mud-man but a shit-man.

The question was, did he have another choice?

Well, yes. He could sit here, trying to persuade himself that rescue probably *would* come after all. The cavalry, like in the last reel of an old western. Only he thought it was more likely that The Motherfucker would come back, wanting to make sure he was still . . . what had he said? Snug in his little housie. Something like that.

That decided him. He looked at the hole in the bench, the dark hole with its evil aroma drifting out, the dark hole with its one hopeful seam of light. A hope as thin as the light itself. He calculated. First his right arm, then his head. Left arm pressed against his body until he had wriggled in as far as his waist. Then, when his left arm was free . . .

Only what if he wasn't able to *get* it free? He saw himself stuck, right arm in the tank, left arm pinned against his body, his midsection blocking the hole, blocking the *air,* dying a dog's death, flailing at the sludge just below him while he strangled, the last thing he saw the mocking bright stitch that had lured him on.

He saw someone finding his body half-plugged into the toilet hole with his ass sticking up and his legs splayed, smeary brown sneaker prints stamped on the goddam toilet cubicle from his final dying kicks. He could hear someone — perhaps the IRS agent who was The Motherfucker's bête noire — saying "Holy shit, he must have dropped something really valuable down there."

It was funny, but Curtis didn't feel like laughing.

How long had he been kneeling there, peering into the tank? He didn't know — his watch was back in his study, sitting by his computer's mousepad — but the ache in his thighs suggested quite awhile. And the light had brightened considerably. The sun would be entirely over the horizon now, and soon his prison would once more turn into a steam room.

"Gotta go," he said, and wiped sweat from his cheeks with the palms of his hands. "It's the only thing." But he paused again, because another thought had occurred to him.

What if there was a snake in there?

What if The Motherfucker, imagining that his witchly enemy might try this very thing, had *put* a snake in there? A copperhead, perhaps, for the time being fast asleep under a layer of cool human mud? A copperhead bite on the arm and he would die slowly and painfully, his arm swelling even as the temperature climbed. A bite from a coral snake would take him more quickly but even more painfully: his heart lunging, stopping, lunging again, then finally giving up.

*There are no snakes in there. Bugs, maybe, but no snakes. You saw him, you heard him.*

*He wasn't thinking that far ahead. He was too sick, too crazy.*

Perhaps, perhaps not. You couldn't really gauge crazy people, could you? They were wild cards.

"Deuces and jacks, man with the axe, natural sevens take all," Curtis said. The Tao of The Motherfucker. All he knew for sure was that if he didn't try it down there, he was almost certainly going to die up here. And in the end, a snakebite might be quicker and more merciful.

"Gotta," he said, once more wiping his cheeks. *"Gotta."*

As long as he didn't get stuck halfway in and halfway out of the hole. That would be a terrible way to die.

"Not going to get stuck," he said. "Look how big it is. That thing was built for the asses of doughnut-eating long-haul truckers."

This made him giggle. The sound contained more hysteria than humor. The toilet hole did not look big to him; it looked small. Almost tiny. He knew that was only his nervous perception of it — hell, his *scared* perception, his *frightened to death* perception — but knowing that didn't help much.

"Gotta do it, though," he said. "There's really nothing else."

And in the end it would probably *be* for nothing . . . but he doubted anyone had bothered to add a steel outer layer to the

565

holding tank, and that decided him.

"God help me," he said. It was his first prayer in almost forty years. "God, please help me not get stuck."

He poked his right arm through the hole, then his head (first taking one more deep breath of the better air in the cubicle). He pressed his left arm to his side and slithered into the hole. His left shoulder caught, but before he could panic and draw back — this was, part of him understood, the critical moment, the point of no return — he shimmied it like a man doing the Watusi. His shoulder popped through. He jackknifed into the stinking tank up to his waist. With his hips — slim, but not nonexistent — plugging the hole, it was now as black as pitch. That seam of light seemed to float mockingly just before his eyes. Like a mirage.

*Oh God, please don't let it be a mirage.*

The tank was maybe four feet deep, maybe a trifle more. Bigger than the trunk of a car, but not — unfortunately — the size of a pickup truck's bed. There was no way to tell for sure, but he thought his hanging hair was touching the disinfected water, and that the top of his head must be within inches of the muck filling the bottom. His left arm was still pinned against his body. Pinned at the wrist now. He couldn't get it free. He shimmied from one side to the other. His arm stayed where it was. His worst nightmare: caught.

Caught after all. Caught head down in stinking blackness.

Panic flared. He reached out with his free hand, not thinking about it, just doing it. For a moment he could see his fingers outlined by the scant light coming in through the bottom of the tank, which was now facing the sunrise instead of the ground. The light was right there, right in front of him. He grabbed for it. The first three fingers of his flailing hand were too big to fit through the narrow gap, but he was able to hook his pinky into the split. He pulled, feeling the ragged edge — metal or plastic, he didn't know which — first dig into the skin of his finger and then tear it open. Curtis didn't care. He pulled harder.

His hips popped through the hole like a cork coming out of a bottle. His wrist came free, but too late for him to lift his left arm and help break his fall. He crashed headfirst into the shit.

Curtis came up choking and flailing, his nose plugged with wet stink. He coughed and spat, aware that he was in a very tight place now, oh for sure. Had he thought the toilet was tight? Ridiculous. The toilet was the wide-open spaces. The toilet was the American west, the Australian Outback, the Great Horsehead Nebula. And he had given it up to crawl into a dark womb half-filled with rotting shit.

He wiped his face, then flung his hands to either side. Ribbons of dark stuff flew from his fingertips. His eyes were stinging, blurring. He wiped them with first one arm, then the other. His nose was plugged. He stuck his pinky fingers up them — he could feel blood running down the right one — and cleared his nostrils as best he could. He got enough out so he could breathe again, but when he did, the stench of the tank seemed to leap down his throat and sink claws into his stomach. He retched, a deep growling sound.

*Get hold of yourself. Just get hold, or it's for nothing.*

He leaned back against the caked side of the tank, dragging in deep gasps of air through his mouth, but that was almost as bad. Just above him was a large pearl of oval light. The toilet hole he had, in his madness, wriggled through. He retched again. To his own ears he sounded like a bad-tempered dog on a hot day, trying to bark while half-strangled by a too-tight collar.

*What if I can't stop? What if I can't stop doing that? I'll have a seizure.*

He was too frightened and overwhelmed to think, so his body thought for him. He turned on his knees, which was hard — the side wall of the holding tank, which was now the floor, was slippery — but just possible. He applied his mouth to the split in the floor of the tank and breathed through it. As he did, a memory of some story he'd heard or read in grammar school came back to him: Indians hiding from their enemies by lying on the bottom of a shallow pond. Lying there and breathing through hollow reeds. You could do that. You could do that if you remained calm.

He closed his eyes. He breathed, and the air coming in through the split was blessedly sweet. Little by little, his runaway heartbeat began to slow.

*You can go back up. If you can go one way, you can go the other. And going back up will be easier, because now you're . . .*

"Now I'm greasy," he said, and managed a shaky laugh . . . even though the dull, closed-in sound of his own voice frightened him all over again.

When he felt he had some control, he opened his eyes. They had adjusted to the deeper gloom of the tank. He could see his shit-caked arms, and a matted ribbon of paper hanging from his right hand. He plucked it off and dropped it. He supposed he was getting used to such things. He supposed people could get used to anything, if they had to. This wasn't a particularly comforting thought.

He looked at the split. He looked at it for some time, trying to make sense of what he was seeing. It was like a split along the seam of a badly sewn garment. Because there *was*

a seam here. The tank was plastic after all —
a plastic shell — but it wasn't a single piece;
it was two. It was held together by a line of
screws that glimmered in the dark. They glimmered because they were white. Curtis tried
to remember if he had ever seen white screws
before. He couldn't. Several of them at the
lowest point of the tank had broken off, creating that split. Waste and wastewater must
have been dribbling out and onto the ground
beneath for some time.

*If the EPA knew about this. Motherfucker,
you'd have them on your back, too,* Curtis
thought. He touched one of the screws still
holding, the one just to the left of where the
split ended. He couldn't be sure, but he
thought it was hard plastic rather than metal.
The same kind of plastic the toilet-ring
flanges were made of, probably.

So. Two-piece construction. The tanks put
together on some portable-toilet assembly
line in Defiance, Missouri, Magic City,
Idaho, or — who knew? — What Cheer, Iowa.
Screwed together with hard plastic screws,
the seam running across the bottom and up
the sides like a big old smile. The screws
tightened with some special long-barreled
screwdriver, probably air-driven, like the
gadget they used in garages to loosen the lug-
nuts holding on your tires. And why put these
screwheads on the inside? That was easy. So
some merry prankster couldn't come along

with his own screwdriver and open a full tank from the outside, of course.

The screws were placed about two inches apart along the seam, and the split was about six inches long, causing Curtis to deduce that three of the plastic screws had snapped. Bad materials, or bad design? Who gave a shit?

"To coin a phrase," he said, and laughed again.

The screws still holding to the left and right of the split were sticking up a little way, but he could neither unscrew them nor snap them off as he had the toilet seat. He couldn't get enough purchase. The one on the right was a little loose, and he supposed that if he worked at it, he might be able to get it started and then unscrew it the rest of the way. It would take hours, and his fingers would probably be bleeding by the time he managed the job, but it could probably be done. And what would he gain? Another two inches of breathing space through the seam. No more than that.

The screws beyond the ones bordering the split in the seam were firm and tight.

Curtis could stay up on his knees no longer; the muscles in his thighs were burning. He sat down against the curved side of the tank, forearms on his knees, filthy hands dangling. He looked at the brightening oval of the toilet hole. That was the overworld, he supposed, only his share of it had grown very small. It smelled better, though, and when his legs felt a little stronger, he supposed he would clamber back through the hole. He wasn't going to stay in here, sitting in shit, if there was nothing to be gained by it. And it seemed there was not.

A jumbo cockroach, made bold by Curtis's new stillness, scuttled up his filthy pant leg. He flapped a hand at it and it was gone. "That's right," he said, "run. Why don't you squeeze out through the hole? You'd probably fit." He brushed his hair out of his eyes, knowing he was smearing his forehead, not caring. "Nah, you like it in here. You probably think you died and went to cockroach heaven."

He would rest, let his throbbing legs calm a little, then climb out of Wonderland and back into his phone-booth-sized piece of the over-world. Just a short rest; he wasn't staying down here any longer than he had to, that was for sure.

Curtis closed his eyes and tried to center himself.

He saw numbers scrolling up on a computer screen. The stock market wouldn't be open yet in New York, so these numbers must be from overseas. Probably the Nikkei. Most of the numbers were green. That was good.

"Metals and industrials," he said. "And Takeda Pharmaceutical — that's a buy. Anyone can see . . ."

Curled against the wall in what was almost a fetal position, his drawn face streaked with brown warpaint, his butt sunk almost to the hips in muck, his filth-caked hands still dangling from his drawn-up knees, Curtis slept. And dreamed.

Betsy was alive and Curtis was in his living room. She was lying on her side in her accustomed place between the coffee table and the TV, snoozing with her latest half-chewed tennis ball near to hand. Or paw, in Betsy's case.

"Bets!" he said. "Wake up and fetch the idiot stick!"

She struggled to her feet — of course she struggled, she was old now — and as she did, the tags on her collar jingled.

The tags jingled.

The tags.

He woke up gasping, listing to the left as he leaned against the holding tank's greasy bottom, one hand outstretched, either to take the TV controller or to touch his dead dog.

He lowered his hand to his knee. He wasn't surprised to find he was crying. Had probably started even before the dream began to unravel. Betsy was dead and he was sitting in shit. If that wasn't reason enough to cry, he didn't know what was.

He looked again at the oval light across from and slightly above him, and saw it was quite a lot brighter. Hard to believe he'd been asleep for any length of time, but it seemed he had been. An hour at least. God knew how much poison he was breathing, but —

"Don't worry, I can deal with poison air," he said. "After all, I'm a witch."

And, bad air or no bad air, the dream had been very sweet. Very *vivid.* The jingling of those tags —

"Fuck," he whispered, and his hand flew to his pocket. He was terribly sure he must have lost the Vespa key in his tumble and would have to feel around for it down here, sifting through the shit with nothing but the scant light coming in through the split seam and the toilet hole to help him, but the key was still there. So was his money, but money would do him no good down here and the clip wouldn't, either. It was gold, and valuable, but too thick to qualify as an escape aid. So was the key to the Vespa. But there was something else on the keyring. Something that made him feel simultaneously bad and good every time he looked at it, or heard it jingle. It was Betsy's ID tag.

She had worn two, but this was the one he'd slipped off her collar before giving her a final hug goodbye and turning her body over to the vet. The other one, state-required, certified that she'd had all her shots. This one was more personal. It was rectangular, like a GI's dog tag. Stamped on it was

BETSY
IF LOST CALL 941-555-1954
CURTIS JOHNSON
19 GULF BOULEVARD
TURTLE ISLAND, FLA. 34274

It wasn't a screwdriver, but it was thin, it was made of stainless steel, and Curtis thought it just might serve. He said another prayer — he didn't know if what they said about no atheists in foxholes was true, but there seemed to be none in shitholes — then slipped the end of Betsy's ID tag into the slot of the screw just to the right of where the split ended. The screw that was a little loose to begin with.

He expected resistance, but under the edge of the ID tag the screw turned almost at once. He was so surprised he dropped his keyring and had to feel around for it. He slotted the end of the tag into the screwhead again, and turned it twice. The rest of the length he was able to loosen by hand. He did it with a big, unbelieving grin on his face.

Before beginning on the screw at the left end of the split — a split that was now two inches wider — he wiped the metal tag clean on his shirt (or as clean as he could; the shirt was as filthy as the rest of him, sticking to his skin) and kissed it gently.

"If this works, I'll frame you." He hesitated, then added: "*Please* work, okay?"

He slipped the end of the ID tag into the screwhead and turned. This one was tighter than the first . . . but not *that* tight. And once it started turning, it came out in a hurry.

"Jesus," Curtis whispered. He was crying yet again; he'd turned into a regular leaky faucet. "Am I gonna get out of here, Bets? Am I really?"

He moved back to the right and started on the next screw. He went on that way, right-left, right-left, right-left, resting when his hand got tired, flexing and shaking it until it felt loose again. He had spent going on twenty-four hours in here; he wasn't going to hurry now. He especially didn't want to drop his keyring again. He supposed he could find it, the area was small, but he still didn't want to risk it.

Right-left, right-left, right-left.

And slowly, as the morning passed and the holding tank heated up, making the smell ever thicker and more noisomely rich, the split in the bottom of the tank widened. He was doing it, closing in on getting out, but he refused to hurry. It was important not to hurry, not to bolt like a frightened horse. Because he might fuck up, yes, but also because his pride and self-esteem — his essential sense of self — had taken a beating.

Questions of self-esteem aside, slow and steady won the race.

Right-left, right-left, right-left.

■ ■ ■ ■

Shortly before noon, the seam in the dirt-caked bottom of the Port-O-San bulged open, then closed, then bulged and closed again. There was a pause. Then it split open along four feet of its length, and the crown of Curtis Johnson's head appeared. It drew back, and there were clatters and scratches as he went to work again, removing more screws: three on the left, three on the right.

The next time the seam spread apart, the matted, brown-streaked crown of his head continued to thrust forward. It pushed slowly through, the cheeks and mouth drawn down as if by terrible G-force, one ear scraped and bleeding. He cried out, shoving with his feet, terrified that now he *was* going to get stuck half in and half out of the holding tank. Still, even in his fear, he registered the sweetness of the air: hot and humid, the best he had ever breathed.

When he was outside to his shoulders, he rested, panting, looking at a crushed beer can twinkling in the weeds not ten feet from his sweating, bleeding head. It looked like a miracle. Then he pushed again, head lifted, mouth snarling, cords on his neck standing out. There was a ripping sound as the gaping split in the tank tore the shirt off his back. He hardly noticed. Just ahead of him was a baby scrub pine no more than four feet high. He stretched, got one hand on the base of its thin and sappy trunk, then the other. He rested for another moment, aware that both of his shoulder blades were scraped and bleeding, then pulled on the tree and pushed one final time with his feet.

He thought he might pull the small pine right out by the roots, but he didn't. There was a searing pain in his buttocks as the seam through which he was wriggling tore his pants down, bunching them around his sneakers. In order to get all the way out, he had to keep pulling and twisting until the sneakers finally came off. And when the tank finally let go of his left foot, he found it almost impossible to believe he was actually free.

He rolled over on his back, naked save for his underpants (askew, the elastic hanging in a limp flap, the seat torn open to reveal badly bleeding buttocks) and one white sock. He stared up at the blue sky, eyes wide. And began to scream. He had screamed himself almost hoarse before he realized he was screaming actual words: *I'm alive! I'm alive! I'm alive! I'm alive!*

Twenty minutes later, he got to his feet and limped to the defunct construction trailer sitting on its concrete blocks, a large puddle from yesterday's shower hiding in its shadow. The door was locked, but there were more blocks lying to one side of the raw wooden steps. One was cracked in two pieces. Curtis picked up the smaller chunk and bashed it against the lock until the door shuddered open, letting out a puff of hot, stale air.

He turned before going in and for a moment surveyed the toilets on the other side of the road, where pothole puddles flashed back the bright blue sky like shards of a dirty mirror. Five Port-O-Sans, three standing, two lying face-down in the ditch. He had almost died in the one on the left. And although he was standing here in nothing but a pair of tattered underpants and one sock, shit-streaked and bleeding in what felt like a hundred places, that idea already seemed unreal. A bad dream.

The office was partially empty — or partially ransacked, probably only a day or two ahead of the final project shutdown. There were no partitions; it was one long room with a desk, two chairs, and a discount-store couch in the front half. In the back half there was a stack of cartons filled with papers, a dusty adding machine sitting on the floor, a small unplugged fridge, a radio, and a swivel chair with a note taped to the back. SAVE FOR JIMMY, the note said.

There was also a closet door standing ajar, but before checking it, Curtis opened the little fridge. Inside were four bottles of Zephyr spring water, one of them opened and three-quarters empty. Curtis seized one of the full bottles and drank the entire thing down. It was warm, but it tasted like the kind of water that might flow in the rivers of heaven. When it was gone, his stomach clenched. He rushed to the door, hung out by the jamb, and vomited the water back up to one side of the steps.

"Look, Ma, no gagging necessary!" he cried, with tears running down his filthy face. He supposed he could have vomited the water right onto the deserted trailer's floor, but he didn't want to be in the same room with his own waste. Not after what had happened.

*In fact, I intend never to take another dump,* he thought. *From now on I'm going to empty myself the religious way: immaculate evacuation.*

He drank the second bottle of water more slowly, and it stayed down. While he sipped, he looked into the closet. There were two pairs of dirty pants and some equally dirty shirts piled in one corner. Curtis guessed that at one point there might have been a washer-dryer back there, where the cartons were stacked. Or maybe there had been another trailer, one that had been hitched up and hauled away. He didn't care. What he cared about was the two pair of discount-store overalls, one on a wire hanger, the other dangling from a wall hook. The pair on the hook looked much too big, but the one on the hanger might fit. And did, more or less. He had to roll the cuffs up two turns, and he supposed he looked more like Farmer John after slopping the hogs than a successful stock trader, but they would serve.

He could call the police, but he felt he had a right to more satisfaction than that after what he had been through. Quite a lot more.

"Witches don't call the police," he said. "Especially not us gay ones."

His motor scooter was still out there, but he had no intention of riding back just yet. For one thing, too many people would see the mud-man on the red Vespa Granturismo. He didn't think anyone would call the cops . . . but they'd laugh. Curtis didn't want to be noticed, and he didn't want to be laughed at. Not even behind his back.

Also, he was tired. More tired than he'd ever been in his life.

He lay down on the discount-store sofa and put one of the pillows behind his head. He had left the trailer door open and a little breeze frisked through, stroking his dirty skin with delicious fingers. He was wearing nothing but the overalls now. He had stripped off his filthy undershorts and the remaining sock before putting them on.

*I don't smell myself at all,* he thought. *Isn't that amazing?*

Then he fell asleep, deeply and completely.

He dreamed of Betsy bringing him the idiot stick, the tags on her collar jingling. He took the controller from her, and when he pointed it at the TV, he saw The Motherfucker peering in the window.

Curtis woke four hours later, sweating and stiff and stinging all over. Outside, thunder was rumbling as that afternoon's storm approached, right on schedule. He made his way down the makeshift trailer steps side-saddle, like an old man with arthritis. He *felt* like an old man with arthritis. Then he sat down, looking alternately at the darkening sky and at the portable toilet from which he had escaped.

When the rain began, he stepped out of the overalls, threw them back into the trailer to keep them dry, and then stood there naked in the downpour, his face turned upward, smiling. That smile didn't falter even when a stroke of lightning forked down on the far side of Durkin Grove Village, close enough to fill the air with the tang of ozone. He felt perfectly, deliciously safe.

The cold rain sluiced him relatively clean, and when it began to let up, he slowly climbed the trailer steps again. When he was dry, he put the overalls back on. And when late-day sun began to spoke through the unraveling clouds, he walked slowly up the hill to where his Vespa was parked. The key was clutched in his right hand, Betsy's now-battered ID tag pressed between the first two fingers.

The Vespa wasn't used to being left out in the rain, but it was a good pony and started after only two cranks of the engine, settling at once into its usual good-natured purr. Curtis mounted up, barefooted and helmetless, a blithe spirit. He rode back to Turtle Island that way, with the wind blowing his filthy hair and belling the overalls out around his legs. He saw few cars, and got across the main road with no problems at all.

He thought he could use a couple of aspirins before going to see Grunwald, but otherwise he had never felt better in his life.

By seven o'clock that evening, the afternoon shower was just a memory. The Turtle Island sunsetters would gather on the beach in another hour or so for the usual end-of-day show, and Grunwald expected to be among them. For now, however, he lay in his patio hot tub with his eyes closed, a weak gin and tonic near to hand. He had taken a Percocet prior to climbing into the tub, knowing it would be a help when it came to the short walk down to the beach, but his sense of almost dreamy satisfaction persisted. He hardly needed the painkillers. That might change, but for the time being, he hadn't felt so well in years. Yes, he was facing financial ruin, but he had enough cash socked away to keep him comfortable for the time he had left. More important, he had taken care of the queer who had been the author of all his misery. Ding-dong, the wicked witch was d—

"Hello, Grunwald. Hello, you mother-fucker."

Grunwald's eyes flew open. A dark shape was standing between him and the westering sun, looking cut from black paper. Or funeral crepe. It looked like Johnson, but surely it could not be; Johnson was locked in the overturned toilet, Johnson was a shithouse mouse either dying or dead. Also, a smarmy little bandbox dresser like Johnson would never have been caught dead looking like an extra from that old *Hee-Haw* show. It was a dream, it had to be. But —

"You awake? Good. I want you to be awake for this."

"Johnson?" Just a whisper. It was all he could manage. "That's not really you, is it?" But now the figure moved a little — just enough to allow the late-day sun to strike across his scratched face — and Grunwald saw that it was. And what was that he had in his hand?

Curtis saw what The Motherfucker was looking at, and considerately turned a little more, so that the sun struck across it, too. It was a hair dryer, Grunwald realized. It was a

584

hair dryer, and he was sitting chest-deep in a hot tub.

He grabbed the side, meaning to pull himself out, and Johnson stepped on his hand. Grunwald cried out and jerked his hand back. Johnson's foot was bare, but he had brought it down heel first, and hard.

"I like you right where you are," Curtis said, smiling. "I'm sure you felt the same about me, but I got out, didn't I? And I even brought you a present. Stopped by my house to get it. Don't refuse it on that account; it's only slightly used, and I blew off all the gay-dust on my way over here. By way of the backyard, actually. Convenient that the power's off in the stupid cattle-fence you used to kill my dog. Here you go." And he dropped the hair dryer into the hot tub.

Grunwald screamed and tried to catch it, but he missed. The hair dryer splashed, then sank. One of the water jets turned it over and over on the bottom. It bumped Grunwald's scrawny legs and he jerked away from it, still screaming, sure he was being electrocuted.

"Take it easy," Johnson said. He was still smiling. He unsnapped first one strap of the overalls he was wearing, then the other. They dropped to his ankles. He was naked beneath, with faint streaks of filth from the holding tank still on the insides of his arms and thighs. There was a nasty brown clot of something in his navel. "It wasn't plugged in.

585

I don't even know if that old hair-dryer-in-the-tub thing works. Although I must admit that if I'd had an extension cord, I might have made the experiment."

"Get away from me," Grunwald rasped.

"Nah," Johnson said. "Don't think so." Smiling, always smiling. Grunwald wondered if the man had gone mad. *He* would have gone mad in circumstances similar to those in which he'd left Johnson. How had he gotten out? *How,* in God's name?

"The rain shower this afternoon washed off most of the shit, but I'm still quite dirty. As you see." Johnson spied the nasty wad in his navel, pried it out with a finger, and flicked it casually into the hot tub like a booger.

It landed on Grunwald's cheek. Brown and stinking. Starting to run. Good God, it was shit. He cried out again, this time in revulsion.

"He shoots, he scores," Johnson said, smiling. "Not very nice, is it? And although I don't exactly *smell* it anymore, I'm very tired of *looking* at it. So be a neighbor, would you, and share your hot tub."

"No! No, you can't —"

"Thanks!" Johnson said, smiling, and jumped in. There was a great splash. Grunwald could smell him. He *reeked.* Grunwald floundered for the other side of the hot tub, skinny shanks flashing white above the bubbling water, the tan on his equally skinny legs looking like taupe nylon stockings. He flung one arm over the edge of the tub. Then Johnson grabbed him around the neck with one badly scratched but horribly strong arm and hauled him back into the water.

"No no no no *no!*" Johnson said, smiling. He pulled Grunwald against him. Little brown-black flecks danced on the surface of the bubbling water. "Us gay guys rarely bathe alone. Surely you came across that fact in your Internet researches. And gay *witches?* Never!"

"Let me go!"

"Maybe." But Johnson hugged him closer, horribly intimate, still stinking of the Port-O-San. "First, though, I think you need to visit the gayboy ducking stool. Kind of a baptism. Wash away your sins." The smile became a grin, the grin a rictus. Grunwald realized he was going to die. Not in his bed, in some misty, medicated future, but right here. Johnson was going to drown him in his own hot tub, and the last thing he'd see would be little particles of filth floating in the previously clean water.

Curtis grabbed Grunwald's naked, scrawny shoulders and shoved him under. Grunwald struggled, his legs kicking, his scant hair floating, little silver bubbles twisting up from his big old beak of a nose. The urge to just hold him there was strong . . . and Curtis could do it because *he* was strong. Once upon a time, Grunwald would have been able to take him with one hand tied behind his back, age difference or not, but those days were gone. This was one sick Motherfucker. Which was why Curtis let him go.

Grunwald surged for the surface, coughing and choking.

"You're right!" Curtis cried. "This baby *is* good for aches and pains! But never mind *me;* what about *you?* Want to go under again? Submersion is good for the soul, all the best religions say so."

Grunwald shook his head furiously. Drops of water flew from his thinning hair and more luxuriant eyebrows.

"Then just sit there," Curtis said. "Sit there and listen. And I don't think we need this, do we?" He reached under Grunwald's leg — Grunwald jerked and uttered a small scream — and snagged the hair dryer. Curtis tossed it over his shoulder. It skittered beneath Grunwald's patio chair.

"I'll be leaving you soon," Curtis said. "Going back to my own place. You can go down and watch the sunset if you still want to. Do you still want to?"

Grunwald shook his head.

"No? I didn't think so. I think you've had your last good sunset, neighbor. In fact, I think you've had your last good day, and that's why I'm letting you live. And do you want to know the irony? If you'd let me alone, you would have gotten exactly what you wanted. Because I was locked in the shithouse already and didn't even know it. Isn't that funny?"

Grunwald said nothing, only looked at him with his terrified eyes. His *sick* and terrified eyes. Curtis could almost have felt sorry for him, if the memory of the Port-O-San was not still so vivid. The lid of the toilet flopping open like a mouth. The turd landing in his lap like a dead fish.

"Answer, or you get another baptismal dunk."

"It's funny," Grunwald rasped. And then began to cough.

Curtis waited until he stopped. He wasn't smiling anymore.

"Yes, it is," he said. "It is funny. The whole thing's funny, if you see it from the right perspective. And I believe I do."

He boosted himself out of the hot tub, aware that he was moving with a litheness The Motherfucker would never again be able to match. There was a cabinet under the porch overhang. There were towels inside. Curtis took one and began to dry off.

"Here's the thing. You can call the police and tell them I tried to drown you in your hot tub, but if you do that, everything else comes out. You'll spend the rest of your life fighting a criminal case as well as dealing with your other woes. But if you let it go, it's a reset. Odometer back to zero. Only — here's the thing — I get to watch you rot. There will come a day when you smell just like the shithouse you locked me in. When other people smell you that way, and you smell that way to yourself."

"I'll kill myself first," Grunwald rasped.

Curtis was pulling the overalls on again. He had decided he sort of liked them. They might be the perfect garment to wear while watching the stock quotes on one's computer in one's cozy little study. He might go out to Target and buy half a dozen pairs. The new, non-compulsive Curtis Johnson: an overall kind of guy.

He paused in the act of buckling the second shoulder strap. "You could do that. You have that gun, the — what did you call it? — the Hardballer." He finished with the buckle, then leaned toward Grunwald, who was still marinating in the hot tub and looking at him fearfully. "That would be acceptable, too. You might even have the guts, although, when it comes right down to it . . . you might not. In any case, I'll listen with great interest for the bang."

He left Grunwald then, but not the way he had come. He went around to the road. A left turn would have taken him back to his house, but he turned right, toward the beach. For the first time since Betsy died, he felt like watching the sunset.

Two days later, while sitting at his computer (he was watching General Electric with especial interest), Curtis heard a loud bang from next door. He didn't have his music on, and the sound rolled through the humid, almost-July air with perfect clarity. He sat where he was, head cocked, still listening. Although there would be no second bang.

*Us witches just know shit like that,* he thought.

Mrs. Wilson came rushing in, holding a dishtowel in one hand. "That sounded like a gunshot!"

"Probably just a backfire," he said, smiling. He had been smiling a lot since his adventure at Durkin Grove Village. He thought it wasn't the same sort of smile as the one he had worn during the Betsy Era, but any smile was better than none. Surely that was true?

Mrs. Wilson was looking at him doubtfully. "Well . . . I guess." She turned to go.

"Mrs. Wilson?"

She turned back.

"Would you quit me if I got another dog? A puppy?"

"Me, quit over a puppy? It'd take more than a pup to drive *me* out."

"They tend to chew, you know. And they don't always —" He broke off for a moment,

591

seeing the dark and nasty landscape of the holding tank. The underworld.

Meanwhile, Mrs. Wilson was looking at him curiously.

"They don't always use the bathroom," he finished.

"Once you teach them, they usually go where they're supposed to," she said. "Especially in a warm climate like this one. And you need some companionship, Mr. Johnson. I've been . . . to tell the truth, I've been a little worried about you."

He nodded. "Yes, I've kind of been in the shit." He laughed, saw her looking at him strangely, and made himself stop. "Excuse me."

She flapped her dishtowel at him to show he was excused.

"Not a purebred, this time. I was thinking maybe the Venice Animal Shelter. Someone's little castoff. What they call a rescue dog."

"That would be very nice," she said. "I look forward to the patter of little feet."

"Good."

"Do you really think that was a backfire?"

Curtis sat back in his chair and pretended to consider. "Probably . . . but you know, Mr. Grunwald next door has been pretty sick." He lowered his voice to a sympathetic whisper. "Cancer."

"Oh, dear," Mrs. Wilson said.

Curtis nodded.

"You don't think he'd . . . ?"

The marching numbers on his computer screen melted into the screen saver: aerial photos and beach scenes, all featuring Turtle Island. Curtis stood up, walked to Mrs. Wilson, and took the dishtowel from her hand. "No, not really, but we could go next door and check. After all, what are neighbors for?"

# SUNSET NOTES

According to one school of thought, notes such as these are unnecessary at best, and suspect at worst. The argument against is that stories which need explanation are probably not very good stories. I have some sympathy with the idea, which is one reason to put this little addendum at the back of the book (putting it here also avoids those tiresome cries of "spoiler," which are most commonly uttered by spoiled people). The reason to include them is simply that many readers like them. They want to know what caused a story to be written, or what the author was thinking when he wrote it. This author doesn't necessarily know either of those things, but he can offer some random thoughts that may or may not be of interest.

**"Willa"** This probably isn't the best story in the book, but I love it very much, because it ushered in a new period of creativity for me — as regards the short story, at least. Most of the stories in *Just After Sunset* were written subsequent to "Willa," and in fairly quick succession (over a period of not quite two years). As to the story itself . . . one of the great things about fantasy is that it gives writers a chance to explore what might (or might not) happen after we shuffle off this mortal coil. There are two tales of that sort in *Just After Sunset* (the other is "*The New York Times* at Special Bargain Rates"). I was raised as a perfectly conventional Methodist, and although I rejected organized religion and most of its hard and fast assertions long ago, I hold to the main idea, which is that we survive death in some fashion or other. It's hard for me to believe that such complicated and occasionally wonderful beings are in the end simply wasted, tossed away like litter on the roadside. (Probably I just don't want to believe it.) What that survival might be like, though . . . I'll just have to wait and find out. My best guess is that we might be confused, and not very willing to accept our new state. My best hope is that love survives even death (I'm a romantic, so fucking sue me). If so, it might be a bewildered love . . . and a little bit sad. When love and sadness occur to my mind at the same time, I put on the country music: people like George Strait, BR549, Marty Stuart . . . and the Derailers. It's the latter who are playing in this story, of course, and I think they're going to have a *very* long engagement.

**"The Gingerbread Girl"** My wife and I live in Florida for part of the year now, near the barrier islands just off the Gulf of Mexico. There are a lot of very large estates there — some old and gracious, some of the bloated *nouveau* sort. I was walking with a friend on one of these islands a couple of years ago. He gestured at a line of these McMansions as we walked and said, "Most of these places stand empty six or even eight months of the year, can you imagine that?" I could . . . and I thought it would make a wonderful story. It grew out of a very simple premise: a bad guy chasing a girl along an empty beach. But, I thought, she'd have to be running away from something else to start with. A gingerbread girl, in other words. Only sooner or later even the fastest runners have to stand and fight. Also, I like suspense stories that turn on crucial little details. This one had a lot of them.

**"Harvey's Dream"** I can only tell you one thing about this story, because it's the only thing I know (and probably the only thing that matters): it came to me in a dream. I wrote it in a single sitting, doing little more than transcribing the tale my subconscious had already told. There's another dream-story in this book, but I know a little more about that one.

**"Rest Stop"** One night about six years ago, I did a reading at a college in St. Petersburg. I stayed late, and ended up driving home on the Florida Turnpike, after midnight. I stopped at a rest area to tap a kidney on the way back. You'll know what it looked like if you've read this story: a cellblock in a medium-security prison. Anyway, I paused outside the men's room, because a man and a woman were in the ladies', having a bitter argument. They both sounded tight and on the verge of getting physical. I wondered what in the world I'd do if that happened, and thought: *I'll have to summon my inner Richard Bachman, because he's tougher than me.* They emerged without coming to blows — although the lady in the case was crying — and I drove home without further incident. Later that week I wrote this story.

**"Stationary Bike"** If you've ever ridden on one of those things, you know how bitterly boring they can be. And if you've ever tried to get yourself back into a daily exercise regimen, you know how difficult *that* can be (my motto: "Eating Is Easier" — but yes, I do work out). This story came out of my hate/ hate relationship not just with stationary bikes but with every treadmill I ever trudged and every Stairmaster I ever climbed.

**"The Things They Left Behind"** Like

almost everyone else in America, I was deeply and fundamentally affected by 9/11. Like a great many writers of fiction both literary and popular, I felt a reluctance to say *anything* about an event that has become as much an American touchstone as Pearl Harbor or the assassination of John Kennedy. But writing stories is what I *do,* and this story came to me about a month after the fall of the Twin Towers. I might still not have written it if I had not recalled a conversation I had with a Jewish editor over twenty-five years before. He was unhappy with me about a story called "Apt Pupil." It was wrong for me to write about the concentration camps, he said, because I was not a Jew. I replied that made writing the story all the more important — because writing is an act of willed understanding. Like every other American who watched the New York skyline burning that morning, I wanted to understand both the event and the scars such an event must inevitably leave behind. This story was my effort to do so.

**"Graduation Afternoon"** For years following an accident in 1999, I took an antidepressant drug called Doxepin — not because I was depressed (he said glumly) but because Doxepin was supposed to have a beneficial effect on chronic pain. It worked, but by November of 2006, when I went to

London to promote my novel *Lisey's Story,* I felt the time had come to give the stuff up. I didn't consult the doctor who prescribed it; I just went cold turkey. The side-effects of this sudden stoppage were . . . interesting.[*] For about a week, when I closed my eyes at night, I saw vivid panning shots, as in a movie — woods, fields, ridges, rivers, fences, railroad tracks, men swinging picks and shovels on a stretch of road construction . . . and then the whole thing would start over again until I fell asleep. There was never any story attached; they were simply these brilliantly detailed panning shots. I was sort of sorry when they went away. I also experienced a series of vivid post-Doxepin dreams. One of them — a vast mushroom cloud blossoming over New York — became the subject of this story. I wrote it even knowing that the image has been used in countless movies (not to mention the TV series *Jericho*), because the dream had a documentary matter-of-factness to it; I woke with my heart pounding, thinking *This could happen. And sooner or later, it almost certainly* will *happen.* Like "Harvey's Dream," this story is more dictation than fiction.

**"N."** This is the newest story in the book,

[*]Do I know for a fact that quitting the Doxepin was responsible? I do not. Hey, maybe it was the English water.

and published for the first time here. It was strongly influenced by Arthur Machen's *The Great God Pan,* a story that (like Bram Stoker's *Dracula*) surmounts its rather clumsy prose and works its way relentlessly into the reader's terror-zone. How many sleepless nights has it caused? God knows, but a few of them were mine. I think "Pan" is as close as the horror genre comes to a great white whale, and that sooner or later every writer who takes the form seriously must try to tackle its theme: that reality is thin, and the *true* reality beyond is a limitless abyss filled with monsters. My idea was to try and wed Machen's theme to the idea of obsessive-compulsive disorder . . . partly because I think everyone suffers OCD to one degree or another (haven't we all turned around from at least one trip to make sure we turned off the oven or the stove burners?) and partly because obsession and compulsion are almost always unindicted co-conspirators in the tale of horror. Can you think of a single success-ful scary tale that doesn't contain the idea of going back to what we hate and loathe? The best overt example of that might be "The Yel-low Wallpaper," by Charlotte Perkins Gilman. If you ever read it in college, you were prob-ably taught that it's a feminist story. That is true, but it's also a story of a mind crumbling under the weight of its own obsessive thought. That element is also present in "N."

**"The Cat from Hell"** If *Just After Sunset* has the equivalent of a hidden track on a CD, I guess this would be it. And I have my long-time assistant, Marsha DeFilippo, to thank. When I told her I was going to do another collection, she asked me if I was finally going to include "The Cat from Hell," a story from my men's magazine days. I responded that I surely must have tucked that story — which was actually filmed as part of *Tales from the Darkside: The Movie* in 1990 — into one of the previous four collections. Marsha provided tables of contents to show that I had not. So here it is, finally between hardcovers, over thirty years after it was originally published in *Cavalier.* It came about in an amusing way. The fiction editor of *Cavalier* back then, a nice guy named Nye Willden, sent me a close-up photograph of a hissing cat. What made it unusual — other than the cat's rage — was the way its face was split down the middle, the fur on one side white and glossy black on the other. Nye wanted to run a short story contest. He proposed that I write the first five hundred words of a story about the cat; they would then ask readers to finish it, and the best completion would be published. I agreed, but got interested enough in the story to write the entire thing. I can't remember if my version was published in the same issue as the contest winner or later on, but it has since been anthologized a number of times.

**"*The New York Times* at Special Bargain Rates"** In the summer of 2007, I went to Australia, leased a Harley-Davidson, and drove it from Brisbane to Perth (well . . . I stuck the bike in the back of a Toyota Land Cruiser for part of the Great Australian Desert, where roads like The Gunbarrel Highway are what I imagine the highways look like in hell). It was a good trip; I had lots of adventures and ate a lot of dust. But getting over the jet-lag after twenty-one hours in the air is a bitch. And I don't sleep on planes. Just can't do it. If the stewardess shows up at my seat with those funky pajamas, I make the sign of the cross and tell her to go away. When I arrived in Oz after the San Francisco to Brisbane leg, I pulled the blinds, crashed out, slept for ten hours, and woke up bright-eyed and ready to go. The only problem was that it was two a.m. local time, nothing on TV, and I'd finished all my reading matter on the plane. Luckily, I had a notebook, and I wrote this story at my little hotel desk. By the time the sun came up, it was done and I was able to sleep for another couple of hours. A story should entertain the writer, too — that's my opinion, we welcome yours.

**"Mute"** I read a story in my local newspaper about a high school secretary who embezzled over sixty-five thousand dollars in order to play the lottery. My first question was how her husband felt about that, and I wrote this story to find out. It reminds me of the poison bon-bons I used to sample weekly on *Alfred Hitchcock Presents.*

**"Ayana"** The subject of the afterlife, as I have said earlier in these notes, has always been fertile soil for writers who are comfortable with the fantastic. God — in any of His supposed forms — is another subject for which tales of the fantastic were made. And when we ask questions about God, one near the top of every list is why some people live and some die; why some get well and some do not. I asked it myself in the wake of the injuries I suffered in 1999, as the result of an accident that could have easily killed me if my position had been different by only inches (on the other hand, if my position had been different by other inches, I might have escaped completely). If a person lives, we say "It's a miracle." If he or she dies, we say "It was God's will." There is no rational response to miracles, and no way to understand the will of God — who, if He is there at all, may have no more interest in us than I do in the microbes now living on my skin. But miracles do happen, it seems to me; each breath is another one. Reality is thin but not always dark. I didn't want to write about answers, I wanted to write about questions. And suggest that miracles may be a burden as well as a blessing. And maybe it's all bullshit. I like the story, though.

**"A Very Tight Place"** Everyone has used one of those roadside porta-potties from time to time, if only at a turnpike rest area in the summertime, when state Highway Departments have to put out extra bathrooms to cope with the increased flow of travelers (I'm smiling as I write this, thinking how marvelously excretory it sounds). Gosh, there's nothing like stepping into one of those dim little roomettes on a hot August afternoon, is there? Toasty-warm, and the smell is *divine.* In truth, I have never used one without thinking of Poe's "The Premature Burial" and wondering what would happen to me if the shithouse fell over on its door. Especially if no one was around to help me get out. Finally I wrote this story, for the same reason I have written so many rather unpleasant tales, Constant Reader: to pass on what frightens me to you. And I cannot close without telling you what childish fun this tale was. I even grossed myself out.
  Well.
  A little.

■ ■ ■ ■

And with that, I bid you a fond farewell, at least for the time being. If the miracles keep happening, we will meet again. In the meantime, thank you for reading my stories. I hope at least one of them keeps you awake for awhile after the lights are out.

Take care of yourself . . . and say! Did you maybe leave the oven on? Or forget to turn off the gas under your patio barbecue? What about the lock on the back door? Did you remember to give it a twist? Things like that are so easy to forget, and someone could be slipping in right now. A lunatic, perhaps. One with a knife. So, OCD behavior or not . . .

Better go check, don't you think?

Stephen King
March 8, 2008

# ABOUT THE AUTHOR

**Stephen King** is the author of more than forty books, all of them worldwide bestsellers. Among his most recent are *Duma Key, Dark Tower VII: Dark Tower, Dreamcatcher, On Writing, Hearts in Atlantis, From a Buick 8, The Girl Who Loved Tom Gordon, Bag of Bones,* and *The Green Mile.* He lives in Bangor, Maine, with his wife, novelist Tabitha King.